About th

Rebecca Hunter is the award-winning author of sensual, emotional adventures of the heart. She writes sexy stories about alpha men and spirited women for Mills & Boon Dare line, and her books reflect her love of travel. To find out more or to join her newsletter, please visit rebeccahunterwriter.com

Julie Danvers grew up in a rural community surrounded by farmland. Although her town was small, it offered plenty of scope for imagination, as well as an excellent library. Books allowed Julie to have many adventures from her own home, and her love affair with reading has never ended. She loves to write about heroes and heroines who are adventurous, passionate about a cause, and looking for the best in themselves and others. Julie's website is juliedanvers.wordpress.com

Clare Connelly was raised in small-town Australia among a family of avid readers. She spent much of her childhood up a tree, Mills & Boon book in hand. She is married to her own real-life hero in a bungalow near the sea with their two children. She is frequently found staring into space – a surefire sign she is in the world of her characters. Writing for Mills & Boon Modern is a long-held dream. Clare can be contacted via clareconnelly.com or on her Facebook page.

Workplace Romance

Workplace Romance:

Irresistible Attraction

REBECCA HUNTER

JULIE DANVERS

CLARE CONNELLY

MILLS & BOON

First Published in Great Britain 2024
by Mills & Boon, an imprint of HarperCollins*Publishers* Ltd,
1 London Bridge Street, London, SE1 9GF

www.harpercollins.co.uk

HarperCollins*Publishers*
Macken House, 39/40 Mayor Street Upper,
Dublin 1, D01 C9W8, Ireland

Workplace Romance: Irresistible Attraction © 2024 Harlequin Enterprises ULC.

Pure Temptation © 2020 Rebecca Hunter
From Hawaii to Forever © 2020 Alexis Silas
Off Limits © 2018 Clare Connelly

ISBN: 978-0-263-32484-6

This book contains FSC™ certified paper and other controlled sources to ensure responsible forest management.

For more information visit: www.harpercollins.co.uk/green

Printed and Bound in the UK using 100% Renewable Electricity at CPI Group (UK) Ltd, Croydon, CR0 4YY

PURE TEMPTATION

REBECCA HUNTER

To Megan and Maneesha, who entertained the topics of free climbing, adrenaline sports, and cautionary tales on an Inspiration Point hike, and to the group of climbers I accosted while on a walk in the Berkeley Hills, especially Alicia, who answered all my probing questions. Thanks to Kim Ryan, former hotshot and current hotshot wife, for detailed clarifications (all mistakes are my own, of course), and thanks to both Stacy Finz and Kira for yet another round of insightful beta comments. Can you tell that it truly takes a village to build a book? I'm so lucky to have mine.

CHAPTER ONE

TAP, TAP.

The knock on the front door of the cabin came in the open window, cutting through the sounds of the shower just as Daxon Milcs was turning it off. He scrubbed his face and searched the ultramodern bathroom for a clock, but all he saw was tile, glass, and the wooden box filled with hibiscus-scented soaps and shampoos he had passed over earlier. How long had he stood under the shower, letting the water run over his body? After a long plane ride, it was surprising just how satisfying something as simple as hot water felt.

Tap, tap.

"Just a minute," he called.

Daxon grabbed a towel and scrubbed the water from his hair, then wrapped it around his waist. The towel was just long enough to secure, though not by a wide margin. He would have thought that a super-exclusive resort like this would lean toward overindulgent for everything, including towel length, but like the rest of the bathroom, minimalism seemed to be the guiding principle. He stepped out through the glass door, his body drinking in the humid Hawaiian heat.

"It's your *personal healing coach*."

The sentence wafted through the window, hitting him hard in the middle of his chest. Daxon froze midstride. What the hell? It wasn't the sarcasm dripping from those last three words that had his heart jumping in his chest. It was the voice.

Her voice. The sound of it flooded him with the same liquid heat he had fought off six months ago.

Impossible. It couldn't be her...could it? No, it couldn't. The hot shower, the beautiful beachside location, the Kalani Resort itself with its wish-fulfillment promise must have lulled him into a fantasy world where *she* was here, too. But that couldn't be right.

The doctor's strict orders to put his well-known focus on chilling out must be messing with his head. Why else would his mind have wandered to Kendall Clark? Back to those days in his suite in a different resort, the lush breeze blowing the curtains, when she was his physical therapist and he was trying not to be yet another douchey client with a hard-on. But her hands had felt soft and good in a way no physical therapist's should—or had. And he had spent too much time wondering if the rest of her body was just as soft. Oh, how he had wanted to take her to bed on his final night there when they'd kissed, spend the whole night exploring her…except it didn't happen. Which must be why he was hearing her voice, six months later, on the other side of the world.

"Be right there," he called, pushing those memories away.

His focus here at the Kalani was getting himself back in top shape for the Moonlight Buttress free solo that'd be filmed live in two weeks. No ropes, no safety measures to fall back on. And absolutely no distractions. Which meant no thinking about Kendall Clark.

Daxon headed out of the bathroom, into the main room of his private cabin. Halfway across the floor, it occurred to him to grab a hold of his towel to keep it in place—because he didn't need his junk hanging out. He made his way to the door, took a deep breath and turned the handle.

"Listen, I lost track of—" Daxon stopped mid-sentence, mouth gaping as he swung the door open and he caught sight of the woman standing in front of him.

Kendall Clark.

Was it really her? She seemed very real in the little entryway, cheeks flushed, her big brown eyes round, framed by the longest lashes—just like he remembered. He stared at those eyes, blinking, a little dazed. Her gaze swooped down, over his bare chest, then up again to his mouth, and his whole body prickled with awareness. His ultimate distraction was standing right in front of him…wasn't she?

He lifted a hand to reach for her, to make sure she was real. Halfway there, he thought better of it, so he rested that hand on the doorframe, trying to jump-start his stalled thoughts.

What the hell was going on right now? Was all this Hawaiian heat having some sort of rock-to-the-head effect? Because what he was seeing was Kendall, dressed in a red Kalani Wellness polo shirt and shorts that exposed miles of her lean, tanned legs. The same legs he had ached to touch for one, tantalizing week. Her long hair was back in a ponytail, the way she'd worn it in Costa Rica when she had knelt down... Shit. Not what he should be thinking about.

Daxon blinked a couple times, but Kendall was still there, staring at him. She was holding a tablet and looking all business. Or at least, she had been a few moments ago. Now she was gaping at him, too.

Her eyes narrowed. "Is this your way of saying hello?"

What? He gave himself a little shake and furrowed his brow. As her gaze traveled down his body, instinctively he looked down, too, and—fuck.

His hand was resting on the doorframe, which meant it was no longer holding his towel up. His brain hadn't even registered that he dropped it, but clearly, his dick had been a lot quicker to believe that she was real.

"Shit," he muttered. Daxon grabbed his towel off the floor and wrapped it around his waist again, but that did nothing to hide his growing hard-on.

Slick, Dax. Really subtle.

He straightened up and met her eyes again. "You might not believe this, but that was an accident."

She gestured to his cock. "And that is, too?"

"In a manner of speaking, yes." Daxon rubbed the back of his neck—with his free hand this time.

Then he found himself just staring at her again, his brain still malfunctioning, trying to process the fact that Kendall was really here. She stared back for a bit, and then a burst of laughter came from her sexy mouth. He blew out a breath and smiled. This was ridiculous. Thank God she didn't look too pissed. Maybe he wasn't the first asshole to drop his towel for her, though he really hoped this wasn't one of her occupational hazards.

Finally, she caught her breath and gave him a look that suggested something between amusement and exasperation. "Classy."

"That's me. Come on in," he said before his mind could fall into another gutter.

He stepped aside, and Kendall wandered into the main room of his cabin. A zing of raw attraction ran through him as she passed by, and Daxon paused in the hall and ran a hand through his hair, trying to get a handle on the situation. He had come to the Kalani to fully heal, away from public eyes, and *she* was his physical therapist? Either this was the world's most improbable coincidence…or something else was going on. Daxon was betting everything on the latter, and he needed to figure out what that *something* was.

He watched her as she wandered over to peek at the view of the ocean through the French doors. She looked…different. What was it? Her hair was lighter, streaked with hints of blond. The taper of her waist, the curve of her hips, those fit legs—her body was just as distracting as before. Her skin tone was a little darker, from all the Hawaiian sun no doubt, but there was something else.

"You look good," he said, following her in. "More…relaxed."

That's what it was. There was an ease to her that he hadn't seen the last time.

Kendall turned. "Thanks, I think. You look very… relaxed, too." She gestured to his current state of undress. "Well, most of you."

There was a hint of a smile on her lips, a good sign. But after that full-frontal greeting, he needed to tone this the fuck down.

"I'll put on some clothes. In case you've seen enough of me for the day."

She waved him off. "Nothing I haven't seen before."

Daxon frowned. She had thrown out that comment in the most casual tone, like getting a peek at him naked was just another part of her day, somewhere between taping up an injured wrist and paperwork. Not that she was supposed to be jumping with joy at seeing his dick, unsolicited, but, well, wasn't she at least a little…impressed?

"I'll be out in a minute," he grumbled over his

shoulder. But as he turned away, he caught her gaze wandering lower, like she was checking him out. Or at least he thought he saw it. Maybe that was his ego talking, but a guy could hope.

Daxon headed for the bedroom and shut himself in the large walk-in closet. He rested his forehead against the door and let out a quiet groan. *Focus.* Kendall Clark, the star of far too many of his fantasies, was sitting on the couch, a dozen steps away from his bedroom, and he still had the lingering remains of a hard-on. Time to get this situation under control.

Goal number one: fully heal his injured calf so he could face off with Moonlight Buttress on schedule. Goal number two: keep his overeager cock down and safely covered. Because Kendall didn't strike him as the kind of woman who enjoyed a flasher. Even if she may have been checking him out.

He grabbed a pair of shorts and T-shirt and slipped them on. He ran his hand through his wet hair a couple times and hung his towel on a hook, then rested his hand on the door handle.

Apparently his brain had started working again because he was almost sure he knew who had set this up. Calvin. His business partner and producer's last words before he got on the plane to Hawaii sank in. *I arranged a special wish for you, one I know you'll love.* The asshole had set this up, probably assuming that Daxon had, in fact, slept with her back in Costa Rica and wouldn't mind a repeat. Dax had guessed Calvin's wish for him would be misguided, but this was an epic miss. Because spending hours a day with hot-as-hell Kendall Clark was the polar opposite of relaxation. More like excruciatingly tense. Hard in every way.

Kendall Clark didn't do hesitant, fumbling girlishness. Definitely not around high-profile men in general, and especially not around Daxon Miles in particular. So as soon as Daxon left the room, Kendall plopped down on the sofa and took deep breaths, trying to get her runaway pulse under control. Because despite all the rehearsals in front of her bathroom mirror, that greeting didn't go anything like the one she'd planned.

In the entryway, as her eyes had wandered south, a rush of tempting heat had spread through her, shutting off all reasonable thought. Then the memories of Costa Rica flooded back. Seven long days of trying to ignore all those perfect, taut muscles. That sharp pull of sexual interest that came anyway each time she touched him, each time she felt him move under her hands. As she tried like hell to focus on her job.

She could sense it all starting again: the client crush she never should have had, the one she had tried so hard to resist, was taking hold. And she definitely didn't do celebrity client crushes.

Plus, Daxon Miles made her nervous. Kendall had assumed his love of danger was all an act, a show he put on for his bazillions of YouTube followers. Who the hell in his right mind would actually want to dive off cliffs just for fun? But after a week in Costa Rica with him, she was forced to admit that, number one, he truly did love these stunts, and number two, he wasn't crazy. Okay, number three, he was hot as sin, but she wasn't counting that realization.

She might have even written him off. It wasn't like she'd never had a hot, ultra-fit client before. But the conversation she'd had with him back then about the difference between high risk and high consequence—the one that stretched long beyond working hours—had her questioning all her safe choices. The things he had said that last night in Costa Rica had stayed with her, bubbling inside when she was debating whether or not to accept a job at the Kalani Resort and move to Hawaii. With enough preparation, Daxon really was up for just about anything, and she...well, over the past six months, she was trying harder to be. But ignoring her risk-averse nature certainly didn't come easily.

When Sheila Alleyne, the Kalani's mysterious "wish maker," had contacted her about this assignment, she'd said Daxon Miles had specially requested her. Though each guest at the resort was entitled to a "wish"—a special request to be fulfilled during their stay—she had never heard of a personal request like this. Wishes were usually more along the lines of a personal chef or a paragliding instructor, and Sheila and the staff took care of it. Kendall had tried hard not to waste her time contemplating questions like

How the hell did he know I was here? or *Do I just ignore the scorching-hot kiss that happened in Costa Rica while my hands are on his thighs?* Instead, she'd focused on the reason she hoped he'd requested her: because she was a damn good physical therapist. Thorough, methodical and careful.

But for a guy who had personally asked for her, Daxon had seemed awfully surprised to see her at his door. Then again, her first clue that she wasn't getting the full story was in Sheila's words: *he also wished for you as a personal healing coach.* The Daxon Miles she knew would never use words like that. The man wasn't really the type to wish for help with anything. And what the hell did that title mean? The only service she was giving him this week was physical therapy.

Her last assignment with him in Costa Rica had been her most memorable as a travelling physical therapist for many reasons... Daxon being one of them. Kendall had started to think her memories had mixed with fantasy, overexaggerating his appeal. But no. When he opened the door earlier, tousled wet hair, strong jaw and piercing grey-green eyes, she remembered why she had turned him down that last night. Daxon Miles was trouble. Shirtless, his hard, lean muscles flexed in stark relief. Up close, the raw sexuality of his body was almost irresistible. Another wave of heat rippled through her. Trouble. Especially for her, who seemed to have been born with an extra-large caution gene.

Daxon entered the room again, and the scent of him—freshly showered and very male—wafted in the air. She shivered as he brushed by her. Definitely trouble.

He took a seat at a safe distance on the couch and leaned forward, resting his forearms on his thighs. All the surprise from their greeting was gone, and in its place, he was giving her that smile. The one that said he knew exactly what effect he had on women. He had been melting panties with it for years between all the skydives and cliff dives and free climbs, if the tabloids were to be believed. She should know better, but that look was pulling her in.

"I promise I won't flash you again," he said, eyes glittering. "Unless you ask for it."

"You know, most people start conversations with 'hello' or 'how have you been?'"

His smile spread wider. "Do you really think I'm aiming to be like most people?"

Everyone with internet access knew the answer to that.

"Let's just get this started." Kendall opened her tablet and found the bullet points for the introduction. "Welcome to the Kalani," she said, reading straight from the notes, in her best professional voice. "I want to make sure your stay is everything you want it to be."

Kendall almost rolled her eyes. *Everything you want it to be.* Yeah, that definitely had sexy overtones.

She scanned the rest of the key talking points

Sheila had given her for the meeting. The wording of the resort's welcome was carefully chosen so as to flatter—and not to bruise any egos. God forbid. But she got the feeling that the whole *Fantasy Island* appeal of the Kalani Resort would take this conversation in the wrong direction. Time to go off-script.

"What are you doing here, Daxon?"

He blinked at her in surprise, then frowned. "Taking a break, healing my calf. *Relaxing*." He said that last word with plenty of sarcasm. "Lying low before my next filming. My producer's the cautious type, and he thinks this is the best option."

"I see," she said slowly. "He's the one who booked your stay here, right?"

Daxon nodded.

"So you don't want to be here?"

He hesitated, rubbing his jaw. "I do." His gaze was laser-sharp, and she squirmed under his scrutiny. It felt like he was planning, calculating, waiting for the right moment to…what? Drop his towel? No, he already did that. But the pull she had felt six months ago was just as strong now, like they were picking up right where they left off that last night.

In the hallway of a luxury hotel in Costa Rica, lit by the setting sun, oh, Lord, what a kiss they'd had. The whole world had been his soft mouth and his hard body, moving against hers. The feel of it was still so easy to recall, the physical memories, dreamy and ethereal. His big calloused hand cupping her jaw. Hungry strokes of his tongue as their hips fit together. Gasping for breath as he came in for more. And the hunger in his eyes as she broke the kiss off, long after it had gotten out of hand. The memory was still vivid. Very vivid. But she could think about that later…after she got through this first session.

"Let's get started," she said again. She scrolled through his files on her tablet until she found the one she was looking for: the doctor's report she'd reviewed a few days before. "You tore your calf a few weeks ago, Grade 1, and it still hasn't fully healed." She looked up at Daxon. "The doctor thinks the slow healing is a combination of not enough physical rest and possibly stress."

Daxon shrugged. "I doubt it's stress. I have the best job in the world. Cliff diving last season, rock climbing this season and a bunch of other adventures planned for the future."

"But a free solo climb has absolutely no margin for error. One missed foothold, one loose rock, one bee sting—if anything goes wrong, you could die."

He nodded solemnly, and for a moment she thought she was getting her point through to him, but then he smiled. "That's why people love to watch it."

His raspy voice strummed something inside her, but Kendall was trying hard not to be swayed by it, or his enthusiasm. He made it all sound so natural, so…sane. "You're talking about the rush of all this, but you have to understand that at some level this is stressful, both physically and mentally, even if it's fun. You jumped out of an airplane with no parachute a few months ago, for God's sake."

Daxon flashed her a cheeky grin. "Did you watch?"

This man was incorrigible.

"Maybe," she hedged. "Just to make sure you got to the ground safely."

Daxon waved off the comment. "I trusted my partner enough to put my life in his hands. Besides, Calvin wouldn't have shown the footage if I didn't make it."

"Good point," said Kendall.

He winked at her mischievously. "Which is why my free climb of Moonlight Buttress is going to have a live broadcasting element. Everyone will be watching, wondering if I'll make it. One slip of my fingers and..." He lifted his hands in surrender, adding, "It ups the stakes."

"Aaaand now we have the answer to where your added stress level is coming from."

Daxon's smile turned cocky.

"Not a chance. I thrive on the pressure. And I perform best that way, too." He lifted his eyebrows as that last sentence left his lips. "Just in case you're wondering."

It was the kind of thing a guy said right before he headed into bedroom talk. She could tell Daxon's mind went there for a moment by the way his eyes glittered with heat. And despite the fact that it was one step away from a bad pick-up line, that tempting heat traveled right through her body. *Don't get distracted.*

"I'm sure your performances are…fine," she said evenly. His eyes narrowed at that last word. "But that's still stress, and it has to come out somehow. In your case, it could be taking on physical manifestations."

"Like tension, which means the slow healing of my calf muscles?"

"Exactly."

"I see," said Daxon.

He actually looked serious, like he was really considering what she was saying. He was quiet, staring out the open French doors at the ocean, but she got the feeling he wasn't seeing it.

And for just a moment, she wondered what it was like to be Daxon Miles. He probably didn't even let himself think about his own vulnerabilities two weeks before a free solo climb. He'd have to have shut all his doubts out long ago, build a wall so they didn't creep in. Kendall knew exactly how people like this worked. She'd grown up with a man like this in her very own home.

She studied Daxon for an extra beat. "Can we rewind back to when you answered the door a bit ago?"

"Sure."

"What would you have done if someone else had been standing outside your door, someone you didn't know?"

Daxon laughed. "Well, for starters, I wouldn't have dropped my towel."

Yeah, right. Her face must have said exactly that because he tilted his head to the side, his brow wrinkling.

"Truthfully, I probably would have sent someone else away today. I'd also probably dodge them a few times this week, just for a little space." His mouth turned up, sliding back into his signature grin. "But I'm definitely not going to dodge you."

Damn. One-on-one with this man for seven days? He was already distracting her after fifteen minutes. It was time for a new plan, a better one. The plan she had decided on before she knocked on the door— *resist his charm*—wasn't going to hold up for long. At this point, she wasn't sure if she even wanted to avoid this particular brand of trouble anymore...

"My turn for a question," he said. "At dinner that night in Costa Rica, you said you were traveling to Hawaii for your next assignment. Is that when you got this job?"

Kendall shook her head slowly. She was a little thrown off by the fact that he actually remembered a detail like that from their conversation. But she shouldn't be. There was an intensity to him when they were alone, like every ounce of his attention was on her.

"That assignment never panned out," she said. "But I couldn't get Hawaii out of my mind."

He looked out the window, and she did, too.

Across the patio and his private pool, through the palm trees, the ocean spread out in front of them, a sparkling blanket of blue.

"I understand why," said Daxon softly.

"Costa Rica was gorgeous, too," she said. "That night at dinner, I got the feeling you loved it there, like you were considering staying. What's stopping you?"

Daxon's forehead wrinkled as he seemed to consider his answer. "I don't have any desire to stop traveling, to stop exploring new places, but I wouldn't mind a little beach house somewhere to come back to."

"You could still get one."

He tilted his head, studying her. "My turn again. And tell the truth."

Kendall crossed her arms, trying to resist the twitch at the corners of her mouth. "Ask away."

"I want to go back to that hallway in Costa Rica. That kiss was…" His voice trailed off, and his smile turned hungry. "You can fill in that last word yourself. But something made you stop. What was it?"

Of course he wanted to discuss that. Though she supposed it was better to get this topic out of the way from the start.

"The obvious. You hired me." She shrugged, as if that kiss hadn't been a big deal. As if she hadn't replayed it in her mind too many times.

"But the job was over," he said. "And I'm not into mixing work with pleasure, either. The idea of you feeling obligated in some way to have sex is a boner-killer for me."

She shook her head. "Thank you for that TMI moment."

Daxon's laugh was so real, so deep and easy and infectious, and Kendall found herself smiling, too. His laughter waned, leaving a glint of determination in his eyes.

"Do the same rules apply between us now?" His voice was low and sexy, making this question even more torturous.

Lord, he was tempting. Could there possibly be a way to explore this attraction and still keep her principles firmly in place? Kendall sighed. "I haven't decided."

"If we chose to explore...mutual pleasure this week, could it in any way interfere with your career? In theory, of course."

The word *pleasure* rolled off his beautiful lips, echoing through her. More physical memories came back. The hard, defined muscles of Daxon's biceps moving, flexing beneath her hands as he slid his tongue over hers. She shook her head again. "Not that I'm aware of. Though it's not exactly the reputation I'm cultivating here."

"Noted," he said, and he sounded a little more serious. At least he seemed to understand that part. "I can keep my mouth shut."

"Noted," she said, giving him what she hoped was a dry smile. "I'll take it under consideration."

His signature grin curved seductively at the corners of his mouth, like he was considering it, too. In detail.

His sharp gaze was on her again. His hand stopped halfway down his jaw. There was heat in his eyes along with something that looked an awful lot like resolve. He was deciding something, and she was almost sure it was about her.

He rose from the couch and stretched, his T-shirt lifting, exposing the sculpted abs and dark trail of hair that led into his shorts. Was she gawking at him again? Kendall swallowed and met his eyes.

He flashed her a smile, a mix of amusement and challenge. "Well, if stress is why my muscles aren't relaxing, I think we should start right away with my welcome massage."

Kendall's face flushed as she leveled her gaze on him. "This isn't the kind of massage that has a happy ending."

When Daxon's smile broadened, still hot and even more determined, she knew she was in so much trouble. "If anyone's getting a happy ending today, it's you."

CHAPTER TWO

Was that last comment a little too much? Maybe, but Daxon had made a decision, and once he put his mind to something, he couldn't let up. His brain had kicked back into gear, and he had decided to pursue the most obvious route, the perfect relaxation plan, one they'd both enjoy. He had never had much success at reducing his intensity level, but he could switch his focus.

His attraction to Kendall was a little dizzying, but that was likely just because he had resisted it—of course, her appeal had intensified when she walked away after a hot-as-hell kiss. His mind had filled in all the details that his body had missed out on that night. Solution: instead of spending another week trying *not* to picture Kendall Clark underneath him, they could have a little fun, get this thing between them out of their systems.

Besides, he needed a really good distraction, something to take his mind off the fact that he'd rather be in Zion National Park right now, preparing to climb Moonlight Buttress. Thinking about that had driven him crazy today. Thinking about sex with Kendall was a stellar alternative, and he had one glorious week to divert himself with it. But she looked far from convinced, which meant he had to get this next part right: keep her laughing and figure out her hesitations and limits. Make it clear from the beginning that getting naked with him meant plenty of fun for her, too. *And no more flashing your hard-on, buddy.*

Daxon gave her a playful wink. "Satisfaction guaranteed."

She cracked a little grin. Slowly, it grew wider until her whole face lit up in a beautiful, thousand-watt smile. "You're relentless."

"That's my strength," he said. "For better or for worse."

It felt so good to see her again. A whole week with Kendall stretched in front of him, and his smile just wouldn't quit. She stood, smoothing her tiny shorts over her long legs. Daxon loved any challenge, and this one involved a hot woman whom he'd thought about too much…in the shower, most often. His mind was going in a dozen different directions right now, but it was time to focus and let her do her job.

He rubbed his hands together, quirked an eyebrow at her and nodded to the massage table. "You can go first if you want."

She rolled her eyes. "Climb up, champ. I want to check out your leg." She walked over to the table and spread a towel over one half, and he climbed on. "I'm going to start by feeling around and moving your leg to get a sense of what's going on. Let me know how it feels."

He nodded.

Kendall moved to his left side, her attention focused completely on his leg, which meant he was free to watch her work. And not stare down her shirt, since he was pretty sure that would fall under obnoxious client behavior. He respected that. After a few unsolicited kisses by women when he was in front of the camera, he understood that there were many reasons why it could put her in a tricky position. So seeing her off duty was the—

"Ooooh," he groaned as her fingers gently kneaded the top of his calf. "Right there."

"Does it hurt?" She moved her hands farther down and to the sides, testing.

Daxon shook his head. "Just a little tight."

She moved to the base of the table and picked up his foot, flexing it gently.

"Still okay?"

"Yeah," he said. "Rarely hurts anymore. I'm just trying not to push it too hard this week. Which means mandatory R&R for me." Daxon sighed. Some people just weren't built to relax, and he was one of them. This week he'd work on his core and hand strength while going easy on his legs—that was the best he could do.

She put down his foot and rested her hands on the

table. "I don't see anything worrisome at this point, but I agree that three weeks is a bit long for a Class 1 tear to heal. Though if you're still the same person as you were in Costa Rica, I'd guess the reason for the slow recovery is that you're still pushing yourself too hard."

"Which is what my 'personal healing coach' is supposed to help with?"

Kendall laughed. "Who came up with that title?"

Daxon shook his head. "That would be Calvin. Definitely his sense of humor."

"Calvin, your producer?" She frowned a little. "Does he think we…?" Her sentence drifted off as she gestured between the two of them.

He paused, considering his answer carefully. "I think he assumes I sleep with a lot of women." Kendall's frown grew deeper. "Shitty, I know. Still, assuming we slept together is not enough for him to arrange this."

Her expression softened. "Then why did he specifically request me?"

Daxon shrugged. "Probably because I actually followed what you said I should do back in Costa Rica."

"And you don't follow orders?"

He heard the hint of sarcasm in her voice, but he ignored it. "I'm not being a dick about this, just honest. I need someone who takes lots of things into consideration, including working within my business obligations." He paused. "I've been told I'm frustrating to work with."

"I see."

"You're a great physical therapist, Kendall," he said softly. "And I'm not just saying that to get into your pants. Though I wouldn't say no if that's an option."

"Thanks, Daxon," she said, then, with a smirk, added, "for the professional compliment, of course."

The compliment was the unfiltered truth. In Costa Rica, Kendall went beyond the physical aspects of healing and actually listened when he said he couldn't make a particular accommodation.

She was also hot, of course, but there were plenty of hot women in the world and only one Moonlight Buttress to free solo. Not that he was celibate these days, but it had been a while…which probably wasn't a good thing since Kendall was about to put her hands on him again.

This would likely turn into the world's most torturous PT session. Daxon tried to clear his mind of the lusty haze that was still lingering. He—or Calvin, actually—had pushed her into this setup. If he wanted to propose after-hours fun, Dax needed to figure out how to give her a real choice, the freedom to opt in or opt out. Hopefully it wouldn't be the latter, but this would only work if she was all in.

"Look, I've made it clear that I find you incredibly attractive, and maybe you're feeling this vibe, too." He lifted one eyebrow, and he got a wry smile from her in return. "But I respect that you probably don't want to fool around on the clock."

She gave a little nod, which hopefully meant he was on the right track. Now for the solution.

"I have an idea for you to think about," he continued, keeping his gaze steady on her eyes, not letting it wander down to her mouth, no matter how tempting it was. "I'm not looking for an answer right now, just something to consider. You check out my leg and do your job, and I won't come on to you." She gave a little snort, but he pushed on. "When you're finished, you walk out my cabin door. Then you have a choice—you can keep walking, or you can turn around and come back in for that happy ending I'm dying to give you. Off duty."

She lifted her gaze to his, and her eyes were filled with heat. She licked her lips, and his eyes went straight there, fixating on her tongue. A bolt of heavy lust ran through him. Fuck, he had to keep this decent. He forced his gaze back up, and a smile quirked at the corners of her mouth.

"Just think about it," he whispered.

The body was a truly miraculous instrument, intricate connections of nerves and muscles and ligaments and bones. They all worked together to do the simple movements humans took for granted... until the system broke down. Then the different parts came into painful relief.

Kendall had seen the toll this breakdown could

take on someone, how it could crush a person. Her
father had come so close to that breaking point during one awful fire season, when the worst came so
close to happening. Being a hotshot firefighter came
with a ticking clock, and both her parents knew that
when they started. In the intimate game with nature's
forces, nature always won. The night the tree limb
fell and crushed her father's arm, ending his hotshot
career, was a reminder neither she nor her mother
would ever forget. Her dad got out alive, thanks to
his team, and after a long, painful recovery period—
thanks to both his physical therapist and Kendall's
mother—he had moved on. Still, all these years later,
her father missed it, some days wistfully, other days
fiercely. Kendall tried not to get hung up on the question she had asked too many times: Why the hell did
he still want to run toward danger instead of away
from it?

All this had unfolded when she was in her tweens,
and she had decided to become a physical therapist.

Her family history had probably made her a better one, or at the very least, a more dedicated one.
Each client was a new path into the intricate art of
movement. Each client meant learning the ways that
a person could heal.

Her fingers brushed the dusting of hair on Daxon's
thighs. His body was truly a wonder. She moved her
hands up and down his leg, over all that golden skin,
those well-defined muscles. She was trying hard not
to get distracted by his off-duty idea, but every time

her fingers moved up to his thighs, he sucked in a breath, reminding her of where this could go. Later.

Concentrate.

She had seen her fair share of men in amazing shape as a traveling physical therapist, athletes with bodies fine-tuned for sports. This was different. The switch had flipped that night in Costa Rica, and she couldn't figure out how to flip it back. She was no longer studying Daxon's body the way she would study a work of art. She was thinking about what it could do. What his muscular thighs would feel like pressed against hers. How it would feel to run her hands over those biceps as he lowered himself over her with each heavy thrust.

She glanced up at Daxon. His eyes were fixed on her, hot and intense. Holy hell. His hands gripped the sides of the massage table, his knuckles white. Still, he said nothing. Kendall smiled. She had to admit the man had impressive focusing skills. Much better than hers, clearly. Still, it was amusing to see him all worked up like this.

She quirked her eyebrow at him. "Not your best day for relaxing?"

He gave her a wry smile. "It's not a strength of mine, even on a good day."

"I think if you spend this week with a little stretching, massage and low-strain exercise for your legs, you'll be fine," she said, rocking back onto her heels, putting a little distance between them. "The real challenge is to go easy on your calf during the rest of the day. Try to stay off your feet as much as possible."

"I'll think of something."

She narrowed her eyes, and he put up his hands in surrender, laughing. "I wasn't coming on to you. Just a guy and his 'personal healing coach'—" He put air quotes around those last words "—having a conversation."

"Can we stop with the job title? It sounds like I'm part of some sort of cult fitness retreat."

He chuckled. "I already told you you're an amazing physical therapist," he said. "But the truth is I don't want you as a coach. And in the interest of keeping my word, I'll stop before I tell you what I want instead."

She bit her lip as Daxon's proposition came back. Off-hours fun. Low risk and high reward, if their kiss back in Costa Rica was any indication.

Kendall ended the session and packed her bags, taking her time, enjoying the heat of Daxon's intense gaze on her. She scrolled through the tablet, reviewing and adding to his schedule for the next day. She ticked off sailing, snorkeling, and a few more of the Kalani's features that were well suited for a guy with an itch for adventure and a body that wasn't currently cooperating. After all, he wasn't the resort's first guest in this situation.

"Here's a map of the Kalani, and I'll take you on a tour tomorrow afternoon," she said, handing it to him. "You can also use this tablet to book appointments or activities, order food—anything you need."

He scrolled through his options. "Can I book as many sessions with you as I want?"

"Don't push it." She tried to hold back her smile, but Daxon seemed to catch it anyway.

His mouth quirked up. "Thank you for doing this."

"My pleasure," she said, giving him the same playful wink he'd given her earlier. Before he could respond, she turned and walked toward the door.

Daxon followed. He didn't say anything, but she got his message just fine. *Remember how hot it was between us? I'd love to take it further this time.* Or maybe that was her own voice.

She paused at the door, then turned around. "I'll see you soon."

"I hope so." His gaze dipped to her lips, then back to her eyes. He opened his mouth, as if to say something more, then closed it with a little frown. Lord, she wanted to kiss that mouth, so she turned around, opened the door and walked out, shutting it with a click.

Then she came to a full stop on the wooden porch. *Whoa.*

Kendall took a deep breath. In front of her, Mauna Kea, the enormous volcano, rose up in the middle of the island. She was surrounded by miles of untouched hills and beaches, and the only other people anywhere near the place were high-profile guests, equally interested in privacy. A perfect place for escape and fun. Behind her, just on the other side of the door, was the hot, ultra-fit, six-foot-something man who had fueled her sexiest fantasies for the last six months—and that was only after a kiss. The man just had to breathe next to her and she was turned on. Escape and fun? Definitely.

Back in Costa Rica, Daxon had been hard enough to resist. Her employer at the time hadn't forbidden any intimate relations with clients…and she'd heard stories. But until that assignment, Kendall had never once been tempted to cross the line. Daxon didn't make on-the-job advances, but for one aching week, she found herself wondering what it would be like if he had.

Today she was getting a chance to reconsider that night in Costa Rica when she had walked away. She had taken this job as Daxon's physical therapist knowing full well that spending time with him would be intense. All she had to do was walk back in the door.

Kendall took a deep breath. Another breath. Another. Not helping. The anticipation of kissing Daxon again, all that intense energy focused—

The door creaked open behind her. She spun around and stood face-to-face with Daxon.

He blinked at her, lust written all over his face. Then he rubbed the back of his neck and gave her a sheepish smile. "Just checking the weather."

"Liar."

"I *was* checking the weather." He glanced up at

the cloudless sky. Then he stretched out his hand, palm up. "No rain. I *also* might have been checking to see if you had left. In addition."

"Just thinking through my options." Kendall crossed her arms, going for her best casual pose.

"Sure," he said lightly. "Let me know if you want any help thinking through those options. Or trying some of them out."

She raised an eyebrow. "Are you offering to drop your towel again?"

"I'm never going to live that one down, am I?"

"Probably not."

"You know where to find me." He started to close the door.

It was time. Kendall put her hand on the door. "Wait."

The door swung open again, and he was grinning. She stood, facing him, staring into those glittering green eyes. God, those eyes. They were filled with the same kinds of *more* that she had spent a week resisting last time: more games, more sexy, more fun. And right now, that was exactly the kind of *more* she needed.

"Made up your mind?" he asked, his voice soft, low.

She nodded.

"You're coming in?"

She nodded again. "Otherwise, I'll spend another six months wondering what I missed."

CHAPTER THREE

DAXON STEPPED ASIDE, leaving just enough room for her to pass through. Kendall's eyes narrowed, like she saw exactly what he was doing. She stopped in front of him, her body brushing up against his.

"I can play this game, too, you know," she whispered.

Then her hand was on his chest, and she looked up at him with wide brown eyes. He tried to read her expression, but he was sidetracked by her lips, so plush and inviting. His body was on high alert, memories mingling with the immediate sensation of her fingers on him. Her mouth was so close, and he was aching to kiss her. *Just a little more patience*. Last time this ended with him watching her walk away. This time felt…right. But he wanted her to lead.

So he waited as long as he could, which wasn't long. It was too tempting not to brush his fingers over her skin. Spending the last hour resisting her wasn't doing him any favors now. Daxon slipped his hand around her waist, bringing their bodies together, and walked them into the cabin, one slow step at a time. He kicked the door closed and rested his hand on it, leaning over her, breathing in the scent of her hair.

"Will you let your hair down?"

She blinked, a little surprised, it seemed, then nodded and slipped the fastener out. Shiny, sun-streaked chestnut-brown waves cascaded over her shoulders. Daxon groaned as his cock gave an urgent throb. She rested her hands around his neck, coaxing him closer.

He found the shell of her earlobe with his lips. "I got it wrong back in Costa Rica. Tell me how to get it right this time."

Kendall arched against him, their bodies flush. "You didn't get it wrong. I just wasn't ready."

"Are you ready now?" Thinking was getting more and more difficult.

"Mmm."

Oh, that sound out of her mouth… *Focus*. "Is that a yes?"

She tilted her head up and smiled at him. "That's a *hell yes*."

Then finally, *finally* he was pressing his mouth against hers, and she sighed, like she had been waiting for this just as much as he had. She kissed him, her lips brushing against his in achingly slow caresses. Months of pent-up desire flooded through him as he met each stroke, each invitation. He threaded his fingers through all that soft, beautiful hair, grabbing on, pulling her closer. He took a gulp

of air and then dived in for more. He had forgotten
just how good she tasted, like endless sunshine and
warmth. Each hungry stroke of her tongue fueled
another jolt of pleasure to his system.

His muscles tensed as her hands traveled down,
farther, until she found the hem of his T-shirt and
slipped her hands underneath. Goddamn, this was
better than he had remembered. Everything else
faded, and what was left was Kendall. He pressed
up against her, her body trapped between his and the
door, his cock hard and straining inside his boxers.
Her teeth raked over his bottom lip, and she hooked
her leg around him, starting a slow, sensual grind
that made his eyes roll back. He could come like
this, fully clothed and panting in this little hallway,
just from finally kissing Kendall, feeling her body
against his again.

Aaaaand…no. That wasn't where this was going.

Daxon slowed the kiss, reining himself in, loosen-
ing his grip on her hair. She pulled her hands from
under his shirt and settled them on his hips. He rested
his forehead against hers.

"Fuck, sweets. This is really hot, and you haven't
even taken off your clothes."

"Yet," she added, smiling. "You haven't, either."

"You haven't seen enough of me today?"

One of her hands moved lower, down between his
legs, and she stroked his rock-hard cock. Pleasure
rippled through him.

"I've changed my mind," she whispered. "I'd like a closer view."

The image from Costa Rica of Kendall kneeling between his legs came back, his own fantasies layered on, and he groaned. He had to stop thinking about that for now. If this was his only chance to touch her, to enjoy her, to taste her, he wanted to get it right.

"We'll see about that," he said with a wink. "Right now, I want to get you on that table."

Now Kendall remembered exactly why she had walked out of Daxon's room in Costa Rica. She had played back that kiss so many times in her mind, but somehow she had forgotten important details. The way his breath hitched when she touched his bare skin. The hunger in each brush of his lips. The way she lost herself as the tidal wave of want took over, building, threatening to crash through her body. She wanted more of this man, his hard muscles, the weight of him against her, his thick cock that was pressing against her, his mouth everywhere. She wanted *more*.

It had been almost impossible to walk away last time, but when she came up for air, she'd known she had to. Because drowning in a kiss with Daxon Miles had suddenly felt like a different kind of risk, one that had nothing to do with her job. One she knew was dangerous.

And yet here she was again, aching for more. During their sessions, her hands had traveled up and down his legs many times. She wanted to explore further. She wanted to learn his body, how it worked, how his muscles flexed when she touched him, what he sounded like when he came. This was a man with a preternatural ability to focus. What would it be like to feel him let go of all that control and lose himself in pleasure?

She just had to make sure this stayed uncomplicated. People had uncomplicated sex all the time, so why shouldn't this new, more adventurous version of her do it, too?

Kendall laced her fingers with his. "Let's try the bedroom instead. I think it'll be a little more comfortable."

"Maybe we can try the table later," he said. "But I'm happy to start anywhere, sweets, as long as I get to put my mouth on you."

Damn, he sounded so sincere, like he was aching to go down on her. No wonder women tripped over one another for this man.

"Right this way, champ." She led the way to the bedroom, her heart jumping in her chest. After months of watching his videos, just to make sure his previous injury had healed, of course—okay, and possibly using him as fodder for a late-night date with her vibrator because she never planned to see him again—after six months of *not real*, this was about to get very real.

A warm breeze blew through the open windows

of the light, airy room. The bed was enormous, covered with a fluffy duvet and a stack of pillows. A tray of hibiscus flowers lay on the long, narrow bench in front of the windows. He turned to her, tucking her hair behind her ear. The echoes of waves and the brush of palm leaves mixed with the sounds of turned-on male, so close. His hand lingered on her neck.

"I want to undress you."

"Sounds a little impractical."

He laughed. "Sounds sexy to me. As long as you don't mind me staring at you like a hungry dog."

Well, if he wanted to. She might as well get the whole Daxon Miles experience, from start to finish.

"Oooh, hungry dog," she said. "Very sexy."

He tickled her sides, and she yelped and wriggled. His laugh grew huskier.

"You like to tease me?" he said, his hands gentling, urging her to face him. "Just so you know, it only makes me harder for you."

When she turned around, his smile was so full of heat, and it sent a shiver of desire through her. Her eyes met his, and his smile faded. What would this incredible man feel like inside her, thrusting, working her hard? God, she wanted to know.

Slowly he slipped his hands under her shirt and lifted it up, his palms skimming her sides. She raised her arms, and he pulled the shirt over her head, tossing it on the floor. His warm hands rested on her arms, and he ran them up and down a few times, as if he were learning her in the same way that she was learning him back on the table. He traced the outline of her bra, around the curve of her breasts.

She'd always had mixed feelings about her chest size. Her body was a comfortable one to live in, fit, strong, and as a physical therapist, she was reminded daily not to take any of these pieces for granted. But she had been an early bloomer, and having large breasts at an younger age had made her self-conscious long after she should have outgrown it. She still had to fight her instinct to cover them. But with Daxon's eyes hot, his mouth parted as he gazed at her breasts, she didn't want to hide. Not when he was looking at her like she was the only thing on earth he wanted right now.

He traced the straps up to her shoulders, then moved down, exploring her nipples through the silky material. Pulses of heat spread through her, and she drew in a quiet gasp. He slipped his hands around her and unhooked her bra, eased the straps over her shoulders and tossed it on top of her shirt. He ran his fingers down her chest, and she covered his hands with hers. There was so much pleasure in this slow exploration. His eyes fluttered closed, and he leaned forward to kiss her neck, holding her breasts in his palms, kneading, learning them. Then, with a soft bite on her neck, he let go and knelt down in front of her.

"I love getting you naked," he said, reaching between his legs to adjust himself. His voice was getting lower, rougher. "I've wanted to do this for so long."

She spent so much time concentrating on other people's bodies and movements that it was strange to have the roles reversed. But definitely not a bad kind of strange.

He urged her to turn around, so she did, but she could still feel his gaze on her, hot and heavy. His hands moved from her hips, lower. He cupped her rear.

"You have one fine behind, Kendall." The rumble of his voice was making her giddy.

She peered over her shoulder, down at him. "You do, too, you know."

He looked up at her and cracked a cocky smile. "I'm glad you noticed."

"At the risk of inflating your ego, I admit that I've peeked at your ass more than once," she said, laughing.

"I've watched yours, too. Many times." Amusement threaded through the desire in his voice.

Would she ever tell him that she had stood at her dresser that very morning, choosing her outfit and, in the end, selected her shortest pair of jersey shorts, the ones that hugged her ass and showed off her legs, just for this meeting? Maybe. He slipped his fingers under the waistband of her shorts and pulled them down, revealing the scrap of her thong and a lot of her ass.

"Fuck," he whispered. "Just touching you like this makes me want to come."

His hands returned to her ass and his teeth grazed one side as he tugged down her panties. He paused, and she waited, not breathing. Then he got to his feet again. He brushed her hair over her shoulder and pressed his body up against hers, and he nibbled the shell of her ear. "On the bed, sweets."

She climbed up, and he followed her, tugging off his shirt as he settled between her legs. Then he made his way up her body, holding himself over her, his muscles flexing. She pressed her hands against his biceps, feeling the way they moved. When he leaned down to kiss, it was sweet, almost tender. Then he moved to her neck, her chest and, oh, her breasts. His lips closed around one nipple, and he swirled his tongue and dragged his teeth until she squirmed and ground against him. Watching him suck her breast added another erotic layer, and her mouth hung open in anticipation as he moved to the other. New jolts of pleasure shot through her. How close would she get to an orgasm, just like this?

But he moved lower before she found out, his lips on her belly. Her hips. The inside of her legs. She moaned as he came closer, his tongue hungry against her skin. Finally, he pressed his mouth against her clit. The spark was electric, sending shuddering waves of pleasure through her body, bringing her so close to the edge. He was kissing her everywhere, drinking her with endless thirst, his tongue exploring, repeating the strokes she responded to. Learning. When she moaned, he groaned, too, and came in for more.

Oh, *more*. Daxon's mouth was its own category of more. He slipped two fingers inside her and thrust, in and out, driving her mad as he worshipped her with his mouth. It happened so fast. Kendall arched her back and came, crying out, shuddering as Daxon took his last hungry licks of her, drawing out her pleasure.

She sucked in gulps of air as she came back down. The quiet sound of the ocean blew through the windows. Daxon crawled up her body and lay by her side. He propped his head on one hand, his other hand resting on her stomach.

"I've been thinking about doing that for so long," he whispered.

Kendall was trying to get her thoughts together, though her entire body protested. But when his cock pressed against her thigh, her mind skidded back to her earlier question: What would he feel like inside her? She took a couple more breaths and turned to Daxon. "Want to try something else?"

His eyes darkened with desire, but he shook his head. "Some other day, if you want. But I meant what I said earlier. Today is all about your happy ending."

She closed her eyes and let the mix of languid pleasure and the heat from Daxon's body lull her into a rare moment of peace. Was this his plan to get her to come back another time? If so, it was working.

CHAPTER FOUR

"Daxon Miles wished for you specifically?" Alana asked with a burst of laughter. "Based on your past experience together? Sounds like fun."

"Not *that* kind of experience." Kendall chuckled. "But definitely fun. And potentially overwhelming, considering his reputation. Plus, he's even hotter in person."

The words slipped out of Kendall's mouth before she could check her tone, almost definitely revealing her current state of client lusting.

"Just about everyone who walks into this place has an ego and a reputation," said Alana. "If they're hot, too, why not?" She waggled her eyebrows, like it was no big deal. Maybe it wasn't.

Alana, one of the Kalani's chefs, had a few years' experience granting the wishes that made this resort so famous. Visitors' wishes weren't sexual per se, but the whole *Fantasy Island* appeal of the resort set the tone for indulgence of all kinds. Kendall looked over at her friend, with her long purple hair and blunt, irreverent style. If anyone could help her navigate hang-up-free casual sex in this place, it was Alana.

Kendall leaned back on her elbows, sinking into the warm sand, and looked out at the ocean, sparkling in the morning sun. Even after six months in Hawaii, she still hadn't gotten used to this warm and welcoming beach, so different from the ice-cold water and whipping winds of Northern California. But it was time she started to get the hang of the laid-back Hawaiian vibe…and maybe Daxon could help with that.

"Can I ask you a personal question?" she asked. "You don't have to answer it."

Alana leaned back on one elbow, facing Kendall, and a smile curved on her lips. "Now I'm intrigued."

"You ever sleep with a guest?"

"Of course. Sheila must have told you there's no policy against client-employee relations here." Then she gave Kendall a conspiratorial wink. "Come on. You can ask me something better than that. Like the best location or more than one at a time."

A splash of a wave washed over Kendall's feet, and she flicked some water onto Alana's bare legs. "I mean someone you're working with."

"Only if I think it's really going to be worth potential complications."

The day before had definitely felt worth it, especially when she was lying on his bed.

"My turn for a question," said Alana, rolling onto

her side. "Did you sleep with Daxon the last time you worked with him?"

"Nope. Not at all," said Kendall quickly.

Not at all? What kind of wacky answer was that?

A tiny hint of a smile tugged at the corners of Alana's mouth. "I'm guessing it wasn't for lack of interest. But if he didn't talk you into bed the last time, I'm trusting you'll be able to hold out for a week. If that's what you want."

"It's too late for holding out," said Kendall, "though I guess it depends on how broadly you define sleeping together."

Alana drew a little heart with cupid's arrow in the wet sand between them. "I hope that definition includes your orgasm."

"Of course it does," she said with a smirk. "Daxon Miles seems to take pride in mastering *all* of his performances."

"So I'm not seeing the problem." Alana added a "D + K" to her sand art project. "The guests at the Kalani are used to being the masters of their own domains, and they come here looking for something they still haven't found. Sometimes it's explicitly what they ask for, and sometimes it's not. As long as it involves two willing partners, there's nothing wrong with that."

"Willing isn't the problem." Kendall dug her toes deeper into the cool, wet sand, waiting for the next wave to wash it away. She had certainly been willing the day before on his bed. It was just so easy to get carried away when he was close, and she didn't know where that would lead.

"We're just talking about sex, right? What happened to the new, adventurous version of you?" asked Alana, gesturing to the long, sandy beach that stretched out on both sides.

"You're not going to talk me out of this, are you?"

Alana shook her head. "I think you should go for it. Besides, you said Daxon Miles is here because of a torn calf. He's a man who thrives on physical thrills, and if he's not performing some crazy stunt, all that energy has to go somewhere…"

Yes, it certainly did. Why not be the one who enjoyed his reputed endurance performances in bed? Now that she'd seen what else his mouth could do, well, Daxon was the perfect—

Alana nudged her. "Hey, lady, stop daydreaming about hot extreme sportsmen. The real thing is approaching."

Kendall snapped out of her thoughts and looked down the beach. And there was Daxon Miles, tanned, shirtless, his abs flexing with each step as he… jogged? With his injured calf? Slowly, she shook her head. What the hell was he thinking?

"I can't believe you requested Kendall Clark," Daxon muttered into the phone as he closed the door to his cabin.

"You're welcome," said Calvin brightly. Cheers

erupted from some sort of sporting event in the back-ground of the call.

"You stalked her and figured out where she was working now?"

"So you didn't have to."

The path from his cabin curved through flower-ing bushes that wafted their sweet scent. A woman walked by in a bikini, all smiles. The boardwalk crossed a stream and headed into the sand, where the cabins stretched out along the beach…if they could be called cabins. More like small luxury resi-dences. In one direction, the island's highest volcano rose up to a barren, treeless peak, and in the other, the endless blue-green ocean rippled and sparkled in the sunlight. Both tempting, both off-limits for anything remotely interesting. So instead, he was heading to the beach for an easy morning run, the best antidote for the stir-crazy he was already feel-ing, less than a day after arrival.

"You'll thank me," said Calvin, optimism oozing from his voice. "Just do whatever it takes to be ready for filming in two weeks. The Kalani has every ser-vice you could need."

"And which kind of services are you recommend-ing?" This was sounding a lot like *go get laid*.

"The kind that gets you back on the face of Moon-light Buttress for your free solo," he said, his voice turning serious. "I mean it, Daxon. Do whatever it takes. We've built up a lot of hype around this climb, and I don't think I need to tell you that we have a lot riding on it. You are the Pure Adrenaline brand, and people want to see you, shirtless, at the top of your game, in front of the camera. And with the Moonlight Buttress free solo and then the El Capitan free solo, you're giving viewers a peek into the next level of crazy."

"Nice way to put it," Daxon grumbled.

When the Pure Adrenaline YouTube channel began, it had been all about having fun. Daxon had been the young upstart, back when their videos were all about taking each climb or dive or jump to the next level by filming it live. As viewership multiplied and sponsorships exploded, so did the offers for all-expenses-paid trips, endorsement opportunities and other ways to make money. During his mother's hardest years, back before they knew what was wrong, he had been grateful for the money. After years of worrying about her, scrambling to make ends meet, he had taken those opportunities that fell into his lap so he could finally carry the financial burden for her. But none of it would last if the videos didn't keep coming.

Which was why Calvin had come up with a strategy to make Pure Adrenaline into a more permanent business. Instead of putting up videos sporadically, whenever Daxon was ready to film, this new series on his explorations of elite free-climb spots was on a regular streaming schedule to encourage regular viewership. Daxon had already done a set of training videos on smaller routes, and the viewership bump had been impressive. A lot was riding on his ability to deliver a stellar performance on Moonlight Buttress…and then El Capitan. The latter was the ultimate free solo climb, and only one person had ever done it and survived. When Daxon succeeded on live camera, he'd be a legend—a living one. In between the two major climbs, Calvin had worked out a plan for merchandising, guest appearances on television and other publicity boosts. At the other end of all these plans was the hope that he could leverage his Pure Adrenaline image to be less reliant on his next live video. A long-term plan, as Calvin put it. Daxon still wasn't sure about any of it, but he trusted his friend's business instincts. That's what had gotten them this far.

"This is an opportunity to make our business venture last, and it's all resting on your image as a high-risk adventurer. People either want to be you or fuck you," Calvin said with a derisive laugh. "But that attention depends on you in front of the camera. So find a way to redirect that adrenaline impulse for the week."

Earlier that morning, he'd used the tablet Kendall had left for him to scroll through the Kalani's recreational offerings—private dolphin sightings? Just the thought of spending an entire week on enforced relaxation was making him restless. Which was why he was going to focus the entire week on having fun with Kendall. Hopefully naked, at least some of the time. That thought cheered him up a bit.

"Is this the point where you say I need a girl-friend?"

"Nah. I think you're right on that one," said Calvin. "No one looking for a future together wants to watch you dangle from a sheer rock face, over and over again."

Daxon had made this point to Calvin many times, and apparently, it was finally sinking in. Any relationships he had attempted ended not long after the woman understood that extreme adventures were his lifestyle, now and in the future. Plus he couldn't afford to be distracted by someone on the ground. He never said that last part aloud to a woman, but they all seemed to get the message anyway.

"But there are other options for fun of the less serious variety," Calvin continued, chuckling. "Both men and women have come back from this place positively rejuvenated."

"Kendall would probably kick you in the balls if she heard that, even if that's not why you requested her," Daxon grumbled. "Plus, rejuvenated is quite a promise to a guy who's not getting any younger."

He hung up his phone as he wandered along the boardwalk, past more cabins and through a lush tangle of palms and what looked like ferns, until the pathway split. In one direction, arrowed signs pointed him toward Reception, the pool, the spa and various other facilities. In the other direction, a lone sign pointed him toward the beach. He sighed and headed that way.

Daxon glanced at his watch. It was 7:28 a.m., and he was already itching to do something. He had completed a round of pull-ups on the fingerboard he had installed in the bedroom doorway, and he'd do another round when he got back. Then Kendall would show up for his physical therapy session and make everything feel better.

The boardwalk ended, opening up onto the sand. A smattering of palms guided the way to the shore, and everything else in front of him was sand and ocean. No people, no cameras, nothing except him and the elements and his goddamn injured calf.

But it hadn't bothered him at all when he woke up this morning, not sore or stiff, maybe thanks to the massage Kendall had given him yesterday. All attraction aside, she was really good at what she did.

Daxon walked across the soft sand, letting his leg muscles stretch with each stride. The resort was located on a rather remote part of the North Shore, far from other developments, so there was nothing else in sight, just the stretch of beach and greenery that disappeared in the gentle curve of the Hawaiian shoreline. He could probably run for thirty minutes in one direction and thirty minutes back without much strain.

Daxon reached the shore and stopped, facing the ocean, taking the time to stretch on the empty beach. What the hell was everyone else at this place doing? Sleeping? Fucking? Soon this area would be filled with rich, sunburned mainlanders, but for now, at least he was alone.

He used to spend long stretches of time on his own when he first got into adrenaline sports. No one around, just him and the natural world as he climbed a peak or jumped out of a plane and fell toward the ground. And he had liked it that way. Now, for this new venture, everything he did was monitored by a camera crew, with three takes to get better angles and Calvin's direction for maximum viewer appeal.

But right now, it was time to ease some of the tension, both mind and body. Daxon started off at a leisurely pace, nothing like the clip he'd take if he were in top form. If Kendall were here, she'd probably tell him that running was a stupid risk. Maybe it was, but it was also key to keeping him sane in paradise. And she would never know the difference.

The ocean breeze was a warm caress against his skin, a welcome change from the dry heat of southern Utah. He had spent a number of hot days and cold nights in Zion National Park, just hiking around, getting the feel of the place after the summer tourists had scattered. Moonlight Buttress was an old friend, one of his earliest challenges in his home state and off-camera, so he was more than ready for his second free solo of it. Free, with no partner, with no harness. Just the mountain and him. And his camera crew this time, of course.

He had done plenty of practice climbs with ropes, choreographing his route while harnessed in. He wouldn't think twice about this plan if it weren't for the injury. And Moonlight Buttress was calling to him, louder every day. The wide canyons of Zion that stretched out below him, the red rock face rising up on either side, the chalk on his fingers, when the only sounds were the quiet wind and the scrape of rubber soles on the rock.

Pulling the earbuds out of his pocket, he selected one of the focus tracks on his audio app, then slipped his phone into his shorts pocket. Each track was thirty minutes, serving as a perfect timer for his run.

The music began and he was there, at the base, tracing his path up the mountain, seeing it, feeling the rock with his fingertips. The route drew and redrew itself as he moved, one foot at a time, one crevice at a time, one hand at a time as he made his way up. He thought through all possible routes as he ran, focusing on each challenge as it came, problem-solving it in different ways, just to be certain. Daxon saw the mountain, not the sand and the ocean in front of him. The first track ended, and he turned back down the empty beach, back toward the resort, and focused on the last stretch of mountain terrain, factoring in the sun and his thirst and the tingle in his muscles, craving energy.

And then…there she was.

Daxon might have missed Kendall entirely if the audio track hadn't ended. He had seen two figures, but he hadn't really registered them. Now all he could do was stare. His steps slowed as he approached her, and he felt a strange twist in the pit of his stomach.

What the hell was that? It felt almost like…loneliness? Nah. More likely hunger.

But damn, Kendall looked hot. She was lounging on the beach in shorts and a T-shirt, her feet in the water, and another woman was next to her, with purple hair and a string bikini. And they were both looking at him. The other woman's smile sparkled with amusement, but there was no trace of humor on Kendall's face. She sat up, brushing the sand off her hands. Half of his body, the lower half, was thrilled to see her. The upper half had a little more sense than that. He could guess what would come out of her mouth before she even said it.

"What the hell, Daxon?"

That wasn't quite the tone he was hoping for.

"Good morning, Kendall," he tried, flashing her his camera-ready smile. "Lovely to see you, too."

Purple Hair chuckled, but Kendall didn't look pleased.

"I'm supposed to help you, and you're actively countering my efforts." It wasn't a question.

He slowed to a stop in front of her. "That's not what I'm doing. I just needed to get out and go for a run. To clear my head."

Kendall stood up and put her hands on her hips. His gaze traveled down as she moved, to her hips, then farther to her bare, toned legs…but this really wasn't the time to get distracted. He rubbed the back of his neck and looked up again. Her eyebrows were raised, and she was frowning. "You didn't hear when

I told you to take it easy on your calf yesterday? Or you just ignored me?"

That wasn't really a question either, but he ran his hand through his hair and attempted to answer it anyway. "I *was* taking it easy. I could have done this run in half the time."

Kendall rolled her eyes. "Bullshit. You know exactly what I would've said if you had floated the idea of going out on a jog while your calf is recovering. So now you're ignoring my professional opinion after we…"

She let the sentence drift off and looked away as the weight of her accusation sank in. *Shit.* That wasn't a connection he had consciously made, but he could see why it would really sting from her perspective.

He stared down at the sand, trying to think, but his eyes caught something in the sand next to Kendall's friend. A heart and an arrow and… D + K? Daxon covered his mouth to hide his smile. Had they been discussing him? God, he hoped so.

Purple Hair caught where his gaze was and quickly brushed it away, then stood up. "Time for me to stop eavesdropping. I'll catch you later."

"Later, Alana," said Kendall, not looking in her friend's direction. She kept her glare steady on Daxon, and the last of his smile faded. She shook her head. "I'm feeling like an idiot right now."

Daxon grimaced. "Why? I'm the idiot who went running, not you."

"And I'm the physical therapist that got distracted by all this—" She gestured up and down his body.

His shirtless state had been in deference to the climate, but he couldn't deny he liked hearing that Kendall was enjoying the view...

She shook her head. "Daxon, I don't think this is going to work."

Whoa. His thoughts screeched to a halt.

"What's not going to work?" he asked carefully.

"Me as your physical therapist," she said. "I can arrange to get you someone else, someone good."

"No." His answer came out louder than he meant it to, but the idea that he wouldn't see Kendall...well, the thought was like a kick in the stomach, and he wasn't about to sort out why. He took a deep breath and softened his tone. "Please don't back out. I don't want anyone else."

She gave him a sidelong glance. "That's just because you haven't gotten your happy ending yet."

"No. That's not why." *Shit, shit, shit.* This run was shaping up to be the worst idea he had had in a long time. He tried to stanch the feeling of panic that was rising up in him. He couldn't let her leave. "If you want the after-hours part of this to stop, that's your call. But please don't quit. I'll do exactly what you say. I promise."

They were standing close together, and Daxon had no idea who had stepped forward or when it had happened. All he knew was that Kendall looked upset. He was dying to close that last distance, to comfort her in ways he had no business doing right now. Her hair was back in a ponytail again, and her cheeks were flushed. In her eyes, behind everything else, he could see the stubborn wall of determination. If he promised to do exactly what she said, she'd hold him to his promise, no exceptions. And she seemed to be considering it. She raised her eyebrows skeptically. "Exactly as I say?"

He nodded.

"Like—" her expression brightened "—if I said dive in the ocean right now with your clothes on, you'd do it?" She gestured out into the turquoise water.

He blinked at her. "These running shoes are specially made for me, and they're the only pair I brought."

She gave him a look of impatience. "That wasn't a serious req—"

"Never mind. Hold my phone."

"What?"

He unzipped his pocket, picked up her hand, and placed his phone in it, along with his earbuds. His fingers brushed the soft skin of her palm, reminding him just how much he wanted to touch her. Definitely time to cool off in the ocean.

So he turned and walked straight in, special shoes and all.

CHAPTER FIVE

KENDALL WAS NOT going to stare at this perfect speci-
men of a man, mostly naked, entering the water. She
was not going to gape as the muscles of his shoulders
flexed and moved with each step. Nope, she wasn't.

Okay, maybe for just a moment. Purely from a
kinesiology perspective, of course.

A few drops of sweat ran down his tanned back,
following the intricate ridges of his muscles. His
torso was long and lean, and his dark hair curled a
little around his neck. She had shamelessly lusted
after him while watching his videos, but that body in
real life? Holy hell. He waded in until the water was
up to his waist, then lifted his arms over his head and
dived. He stayed under for a while, his underwater
image moving with each stroke he took, those over-
priced orange shoes glowing in the blue-green sea.

Finally, Daxon emerged again. He turned, shaking out his hair, and smiled at her. It was a beautiful smile, a smile that held pure joy, the same smile
millions of viewers had seen when he was in the

middle of doing something he loved. But right now, that smile was aimed directly at Kendall. Her insides fluttered dangerously.

"I'll do exactly what you say, Kendall," he called, swimming back toward her.

He stood up, emerging like some sort of sea god, and walked through the shallow water, back to shore. His body glistened in the morning sun. He stopped in front of her, closer now. His hair dripped on her shirt and then on her nose. He wiped it away with the pad of his thumb.

"Please don't quit," he whispered softly. "We'll do this exactly the way you want. You decide. Just tell me you'll stay."

Kendall was dying to reach out and touch him, to trace the paths of water running down his chest. Maybe even lick them. But before she got carried away—again—the work relationship part of this had to be cleared up.

"If you go back with your calf in worse shape than when you started, what kind of a physical therapist does that make me?" she asked.

He looked down at her, and all traces of playfulness were gone. "I see your point."

"This isn't worth my professional reputation, Dax."

He leaned down, and his lips brushed against her ear, but he didn't touch her. More ocean water dripped from his hair, onto her cheek, and ran down her neck. "I'll behave," he whispered. "And I'll make it worth it. I promise."

Kendall closed her eyes and let herself take in everything at that moment. The shush of waves breaking on the shore, the warm, salty wind, the cool sand under her feet, the sun heating her back, and Daxon, his wet body so close, short-circuiting most of her rational thoughts. The truth was she didn't want to walk away, but she would if she needed to. Even if it would be harder to walk away the longer she spent with him, she knew in her heart she'd do it.

So she leveled a steady gaze at him. "Okay, Dax. We'll give this a try. But the moment you break that promise, I'm out. Both as a PT and anything after-hours."

He nodded, and his intense green eyes were serious, drawing her in. It was just the two of them on a gorgeous morning, standing on the edge of the ocean, all alone. For a moment, she wasn't with Daxon Miles, Pure Adrenaline YouTube phenomenon. They were two people on a precipice. Something was unfolding, something strong and complicated and so, so tempting.

Then he straightened up and gave her another nod. He took his phone out of her hand and looked at the screen.

"It's a little past eight thirty now," he said. "I've got thirty minutes before you show up at my door for PT, so I'm going to hop in the shower and get changed in plenty of time. Just to make sure there's no more towel-dropping."

* * *

Waves of warmth radiated through Daxon's muscles. Kendall's hands on his leg were heaven. This was the ultimate distraction, and he struggled not to groan. If he did, she might mistake it for sexual, and he was trying his hardest not to take things in that direction, despite the fact that the sexiest woman in the world had her hands all over him. And, fuck, it was exactly what he needed.

Lying here in this luxury cabin, with Kendall's hands on his skin, was also easing that knot in his stomach, the one that had formed on the beach. It had stayed with him as he'd waited for her to show up for his morning appointment, wondering if she'd have second thoughts about coming back. But she was here, and her fingers were working their magic.

Daxon gritted his teeth to stop whatever sound was about to come out of his mouth, and Kendall pulled back, softening her touch.

"Too intense?" she asked.

He shook his head. "Not at all. Just sparing you the wild animal noises that are probably going to come out. It feels so goddamn good."

She started moving her fingers again, kneading into his muscles. "I thought you had a physical therapist back in Utah."

"I did," he said. "Not as good as you."

Kendall laughed. "I'm going to assume that comment is about my PT services."

"Trust me, it is," he said with a sigh.

She began the stretching exercises, flexing his foot, changing positions. She had been right about the run, of course; his calf was a little tighter. But what else was he supposed to do with the restlessness that came back when he tried to relax? Without an outlet for all this energy, it was like he was eighteen again, sleeping in the back of his truck, always on the move, always looking for the next rush. But he had to figure out something else, because the idea of her quitting sure as hell hadn't sat well. Daxon frowned.

He really had to leave this place in top shape. Over the last weeks, as the Moonlight Buttress climb grew closer and he hadn't bounced back from his torn calf, more tension had been building. Every free solo was a high-consequence pursuit, and over half of the very best climbers had faced that consequence. Just about every season, an elite climber fell to their death. Sometimes two. That was the reality of the sport, a factor he accepted in exchange for the freedom that came from climbing impossible mountains. But he wouldn't attempt the climb if he wasn't confident he'd live through it.

Still…

Doing Moonlight Buttress again would be full-on intense. Amazing. But the next climb was El Capitan in Yosemite, a mountain face that was much taller, made of unforgiving granite, and it featured a couple spots that were near impossible. Meeting the El Cap challenge would be an accomplishment of a lifetime, a personal achievement that would last beyond the popularity of a YouTube channel. And if Calvin was right, the payoff would be long-term for Pure Adrenaline, too. It would be a huge financial jump, the kind of money that sponsorships and merchandising and everything else Calvin had planned would bring, the kind that would support his mother when her body no longer cooperated. It would make up for all those years he wasn't there for her.

Kendall flexed his foot, gently stretching his calf. Man, that felt good. Then, before he could ask himself why, an image of Kendall watching from the base of Moonlight Buttress as he climbed flashed through his mind. He already knew what Kendall thought about Pure Adrenaline, and as a PT, that probably came with the territory to some degree. But the idea of her watching from the base was both thrilling and disconcerting...which was exactly why relationships didn't work—not just for the woman but also for him. Because a relationship would mean he'd have to consider how she felt about the climb, too.

Why was he even thinking about that?

Probably because that scene on the beach with Kendall had driven home just how much he was looking forward to seeing her. And when she made the point about her professional reputation, he'd felt like a real asshole. He hadn't even considered what it would say about her as a PT if he hurt himself further. Daxon cringed.

"Tell me about your Moonlight Buttress plans,"

said Kendall. "Free solo, so you're going up without equipment."

"Just me and the mountain. I've done it once before."

"Were you climbing when you tore your calf?"

"Yeah. The move I tried was risky, but it was better than falling." Daxon thought he caught a hint of a frown. He didn't take the possibility of death lightly, if that's what she was thinking.

"What happens if you get into trouble this time?" She started to work her hands up his leg now, and he was trying like hell to keep his mind on the conversation.

"It's up to me to practice every single move enough to make sure there's no trouble."

He had given this answer countless times to the media, but unlike the others, Kendall didn't look suitably impressed. In fact, she was definitely frowning now. She was quiet for a while, lifting his leg, stretching it, searching for points of tension. Finally, she lowered his leg back onto the table and then turned to him. Her hand was still resting on his thigh, though she didn't seem to notice it. Daxon certainly did.

"Why?"

He raised his eyebrows. "Why practice?"

"I mean why are you doing this at all?" Her brow was furrowed, as if she already knew the answer and didn't like it. "I get the adrenaline rush thing. When I was younger, I used to stand at the top of the ten-meter platform at the Stanford pool and look down, thinking, *there's nothing like this in the world*. But climbing a cliff face without a rope isn't just that."

Daxon raised his eyebrows. "I thought diving had the highest death rates of any sport."

"I didn't actually jump."

He smiled a little. "That's the difference. I'd jump any day."

He propped himself up on his elbow and looked into her eyes. The outer rims were dark, and there were streaks of yellow that grew brighter toward the center. Beautiful and unlike any eyes he had seen before. "You don't think I know what I'm doing?"

She blinked, staring down at him, the lines still creasing her forehead. Then she opened her mouth, like she was about to speak, but she closed it. Finally, she started to laugh. "We're not going to get anywhere in this discussion, are we?"

"If you're going to try to talk me out of the climbs, then probably not," he said, smiling. "The filming is already scheduled. But I'm happy to discuss whatever else is on your mind."

"What do your girlfriends say about Pure Adrenaline?"

He shook his head. "This lifestyle doesn't leave a lot of room for girlfriends. You can probably imagine why."

Her hand was still on his thigh, and his dick didn't seem to care that it was unintentional.

He cleared his throat. "If you're finished, you

should probably stop touching me so I can keep my promise not to come on to you."

Kendall's brow wrinkled in confusion for a moment, and then she pulled her hand away.

"Sorry," she muttered, a flush creeping up her neck.

Daxon sat up and waved off her apology. "Let's sit out on the lanai and go through what I should or shouldn't be doing here this week."

One of the many appeals of the Kalani was that he never had to leave the cabin if he didn't want to. He and Kendall could spend a meal in the privacy of his own lanai, without any interference from the rest of the world. Off duty.

"I'll order us some lunch, too," he added. "I looked at my schedule, and we have a few hours to kill until you're showing me around the Kalani. We can take a dip in this pool I have all to myself."

He gestured out the door to the private rectangular pool. Her eyes widened a little, bright and glittering, but she shook her head. "I can't. I have an appointment with another client. In fact, he is scheduled…" She glanced down at her watch. "In thirty minutes."

Daxon didn't move, but a grumble somehow still escaped. Another client? *He*—as in, a male client? Holy fuck, he really was a self-centered prick, because this whole time, in his mind, Daxon had assumed that her week was all about him. But of course it wasn't. Other clients could book regular times for her services. Including other *male* clients.

"Something wrong?" Kendall was eyeing him, her expression somewhere between skeptical and amused. Daxon massaged some of the tightness out of his jaw.

"It's nothing," he said roughly, though he knew he sounded petulant and sulky.

But she seemed to know the reason behind the change in the course of this conversation without him saying it. "Did you think being your PT meant my week was dedicated to you and only you?" She had the nerve to smile. "Sorry, Dax. I do have some regular clients I had scheduled before I got this assignment."

Regular clients? Every single week? This really wasn't what he wanted to think about right now. He just grunted in response, trying to cut off the discussion before he said something stupid.

She crossed her arms, and the skeptical look on her face suggested he hadn't quite convinced her yet.

"Fine," he said. "It's not my favorite thought that you would be touching some other guy today. But I know that's stupid and childish and maybe even probably crossing the line. But there it is."

Kendall tilted her head, like she was thinking about what he said…and all of the things he didn't say but that might have slipped through in that confession. *Well, fuck it all.* He had said it, and she could do with it what she wanted.

But she smiled. It was a beautiful smile, so full of laughter and warmth. "Do you have a crush on me?"

Did he? Daxon sighed. This wasn't just about sex so… "Maybe." The corners of his mouth tugged up. "Yes."

"Just checking."

A crush. His smile grew. The great thing about a crush was that it was fleeting. Which meant it would fizzle by the time he left the Kalani.

"So help me out here." He waggled his eyebrows. "Spend more off-hours time with me, tomorrow if you can't today. I promise I'll make it worth your while."

Kendall hesitated. "Um, I'll think about it."

"You'll think about it?" Christ, this woman was killing him.

"I'm your PT, not your babysitter," she said.

"Don't worry. I'm not into the babysitter thing," he said with a straight face. "But I could get into naughty schoolgirl."

Kendall buried her face in her hands, her shoulders shaking with laughter. "Didn't you promise me you weren't going to flirt with me on the clock?"

Oh, right. "Shit. Sorry. Let's get back to the real issue," he said. "Are you going to let me take you on an outing tomorrow? Or the next day?"

"Maybe," she said, her sexy mouth curving up again. He was getting closer.

"You're free to stop by this evening, off duty, and let me know your decision."

"Thanks," she said. "Generous offer."

He had toyed with her, and now she was enjoying toying with him. Time to take it a step further.

"Just think what I'll do to entertain myself while you're off with another man."

Kendall snorted. "The internet is full of wonders, isn't it?"

Daxon let his gaze wander down her body. "I have many ideas," he said softly.

Her cheeks flushed, and pleasure danced on her face. "As long as it doesn't involve any strain on your calf I'm all for it."

"I hope you don't regret saying that later," he said with a lusty laugh. "I've got a dirty mind and too much time on my hands."

"Now I'm curious."

"That's definitely off-duty material," he said, smirking. "Looks like you'll have to come back."

She laughed and then turned for the door. "Bye, Dax. See you later."

And she walked right out without telling him when off-the-clock *later* would be.

CHAPTER SIX

THE LATE-AFTERNOON sun glittered on everything, reflecting off the blue-green water and the white sand beach. It was a beautiful day, the kind Kendall had imagined when she left everything behind in Northern California. The warmth surrounding her as she walked barefoot through the shallow waves, on her afternoon walk with Alana.

"So he asked you on a mystery date." Alana lifted her sunglasses and gave Kendall a look, the kind that said *right on*. "Not really following why you'd say no to this."

"It's not a date. And it's complicated," said Kendall, shading her eyes from the sun. "Though I'm not on the clock, which was my first concern. I'm not *that* kind of professional."

Alana grinned. "But the paid escort game sounds rather fun."

Kendall gave her friend a little shove, and Alana kicked a splash of water her way in return. She opened her mouth to respond when her phone buzzed in her pocket. She pulled it out and looked at the screen. *Home.* Her heart jumped, and an ominous shiver ran through her. Her mother was calling in the middle of the day. Something must be wrong. Kendall frowned and blew out her breath. *Chill out.* Not every unexpected call had to be a tragedy. She'd thought moving across the ocean would make her less jumpy about her father's health, but apparently that part of her psyche was immune to the mellow Hawaiian vibe.

"Sorry. I have to take this," she said to Alana.

Alana waved her off as Kendall waded deeper into the water and accepted the call.

"Mom? Is everything okay?"

"Everything's fine, honey." The lightness in her mother's voice sent a rush of relief through her. After years of anxiety that wore on her family, fire season after fire season, Kendall had learned to read her mother's voice well. "Am I catching you at a bad time?"

"No. This is fine." She tried to shake the last of her worry.

"I thought quitting the traveling PT job and moving to Hawaii was supposed to be relaxing."

"I'm relaxed...most of the time." Or as relaxed as she'd probably ever be. Her father was sure she'd outgrow her goal of becoming a physical therapist after the fear of his career-ending injury had faded, but her mother understood all too well that the mark that night had made was permanent. Who wouldn't err on the cautious side after almost losing her father? Okay, maybe Kendall had leaned just a little too far in that direction, but now she was spreading her wings...safely. "It's just that you usually call in the morning, and I wondered if..." Her voice trailed off. "Never mind."

"You wondered if something had happened to your father?" Her mother's voice was more serious. "He's fine. No emergency."

Kendall hung her head. "Sorry," she mumbled. She let out another breath, then injected a little more cheer into her voice. "How are you?"

"We both took the day off, so your dad's out surfing, and I'm about to sit down on the deck with a book."

"Sounds great," said Kendall, keeping her tone light, but the unease came back. Why did her parents take the day off? Her mother had to be calling for some reason.

"You're still worried, aren't you?" said her mother gently. "Honestly, nothing's wrong. We just got back from your dad's appointment, and I promised I'd call right after."

Her father had begun to feel the long-term effects of smoke inhalation—yet another occupational hazard.

"How's his breathing?"

"No worse than it was on his last visit."

The words settled in, relief spreading through her muscles. Thank God. She didn't spend all her days worrying about her father's health, but these unexpected calls still triggered the same feelings they did when she was a kid, when she and her mother would jump every time the phone rang during fire season. It was the kind of thing she thought would dull after a while, but it didn't. Even years after her father retired from hotshot duty.

"That's great news," she said. "Can I call you tonight, talk to both of you?"

"Of course." Her mother sighed. "You don't have to worry so much about us."

"Old habits die hard, Mom. You know that."

Her mother laughed. "I guess I do. Love you."

"Love you, too."

Kendall shoved her phone back into her pocket and wandered back over to Alana, who was currently inspecting a shell on the beach. Her friend looked up at her.

"Isn't it the parents that are supposed to worry about their kids? How did you get it backward?"

"I've been practicing since I was a kid." Kendall's smile faded. "I don't know how my mom survived all those years of forest fire seasons. She said it's harder to be a hotshot's wife than it is to be a hotshot."

"Your dad must have been worth it."

"She'd say so, but there were some hellish times, too." When the tree limb that crushed his arm fell, her father had been knocked unconscious. For one terrible day, they hadn't known if he would ever wake up. That day had almost broken her mother, and it was the last thing Kendall wanted to think about right now.

"Don't most relationships have a few hellish times?" Alana gave her a pointed look.

"Maybe, but marrying a hotshot set her up for more than her share."

But Alana waved off her comment. "Makes the fun times all the better. You don't want to miss a single one of those."

Kendall chuckled. "You're bringing this back to Daxon, aren't you? You think I should get naked with him."

"I certainly do. As soon as possible."

Daxon clung to the hangboard, mounted on the wall of the lanai, holding up the weight of his body with only his first three fingers. The timer beeped, so he shook out his hand, then started another set of pull-ups. Ten...then twenty. This was his last interval. Thirty-five, thirty-six, thirty-seven...just a few more.

Forty-two, forty-three, forty-four... His hands were aching, and each pull-up was slower, but he couldn't stop now. If he was going to make it up Moonlight Buttress, his shoulders, his arms, his hands, his fingers—everything needed to be in top shape. It was his fifth set of pull-ups today, and he was almost done. Three more. Two. One. He let go and his arms fell to his side as his feet found the ground. Daxon leaned back against the wall and wiped the sweat from his forehead. The warm breeze blew off the ocean as he flexed his hands, in and out, stretching out the soreness.

Done. Now it was time for his reward. The lanai formed a U shape, and inside the U, his private swimming pool was glassy-smooth and ocean blue. It wasn't made for laps, just big enough and the right temperature for a quick dip, which would be followed by the oldest relaxation technique known to man.

Daxon set his phone on the side of the pool, stripped and dived in. He stayed under for a few strokes, the rush of the water cooling him off. He emerged for a breath and swam over to the side, where there was a ledge so he could sit chest-deep in the water. The sun shone down on him, reflecting everywhere. Beautiful, but it would be so much better if Kendall were here.

He imagined her swimming up to him. She'd sit next to him on the ledge, work her hands up his leg, much like she did in PT, with that crease between her eyebrows when she was concentrating. But instead of stopping mid-thigh, she'd keep moving higher. Then, just before her hands reached his cock, she'd look at him, her lips parted with just a hint of a smile.

"You want the deluxe treatment today?" she'd ask with a little laugh.

"Hell, yes," he'd say.

And now he was hard. He'd need to climb out of the pool...soon. He wrapped his hand around his cock and squeezed.

Kendall's words from the bedroom came back.

Your turn now. Her voice had been husky with pleasure, pleasure he had given her. Daxon gritted his teeth and moved his hand up and down. Next she'd run her hand up his cock, exploring his length before she reached for the strings of her bikini. Then, slowly, she'd—

His phone dinged, jolting him out of his fantasies. He glanced at his phone, lying on the pool deck. Another ding. Who the hell was calling him? Kendall had his number, and that call would be worth answering. Daxon reached for his phone.

The Kalani concierge.

Daxon sighed and answered it.

"Mr. Miles, I hope I'm not catching you at a bad time," said the woman. "You told me to call when I had an update about your requests."

"Perfect timing," he deadpanned.

"Great. Just wanted to let you know that I located the exact convertible model you requested in red. Would you like me to have it delivered to the Kalani tomorrow morning?"

Kendall hadn't given him an answer about the outing. Should he plan it anyway? Better than the opposite—she agreed to go and he wasn't ready.

"Yes, please reserve the car for a few days," said Daxon. "And I'll send you the other items I'd like to have picked up."

"Very good, sir."

Daxon hung up and set down his phone. His dick had mellowed out a bit, and a little more of his reason flooded in. As far as distractions went, Kendall was a very effective one. Daxon frowned. He sounded like an asshole when he called her a distraction, even in his own head. She was funny and sexy, and being with her was so much more than just passing the time.

There was this niggling thought in the back of his mind that it might not be very easy to just shut off these days with Kendall when he left the island. But he had to, and he would. Climbing demanded every ounce of his concentration, which meant shutting everything else—and everyone else—off. He had never had a problem blocking out everything once he got on the mountain. Whatever happened this week wouldn't change that.

"You're not getting dressed for this?" Kendall's gaze raked down Daxon's bare torso, then snapped back up to his face.

Daxon bit back a grin and flashed an innocent smile. "What? This?" He gestured to his chest and his abs.

Kendall rolled her eyes. "Put a shirt on, Dax."

"Whatever you want, sweets."

He hadn't really planned to take his private Kalani tour shirtless, but he was loving this habit of answering the door in various stages of undress. Did it count as a come-on? Naaah.

Daxon grabbed the shirt he'd left on the table by the door and pulled it over his head. Then he tugged on a baseball cap and picked up his sunglasses. "Better?"

"Come on, champ. Let's do the tour."

The path to Daxon's cabin opened onto a private road, lined with tall palm trees and flowering bushes. From his glance at the map of the resort when he first arrived, he knew the resort spread out for miles along the northeast shore of the island. Much of the property was untouched coast. The buildings were clustered on a narrow peninsula, lined with white sand beaches, and the guest cabins of various sizes were tucked away just inside the trees, dotting both shores. On the stretch of land between these strings of cabins were the bar, the tennis courts and other resort offerings for guests who were feeling social. The head of the peninsula was mostly undeveloped, with a few trails, an ocean-side restaurant and an un-marked building that looked like a private residence.

"I assume you got a glimpse of some of the facili-ties when you came in," said Kendall as they walked past the trail to the large pool. "As you've seen, guest cabins have pools that overlook the ocean, and the main pool is for guests looking for something larger."

The stone-lined path led to an area built up an incline, with different levels of pools, connected by waterfalls, one leading to the next. At the base was the largest. One side was rectangular and well-suited for lap swimming, while the other seemed to be shallower, curved with seating along the edges. More splashes of waterfalls fell along the rocky incline, and the pool was surrounded by leafy plants and palms. Nicely done for people who liked to sit around. Daxon didn't.

They wandered on, past the tennis courts and the spa, as Kendall continued to list the luxury services the Kalani offered and how to access them. Daxon wasn't paying close attention to what she said. In fact, he was almost sure he wasn't going to use any of this during his stay. He was more at home out in the wilderness, and what the resort had to offer him— discretion while his calf healed—had nothing to do with the facilities. He supposed it would've been the nicest thing to decline Kendall's tour, but the truth was that he wanted to spend a little more time with her. Climbing was a social activity, despite the list of very individual skills it required, and he was used to being around other people, doing what he loved. Now he was alone and practically on house arrest, granted it was pretty much the best location for it. But he wanted to talk to someone. No, not just *someone*. He wanted to talk to Kendall.

"Inside that building is the gym, in case you want to do...whatever it is you do that doesn't involve your calf."

He cracked a little smile. "Is that a hint that I should work out a little more?"

Kendall smirked. "Are you fishing for a compliment?"

"From you? Always."

"You look just fine the way you are," she said

evenly. The word *fine* came out the same way it had when she had called his performance *fine* in his cabin yesterday. But this time she said it with a little grin.

He laughed. "Thanks for that lukewarm praise. But I won't be using the gym this week. I brought everything I need to keep up my strength."

The truth was that he didn't need much in the way of equipment. Climbing favored lean muscle strength, not bulk, which made pull-ups on his fingerboard his top activity, not lifting weights.

They passed the last of the cabins, but the road continued a ways, up a slope and into a lush tangle of green, and then forked. Kendall chose the road to the left.

"What's up that way?" he asked, nodding to the right.

"There's a waterfront restaurant up there, the fine dining option, if you're interested in that."

Daxon shook his head. Growing up without money, he and his mother never once ate anything fancier than In-N-Out Burger. Though he had more than enough money now, he still avoided any place that might require a button-down shirt. Did he even own a tie? Not likely. If he did, it was long forgotten at the back of his closet at home.

"The rest is hiking trails and lookouts except for that area." Kendall pointed up to the hillside, where a gate peeked out over the foliage. Probably leading to the unmarked building from the map. "That's where Byron Keahi lives."

"The owner?" Daxon knew just the basics about him: ultra-successful businessman with Hawaiian roots. "I read the *New York Chronicle* article about him. Interesting guy."

"Probably." She shrugged. "I almost never see him around the resort, though he surfs early every morning when he's here. Actually, I think he bought this land because of its waves."

"He doesn't hang around the bar?" He'd read that Keahi was known for enjoying all of life's pleasures. Often.

"He meets with a few guests and works the jobs around here every now and then, but he definitely keeps a low profile."

Good. Because the idea of Byron Keahi flirting with Kendall wasn't sitting well with him.

"So no staff Christmas dinners at the boss's house?"

Kendall shook her head. "Nope. But a good Christmas bonus more than makes up for it."

The road took them to the shore and turned, heading along the stretch between the beach and the forest, toward the tip of the peninsula. They were high above the ocean and still climbing, high enough to see the curl of each wave, rolling around the point and breaking in long-running tubes to-ward shore.

Kendall stopped at the turnoff to a trail that zig-zagged down to the beach, weaving through the rocky hillside. He stopped next to her, close enough to settle his hand on her waist or against the small of her back. He was dying to touch her.

But he couldn't, so he just leaned closer. "If we continued heading uphill, where would the path take us?"

"If you keep left on the trail, you get to one of my favorite places. Maybe I'll show it to you one day."

"As my reward for behaving?"

She gave a little snort. "Your life is already full of rewards, Dax."

It was true, so why did he still have this hole inside him, this need he couldn't seem to fill in any lasting way? There were moments of real satisfaction, like right now, standing here with Kendall. But mostly they came when he was doing something physical, something that took every bit of his concentration, every ounce of his focus. The satisfaction used to last longer, but lately it faded too quickly. And it was a selfish kind of satisfaction, which Kendall had gently pointed out to him six months ago.

"Remember that conversation we had back in Costa Rica?" he asked.

"The one about high risk versus high consequence?"

He nodded. It began at the end of a PT session and continued so naturally and easily into dinner, unfolding as the evening darkened in that beachside restaurant. Hell, he'd wanted her badly that night. He had replayed that conversation in so many different ways, but right now, he was thinking about the part where she had pointed out some gaping holes in his ideas.

"You know, that conversation was one of the reasons I took the job at the Kalani," she said softly.

His eyebrows shot up. There had been an intensity between them that night, and he was pretty sure she wouldn't have forgotten it. But he hadn't been sure if the night had stuck with her in the same way it had with him. Maybe it had.

"I loved visiting new places as a traveling PT, but I didn't love the impermanence of it. There was always this idea in the back of my mind that someday I'd move somewhere new, stay there." She looked out at the ocean, like she was debating how much to say. Then she turned to him again. "At dinner that night, you told me that I was mixing up risk and consequence, and you were right. I had never differentiated the two. I used high risk as a reason for not trying things, things that I wanted, when I really should have been looking at consequence. The risk of moving, that my life would change drastically, that I would be far away from my parents if anything happened—those risks could be high. But the consequence was low. I could get on a flight and go see them at any point. And I could probably even get my old job back."

"And the move turned out fine?"

"Better than fine." She smiled. "What made you think of that night?"

There was the fact that he wanted to kiss her just

as badly then as he did right now, but that probably wasn't the connection she was looking for at the moment.

Daxon ran a hand through his hair. "I just wanted to say that you were right that day, too. That my assessment of risk and consequence was based on how things affected me. But the decisions *don't* just affect me."

Kendall laughed. "Sounds a little harsh now, out of context."

He shook his head. "Just honest. And understandable, considering what you and your mom went through when your dad was in the middle of fire season, choosing to go back, again and again."

She smiled a little. "I wasn't sure how closely you were listening that evening. Especially when I caught you looking down the front of my dress."

He chuckled. "I was multitasking."

Then his smile faded. He wanted her to know that he hadn't forgotten a word she'd said that day about what it was like to watch someone she loved choose a high-consequence profession. Nor had he forgotten the reservations she voiced that came from having clients who were injured in high-consequence situations. But in the end, her drive to help these people was stronger than her personal opinion. No, he had not forgotten any of that.

"I talked with my mother after that conversation," he said quietly. "I wanted to hear what she thought about what you said."

Kendall nodded, but she said nothing.

"She said it was hard sometimes, watching me do the things I did. But she trusted me to make the right decisions." He rubbed the back of his neck. "I was hoping she'd give me a definite answer, but she pushed it back on me. I hope I'm making the right choices for her."

"Everyone hopes that, right?"

Kendall was looking up at him, her big brown eyes pulling him in. He felt the shift between them, the tension, the awareness. Her long dark lashes fluttered, like they had just before she kissed him.

"Are we on the clock right now?" he whispered.

Her eyes sparkled with humor. "I'm afraid so."

"Just checking."

Damn, she was tempting. And she looked like she might give in. But he had promised not to make the first move, so he held back.

"It's a beautiful view from here," he said softly, keeping his gaze focused on her deep brown eyes. He smoothed her hair off her face. "Come visit me tonight. Please."

Slowly, her mouth curved up into a smile. "I'll think about it."

CHAPTER SEVEN

KENDALL HAD TAKEN the safe route for as long as she could remember. She had chosen San Francisco State University, closest to home, instead of the school with the best kinesiology program. She had taken the summer internship at San Francisco General instead of the internship with the WNBA. Even the traveling physical therapy job had been a compromise. She had chosen it instead of a position on the location of a movie set because of the lack of job security. At the time, Kendall had thought of each one of these decisions as logical, as strategic, as better financially, especially considering her dad's health limited his work possibilities these days. But deep down, she knew why she made all of these decisions: fear.

The evening breeze was warm as she walked down the path through the trees toward Daxon's cabin. Every decision she made was run through some sort of internal risk-assessment monitor that played in the background of her mind. Boyfriends, travel plans, airplane rides and of course, her move to Hawaii, which she had come so close to backing out of.

That evening, as she stared in the mirror, tracing her mouth with lip gloss, she had tried to calculate the risks and consequences of this evening visit. The risk of liking Daxon a little too much, the consequence. What exactly were the hidden risks of a really hot man who was amazing at…well, just about everything? It was impossible to weigh them when her mind kept wandering back to the kiss in his hallway the day before. Pulling back from the kiss, his thumbs brushing against her skin, rough, calloused, she had looked up into his eyes, and she had seen something she wanted.

So here she was, on this beautiful Hawaiian night, heading to Daxon's cabin to proposition him. The ticking clock of his stay was why she'd finally decided to come. She knew that no matter what it felt like between them, he was leaving to climb a mountain without ropes, and he had decided that this was worth the consequence of death. Every free solo climb could end his life, and she would never, for one minute, forget that. That was enough to keep this casual. At least that was her thinking as she headed out of her little rental cabin, down the hill and over to the guest lodgings.

The walkway turned off to Daxon's place, and Kendall approached the front patio, slowing with every step. The Kalani was a truly beautiful resort, every building exuding the kind of exclusive luxury it was known for. Modern, simple, sustainably built with reclaimed mango wood beams.

Kendall stopped in front of Daxon's door and smoothed the wrinkles of her spaghetti-strap hibiscus-print dress. She had paired it with her cowboy boots in a sort of mainland-meets-Hawaii effort, but now she was having second thoughts. Too cute? Too revealing? Her breasts weren't really made for a strapless bra, but if things went the way she hoped they would, the bra wouldn't stay on for long. Her heart was jumping in her throat, fluttering, her breath coming quicker.

She swallowed and tapped on his door. Nothing. She tried again, louder. Still nothing. *Damn*. She had spent her afternoon debating whether or not she should come, and he wasn't home? She wasn't giving up this easily. Maybe she could break in and wait for him. Naked on his bed? No, too cliché. She could do better than that. She turned, leaning against the door, and blew out a breath.

But just as her back touched the wood, the door opened from behind her, hitting the heels of one cowboy boot and pushing her forward. She stumbled across the porch, grabbing the support beam in front of her, clutching it.

"Fuck." Daxon's low mutter came from behind her, followed by a rush of footsteps. Then his hands were on her waist—large, warm hands. Slowly, Kendall let go of the beam and turned around. In front of her was a stunned Daxon Miles dressed in a pair of board shorts and nothing else. His washboard abs and his broad, muscular shoulders were on full display, but this time, she was sure he wasn't just showing off. He blinked, as if she were the last person he ever expected to see at his doorstep.

"Kendall?" he whispered as he searched her face, his forehead lined with concern. "Are you hurt?"

She shook her head, but he didn't look convinced. He lifted his hands to her forehead, which was probably bright red at this point, then touched her cheeks. His fingers tested her bare shoulders, then worked their way down her arms, gently probing.

"Where did I hit you?"

"Just my boot," she said, the corners of her mouth tugging up. "Good thing I came prepared. Most people around here wear sandals."

He was so close, his body warm, his muscles flexing as he touched her, lines of worry across his forehead. Each brush of his fingers sent a delicious shiver through her. His hair was wet, she noticed for the first time, the water dripping onto his shoulders and sliding down his bronzed skin in trails. It looked like he had come straight from the shower to the door, without bothering to towel off.

He touched one of her palms, then the other, and she flinched. Daxon frowned and lifted her hand, inspecting it. He found a little splinter—she hadn't noticed it in the rush of his nearness—and pulled it out.

Kendall sighed. "The perils of reclaimed wood. Thanks."

He smiled a little but continued his inspection. His hands skimmed her body and wrapped around her back, testing, until finally he seemed satisfied.

"I'm sorry." He stroked her cheek.

"I'm fine, really. You just surprised me, that's all."

Slowly he nodded, and then he broke out into a grin. "You're here."

His smile was infectious, and the corners of her mouth turned up. "I'm definitely here."

One arm was still around her, his thumb gently stroking her back, and he was looking at her like he was about to kiss her. Like he was dying to but holding himself back.

"You want to come in?"

"I walked all the way over here in my dress, after hours," she said with a little smile. "I suppose I'll come in."

Daxon started to laugh, a low rumble that shook his shoulders and crinkled at the corners of his eyes. But he didn't move. He looked at her, his eyes searching. His hand moved to her waist, sliding up and down her sides. Finally his mouth turned up into his signature grin, tinged with teasing and humor and desire. "Well, by all means, let's go inside."

The sunset colored the white walls shades of pinks and oranges and purples, and the evening breeze blew through the open room, warm, bringing the scents and the sounds of the ocean closer. Kendall had never been inside one of the guest cabins in the evening. The pool on the lanai sparkled in the evening light.

It was as if they had been transported, not here at the Kalani but somewhere else, just the two of them.

"It's lovely here tonight," she said, walking into the large room.

"Lovelier now that you're here." He rested his hand on her hip. "I can say that now that we're after hours, right?"

Kendall chuckled. "You can get a lot dirtier than that."

His hand traveled lower, down around her ass, his thumb still stroking, reminding her of how close he was. It was almost as if he didn't want to stop touching her, as if waiting the whole day had made him just as hungry as it had made her. And there was satisfaction in that idea, that this driven, highly focused man wanted *her*.

"I hope the rest of your day went well," she said, looking up at him.

"I would've preferred to spend it with you, but you were busy with another guy," Daxon grumbled.

"We don't always get exactly what we want, do we?"

"No, we sure don't," he said, chuckling. "But every once in a while, we do."

Kendall laughed. "Looking forward to your happy ending tonight, champ?"

"I already got what I want. You're here in my cabin," he said softly. Then his familiar grin took over again. "Though I suppose a guy can want more than one thing."

Lord, this man knew exactly what to say. She had imagined what sex with Daxon would be like so many times since Costa Rica, but she hadn't imagined this part, where he'd talk to her, touch her. In her experience, pre-sex time was usually fumbling and awkward conversation. She had never imagined that she would feel so...comfortable with him.

He lowered his head, bringing his mouth to hers. Their lips brushed once, twice. His hands were strong, firm around her, but his kiss was achingly slow, as if he were savoring it. She parted her mouth, meeting each stroke of his tongue. Shivers of pleasure ran through her, heating her up, turning her insides molten hot. She ground her hips against his, trying to get closer. It was happening again, that same thing that had happened in the hallway, as kissing Daxon took over. She was too short, couldn't reach enough of him, couldn't touch enough of his taut, firm muscles. She put her hands on his shoulders and tried to pull him down, closer. Daxon chuckled, kissing her neck.

"I've got you, sweetheart," he whispered. His hands traveled over her ass, finding her bare thighs, and he lifted her, the bottom half of her dress bunched up around her hips. She wrapped her legs around him and wedged his cock between her thighs. He was so deliciously full and hard, and she shamelessly rubbed herself against him. He came in for another kiss, this one hungrier than the last, each stroke of his tongue mimicking the thrust of his hips. His biceps flexed against her, holding her up.

"Your calf," she said breathlessly. "Don't hurt it."

Daxon stopped, slowly blinking down at her. "My calf?"

She nodded. "I just don't want you to strain it. It's already frustrating enough…"

He was looking at her, wide-eyed with wonder. "You're thinking about my calf?" His laugh was rough and full of humor. "I was kind of hoping your mind was elsewhere."

"Actually, it was, which is how I ended up here," she said, squeezing the muscles of his arms, which were currently holding her up. "I shouldn't forget. This climb is everything to you, and I'm your physical therapist, even if I'm off duty." She smiled. "I'm supposed to heal, not injure you further."

But he didn't put her down. He just looked at her, waiting, like he was still a little stunned.

"Sorry to ruin the mood," she added.

"Not at all." He shifted his weight to balance her on one arm and slipped his other hand behind her neck, caressing her with his thumb. His gaze swept over her face. "The mood is perfect."

She was still thinking about his calf. Despite the hunger in her kiss, the way she moved against his body, sighing, moaning, she was thinking about his injury. His first reaction was that he wasn't anywhere near giving her a performance she couldn't forget.

But then the concern in her voice hit him, along with this realization: never once had a woman stopped to worry about *him* in the middle of sex. It wasn't like he had been harboring unspoken complaints about it, but at this moment, it occurred to him that all along, he was just expected to…perform.

Well, that's what he got for living relationship-free.

The irony of it all was that for once, he hadn't been thinking about performance. He hadn't been thinking about anything except kissing Kendall, about those full lips and her soft skin and her sweet body moving up and down against his, with only a thin layer of panties and his board shorts between them. All he was thinking about was how goddamn good it felt to get lost in her.

He had been moments away from dropping his pants and sinking into the sweet, wet heat of her right there, in the middle of the living room. He probably would have done it if she hadn't stopped him, and frankly, with her legs wrapped around his waist, grinding against him, he doubted Kendall would protest. But she was right. He should put her down and get himself together.

This was a woman he wanted to take his time with. And he wasn't just topping his performance reputation, making sure he exceeded expectations. This wasn't a personal challenge. He could slow the hell down and make sure they were right together.

Daxon let her slip down onto the floor, keeping

his hands on her hips, making sure she was stable on her feet. Then he bent down for a languid kiss, full of promises.

He found her hand and squeezed it. "Let's go out on the lanai."

She tilted her head up for another kiss and then turned toward the French doors, giving his hand a tug.

"Give me one minute," he said, letting go.

She nodded, and he took off for the bathroom to find his stash of condoms. When he walked back out onto the lanai, he found Kendall on the couch facing the pool, one sexy leg crossed over the other, cowboy boots and short dress giving the whole scene a fantasy fuck vibe. Except she was so very real. He sat down next to her, and she smiled. Damn, that smile. It was beautiful, and it was for him. *He* was making her happy right now, and he hadn't even taken off his shorts. It had been a long time since he had thought about pleasing a woman outside of the bedroom, so long he had forgotten he had ever even wanted to.

"You look so sexy, Kendall," he whispered. "Relaxed."

"I have almost as much trouble relaxing as you do. Almost." It felt so good to see her at ease with him. He could stare at her all night.

"Then we know what we're aiming for." He motioned with his hand. "Come over here, cowgirl."

CHAPTER EIGHT

KENDALL GOT UP on her knees and climbed onto Daxon's lap, straddling him. She pulled off her dress and dropped it on the sofa, leaving her in panties, a bra and cowboy boots. Then she ran her fingers over his shoulders, feeling his muscles twitch. His big hands rested on her waist and moved lower, around her ass, pressing against her thighs.

"Hey there," he said, pulling her closer. "What's a nice girl like you doing in a place like this?"

"Slumming it. Clearly." She smiled up at him. "I have terrible taste in luxury resorts."

His laugh rumbled in his chest. "And men."

"The worst."

"Thanks for coming." He leaned in and kissed her on the base of her neck, right where her pulse was kicking and jumping. "If you had seen me ten years ago, you probably wouldn't have given me the time of day." His hands began to move up and down her sides, the calluses rough against her skin. "I was the kind of dude with a big truck and a fondness for old

'80s music. Actually, those parts haven't changed. I'm just no longer living in that truck."

He said that all with a laugh, but she detected some seriousness in his voice. Like he was opening up a more private part of his life, just a little bit. His hands moved lower, over her panties, palming her ass. It felt so good to be touched by him, so easy to be with him, just like this, half-dressed and straddling his lap.

"You never can tell what a girl might like," she said after a while. Her voice was starting to sound breathless.

He chuckled. "I can think of a few things that I'm pretty sure you'd like."

"Of course." Kendall smiled. "Even with a mullet, you'd probably still know how to please the ladies."

Daxon pulled back and gave her a mock-offended look. "Hey, I didn't say I had a mullet. A guy can like '80s music without the hair."

"Sure."

He'd probably look great, either way. She slid her hands into his hair. It was soft and thick, and he let out a sigh each time she moved her fingers against his scalp. His hands were exploring, too, skimming over her skin, caressing. His eyes were heavy with desire, and the way he was touching her felt very… intimate.

"Besides, living out of my truck while I'm out looking for the next adrenaline rush doesn't leave room for lots of styling."

"Too late. I can't unthink it now," she said, messing up the top until his hair stuck up in all directions. "Business in the front, party in the back."

He tickled her sides, and she squirmed on his lap, pressing herself hard on his erection. The intensity in Daxon's gaze grew stronger, so she did it again. She felt so lucky to be here right now, but she didn't want him to misunderstand. This wasn't about getting naked with Daxon Miles, Pure Adrenaline star. The chemistry between them had been electric from the start, but it was all the touching and laughing, the comfortable intimacy together, that had her beyond turned on.

"Still thinking about my hair?"

Kendall laughed. "Not quite as much."

It was on the tip of her tongue to say how good this felt, just laughing with him, but luckily, her brain caught up with her. This was Daxon Miles, who would leave in a few days on his quest to climb up another mountain with no ropes. She had to keep this light.

So she distracted him the best way she knew how. She reached behind her back and unfastened her bra. And, *surprise, surprise*, it worked. Daxon's gaze wandered down her body as she arched toward him, his eyes on the cups as she slid them down, slowly revealing the tops of her breasts.

"Fuck, Kendall. Your tits make me so hard," he muttered. "And the cowboy boots are really doing it for me."

Her nipples were sensitive, always had been, and when his thumbs brushed over them, a shiver ran through her body. He did it again, a little harder, rougher. She moved up and down on his lap, getting more of that delicious friction against his erection. God, yes.

Their height difference wasn't nearly as pronounced when she sat on his lap, so they were almost eye to eye. She closed her eyes and opened her lips. His mouth was so hungry, so eager, soft and warm as he opened for her. He met each stroke of her tongue, but it felt like he was holding back, letting her lead. She threaded her hands behind his neck, tilting her head a little, exploring. She got the sense that he usually just took charge, but today, he didn't. It was as if he was saying, *learn more of me, look closer.* His palms moved up her thighs, over her ass, feeling her. He was learning more of her, too.

"You're a good kisser," she said when she broke away. "Really good."

Daxon chuckled. "I'm just really into kissing you."

"Smooth talker, too."

"You hoping I can back it up?"

"Of course." Her cheeks flushed.

"Are you asking me to pull it out?"

"Okay, yes," she said with a little laugh. "I've been a bit curious since you flashed me." She held up her thumb and finger a centimeter apart. "Just a little bit."

He chuckled. "Then feel free to explore. Just a little bit."

"Purely as a professional, of course," she said, her hands moving down his chest. "I mean, your body does some amazing things."

Her heart was pounding hard. She was teasing him, but there was true admiration behind it, too. After years as a physical therapist, she knew intimately the kind of dedication it took to do the things he did.

Her fingers moved down the ridges of his abs, down his stomach. His breath was coming quicker as her fingers trailed lower, lower, to the waistband of his shorts.

A hiss escaped his lips. "That feels good."

"Can I take off your shorts?" She smiled up at him. "Still just professional interest, of course."

"Of course," he echoed, but he made no effort to help.

Kendall drew the tie of his board shorts, and his cock popped out of the opening right away. She blinked a little in surprise but kept unlacing, her fingers brushing against his skin.

"You look skeptical." Daxon's voice was full of humor, but there was a rough undercurrent of need in this voice.

She wanted to tease him, but she couldn't. Not while that intensity burned in his eyes.

"Just admiring," she said. "I never get a chance to look like this."

He gave a hum of satisfaction, so she ventured closer. She ran her hands up his legs, his rough, coarse hair under her fingers. He stilled as she moved higher, higher. He was so hard, all the ridges and colors in stark relief. She had spent the last couple days working on the perfectly formed muscles of his legs, wondering what it would feel like to explore the rest of him. And now she was. She started at the bottom, brushing her fingers against his balls. How sensitive were they? She cupped them, and he sucked in a gasp.

"Are you sure you're doing okay up there?"

"I'm sure," he said, his voice strained. "I'll tell you if it gets too much."

He said the last words through gritted teeth, and something told her he saw this as a challenge of endurance and will, like everything else he did. Which would make this even more fun. How far could she push Daxon Miles, professional adrenaline junkie, his endurance well-known? What were his limits?

She moved her other hand to his cock, testing its feel, its thickness, tracing the veins. His stomach muscles were tense and his thighs, tight, but he held still, all that intense energy coiled, waiting. Kendall took her time. She moved her hand higher, higher, along the smooth skin, up to the head. Drops of precum leaked out the tip, and she had the urge to lick…so she scooted off his lap and did it. Leaning forward, she swirled her tongue around the head, tasting, feeling him with her mouth. He let out a loud groan. Kendall backed up a little, inspecting his entire length.

Daxon was big. The kind of *holy shit* big that legitimized some of the more far-fetched rumors about him. It would take a hell of a lot of blood to keep that thing hard, which meant his other head probably wasn't getting much. She looked up at him, his mouth parted and his eyes heavy-lidded. His arms were spread along the back of the couch, his incredible wingspan on display, muscles flexed, knuckles white as he gripped the pillows.

Her hand closed around his cock, squeezing a little. Then she bent forward and put her mouth on the tip again. She sucked experimentally and then took more, testing him.

His body shuddered, and he muttered a curse. "Yes, sweets. Just like that," he rasped, his big hand coming down to stroke her head. "This is so fucking amazing, Kendall."

She sucked again, hollowing out her cheeks as she pulled out, and another shudder ran through his body. His hands moved through her hair, and at first she thought he was going to guide her, to show her what he liked, but he didn't.

"I want to see your mouth," he whispered.

His last words were mixed with another groan as she took him in, deeper this time. His head hit the back of her throat. She did it a few times, relishing the way Daxon trembled under her fingers, and a surge of energy ran through her. There was so much power in giving him pleasure, so much freedom.

She did it a couple more times, in and out, before he pushed her shoulders gently back. "Enough." His voice was tight in his throat, as if he were one breath away from snapping. Kendall leaned forward, wanting to be the one to make him snap, but he chuckled and held her in place.

"Not a chance, sweetheart," he said. "Not this time. There's no way in hell I am going to come in your mouth if there's a possibility I can come inside you."

Daxon had spent a week in Costa Rica with Kendall kneeling in front of him every day, working on his calf muscle, and he had tried like hell to think of anything but the fact that her mouth was so close to his dick. Each one of those images, memory and fantasy, layered on to the real thing right in front of him. Kendall was kneeling on the ground, staring at his cock, her lips still so close to his head. And that alone was going to make him come if he wasn't careful.

"You finding what you're looking for?"

She smiled. "And more."

A chuckle rumbled from his chest. "Glad to hear it. And I hope you don't mind a little dirty talk."

"I love it." Her smile was wide and genuine, and his heart thudded harder.

He motioned for her to climb up on him, and she did, losing her panties on the way to his lap.

"Because I have a feeling the words are just going to come out," he said, tugging her closer.

He traced a line down her body with his hand, slipping it between them, finding her pussy.

"You're wet," he murmured. "So fucking wet. And I am so goddamn lucky."

"I was just thinking the same thing."

He reached beside him and grabbed a condom that was on the couch. "Put it on me. Please."

She leaned back a little and tore off the wrapper, then placed the condom on his glistening tip, rolling it down carefully. He stared at her hands, his mouth hanging open. Holy hell, he wanted her.

Slowly, her gaze wandered up and met his, and a hard jolt of lust hit him. Daxon let out a groan. "I want you to ride it, sweets. Make us both feel so good."

"I did wear my cowboy boots tonight," she said in an exaggerated Texas accent.

He tipped his head back and laughed. She was the most fun woman he had met in…well, pretty much ever. He brought his lips to her neck, breathing in a little of that sweet scent he had resisted all day long. "Did I mention I really, really like you?"

She shook her head slowly.

He kissed the spot right below her ear. "Just want you to remember that."

Then she raised herself up on her knees, positioned his cock at her entrance, and began to sink down. Holy hell, he wasn't going to survive this. The loveliest woman in the world also happened to have the tightest pussy, which was currently milking his tip, threatening to overpower even his self-control. Or maybe it wasn't the tightness of her pussy or the soft jiggle of her tits that was driving him crazy. Maybe it was just her. But he couldn't process what that meant, and he needed to devote most of his brainpower to not coming right now.

Kendall had her hands on his shoulders, and she was lowering herself, inch by inch, onto him. Her head was tipped back, and her hair fell down her back, tangled and free. She looked like a goddess of sex, sacrificing on the throne of his cock. Yeah, he liked that idea a whole hell of a lot. But even that thought dimmed, along with every other one, as her tight, warm channel squeezed his cock.

"I'll make sure it's good for you," he said, his heart bursting in his chest. "I promise. But take it slow right now."

Lower, lower, she sank onto his aching cock, filling the night air with groans and sighs. His breaths were coming so quickly that Daxon no longer knew which gasps were his. She moved up and down in little movements, stretching to fit him. He held on to her hips, trying hard not to grasp her too tightly, letting her take her time until his entire cock was inside her, all the way to the base. Her breath was shaky, and she wove her hands into his hair and kissed him hungrily. It was as if they were reinventing sex, finding a whole new kind of pleasure.

"This feels so good," she whispered, pulling back, wonder in her eyes.

Daxon chuckled. "It does, and we haven't even started."

She pressed her lips to his for another kiss, slower, luxurious this time.

"Are you ready, sweets?" he whispered when she pulled away.

Kendall nodded. She lifted herself slowly and then sank all the way back down. His fingers flexed against her soft hips as he tried to hold on to this moment, make it last. Thank fuck she had shown up at his door tonight, so lovely and a little nervous. And right now, with his arms around her, buried inside her, it was magical. She slid up his cock again, and he brought her down on him, tilting his hips. She let out a loud cry, hoarse and so hot. He didn't give a shit if the neighboring cabins could hear them. All he could think about was this incredible woman, pleasuring herself with him.

They found a rhythm, up and down, his hips bucking to meet hers. Her eyes met his, half-lidded, and a fresh wave of desire ran through him. He was getting way too close, so he reached a hand between them and found her clit, pressing against it each time he thrust. She was so slippery and wet, his fingers gliding.

"Kendall," he muttered. "Do you feel how much I want you?"

As the last words left his mouth, her orgasm started, clenching his cock, setting him off. His hips bucked, and his cock erupted in hard jolts. Her cries sent more waves of ecstasy through him, warmer, lulling him into bliss. The rush of pleasure turned into languid satisfaction as her body draped over his, her cheek on his shoulder. He buried his face in her hair and took long, steady drags of her scent, letting it fill him.

"Wow," she said against his skin.

The waves crashed on the beach, and the wind blew her hair over her forehead. He brushed it out of her face, tucking it behind her ear. Then he wrapped his arms around her and squeezed her against him.

"Yeah. Wow," he said, kissing her on the top of her head.

What he wanted to say was that she was amazing. That his heart was thumping in his chest, and he never wanted to let her go. That for the first time in a long, long while he felt...content. When she moved to get up, he had the strongest urge to pull her closer. But she had come here just for sex, not more.

"Wait, sweets. I'm not letting you go yet." He took another surreptitious inhale of her scent. "What's your schedule tomorrow?" he whispered into her ear. "Any other clients?"

She shook her head.

"Can I take you somewhere after my morning PT session?"

"Um…"

Daxon's cock was still in her, making it hard to focus, but he pushed on. "I'll make it the best day of your life."

She didn't answer right away, and the longer she was quiet, the more his heart pounded. Finally, she smiled and looked up into his eyes. "Okay, best day of my life. Just to make sure it doesn't involve you doing any life-threatening stunts that might injure your calf."

"Me?" He gave her a mock-innocent look. "Never."

For the first time in years, that hadn't even crossed his mind. All he could think about was that he had less than twelve hours to perfect his plans for a day that would blow her away.

He pulled her close again, breathing in the coconut scent of her shampoo, mingling with the scent of her. He liked this woman. All sorts of ideas were running through his head, ways he could impress her, make her laugh, satisfy her, hold her…and make her want him more. Except their clock was ticking. Loudly. In a few days, there wouldn't be a "more."

So he focused on tomorrow. There was a location he and Calvin had discussed in a planning meeting, right here on the Big Island, and an idea that may or may not fall under the category of crazy stunts. Kendall would either love it or hate it. But if Daxon was going for the best day of her life, it was time to go big. The philosophy "the bigger the risk, the bigger the reward" had been the guiding principle that had gotten him to where he was today. If it worked for his career, it might work on one particular woman... hopefully.

CHAPTER NINE

KENDALL WATCHED DAXON from across the lobby of the Kalani. He was talking to the woman at the concierge desk. It was too far to hear what she said, but the low, soft tones of her voice drifted on the warm breeze of the open-air lobby. The low-cut dress, the flower behind her ear, the seductive smile…ugh. Daxon wasn't encouraging her, and still it was painful to watch. Anyone who signed up to be his girlfriend would have to be okay with this kind of ogling.

Plus a lot of other challenges. And a lot of fun. Hypothetically speaking, of course.

This was the point where Kendall had to be very, very careful. She was a worrier, both by nature and by circumstance, and after twenty-eight years, she had been around herself enough to know that wasn't going to change. After she'd left his cabin the night before, she had had a dream where Daxon was scaling the mountain face with no ropes. When he turned to wave to her, smiling that easy smile of his, he lost his grip and plunged toward earth. She had awoken with a start right before he hit the ground. Morbid and completely on par for her worst-case-scenario brain.

Just one sexy night together poked at her deepest fears. Soon, he would leave the Kalani and go back to putting his life on the line—not just in her nightmares but for real. Which meant the consequences could be real, too. After too many years of watching her father head back to the most dangerous jobs, over and over, she knew that itch to take risks wouldn't go away. Which meant the days at the Kalani were going to be a true test of her new, adventurous approach to living in the moment, not worrying about the future. She was going to enjoy the hell out of this day with Daxon, no matter what.

Because the more time she spent with him, the more she was sure that if she didn't try, she'd spend the rest of her life regretting it. There were so many things about Daxon that surprised her. He was much more considerate than she had expected. Not that she thought he would be an asshole, but for a person who did so many reckless stunts, who treated his own life so carelessly, she had expected him to be a little more self-centered. Instead, he was unselfish, particularly in bed. And on his moonlit lanai. And maybe in other places today…wherever they were going.

Daxon finished what he was saying to the concierge and turned around. Kendall could see the moment he caught sight of her. His eyes raked down her body, and then he gave her a slow smile like she was still naked. She glanced down, just to make sure, but she did indeed have clothes on. Of course she did. But that look he gave her... He crossed the room, and when he came close, he reached out, as if he was going to wrap his arms around her. His gaze dipped to her lips, his mouth parted, and she was almost sure he was thinking about kissing her. Right here, in the middle of the lobby. But then his hand fell to his side again.

"Hey," he said. "I was just arranging a few last-minute things."

"Are you going to tell me where we're going?"

"Hmm..." He pretended to give that idea some thought. "Nah. But if you guess correctly, I'll tell you."

Kendall raised an eyebrow. "Are we climbing Mauna Loa?"

He shook his head. "Not a chance with my calf."

"Hiking to one of the waterfalls?"

He shook his head again. "Same. I'd rather save it for a time when I don't have to hold back."

"Surfing?"

"Sounds fun. Maybe next time." He waggled his eyebrows. "You're getting closer."

Kendall wrinkled her brow. "Boogie boarding?"

Daxon cringed. "Isn't that the B-level version of surfing?"

"Says the guy who's never tried it, right?"

He didn't look convinced. "Fine, you're right. It

sounds like fun. Then maybe we can try water aerobics in the shallow end of the pool?"

"I'm sure I can arrange that if you want," she said, smiling sweetly. "I'm done guessing. Let's just go."

They walked out of the open-air lobby and into the sun. The entranceway to the Kalani was full of palms and bright, blooming flowers, and the driveway was made of large stones, just a little darker than the sand. In the middle of the drive, a red convertible was parked, shiny and inviting.

"You like it?"

She swallowed the thump of excitement in her throat and tried to sound bored. "It's okay."

His hands slipped around her waist, and he tickled her until she burst out into laughter.

"All right, it looks like a lot of fun," she said between gasps.

He beamed at her. "I thought so, too."

Was there a hint of pride in his voice? She was getting the feeling that he really did want to please her. A lot. Which was probably just his competitive spirit at work. But a convertible sports car did look like a fun way to drive around the island.

"You know how to get where we're going?" she asked.

"Of course I do," he said. "Do you really think I'd go into an adventure unprepared?"

"Probably not."

He winked at her. "The right answer is *hell, no.*"

Daxon slipped on his sunglasses, walked over to

the passenger-side door and opened it for her. She had never really seen the point of this chivalrous gesture, since she could easily open a door for herself. But with Daxon watching as she hesitated, his smile faltering a little, she was starting to understand his message: *I'm paying attention to every detail.* Which she was *not* going to overthink. Not even a little bit.

The seat was warm from the morning sun, shining down, filling the air with the kind of sultry heat that made everything nicer...and sexier. It was one of the things she loved most about living here. Back in Northern California, it was as if the thermostat never was cranked quite right. Foggy and cool in the summer, winter alternating between warm sun and rain, and just when the spring seemed to get it perfect, the fog would roll in again, cutting through the bliss of warmth. But here in Hawaii, even the rain didn't interfere with the lazy heat. Maybe someday she'd get tired of the perpetual good weather, but that day wasn't coming anytime soon.

Daxon climbed into the driver's seat, his long, muscular legs on display. If she wasn't careful, she'd spend the whole day gawking at him.

"Did you bring your bathing suit?" he asked, catching her mid-ogle.

Kendall pulled the collar of her T-shirt over to reveal a strap. "That was my only clue about our destination."

"Unless you can think of a way to coax more hints

out of me." He lifted his sunglasses, his gray-green eyes sparkling. "Ready for the best day of your life?"

She laughed. "Impress me, Daxon."

"I will." He lowered his sunglasses and started the car.

The resort's long driveway wound through more palms and bushes before they came to the main road and turned, heading south. The landscape of the north end of the island was drier, and when left alone, without fancy resort plantings, a lot of it was barren, with long stretches of grassy fields that barely covered the lava beds. But they were headed south, toward the greener, rainier side, with the kind of tropical hillsides she had expected when she first came.

From the moment they turned onto the highway, Daxon peppered her with questions. He wanted to know everything about her—growing up just outside San Francisco, her adventures as a physical therapist, and all her memories from when her father would disappear for weeks into wildfire territory.

"How did your mother feel about it?" he asked as he turned off the main road, heading for what was supposed to be the best smoothie place on the island, according to the hand-painted signs on the side of the road.

"It was really hard on her. But complicated. She was a hotshot, too, before they had me, so she understood why he wanted to be there, on the front lines of the fires."

Her mother's experience also gave her mother a well-honed sense of when to worry. There were days of silence, where her father's absence took up all the air in the house, all the space at the dinner table, suffocating them both. Then, when he finally called, the relief came first. Meals were filled with bright bursts of a week's worth of conversation, finally freed, now that her father was safe. But there were nights, not long after, when that relief turned to anger, usually when she caught sight of her mother's expression, worn and weary. Why did her father keep going back when he knew how much they worried?

Kendall didn't reveal all these details, but she could tell she had said enough that Daxon understood. When they pulled over by the smoothie place, under the shade of the palm trees that lined the parking lot, he turned off the engine but stayed in his seat.

"You didn't tell me all of this when we were in Costa Rica," he said.

She shrugged. "It's not a secret. But we were talking in general terms, not about my situation. I didn't think it was relevant."

He was quiet for a moment, and then he nodded. "But it's relevant to me."

The little smoothie shack was on the edge of a farm, with a grove of banana trees where guests could wander and spiky pineapple bushes sprouting out of the ground. They walked around the grounds, sipping smoothies, as he asked more questions about San Francisco State University, about her traveling physical therapy job, about boyfriends and friends. Then they climbed back into the car, and as they headed back to the main road, she thought it was fair to turn the inquiry tables on Daxon.

She knew the basics about his past—just about everyone did: growing up with only his mother, adventurous from a young age, never much for school. He entertained her with stories about his travels while filming, trying local foods and local activities all over the world, and she got the sense that he played down the more dangerous parts of these stories.

"How many people would you say do what you do, climbing the faces of mountains without ropes?" she asked.

"Expert-level free soloists? Not sure. Probably under fifty."

"How many died this year?"

There was a long pause. "One."

"How about last year?"

"One."

And he was going to follow up his Moonlight Buttress ascent with El Capitan, the most dangerous climb of them all. Didn't he see that these crazy stunts would probably lead to his death? One glance at him told her he knew exactly what she was thinking, and he didn't agree. Kendall opened her mouth to argue, then closed it. Not her battle. And she wasn't going to let it ruin her day, either.

They continued south, past Hilo, past the active volcanoes. Kendall looked out the window at the lush, green hills that rose up on one side. The dormant volcanos were steep, green and treeless, and the road cut into the side of them, winding around each cone. There was nothing in sight but the sea and the grass and an occasional cow grazing on the mountainside. It was gorgeous, but where were they going? For most of the ride, she had assumed that they'd go to the active volcano, but they had passed that turnoff miles ago. They had also passed the Black Sand Beach, another attraction in the area. What else was there?

"You're still not going to tell me where we're going?"

"You haven't guessed yet?" he said, glancing over at her with a little smile. "We don't have far to go before we start heading north, up the other side of the island."

"Exactly. So whatever it is must be coming soon."

Daxon pointed to a sign in the distance. "That's where we're going."

It read South Point, 12 Miles, with an arrow pointing to a turnoff on the left. The southernmost point in the US?

This was the destination Daxon had chosen for the best day of her life? It was…a little underwhelming.

"You've never been there, have you?" he asked, turning down the narrow road.

Kendall shook her head slowly. She hadn't even considered visiting this spot.

"Good. I checked with Alana," said Daxon.

Her eyebrows shot up. "You talked to Alana about this?" she asked, motioning between them.

He looked a little guilty, but not nearly guilty enough. "It, um, depends upon what part of this—" he motioned between them like she had "—you're referring to. I would've just asked you but you were busy with a client."

There was a hint of mocking in his tone.

Kendall let out a breath and steered the conversation back on track. "Well, Alana was right. I've never been here."

The grin was back on his face. "I was hoping so. There's something here that I thought might be fun to watch."

Daxon Miles, the man who threw himself out of an airplane with no parachute, thought it would be fun to watch...the southernmost edge the United States, where it met the ocean? Was she missing something?

Daxon reached over and squeezed her leg. "I hope you love it. It's either that or you hate me for bringing you here, which will make for a very long car ride back."

Okay, now she was really curious.

They drove for miles, past houses and little stores until finally they reached the ocean. Daxon pulled into a dusty area and parked the car. He took off his sunglasses, and he opened his mouth to speak but hesitated. Shaking his head, he removed her seat belt, then his, shifting in the seat to face her. He leaned forward, putting his hand on her thigh.

He brushed his lips against hers, so achingly slow. Her pulse jumped, and she reached for him, pressing her hands against the soft stubble of his jaw. He opened his mouth and kissed her, his teeth tugging at her bottom lip as his hand slid farther up her thigh. She tilted her head and stroked his tongue with hers. Her whole body ached for this man…and they were in the middle of a parking lot.

He backed up, and she swallowed. "Did we come all this way for a nice make-out spot? It would have been easier just to stay back at the Kalani."

The corners of his mouth tugged up into a hint of a smile. "It's not what we came for. But I wanted to kiss you before we get out, just in case you get mad at me for this."

Kendall threw up her arms in resignation. "What the hell are you taking me to do, Dax?"

"The southernmost point also happens to be a popular cliff diving spot," he said with a mischievous smile. "I thought it might be fun to watch."

He pointed to the edge of the cliff. Now that he mentioned it, there were groups of people in bathing suits standing awfully close to the edge. Right around a platform of some kind.

"Or we could jump," she deadpanned, narrowing her eyes at him.

Daxon just shrugged. "Only if you want, but not on my account. I can always come back another time, but you probably won't. Not without someone to nudge you a little."

She stared at him, stunned. He was taking her to watch cliff diving, thinking it might look like enough fun to join in? Jesus.

"What do you think?" he asked, assessing her closely.

"I'm thinking that you're crazy if you think I might jump off that cliff in the name of adventure."

Daxon laughed.

"What?"

"I was prepared for much worse." Then he leaned forward and kissed her again. "I'm not going to pressure you at all. Seriously. I brought drinks and a pad we can sit on. I figured it would be fun to just watch."

"In our bathing suits?"

"Yep."

"Okay," she said slowly.

Daxon grabbed bags out of the trunk of the car, and they headed toward the water. The day was clear, and the blue ocean sparkled in front of her. The coast was different on this side of the island, the water deeper, and the cliffs riding high above it. She walked along the black rock, watching the people near the platform, letting Daxon lead the way. He stopped a little farther down, at a spot where they could watch the others without hanging over the edge, and laid out a large pad to sit on.

"Just out of curiosity, how high up is this spot?" she asked as she plopped down.

"About ten meters." His voice was casual, but she caught a glimpse of a grin that told her just how carefully he had planned this out.

Her heart stuttered. He hadn't chosen something truly crazy, a jump that she might barely survive from. Instead, he chose the height of the platform at every Olympic diving well. The height she had contemplated at the age of thirteen—and then backed down from, while all the rest of her friends jumped. Daxon knew this was the height she'd chickened out from before. He had been listening to her, really listening, and he had taken a risk, designing today around a thrill that was just outside of her comfort zone. She wasn't sure if she loved him or hated him for it—and Daxon probably knew that.

Kendall teetered on that brink, back and forth. Then, finally, she did the only thing she could do—she buried her face in her hands and laughed. The wind was blowing gently and the sound of the waves crashed around them, and she just let go. "You are trouble, Daxon Miles," she said.

His mouth quirked up into a cocky smile. "The best kind of trouble, hopefully."

"Yet to be determined."

He could do this all day long. Just sit here with Kendall's long, tanned legs resting across his, the ocean at his side, watching as groups of people climbed out of their cars, peeked over the edge of the cliff, debated, backed away or, finally, jumped.

Daxon meant what he had said. He had absolutely no intention of pressuring her. That wasn't the point of this trip, though if she did jump, he was betting that it would transform a beautiful day into an amazing one. But in truth, he had chosen this destination with something completely different in mind.

He had wanted to show Kendall a new way to see her experiences. That first day at the Kalani, she had asked him questions he hadn't fully answered. Why climb a mountain without ropes? Why jump out of an airplane with no parachute? Behind those questions and every other one like it was one basic question: Why risk his life for these experiences? After being asked variations of this for years, Daxon had realized that this wasn't *his* question. He was asking something completely different: What made him feel alive?

He respected that jumping out of airplanes wasn't everyone's thing. Some people pushed themselves to stand up in front of an audience and tell jokes, hoping that everyone would laugh. Before she got sick, his mother's job as an emergency room nurse had made her come alive. Kendall was looking for the same thing, too: an experience that transcended time, moments when the mind and the body and the world around were all one. Moments like this were worth years and years of a life without them.

He'd heard hints about her aversion to risks back in Costa Rica, and after their conversation in the car today, he understood it much better. He hadn't said much when she talked about her father's absences, just listened, but Daxon supposed this day was the closest he had to an answer as to why a person might choose work that involved danger.

Not that this trip was conceived that way. When he first suggested a day together, he was thinking about sex. On the beach, maybe in the convertible with the top down—lots of fantasies ran through his head, some more than once. But, as usual, he had to take the challenge to the next level. It was then that the little snippet of conversation had come back to him, where she was standing on top of the diving platform, so curious, so ready to jump, so afraid. He knew that feeling. He had lived with it inside, explored it, leaned into it. He had learned more about it—and himself—doing stunts like skydiving, where the real risks weren't high but the fear factor was. Then, once he had understood fear, learned how to work with it, he had moved on to adventures where the consequences were higher. He had learned to trust himself, to harness that fear and turn it into learning what he needed to stay in the moment.

But he hadn't forgotten that messy mixture of fear, temptation and exhilaration, that feeling of standing on top of that ten-meter platform, ready to jump for the first time.

This day's success had nothing to do with whether or not Kendall jumped. Together, they were watching others in that moment, the thoughts written on their faces. While they talked to each other, touched each other, skin on skin. These new explorations were so fresh and alive as they studied each person looking over the edge. This, right now, was what he searched for: the moments when what he said and thought and did were all perfectly aligned. And for once, he was experiencing this fully dressed and sitting down.

Daxon was hoping like hell that she was feeling it, too. That when she leaned over to kiss him after he made her laugh, it was because that was exactly what she wanted to do right then.

"Check out that kid over there," said Kendall. She nodded to the far platform where a group was gathered. "He can't be more than thirteen or fourteen. You think he's going to jump?"

The small wooden platform stuck out a few feet beyond the rocky cliff with a rickety-looking railing. Next to it, a long metal ladder extended the entire ten meters down to the water. The kid was wiry and determined-looking, dressed in board shorts and bare feet, and he was gripping the railing of the platform hard as he peered over the edge. Behind him were two kids, a little older, maybe brothers, who were egging him on.

"He's definitely going to jump," said Daxon, chuckling. "Those guys behind him are making sure of it."

The teens behind the boy said something Daxon didn't catch, and the kid straightened up. He turned to the others, smiled, and then, with a whoop of glee, he jumped. Kendall leaned forward, watching him descend, flailing, until he hit the water. The other kids came to the edge, watching, cheering as the boy emerged from the surface. He swam over to the ladder and called his own taunts back up to the others.

"Now I really can't claim that this is too risky," said Kendall with a smirk. "If a thirteen-year-old kid can do it, it can't be that bad, right?"

Daxon laughed. "You sure you want to use a teenage boy as a risk-assessment gauge? Speaking as a former member of that group, we do a lot of stupid things."

She smiled. "And have a lot of fun along the way."

Daxon ran his hand along her cheek and then tugged softly on her ponytail. "It is a relatively low-consequence thrill, especially on a calm day like today. I think the only way to know whether or not to jump is to ask yourself, will this be fun? Will the thrill of it be worthwhile enough to fight the fear?"

Kendall looked at him. "You're really not going to talk me into this, are you?"

"Nope." He leaned over and kissed her. "But if you decide to jump, I'll go first. I'll be there at the bottom for you."

She was quiet a while, and they watched as the second guy stood at the ledge, the third throwing out comments, half encouragement, half insult. The guy walked forward, calling down to the kid at the bottom, wringing his hands, all nerves and pride, and then he jumped, too. Finally, the last kid looked around as the other two called to him.

"He wants witnesses," said Daxon as the kid looked their way. "Someone to be in this moment with him."

Daxon pumped his fist in the air, cheering the guy on. He stepped forward, standing on the edge, backed up, and with a resigned shrug he jumped off the cliff. When he came up for air, the three boys gathered at the bottom, laughing, giving each other high fives.

"I want to check it out," said Kendall.

"You sure?"

"Just a peek. I still might change my mind."

"No pressure. But just in case, let's strip." Daxon waggled his eyebrows salaciously. She pinched his side, but a smile tugged at the corners of her mouth. Making Kendall smile was becoming his new favorite pastime. The rush he got when her lips curved up and her eyes crinkled at the corners as she looked at him—that rush was addictive, different from anything he had felt in a long, long time. If ever.

He reached inside one of the bags, searching around. "The biggest risk in this jump is probably smacking your feet or cutting them on the barnacles on the way up the ladder, so I brought some water shoes for us, just in case." He pulled out a pair and handed them to Kendall. "That was the reason I contacted Alana in the first place, by the way—to get your shoe size."

But Kendall didn't take the shoes. Instead, she got that look in her eyes like she did the night she came over, like she was about to have her way with him. She shifted onto her knees and climbed onto his lap, straddling him. She was warm from the sun, and her lips still tasted of pineapple and mango as she brushed her mouth against his. Relief rushed through him, relief at kissing her again. Her tongue stroked his in slow, deep moves, like she was showing him what she wanted from him right now. And fuck, he wanted it, too. He slipped his hands onto her hips and helped her ride, pulling her against his cock. Hell, this woman drove him crazy.

The sound of teenage voices broke into their kiss, and Kendall pulled away.

"Damn." Daxon gave her one last squeeze. "I should buy you water shoes more often."

"What can I say? I'm easy to please."

Yeah, right. "Or maybe you're trying to distract me from the jump? Because I'm not against this kind of distraction."

She shook her head. "No distracting. I'm doing it. I just needed a little fortification first."

Daxon set aside his sunglasses and pulled off his shirt, then watched as she stripped down to her swimsuit and tugged on her booties. But watching her was getting him even more worked up, and they were in public. He stood up and offered Kendall a hand, and when she took it, he pulled her close, into his arms.

"I'm almost sure this won't strain your calf. It's almost healed."

He nodded his head slowly. "It feels great. My calf will be fine."

She slipped her hands onto his waist so naturally, as if they were meant to be together like this.

"I'll be there for you, sweets," he murmured into her ear. "You're safe with me."

She stilled in his arms, and for a moment, he wondered if he had said the wrong thing. But when he pulled back, she was smiling. "Let's do it."

They walked along the rocky cliff, over toward the platform where the boys had jumped. The three kids had climbed up the ladder and headed back to a spot farther along the warm black rocks, their cheering and needling still loud, adrenaline-filled.

Kendall walked to the edge of the platform and hung on to the railing as she peeked over the edge. "Holy shit. That's a long way down."

"You sure you want to do this?"

She nodded decisively. "Just working myself up to it."

He smoothed a hand over her cheek and kissed her. "Okay. I'll go first and wait for you at the bottom. Just remember to keep your arms close to your sides and go in straight so you don't smack anything."

"I still remember all the warnings from years ago."

Daxon laughed. "I'm sure you do."

"You've jumped from higher than this, haven't you?"

"Still gives me the same thrill." Even more right

now, when Kendall was next to him. "If you change your mind, just let me know and I'll come back up. But otherwise, I'll wait for you at the bottom for as long as you need me to. Take your time."

He leaned over, cupping her neck with his hand for one more kiss, hard and fast. Her eyes were closed when he backed away, and she sighed. His heart thudded harder in his chest as the thrill of her nearness amped the thrill of the height. This, right here, was the ultimate rush. He took one more breath, soaking in this moment, and then turned to the Pacific Ocean, wide open in front of him, glittering in the afternoon sun. *Best day ever.* The thought filled him as he curled his toes over the edge of the platform for grip and threw himself out into the endless blue sea.

CHAPTER TEN

HOLY SHIT. SHE really was doing this. Kendall was going to jump from a height that looked crazy-high. Though logically, she knew it wasn't life-threatening, her body was still in panic mode. She so, so wanted to do this, but could she actually make herself take that last step off the cliff?

That day years ago on the ten-meter platform wasn't the only time she had considered jumping off the high dive. She had talked herself into similar situations—and then out of them—at least a dozen times before. This time, she was finally following through because Daxon Miles was waiting for her at the bottom. He was probably the most famous risk-taker in the world, and yet she trusted him right now. She trusted he wouldn't bring her here if she couldn't handle it.

Daxon hit the water with a yell and a splash, then disappeared into the darkness. She held her breath, waiting, until he emerged with another shout of glee.

"It's amazing," he yelled up to her. "Best jump ever."

His words pumped another rush of adrenaline through her, as she watched him swim over to the ladder on the side of the cliff. She was standing at the southern tip of Hawaii, ready to jump off into nothing. If she chickened out now, she would regret it for the rest of her life.

"Ready?" she called down to him.

"Ready when you are, beautiful."

Kendall drew in a deep breath and let it out. She wasn't backing down. If she died now, she would die a happy woman, in the middle of the best day of her life. Stepping off the ledge was the hardest part, and the more she stalled, the harder it would be. Deep breath. One more. Kendall shut off her thoughts and pushed off the edge, plunging toward the water.

Words, yelps and squeals came out of her mouth in a tangled cry as the water rushed toward her, too fast. Her heart pounded in her chest and her whole body tingled as she tried desperately to keep her arms by her side, but it was hard to think when she felt so free.

She hit the water with a startling crash, the impact almost knocking the wind out of her. The ocean swallowed her in one quick gulp, and she went down, down, into the dark water. So far down...

Her brain kicked back into gear. She needed to breathe. Which meant she needed to swim like hell for the surface. Her survival instincts took over, and she kicked, but her booties made it hard. Almost there. Finally, finally, she popped out and gasped for air. Her heart thumped as she stared out into the endless blue ocean, sucking in breaths.

Lying back in the cool water, the rush of adrenaline pumped through her. Holy hell. She had done it. She actually jumped.

Kendall didn't register the splash of Daxon's strokes until he was right behind her. His hands came to her waist, lifting her. "You okay, sweets? It took a while for you to come up."

He sounded shaky, worried. She turned around, and he was right there, so close. Another surge of excitement rushed through her.

"It was incredible," she said. "I'm so glad I did it."

She leaned forward and kissed him, a giddy, fumbling kiss full of water and joy. The worry in his expression eased a little, and he smiled, kissing her back, harder. "Fuck. I think I'm the one who came closest to a heart attack today."

He moved closer, their bodies brushing as they treaded water. He touched her cheek, her arms, her waist, like he was checking to make sure she was okay. She treaded water, trying not to kick him, as she stared into the deep pools of his eyes. Maybe it was all the adrenaline pumping through her, but right now, there was nothing else in the world but Daxon, staring right back, his eyes filled with smoldering licks of flames. Finally, he whispered, "Let's get out and find somewhere more private."

Oh, Lord, she wanted that right now. She glanced over at the long ladder up the cliff.

"Right after we climb back up those ten meters."

Kendall's body was still a rubbery mess. As it turned out, climbing ten meters worth of rickety metal ladder was more frightening than jumping, especially if you kept glancing down to see how high the fall would be. If Daxon hadn't been right behind her, talking her through it, she'd probably still be at the bottom of that ladder, treading water until the Coast Guard arrived. But she wasn't. Instead, she was standing on the empty Green Sand Beach, and Daxon was next to her, spreading out a blanket. He ran a hand through his salty, windblown hair, his biceps flexing, but that didn't do anything to tame it. He was all suntan and messy hair and laid-back, sexy male. He was beautiful.

"I read that this was one of the less visited beaches on the island," he said. "Of course, that was publicized on the internet, so I'm not sure how accurate that is, but it's nice so far."

The empty beach was nestled into a sea-etched cove, surrounded by cliffs. The middle of it sloped down gradually, as if nature had designed its own rocky amphitheater for a perfect view of the ocean. They were sitting in the only shaded, semi-secluded spot, where the cliff jutted out. The sand was coarse, more yellow than green, and the water was a bright, shimmering turquoise.

"I'd like to come back to that spot where we jumped sometime," he added, scanning the coastline. "Scope it out for a free climb, right over the water."

"I'm impressed, Dax," she said, rolling onto her side. "All of this is amazing. The drive, the jump, the beach…"

She was expecting a snappy comeback, but his smile was soft. He took off his sunglasses and looked into her eyes. "The best day of your life, remember?"

The words echoed deep inside, shaking her at her core. It was getting harder and harder not to let this mean anything more. But thinking about anything beyond this week was a reminder that Daxon Miles, an incredible man who created this amazing day just for her, could very well die on the mountainside in a few weeks. He would risk everything in the stupid pursuit of man versus the elements, for everyone to watch, livestreamed. In the end, everyone knew how these battles went. Nature always won. It was only a matter of time, and nature had all the time in the world. Daxon Miles didn't.

Which meant she needed to be enjoying the hell out of their day together instead of wasting it worrying.

Kendall got up on her knees, facing him, and rested her hand on his cheek. His body was a warm, welcoming wall of muscles. She leaned over so her mouth was close to his, and his gaze wandered over her face, to her lips.

"Thank you," she whispered. "For all of this."

Then she closed that last distance, pressing her lips against his. His mouth was warm and hungry as he opened it to hers. Kissing Daxon was its own language, each stroke of his tongue a new word, each sigh or moan the punctuation. He strung kisses together into sentences, fresh, like no other one before it. Kendall immersed herself in his dialect of wants and responses while she showed him her own.

This kiss on an empty beach, with the ocean breeze blowing over her skin, this one was all new. The hunger and the desire were there, the undercurrent to everything they did together. It would probably always be that way, even if they kept doing this for hundreds of years. But she felt something else, something like the ache of loneliness, exposed. His? Hers? Maybe both of theirs. He took the kiss deeper, following her lead, unleashing more of that hunger he had been holding back all day. He growled as her tongue swept against his, her heart thumping harder. Then he pulled back, resting his forehead on hers.

"This is supposed to be the best beach for skinny-dipping on the island. Just in case you're interested."

Kendall smiled. "Is this best day mine or yours?"

"The two aren't mutually exclusive."

She pulled back a little, studying him, and raised

an eyebrow. "I think you're making up the skinny-dipping thing."

"Okay, maybe it's not known as that *officially*," he conceded, his eyes alive with mischief. "But *I* certainly think it makes the best beach to get naked."

She gave him a little shove, and he tumbled to the side. Lazily, she turned and stretched out her legs in front of her, staring out at the ocean, trying hard not to stare at Daxon. He pulled off his shirt, and his sculpted muscles flexed underneath sun-kissed skin. Okay, maybe just a little glance. Oh, *Lord*, he was incredible. And probably showing off again.

He scooted back onto the blanket and reached for the cooler bag he had pulled from the trunk of the car.

"I had the resort pack up a few things for us. All healthy, of course," he said, his gray-green eyes crinkling at the corners. His smile for her right now was so different from the one she had watched too many times in his videos. It was relaxed. Intimate. After taking out little dishes of nuts and fruits and a couple canteens of drinks, he unwrapped a baguette sandwich and handed it to her, then unwrapped one for himself.

"Where do you live?" he asked, taking a bite of his sandwich. "You just appear at my place every morning, so either you're getting up at the crack of dawn to drive in, or you're not that far."

"The Kalani has cabins for staff, visiting or long-term. It's one of the perks, since it's so expensive to move to the island."

"By the beach?"

"Yep." She glanced over at him. "You probably passed the area when you went for your illicit run."

"Which I promised I won't do again." Daxon chuckled. "I've followed every single one of your directions. I'll do whatever you ask."

He gave her a sexy, mock-serious look. On anyone else, it would have come off as ridiculous, but Daxon managed it with exactly the right amount of confidence and humor.

"Whatever I ask?" She mimicked his sexy overtones in his question.

"Oh, yeah." His smile was so lazy and sensual.

What if she asked him not to free climb Moonlight Buttress? The question popped into her mind before she could quash it. Kendall wasn't even tempted to voice this unwanted jolt of reality, so far out of bounds of this playful discussion. The thought was another cliff, but when she crashed into the bottom of this one, Daxon wouldn't be waiting.

Plus, she had no right to bring this up, to push him. He was free to make his own choices, just like everyone else. The warm wind blew strands of hair in her face, despite the tight ponytail she had fastened. She closed her eyes and pushed her worries out of her mind. Instead, she found a different question, one she had been thinking about ever since the Costa Rica trip.

"I read about how you started the Pure Adrenaline videos," she said. "About wanting to experience life in the moment. I think you even quoted Sartre."

Daxon groaned. "I'll never live that interview down. God, what a pompous ass I come off as."

She gave him a skeptical glance. "You did call your stunts existentially enlightening."

He laughed. "Aaah, you memorized my words."

"You *would* see it that way." She took another bite of her sandwich.

"Absolutely." Daxon's smile faded. "Seriously, that guy was out to make me look like a fool, but it's my fault I took the bait. He kept pushing me about why anyone in their right mind—his words—would want to do high-risk stunts."

"So you're not after existential enlightenment?"

"I detect some judgment in that question," he said, humor dancing in his voice. "Go ahead, judge away. I wouldn't expect anything less from the person who's supposed to help me recover from my injuries."

Kendall frowned. Was she judging him? The truth was that she actually admired him. He had pushed himself to take risks, and even after years of raising the stakes in each Pure Adrenaline episode, he still hadn't yet reached his breaking point.

"I'm not being judgmental, really," she said. "I want to understand. Why do you take these risks, over and over again?"

"I do love the thrill of it, of course," he said. "That

existential awakening thing isn't complete bullshit, even if it sounds like it."

For a moment, Daxon's smile faltered. "But I didn't need the Pure Adrenaline show to do all that. I would've been happy rock climbing and sky diving and living out of my truck for years, with no one watching."

He took a bite out of the baguette and stared down at the sand. He had put his sunglasses back on, and she wished that he would take them off so she could look in his eyes when he said this. But he didn't.

"What changed?" she asked.

He swallowed, his Adam's apple bobbing in his throat. "My mother got sick."

Oh.

"I'm sorry," she said softly. Kendall wasn't sure what she had been expecting him to say, but this definitely wasn't it.

Daxon gave a little nod, but he didn't say anything. She had basically cyber stalked this guy, read all the articles she could find on him, but she had never seen even a hint of this part of his story. In fact, it occurred to her that she knew nothing about his family. Did he have siblings? Where did his father fit in? She had been so caught up in the excitement of sex and fun that she hadn't thought to ask.

She wasn't sure if they were done with this topic, but after a while, Daxon continued.

"It took me a while to notice she was sick. I had dropped out of college, and I was just driving around to different locations, hanging out with other people doing the same thing. I'd come by her house from time to time, do my laundry, hang out with her for a few days and then leave again. I was getting some sponsorships, making enough money to eat and buy gas, but not much more." Daxon sighed. "Even she didn't know what was wrong for a while, either. She was just tired in the beginning. I guess no one really thinks of Parkinson's at that age."

Oh. Kendall had worked with some Parkinson's patients back in school, so she had an idea of what that could mean. And just how hard it could be on families.

"How's she doing these days?" she asked.

"Surprisingly well, though some days are better than others. It's hard to tell how fast the illness will progress. And the medications seem to work well for her, which isn't always the case."

Kendall was trying to digest this story. She tried to picture a younger Daxon, living out of his truck and looking for the next big thrill. His mother's illness could have made him reconsider high-risk stunts, but apparently he didn't. Instead, he started filming them.

Daxon looked at her, his expression serious. "We had to face the fact that there would be a time when she would no longer be able to work, maybe soon. And then what? Disability doesn't get you far. With my dad long out of the picture, well, I needed to figure something out. I'm a college dropout with a shaky work history, and I really don't like to follow orders. I liked to push myself, test the limits. Not many people's ideal job candidate."

"Depends on what kind of job you're looking for." Kendall gave him a salacious wink. "I think Las Vegas is always looking for hot, fit men pushing limits with their endless endurance."

Daxon chuckled. "I never considered that angle."

She smiled. "And so you got creative."

"And so *Calvin* got creative," he said wryly. "He came up with the idea, he filmed it and got everyone in the community to boost it. I owe him a lot, though he has certainly made out well in all of this, too."

"And now you have money," said Kendall. "And the world is graced with videos of Daxon Miles doing half-naked stunts."

He leaned over her and tickled her side. "Which you watched."

She shrieked and scooted away. "I sure did."

He scooped her up by her waist and put her down on her back, underneath him. He rested on his elbows, his bare torso pressed against her. His muscles flexed under his weight, seductively. Was he distracting her now, steering them away from the more serious territory they had treaded into?

Daxon leaned down and brushed his mouth over hers. "Pure Adrenaline has been a wild ride, and I'm incredibly grateful for it. Calvin has a great plan for making it more sustainable, long term…"

He pulled off his sunglasses and set them aside,

then stared down at her. His eyes were so serious now. What kind of future was he planning? One with fewer risks, with lower consequences?

"We're going to use my free solo of Moonlight Buttress to make the El Capitan climb bigger, far beyond YouTube."

The words shattered that crystal of hope into shards, tearing at her in new places inside. Of course he wasn't going to stop doing high-consequence stunts. No matter what happened between them this week, she knew how this worked long term. Her parents had fought about her father's job for years, but he didn't stop until his arm was crushed...and he was lucky that he got out of it alive. She had known all this when she said yes to this whole slippery slope of intimacy with Daxon.

Stop worrying and just enjoy the goddamn day.

Daxon looked lost in his own thoughts, too, but then he lowered his head for a warm kiss. "Fuck. I really like this position."

She untangled her hands from his hair. "It's hot. I think we need a swim to cool off."

His eyes widened, hazy with lust, as she wriggled out from under him and stood up, brushing off the sand. They had a few more days for sex, but this was probably her only chance to skinny-dip with him. Kendall tugged off her tank top and shimmied out of her shorts, dropping them on the blanket next to Daxon. Next, she slipped the straps of her swimsuit off, and her breasts bounced out. She didn't have to look to know he was watching her as she pulled it down her thighs. She bent over, giving Daxon a show, then headed for the water.

"You coming?" she called over her shoulder.

After a moment, his voice came, rough and full of humor. "Hell, yes."

So she took off, her feet digging into the sand. The water was clear, the bottom sandy, so she ran in, splashing everywhere. It got deep quickly, so she dived under the cool water, closing her eyes. Hawaii was amazing. After living her life next to the foggy, frigid Northern California beaches, the warmth was a pleasure she couldn't get enough of.

Kendall took another long stroke underwater and then came up for air. She found the bottom with her feet and turned around. Daxon was heading straight for her. He was a powerful swimmer, because of course he was. Mastering some stunt had probably required him to hone his skills from good to impressive. Was there anything this man wasn't good at?

He caught up to her and stood, his body against hers. His hands came to her waist, and he pulled her against him, trapping his cock between them.

"I thought it would take a lot more convincing before you skinny-dipped," he said, his mouth next to her ear. His lips closed around her earlobe.

Kendall laughed. "I'm not the famous YouTube phenomenon. No one cares if I'm caught naked on camera. You should be worrying about yourself."

"Calvin would have a heart attack if he knew I was doing this." He pressed his lips against her neck. "But right now, I don't care."

Her heart stuttered in her chest as his words sank in. The water was shoulder-deep, and she wrapped her legs around him, the waves lapping between them.

She brushed her lips against his. "You taste good."

Her body slid against his, and his hands moved down, one on her back and the other on her ass, holding her against him. The water was warm, but his body was warmer. Every time the water slipped between them, she pressed herself against him again, trying to get closer. Their kisses were slow and deep as the thrill of the jump and the pull of their nearness turned into something more intense. Her breaths and his groans all mingled with the sounds of the water. It was incredible just to touch, just to feel every part of him. It was just the two of them, so light, so free, unattached to anything that existed on land.

A larger wave hit them from the side, splashing everywhere, and she pulled away, laughing, but he guided her back against him. He took his cock in his hand and lined it up, and she wrapped her legs around his waist. Slowly, he pushed in. Oh, Lord, the feeling of him inside her was like nothing else. She couldn't get close enough to him, the water winding between their bodies, keeping her away from that sweet friction of his skin against hers.

His hands were on her hips, and his cock was filling her in slow thrusts, the water setting the pace.
He smiled at her, his gray-green eyes sparkling like
the ocean around them, full of warmth and wonder.
The sun beat its languid heat down on her shoulders as he slid in and out of her. This was heaven.
It was a whole new kind of sex, not goal-oriented.
Each thrust, each tightening of her legs around his
hips, wasn't just one step toward an orgasm. It was
simply an exquisitely pleasurable moment. And another. And another. Floating in the warm water with
Daxon's body pressed against hers, his cock slowly
moving inside her, turning her insides into liquid the
way only he seemed to be able to do: each of these
moments was worth the risk of whatever came in
the future.

The intensity in his eyes was growing, and he
opened his mouth, like he was about to say something, something serious and beautiful. Something
she wasn't sure she could keep in perspective right
now, with her heart so full and free. So she pulled
him close and whispered in his ear, "I think I'm done
swimming now."

He nodded against her but didn't let her go. Kissing the top of her head, he turned and started toward
the shore. The water got shallower, revealing her ass.
She was left clinging to him, naked and still with his
cock inside her, so she unwrapped her legs. He gave
her a playful smack on her rear before easing her
back into the water. Laughing, she turned around,

and he placed his hands on her hips, keeping her close as they start walking toward shore.

"I can't believe we're still alone on this beach," she said over her shoulder. "How long do you think that will last?"

He grinned. "We're about to find out. What are your feelings about getting caught?"

Kendall's heart kicked up another notch. She had never considered herself an exhibitionist, but today was all about risk, wasn't it?

"I don't know," she said, biting her lip. "I guess I'm willing to see where this takes us."

Daxon laughed. "I'm pretty sure I know where this will take us, with or without spectators."

His body brushed against her as she came out of the water and walked across the beach, to the sliver of shade underneath the rocks. The soft blanket lay, waiting. Was this whole scenario going exactly as planned, the way that he seemed to plan so carefully for everything else? Or were there parts of today that were just as much a wonder to him as they were to her?

He came to a stop in front of the blanket, and she pressed her body against his for a slow, deep kiss. His skin was wet and salty from the ocean, and her fingers glided over his muscles, warm and hard and so satisfying.

She kissed his jaw, then his lips, opening for more. His tongue swept over hers, and he rocked his hips with the same thrust. If the water was about languid pleasure, this was about hunger and satisfaction. His cock was hard against her belly, and his groans were deep, resonating inside her. She dug her fingers into the muscles of his arms, testing the resistance, and he let out a deep growl as he thrust his hips hard.

"We've got to lie down, sweets," he grumbled. "I'm losing my mind here. I need to lick your pussy." She shuddered at the erotic image of watching him pleasure her.

Kendall looked up into his eyes and smiled. "I love being what you desire, hearing all the things you want to do to me."

His eyes narrowed, sparkling with mischief, and he tickled her sides, sending her into a fit of laughter. "Good. Because it's about to get a hell of a lot dirtier."

They tumbled onto the blanket, a tangle of legs and arms, clumsy and yet unbearably sexy. She lay back as he propped himself over her, his hard muscles straining. He bent down and brushed his lips over hers, kissing her neck.

"I want to lick and suck and devour your body," he rasped, moving lower. "I want you to come so long and hard and good that you never forget what it's like when we're together."

She gasped in a shaky breath as his words hit her. He didn't want her to forget him. Ever. But before that thought could gain momentum, his mouth descended on her breast, just as his fingers brushed between her legs and all rational thought left her.

"*Oh God*, Dax," she cried as his teeth raked over her nipple.

He shifted lower, kissing a trail down her belly. "You can say that as much as you want."

He rested his hands on her thighs and looked up and down her body with that intense stare he had. "I want to get you all worked up and make you feel good. But I'm not gonna let you come. I'm going to make you wait until my cock is deep inside you." His words were like a tuning fork vibrating in her body, pitch-perfect, resonating deep inside. "Tell me now if you want the condom."

"No, no condom."

He swore, or at least she thought he did, because nothing fully registered after that. His mouth descended onto her clit, coaxing it, sucking it, *enjoying it*, like he was enjoying this just as much as she was. The building pleasure was dizzying, lighting her body on fire, turning into that molten liquid of need and want, pushing her quickly to the edge of an orgasm. Then just as her legs began to shake, he pulled back, looking down at her with a wolfish smile.

"You want my cock?"

"Yes, Dax."

"How much?"

She gave an impatient groan. "You're not playing fair."

He was making her ask for it, maybe even beg for it, and he didn't look one bit sorry. Instead, he reached between her legs, running his hand up her thigh for another burst of pleasure, coating his fingers with her wetness. Then he gave his cock a couple sharp tugs. "Don't worry, sweets," he said through gritted teeth. "I am going to give us both what we want."

He lined his blunt head with her, and in one slow, insistent thrust, he pushed into her, filling her.

"You feel so good," she whimpered as he stretched her, rubbing against her G-spot, making her body sing. The pleasure was overwhelming, and she wrapped her legs around him, pulling him closer. Her mind registered a car engine in the distance, but she was too far gone in the haze of need to care. She dug her nails into the tight muscles of his back as his hips thrust against hers. She met each thrust, begging for *harder, more*.

"You gonna come with me, beautiful?" He bit out the words in a sandpaper-rough voice. "Is your pussy going to beg my cock for more? You want me to fill you up, over and over?"

"Yes," she cried. "Please, yes."

The orgasm came fast and hard, red-hot pleasure crashing through her body in wave after wave, spurred on by Daxon's deep, guttural moan.

"Kendall," he bit out, his voice heavy with satisfaction, as he buried his face in her neck. Breathless gasps slowed into dreamy kisses…

A car door slammed. Daxon pulled away. "I'd love to stay here like this for the rest of the day. But I'm pretty sure we're about to be discovered, naked, with my cock in you." He nodded up the slope.

Right. She shifted out from under him, despite every protest from her body. She grabbed a towel out of one of the bags and wrapped it around her. When she glanced back at Daxon, he hadn't moved. He was still lying naked on the blanket, watching her.

"You gonna do something about that?" She gestured to his half-hard, fully exposed cock. Voices traveled down the slope. Soon they'd be in sight.

"Am I making you nervous?"

Kendall threw him his shorts. "I should have known you'd have an exhibitionist streak."

He shook his head as he leisurely put a foot into his board shorts, like he had all the time in the world. "Not particularly. But I definitely have a test-Kendall's-limits streak."

The convertible's top was down, and the wind was blowing everywhere as they headed north along the winding highway on the island's eastern coast, making conversation a challenge. But Kendall had insisted on the open-air drive, and hopefully that meant she was just making the most of the experience.

The quiet between them left Daxon with his thoughts. He had said some intense things back on the beach. Like telling her that he loved being the best at everything, especially when it came to her. *I want you to come so long and hard and good that you never forget what it's like when we're together.*

This was supposed to be a fling, but the silver lining in the dark cloud of a restless week of recovery was turning into something else. Something he wasn't in any position to think further about...unless she was willing to wait out the next six months of training and travel and guest appearances.

Yes, waiting would be shitty for both of them, but they could work that out, couldn't they?

His ideas about the future had always been about exploring, pushing himself further. Before today, he hadn't consciously considered a future with Kendall—with anyone—and yet the moment this thought crossed his mind, the images came, fully formed, as if they had been lurking in his brain all this time, just waiting to be acknowledged. The images weren't all horizontal, though most of them eventually involved sex at some point. But there were others, too, like sitting on a beach with her, much like they had today, but on the banks of Lake Powell. They'd take the trailer he lived out of at climbing sites and go off on their own, just the two of them, with no one else around. And he could visit her in Hawaii, maybe buy a place here? In that scenario, Kendall was leaning back against him on an outdoor sofa...yeah, that one definitely ended horizontally.

He glanced over at her, in the passenger seat next to him, her chin propped on her hand, staring out at the ocean. Damn. Riding along the beautiful coastline, just the two of them, felt so right. The whole day did. He wanted a thousand more days just like this.

But how the hell did he fit that into reality, where he was getting on the plane soon to prepare for his live free solo climb up Moonlight Buttress? Kendall had made it clear that this kind of high-consequence adventure was pretty much her worst nightmare. Which meant any talk beyond this week brought them to an impasse. What the hell was he supposed to do next?

The sun was setting as they reached the north end of the island, and Mauna Kea glowed in oranges and reds. Kendall pointed to a drive along the Kalani's entrance, and he turned in. The string of wooden, no-frills cabins didn't have the same high-end vibe as the one he was staying in. But they looked welcoming, at least from the outside. Lush green trees cast long shadows on the narrow road, and the little groups of cabins were mostly unlit.

Kendall pointed to a cabin tucked back from the road, closer to the beach, and he pulled up on the sandy shoulder.

"It's dark here," he said, looking around.

Kendall shrugged. "I didn't leave the front porch light on. I thought we'd be back earlier."

It looked peaceful enough, but that wasn't a guarantee. How often did she come home alone? Had she taken self-defense courses? Did she carry Mace? The risk of attack was probably low, but the consequence was high. He frowned. His rationale about risks versus consequences sounded a lot more reasonable when it was about his free climbs. It didn't sit nearly as well with him when applied to Kend-all's safety.

None of these safety questions were any of his business anyway. Kendall had a life here in Hawaii, and she'd go on living it just the same way she had before he'd come. The thought unsettled him, but what could he do about it? Unless he came up with a brilliant solution, in a few days, he would leave, going back to Zion to prepare for the big climb. And Kendall would go back to walking on the beach with Alana and physical therapy appointments with her clients. Her male clients. Daxon clenched his teeth.

They still had time. That's what he should be fo-cusing on, not all the things that wouldn't change. Where was that live-for-the-moment wisdom he had spouted in that interview years earlier?

He climbed out of the car and followed her up the path to her cabin, his hand on the small of her back. She turned to him, silent in the darkness. The sounds of the trees and the waves whispered in the back-ground, but all he was thinking about was Kendall. Her hair was mussed and her cheeks were pink from the sun. She looked happy. And so lovely.

"So…" She smiled a little at him. "Here we are."

"Here we are," Daxon whispered, smoothing the salty strands of hair out of her face.

She didn't look away, and neither did he, just stared, letting his gaze wander down to her mouth. He thought about how red her lips were, how good it felt to spend time just kissing her, feeling her. The longer they stayed in this silent purgatory of desire, the more the intensity built inside him.

Finally, he leaned forward and kissed her, brushing his lips against hers. The hunger for her should have gone by now after a full day of touching and kissing and laughing and sex, but it hadn't. He was ready for more, ready to lie down beside her, to take his time. He could—

"I'm tempted to ask you in, but part of me thinks it's not a good idea."

The words cut into his little fantasy. "Why not?"

He waited for an answer, but she didn't speak. She just shook her head slowly, and there was a hint of sadness in her smile. He opened his mouth to protest, but the look on her face stopped him. He was supposed to be giving her the best day of her life, and that probably included listening when she said stop.

"Maybe tomorrow night instead?"

Her smile widened. "Maybe."

He kissed her one more time, slowly, reminding her of all the reasons she should say yes. Then he sighed and pulled away before he took it too far.

"Best day ever," she whispered. "Thank you."

Then she turned around and walked inside, giving him one last smile over her shoulder before shutting the door behind her. Daxon stared at the cabin, blinking, still not ready to walk away. He turned and sat down on her front step. His heart was still pumping from the kiss, and his head was full of memories from the day. At the cliffs, at the beach, in the water…shit.

He had to figure this out, to get this right. Unfortunately, he still didn't know what *right* meant for Kendall and him.

CHAPTER ELEVEN

KENDALL STOOD OUTSIDE Daxon's door, her knuckles just inches from the wood, waiting. Why was she hesitating? After the trip to South Point, the days had flowed quickly, with his stretches and massages mixing with the rest of her clients', but their nights were always together. It wasn't like anything had changed, not really. But this was his last full day at the Kalani. She would be his physical therapist for one more morning, and she'd spend one final night with him before he went back to being Daxon Miles, YouTube phenomenon. Before he left to free solo Moonlight Buttress.

After their excursion together, the idea of letting him go was getting harder. He felt so close, so real. *They* felt real together. Kendall shook her head. This week was supposed to be an exercise in living in the moment, not ruining her joy with worries about the future. She had promised herself a fun fling, and that's what this was…right?

In their first conversation about risks and consequences back in Costa Rica, she had been quick to point out that his risk assessment was about him, not others. But now, as she stood outside his door, she understood another layer of this complicated puzzle. People were much better at assessing practical risks, risks that could be measured in statistics, such as how likely it was to die when fighting fires for almost twenty years. But what about those that were less clear, emotional risks? Like the risk that she wouldn't be able to move on easily after he left? The risk that he'd leave a big, gaping hole in the newfound happiness of her life in Hawaii?

Still, every concern was full of unknowns. She had spent so much time worrying about her father getting trapped during fire season that a crushed arm hadn't even crossed her mind. Had it crossed her father's when he had chosen his path?

Kendall massaged her forehead. *Focus on this last day together.* She could spend the next week or ten overanalyzing. Until then, she just had to shut this off. And if she didn't do it soon, Daxon would probably open the door on her again, and this time she wasn't wearing cowboy boots.

Kendall straightened up and knocked, and the knob turned almost immediately. Had he been watching her out the little side window as she angsted over him? Nope, not going to think about that either.

Daxon opened the door, one large hand leaning against the doorframe. Her heartbeat kicked up another notch when she saw him, all ripped muscles and golden tan in a T-shirt and shorts. She had touched him so many times over the last five days, both professionally and personally, that she wasn't expecting for her heart to thump so hard when he stood in the hallway.

The memories from the past week before were clear. The sleek muscles of his forearms, the bulges of his tight biceps against his shirtsleeves. She took in his full lips, his gray-green eyes. He looked like he was drinking her in, too.

Kendall gave herself a little shake, coming to her senses. She was at work.

"Ready for your last day of personal healing coach treatment?" she asked, raising his eyebrow.

Daxon's laugh was an easy rumble. "Not making sexy jokes is killing me."

"The world is a darker place for it," she said drily, but she couldn't stop from grinning, too.

He motioned for her to come into the living room, and she sat on the couch, opening up her tablet. He sat down next to her, not quite touching.

She bit her lip. "I want to start creating a care plan for after you leave."

He nodded, looking a little more serious.

"I don't want you to get hurt again," she added softly.

Daxon sighed. "Believe it or not, I'm getting cautious as I get older. Calvin warned me that I was aging out of the adrenaline sports world."

Kendall frowned. "He's worried your body might break down on you, so he's planning to fit in as many things as possible before that happens?"

"That doesn't make him sound like a very good friend, does it?" His voice was getting tighter.

"He sounds like a great business strategist. But you're the one who has to live with the consequences. Then again, it doesn't sound like you're too worried about it, either."

He paused, then let out his breath. "Point taken."

Daxon looked out through the French doors, at the deep blue ocean in the distance, his expression serious. Then he turned to her, looking at her straight in the eye.

"So what's your recommendation, Kendall?"

The truth was on the tip of her tongue. She wanted to tell him to quit, to back out of the climb, to stay away from any other extreme activities. Lord, she wanted to, and the tightness in his jaw made her suspect that Daxon knew this. Maybe that's why he had asked. She was trying like hell to remain objective. He was a client, and she had to give him professional advice. So she swallowed back her emotions and gave him an answer that could pass as objective.

"You're great at doing exercises on your own, stretching, and you should definitely keep that up. Otherwise, I think you're fine to resume your normal training. It's the best way to tell whether or not that calf will give you problems when you're in the middle of a climb." She took a deep breath, searching for the right way to say this last part, to express her worries while keeping it impersonal. "But I'd still feel better if you waited a little longer. And if it does give you trouble, I think it goes without saying that I'd advise postponing the climb."

Had she kept the ache out of her voice? God, she hoped so.

Daxon had that intense look, like he was reading every single nuance in what she had said and what she hadn't said. He nodded his head slowly.

"I'm willing to consider that." He swallowed. "Would you consider a traveling physical therapist job?"

Kendall's heart leaped in her chest. She shook her head before she could be tempted to give any other answer.

"Not even for a special case?"

Absolutely not. She wasn't going to follow Daxon around, playing nurse while he took more risks. She didn't want this to end, but nothing good could come from that road. Even seeing him again would be so hard. She had already misjudged the consequences of this week, misjudged how much she loved being around him after just a few days. What would it be like if they spent more time together?

So she schooled her expression into a casual smile and shook her head again. "Not even for a superhot adrenaline junkie."

"That's what I thought," he said. "I just wanted to make sure."

His words weren't a surprise, but something in his voice gave her pause. It sounded a lot like determination. She drew in a shaky breath. When Daxon Miles made up his mind, he was relentless. What was he making up his mind about now?

This man had an enormous capacity to harness his attention and focus on it to get what he wanted. She had experienced the power of this during the week. Hell, she had enjoyed it. This week, she had been a very willing participant. But what if he used his powers to get something she was no longer sure she could handle? Something that part of her wanted badly but the other part knew she shouldn't have? It would gut her—that's what would happen.

But this was physical therapy, the time she had promised herself she would not get personal...or more personal than it already was.

So she ignored his determined stare and put her thoughts aside. When she looked up, Daxon was smiling at her.

"You ready for some healing?" she said with a wink.

He laughed. "With you? Always."

He climbed onto the physical therapy table and lounged back onto his elbows. Some clients were quiet, and some were talkers—Kendall could go either way—but today, she needed a distraction.

"Explain to me how the next week will go, leading up to the climb," she said, trying not to think too hard about the hard muscles under her fingers, muscles she had intimate knowledge of. She bit her lip and tuned them out.

"Nothing like a week at this resort, that's for sure," he said with a chuckle. "I'll be living out of my trailer at the base of the mountain while Calvin and a few other crew members and I work out all the specifics."

"I thought the days living out of your truck were over," she said, moving her hands higher. "You have more than enough money to upgrade your accommodations."

From the tension in his jaw, she wondered if he was having trouble focusing, too.

"Money isn't the issue. It's proximity. I need to be close, and Zion hasn't built luxury accommodations next to Moonlight Buttress. Yet. I can't imagine why."

She laughed. "I see. So you get there and then what? Climb it a few times off-camera first?"

"Most of the preparation is long over. At this point, I spend a lot of time visualizing each move, each hold. I'll film a couple live promo trailers, and the crowds will start coming a few days before, which means we need to have our area well staked out beforehand."

"What do you think about the crowds?"

He hesitated, then shrugged. "I'm used to it. I just tune it out. And when I start climbing, there's nothing else. Just me and the mountain."

The sound of the waves floated through the windows as she finished with his leg, lost in thought. She could feel Daxon's gaze on her, and finally, she met it.

"You've been a perfect PT client this week, doing exactly what I told you to."

Daxon smirked. "And then some."

She gave him an amused snort. "Just keep doing these exercises. I'd say take it easy, but we both know that's a stretch."

"Plus, my favorite relaxation method will be gone."

"I'm sure you and your hand will think of something."

"I'm getting good at coming up with ideas," he said, his eyes brimming with lust.

"I'm not sure what to say about that." The laughter bubbled inside her. Lord, this man made her laugh. "We're on the clock, during a physical therapy session."

He made an effort to look scandalized, but it quickly dissolved into a smile. Then his smile faded. "Kendall, I've been thinking…"

She froze. His voice was quiet and serious, and he was looking at her like he was about to suggest something big, something she wasn't prepared for, that didn't belong in a physical therapy session.

"Wait, Daxon," she said. "Not now."

He opened his mouth, like he was going to protest, then he closed it and nodded.

"When?"

"Later."

He frowned but didn't say anything. She would come later. It wouldn't be easy, but staying away from him wouldn't change anything. It would be painful when they said goodbye, no matter what she decided. There was no reason to start that struggle early.

CHAPTER TWELVE

DAXON THOUGHT ABOUT Kendall all day. He thought about her as he did his pull-ups on his fingerboard, he thought about her as he did another set of push-ups on the hanging rings that he had installed on the lanai, and he thought about her as he climbed into his private pool and stared out at the ocean. There were times that morning she had been quiet during his physical therapy session, as if she were just as lost in thought as he was. Something had shifted in her at the end of that spectacular day at South Point, but he still wasn't sure of the direction of her shift.

Either way, he was never one to back down from a challenge. Hell, he thrived on it, testing his limits, seeing how far he could push himself. But this challenge wasn't a mountain, an impersonal object that didn't care whether or not he succeeded. This was a woman, with her own wants, needs and reservations. Whose heart could break, and he would have to live with himself if he broke it. He would never be able to rehearse his approach the same way he rehearsed his climbs, putting every move into a well-choreographed routine, a road map for successful execution. No matter how much he planned, this wasn't something he could master.

The more he thought about this last evening together, the more he realized how unprepared he was for what she might say. Despite carefully hoarding every bit of knowledge about her over this past week, he was only beginning to learn what pleased her and what she cared about, what she wanted. He was so hungry for more, more, more. Every part of him ached for more of her.

But that wasn't the biggest stumbling block. He was no stranger to the drive to satisfy his own wants, anticipating the adrenaline rush that came with it. He had ignored it before, turned it off to focus on the next climb, the next challenge. This was different. He didn't just want more from her; he wanted to *give* her more. Except…what would make her happy was for him to *not* do what he did. For him not to be the man who free soloed Moonlight Buttress in a week. For him not to cause her the kind of anguish that her father's risks had caused her.

He knew all this. It was a puzzle with pieces that didn't belong together, and yet later that night, he still walked along the resort's path with a packed dinner in his hand, heading for her cabin. Because despite the fact that their hurdles seemed insurmountable, he wasn't backing down from the challenge. He had done impossible things before. This was infinitely more complicated, and yet even the hint of a payoff sounded infinitely more satisfying.

He had visualized what he wanted: Kendall lying over him in the narrow bed of his trailer in the middle of the night, running his hands over her bare skin. And when he woke up the next day for the climb, she would be right there with him.

It was a selfish vision. He knew it, he knew that was the crux of their problem, and yet he wanted it. There had to be a possibility that looked something like this…right? After the next six months of publicity plans, after the El Capitan climb, after Calvin's vision for the future of Pure Adrenaline was secure, he could make adjustments, maybe lay off the stunts that had highest consequence. That idea had run through his mind since his injury in Costa Rica, for his mother's sake. Now he had even more reason to consider it.

But he had months before he could change course. Right now, he had less than a day to convince her that maybe she could hang on in the meantime. His focus needed to be on tonight. He had decided what he'd say and do, and as with any other challenge, he would redraw his route as he made progress.

Kendall's cabin was lit up, glowing from the inside, but she didn't answer when he knocked. He followed the little trail around to the lanai and found her on a chaise lounge with a tub of ice cream in her lap.

Health-conscious Kendall was eating straight from a half gallon tub of mint chocolate chip ice cream. Daxon suspected this was a sign of some sort, but he had no idea whether it was a good one.

She turned as he scraped through the large flat leaves of some tropical plant in his path, and he had no idea how to interpret the uneasy look she gave him.

So he flashed her a smile. "Isn't it a little early to be hitting the hard stuff?"

The uneasy look faded. "You can grab a spoon from the kitchen. You know you want some."

"I brought some addition to that dinner." He set the bag next to the ice cream tub and eased into the lounge chair next to her.

She peeked into the bag, then blinked up at him, a little dazed. "Burritos?"

"Alana tipped me off." It wasn't the most luxurious meal, but her friend had said that good burritos were one of the things Kendall missed most about Northern California. So Daxon had gone with the recommendation. From Kendall's expression, he had chosen right.

"Thank you." She was looking at him, almost guarded, but possibly hopeful. Then a smile curved at her lips. "I still had a good hour of agonizing to go before I came over."

"Figured I'd save us both some time." He gave her a playful wink. "There are so many better ways to spend the evening."

She rolled her eyes. "Of course there are. But I just can't seem to help myself."

"That's just you being you. I wouldn't want to change that."

The words just came, but after he spoke them, he was pretty sure he had just stumbled onto what was probably the most profound thing he had said all week. At the most inconvenient time, he was falling in love with a woman who was wary of who he was, and yet, at this moment, it felt perfect. It must be love, because otherwise, it didn't make a hell of a lot of sense.

She watched him through those dark, impossibly long lashes, like she was drinking him in one last time, getting her fill. Daxon frowned. That's not the direction he wanted to go. He searched for a way to divert to a better route.

"You want to eat?"

She shook her head.

"Not in the mood for burritos tonight?"

"Not yet."

She stood up and held out her hand, nodding to the door. *Oh.*

He followed her inside. It was a much smaller version of his cabin, in the same style that mixed modern with the island. But instead of the sleek, impersonal furniture he had found in his living room, Kendall's place was filled with all the details that made it a home. Photographs of her parents hung on the wall, books were neatly arranged on the shelves, and her bright green couch looked comfortable and inviting.

But she wasn't giving him a tour right now. She took his hand and led him straight to her bedroom. The kelly-green duvet covered the bed neatly. Was green her favorite color? There was so much he didn't know about her. Everything in the room was in its place, because of course it was. Kendall was a careful woman with careful boundaries. She worked to keep her life that way, and he was trampling all over it. He still wasn't sure if this was exactly why they fit together or exactly why he should stay away.

But he could worry about that later. Right now she didn't seem to want to talk. She was silent as she turned to face him, her expression warm and serious. She said nothing as she pulled off her shirt, and she said nothing as she unfastened her bra, letting her beautiful breasts free. And yet with each move, he could hear her, loud and clear.

One last time.

She was giving this message off in waves, and despite the fact that he vehemently disagreed, he knew arguing wasn't the right path. Instead, he told her with his body, with his gaze.

Don't worry, sweets. I'll give you what you want. And more. So much more.

She stripped off her shorts and her panties, and then she stood in front of him, solemn.

I'll give you this, she was saying in the silence of the room. *This is what we have together.*

And, fuck, how he wanted it. He wanted that and so much more. So he took off his own clothes, stripping himself bare, and he stood in front of her, naked. His cock had responded to her long ago, and he hadn't bothered to fight it. But standing here, naked in front of her, he was starting to wish that he had. Sex was where this was unquestionably headed, but at this moment, as she watched him, her brown eyes tinged with sadness, sex felt like a distraction.

Daxon took a step forward and rested a hand on her cheek. It was the wrong time to say all the things he had planned to say to her, so instead, he pressed his mouth against hers. He kissed her, trying hard to resist the urge to memorize this feeling. This wasn't the end. It wasn't the last time, even if she was thinking that. It couldn't be...could it? When they had kissed in Costa Rica, thinking it was the only time, they had still managed to find their way back to each other. Or rather, Calvin had managed it. So much had happened since she had walked into his cabin at the Kalani. After all that, they'd reunite again... wouldn't they?

Slowly, he sucked her lower lip into his mouth, scraping his teeth against it, letting her know how much he wanted her. The intensity of this physical attraction was the one thing they both agreed on without hesitation. But it was also the way he could show her this was more.

I want this, he said with each stroke of his tongue, *and not just for tonight.*

He could feel the moment Kendall put aside all of her hesitations and let herself go. She matched each stroke of his tongue with hers, pressing her body against his. The night was warm, and her skin was soft and hot, and kissing her was so goddamn intoxicating. Her hands closed around his shoulders as she tried to lessen the height distance between them, so he lifted her. His cock wedged between her legs, and they both groaned. He turned and laid her on the bed, collapsing against her as their bodies tangled together, laughter and moans filling him with a deep happiness. Daxon's heart was pounding—anticipation, desire and joy all wrapped up into one long adrenaline rush he'd never find anywhere else. They kissed some more, and he cupped her breasts, sucked on them, teasing her. He was trying so hard to resist the dizzying abyss of pleasure, but the feeling was too strong. So he gave in, holding himself over her, resting on his elbows, staring down at her. Slowly, she lifted her gaze and met his. For a moment, she looked so lost, but after a blink, that look was gone.

"On your back," she said. She gave his shoulder a little shove, her eyes twinkling with mischief.

Kendall on top? Yeah, that was more than fine with him. He'd give her anything she wanted... almost anything. Daxon pushed that last thought away. Instead, he tipped onto his back, holding her close, taking her with him. She sat up and arranged herself, wiggling her hips, dragging her pussy against his cock. He let out a quiet groan. Fuck, she was already so wet.

"You wanna ride, sweets?" He flexed his hips and moved his hands down, around her ass. "Use me. Ride my cock, take whatever you want. It's yours."

She smile down at him, her eyes half-lidded with pleasure. Kendall shimmied backward and reached between them, wrapping her fingers around his dick. She gave it an exploratory tug, and his eyes rolled back in his head. She sat back and smiled, like she was admiring it right now.

"I could spend days playing with it. I think I'm a little obsessed with your cock, Daxon." She let out a little huff of laughter. "Don't let it go to your head."

"It's all yours," he rasped. "I won't come until you come first."

"Satisfaction guaranteed, right?"

It was his promise from the first day, but that version of them seemed so far away.

She took her hand away and shifted forward to press herself over his cock again. He was already seeing stars, but damn if he'd give in to that urge to come before she was ready, so he focused on her, naked, moving over him, finding her pleasure. He reached up to palm her beautiful breasts, pinching her nipples, enjoying her sighs and moans.

"Are we using condoms?" she asked, her voice breathless.

"Your call."

She smiled a little. "Then I think we'll go for a careless end to a spectacularly careless week."

Her words grated on him, so light and final, but tonight was her show. They could discuss the future later.

"Then fuck me, sweets," he said. "Let go."

She took his cock in her hand again and positioned it, rising over him. In one slow movement, she eased down onto him, slick and hot and so goddamn tight. Daxon clenched his teeth, resisting the urge to hold on to her hips and buck his way into oblivion. She moved slowly up and down, taking him deeper and deeper, until she'd settled, his cock buried inside her. She paused, gazing at him seriously. Was she hoping for the same things he was?

Then she began to move, and that thought faded. He slipped his hands around her waist and held on, letting her set the pace, meeting her with a flex of his hips. She was clenching around him, and he could feel that she was close, so soon. She closed her eyes and tipped her head back, like a goddess riding her way to the heavens. But he was a selfish prick, because he didn't want her riding to the heavens. He wanted her riding to him.

"Open your eyes, Kendall," he rasped, holding back his thrust.

She let out a frustrated moan and glared down at him.

"That's right, sweets. I want you looking at me when you come."

He punctuated that sentence with a hard thrust of his hips, and she found her release. She cried out, saying his name, over and over. Daxon couldn't wait any longer. He let go, jackknifing forward as the pleasure shot through him, holding her tight against him.

"Kendall," he whispered in her ear. "My Kendall."

They ate burritos in the darkness of her lanai, the ocean and the wind whispering around them. Daxon had pulled his shorts on again, leaving his ripped abs for Kendall to admire as he lay back in the chaise lounge, taking his last bite. She was shamelessly staring because…well, he didn't seem to care, so why should she? This was their last night, and she was getting her last gulp of Daxon Miles.

Plus, she was trying not to think too hard about what had happened between them in her bedroom.

My Kendall.

It was almost as if she had imagined it. But no. He had said it with a reverence that her brain wouldn't have invented. Neither of them had spoken as they lay on the bed, their bodies slick and pressed together.

Daxon set aside the paper wrap that had held the burrito. He parted his legs and then motioned for Kendall to come sit with him.

She settled between his legs and eased back against the hard planes of his chest. He wrapped his arms around her, pulling her closer, and she rested her head against his shoulder. In front of them, the dark ocean shimmered with the last reflections of the sun. His lips pressed into her hair.

If staring at Daxon was a fun pastime, lying with him in the darkness of the night was a whole different class of pleasure. His fingers wandered under her tank top, brushing over her bare skin, radiating warmth through her body. A calm had settled through her, but it was laced with that same undercurrent of attraction that never seemed to fade around him. That was just how it was between them, she supposed. And she had one last night to enjoy it.

"What's on your mind?" she asked.

He kissed the top of her head again. "Transcendent moments."

Right. The topic of his infamous interview.

"You thinking about your climb?" she asked, trying to keep the disappointment out of her voice.

"Not even a little bit."

Oh. Her stubborn heart gave a new jolt.

"Are you?" he asked after a while.

She bit her lip. "Maybe." Now she was.

His hand stilled against her, and his breath in her ear stopped. "I wanted to talk to you about an idea."

His voice was casual, but she could feel tension coming off him. She was almost sure whatever he wanted to say had the power to either make this moment perfect or splinter this peaceful night apart.

Kendall bit her lip. "What is it?"

"I don't want this to end."

She swallowed, waiting, trying to hold back the swell of hope inside her. She had asked so many what-ifs since she tossed herself off that cliff, but each scenario ended in disappointment. Had he thought of a path she hadn't?

"I was thinking how much I'd love it if you came to Utah with me."

The sentence deflated every bit of hope that she had let fizz inside her just moments ago.

But Daxon took her silence as a prompt to press forward. "Maybe, if you have a few vacation days, you could come stay with me. I know living out of a trailer isn't quite Kalani standards, but Zion is incred—"

"The trailer's not the problem, and you know it," she whispered, cutting him off before he indulged in that idea for one more second. If Daxon thought that she was going to follow him around while he scaled mountains without ropes, maybe he really was crazy.

Kendall shifted to sit up, but Daxon's arms were tight around her. He heaved out a sigh and let her go. She turned to face him. A frown tugged down at the corners of his mouth, as if she were the one who was disappointing him. Kendall couldn't believe how angry she suddenly was. It was as if she had saved up all her feelings about his recklessness all week, just for this moment.

She drew in a shaky breath. "You want me to

watch while you risk your life, just for another stunt? For another adrenaline rush?"

Daxon's jaw tightened. "You don't have to watch the climb. I just want you there with me. We could spend some time together there, and maybe you'd understand this part of me."

"But—"

"I won't be doing this forever," he said. "After the El Cap climb, I can rethink what I want to do. We can think through what comes next for us. Together."

There was no hint of Daxon's usual playfulness, that easygoing side of him that he showed the world. What was left was the person who always lurked underneath, serious and determined.

"You knew who I was from the beginning. That's the reason why Calvin sent me to the Kalani in the first place," he said, his voice harder. "So that I could do this climb."

She was so frustrated she could scream. Yes, this was true, and she had reminded herself of this at each step. But hadn't everything shifted since he arrived? She wasn't just his physical therapist anymore, and he was no longer here solely to heal his calf. Or at least she had hoped this was true, but apparently, in the end, it still came down to his goddamn stunts.

Daxon probably meant what he said about finding something that worked, but she had seen a version of this scenario play out between her parents, and she knew that quitting was complicated. How many times did her father talk about taking a less dangerous job only to hop back on a plane the next fire season because they needed the money…or his buddies needed him…or whatever excuse he found? How many fights had she listened to? Enough to know that for someone who loved the rush, quitting was highly unlikely. Her father had waited until his body began to fail. Any failure on Daxon's part would have the ultimate consequence.

All Kendall could think about right now was that one misstep meant he would die. And he was willing to accept the consequence of falling from a sheer wall of stone. They'd never have a chance to really be together. She didn't need to say any of these things aloud, because she was almost sure he knew exactly what she was thinking.

Daxon blew out a breath. "Did you think this would end any other way than me doing these climbs?"

Kendall closed her eyes. Yes, she had hoped. Against all better judgment, all past experience, the hope had formed during the week that there was a way this could end well.

"Where does it stop?" she whispered. "Do you just keep doing these stunts until you die?"

"Either of us could get hit by a car tomorrow, too," he said, scowling. "That doesn't mean we should stop ourselves from living today."

"It's not the same," she said quickly. Was it? Maybe

there was some truth in what he said, but the scale of risk wasn't even close.

His gaze softened a little. "The next six months will be intense, and, yes, I'll be doing a lot of the kind of high-consequence climbing that scares you. But after that, we can take Pure Adrenaline in a new direction. I'm just asking you to hang on until then."

Until after he free soloed two mountains, including the elusive El Cap, the mountain face where experienced climbers died, even with ropes? And he'd climb them without any safety net?

"You're not willing to try?" he added, his voice quiet.

The words hurt. Kendall massaged her temples.

"Let's just say that I accept this crazy premise, that I can stomach knowing you're doing these two insane climbs. What happens next?" She had lived this life as a kid, watching her father run right back into the fire zone, over and over, even after he promised to quit. It was getting harder and harder to keep her voice calm. "That drive to do things like this doesn't just go away. I've seen this firsthand."

His mouth was a hard line, grim and determined. "We could find a compromise if we both want this to work. I know we could."

Right now, he probably believed he'd truly meet her halfway, but when it came to actually quitting, it wouldn't be that simple. Where would all of that energy go? Would it churn inside, curdling into resentment and restlessness? Then the next time that siren song of a new adventure called, he'd find a way to talk her into it.

Kendall swallowed, knowing she had one last card to play. Goddamn him for making her play it, for bringing her to the point where she was desperate enough to ask for it. It wasn't fair of her—it was straight-up manipulative—but this was his *life* on the line. If she didn't ask him and he did die, she'd never forgive herself for not trying.

So she took a deep breath and said it. "You promised to follow exactly what I said. What if I ask you not to do this climb?"

Daxon's expression went hard as stone. He didn't move, but now there was anger in his eyes. "You can't really mean that."

"But that's the problem. I really do."

Maybe he could never forgive her for pushing him like this, or maybe at some point, he would understand just how desperately scared she would have to be to ask it. But even as his cold glare broke her heart, she didn't want to take it back.

He stared at her through a few more fuming breaths. "Are you saying that as my physical therapist, or is that a personal request?"

"Of course it's personal," she whispered. "I know you're going to do this climb and the next one. It's who you are, and I hate that I want to change that. Part of me even wants you to do all these amazing things."

Some of the anger faded from his expression, and in its place, she saw hurt.

Kendall swallowed back the lump in her throat and continued. "But I also know myself. This is my breaking point. I can't let myself fall in love with someone who lets himself be one loose handhold away from death, over and over again."

How many nights had she woken up in the middle of the night, thinking about her father, stuck on a ridge, surrounded by flames on all sides? Enough to know that this feeling didn't get better with time.

How could she even consider a relationship with Daxon, who seemed to love the challenge of high-consequence adventures even more than her father did? This wasn't a rift; it was a chasm, deep and wide, and no amount of discussion was going to bridge it. She had to cut this off now, because she couldn't handle going down that road again.

Kendall had no idea how long they stared at each other, waging silent warfare. And then, suddenly, it ended, or at least Daxon stepped out of it. His eyes softened, and he took a long breath. "I'm going to figure this out. I know you don't believe it, but I will."

Kendall didn't speak. He could do all the figuring out he wanted by himself, but it still didn't change the fact that he was going to go climb a mountain with no ropes. That he chose a path that had led other top climbers to their deaths.

Daxon wrapped his hands around her waist, silently calling her back to him. This was the very last time she would lie with him. This amazing man who was so full of laughter and energy and life might not be alive in a few weeks. Or maybe it would be the El Cap climb that would be his downfall. She had to live with that. But this was their last night, her last chance, so she eased back onto his chest, closed her eyes, and tried like hell to concentrate on the moment she was in. It was a resounding failure.

Kendall must have dozed off because there was no trace of sunlight when Daxon whispered in her ear, asking if he could stay the night. When they lay in her bed for the last time, she curled up next to him, breathing in his scent, memorizing it. His heart thumped wildly in his chest, and his breaths were uneven. She drank in every detail, getting her fill one more time.

He woke her in the middle of the night, hard, his big body flush behind hers, his arm wrapped around her, pulling her against him. His muscles strained as he held her, thrusting, his breath heavy in her ear. She came twice before he followed her, his lips in her hair, whispering things she couldn't hear.

He awoke early. The sun was just peeking over the horizon when he leaned down to kiss her, fully clothed.

"I won't come to say goodbye before I leave for the airport," he said softly. "I'd rather end like this."

She nodded.

"Goodbye, Daxon," she whispered, not wanting to see his expression. But she made herself look at him one more time. "I hope you get everything you're looking for up on that mountain."

He blinked down at her, his gaze searching. But there was nothing to search for anymore.

So she closed her eyes and let him go.

CHAPTER THIRTEEN

KENDALL SAT ON the floor of her tiny living room, staring at the blank screen of her television. The last week since Daxon had left had been miserable, and today was sinking into new depths. She was not going to watch his climb. She was not going to torture herself, analyzing every step he took, watching for each little slip of his foot, looking for signs of fatigue.

But not watching was just as nerve-racking as watching. Daxon could have, at this point, already fallen to his death, and she wouldn't know. As it turned out, it mattered a hell of a lot whether he was alive somewhere else in the world, even if they were never going to see each other again.

Kendall couldn't shake the restlessness that had been building in her, and it wasn't just fueled by fear. What if Daxon did make it to the top of the mountain? Part of her wanted to see his mastery of this mountain, share it with him. Not watching felt…a bit lonely.

God, she missed him, his deep, easy laugh, the intense attention that he had given to her while they were together. During his stay at the Kalani, the world of his next Pure Adrenaline stunt had been on hold, and oh, what a glorious week it had been. That cliff jumping day was the best of her life. Honestly, the entire week had been.

Damn you, Daxon Miles. It wasn't supposed to be this way. Maybe she should just go ahead and watch instead of spending the next few hours staring at the blank screen, making herself miserable.

A knock on the sliding glass door startled her out of her agonizing.

"Kendall?"

Alana's head appeared through the sliding door. Her friend's gaze slid to the dark TV screen, where Kendall had been staring. Alana quirked up an eyebrow. "Busy?"

Kendall shrugged. "Come join the *not-watching* party."

Alana slid opened the door and stepped in, plopping a bag down next to Kendall. "Sounds fun. I brought refreshments."

She headed for the kitchen, and Kendall peeked inside the bag. A bottle of vodka, a jug of orange juice and a box of doughnuts. Hmm…temporary relief from her current mood?

Alana returned from the kitchen with plates, glasses and napkins. "I figured you could use a little breakfast."

"I'm feeling more than a little pathetic, so I guess day drinking over this guy won't be any worse. Or at least I'll have more fun with it."

"That's the spirit," said Alana, opening the dough-nut box.

Kendall groaned as she looked inside. "Oh, yes. Guava."

"I couldn't remember if that was your favorite. Or was it lilikoi? I got both," said Alana, reaching for the vodka. She poured generous shots into each tumbler and topped them off with a few splashes of orange juice. Then she grabbed an old-fashioned doughnut out of the box and held it up. "Cheers."

Kendall tapped hers against Alana's. "Breakfast of champions."

She took a big bite of her doughnut and washed it down with a swig from her glass, wrinkling her nose. The last time she had drank vodka was in college. And even then, it hadn't been in the morning.

Alana took a bite of her doughnut and they sat, staring at the blank screen. "Pretty fun, this not-watching party," said Alana. "Want to know what would be even more fun?"

"A watching party?"

"Yep." Alana smiled brightly.

"Fine." Kendall grumbled. Not watching wasn't really working for her anyway.

She grabbed the remote next to her and flipped on the screen, navigating to the YouTube app. She

clicked on Daxon's channel, and there he was, shirtless and beautiful, halfway up Moonlight Buttress.
With no ropes. She took a long drink of her screwdriver.

"He's still alive. Cheers to that," said Alana, raising her glass.

Kendall clinked her glass with Alana's and took
another gulp.

"Damn, he's hot," said Alana.

She waved off the comment. "I know, I know."

"What? It had to be said."

Yes, he was hot, but she wasn't thinking about
how he looked. She was remembering what it felt
like to lie on the lounge chair, her back against his
hard chest, his arms around her. Or lying in her bed,
half-asleep, the scent of him everywhere.

"He's incredible," she muttered.

"Plus he's good in bed and ultra-attentive to you."

"When he's not climbing up a sheer mountain
face with no ropes, and it's only in preparation for
an even riskier climb."

"There's plenty of time for good sex before that
climb."

"This is ridiculous," said Kendall. "No amount
of sex is worth watching him willingly take these
risks. It's just too much. I watched what living
like that did to my mother. I'm not going to do
that, too."

"But your parents are still together, aren't they?"

"Yes. That's part of why it's so painful. My mom

loves him so much, so she put herself through that, over and over."

"But your mom's no pushover. I've met her," said Alana, with a smirk. "Wasn't she a firefighter a long time ago, too?"

"She was. She quit when she got pregnant with me. Too risky."

"But your dad didn't quit?"

"Not until his arm was crushed. Not until it became personal."

Alana's expression softened. "I see."

Daxon's progress up the mountain was slow, methodical and confident. He had clearly rehearsed this route many times, because he seemed to know exactly where he was going. His muscles flexed as he dipped his fingers into the chalk pouch by his side and then found his grip to climb the next few inches of rock. It was incredible. Of course millions of subscribers tuned in each time, captivated.

Watching him move, his broad back and shoulder muscles as chiseled as the mountain face, bunching, rippling, his focus solely on the rock in front of him, this was about so much more than money and fame. His comments about existential awakening hadn't just been bullshit. As he moved along the face of the mountain, it was as if a part of him came alive. He was at peace, wearing that same look he'd had that day on the beach. Watching it was both beautiful and incredibly depressing. She had asked him to give this up, this part of him. That twist in her stomach came back, the one that had started during their last night together, when she couldn't decide if she was mad at Daxon for taking this risk or angry with herself for asking him to quit. Was this how her mother had felt about her father, too?

Kendall bit her lip and watched the man in front of her. There was a good chance he would die at a young age, like most free solo climbers, unless he wanted to stop. But he didn't want to. That was his path, and she had to respect that. She just didn't want to watch it play out...except here she was, glued to his YouTube channel, despite everything.

Muscles coiling, toes digging into rock, springing up, sideways, fingers catching on ledges with each full-body extension, he rose, concentrating on every move. He paused, and Kendall stiffened, holding her breath. But then he smiled. Hanging by one hand, shaking out the other, he smiled that cocky smile at the camera, the one that said, *I've got it all under control.* Daxon Miles was in his element, working—

And then it happened.

Just as Daxon shifted his weight, the rock loosened under his foot, and it slipped. As he scrambled for a foothold, she saw it. Fear. It flashed across his face. She had watched his Pure Adrenaline videos embarrassingly often, and never once had she seen fear. He knew it, too; he must have, because he stopped and looked away. Something had gone wrong, but this was a live broadcast, and there was nowhere to go. The camera panned back, waiting. How long would she and the rest of the crew just watch?

"Help him," Kendall whispered.

Alana had grabbed her hand somewhere in the last few seconds. Kendall didn't remember it happening, but now she was squeezing it hard. She could see Daxon's shoulders rising and falling. Were these his last breaths?

The simmering regret boiled over, flooding her thoughts. She should have gone with him. Just spent a few more days together. And she had given it up because she was afraid he would die in one of these stunts.

Except the truth was that despite all her fears, she had never really believed that he could die *today*. In her heart, she had believed he had more time. But what if there was no future? What if she had just spent the last week worrying about him from across the Pacific when she could have been worrying about him while she lay next to him? Or under him…

"I should be there right now," she whispered.

Alana shook her head decidedly. "You absolutely should not. If something goes wrong, you shouldn't be there."

Kendall frowned. "Maybe. But what about all those other moments before the climb? I gave up days with him. I chose to give up what could be my very last chance with him."

Alana nodded slowly.

Tears welled in Kendall's eyes, and she fought to hold them back. "If he falls, it won't hurt any less. Staying back doesn't make me care less. But it does make me regret the time I missed."

"You're falling in love with him," she said softly.

"It's ridiculous," said Kendall with a sniff. "I've only spent two weeks with the man, and they were six months apart."

"But those were two very intense weeks, one of which included plenty of spectacular sex, right? If you convert all those hours together to dating time, that's probably months."

"Still." Kendall glanced at the screen. Daxon was still there, in the same position. She took another drink of her screwdriver, but it wasn't helping the jumble of worries and hopes that was stirring in her mind.

The camera zoomed in slowly, and Kendall and Alana fell silent, their gazes fixed on the TV. Then Daxon started to move, slowly at first, then gaining speed. He found his rhythm, climbing with the same confidence she had seen so many times in his videos. Kendall let out a shuddering sigh. If he made it up the mountain, she was going to…do something. She didn't know exactly what, but she had to let him know that she had made a mistake. That she shouldn't have shut him out, because as it turned out, even a few more days of being with him was more important than her fears. But there was no reason to plan her apology yet. He still had a long way to go before he reached the top. Then, if he made it, she'd figure this out. In the meantime, she was going to need another drink.

Daxon Miles had never once been afraid when he filmed a Pure Adrenaline episode. He prepared everything he did meticulously, and if he felt even a twinge of fear, it was a good indication that he needed more preparation. He choreographed every last move so that when the camera rolled, all he was thinking about was the moment he was living in. It was why Calvin had suggested the video series in the first place and probably the reason behind their runaway success: because when Daxon was in the middle of a stunt, anyone who watched could see that he was on top of the world.

Until today. His foothold slipped. It was the kind of thing that could happen during climbs, the kind of thing he was prepared for, and he had been in more perilous situations before. He had walked himself through this scenario so many times and trained his brain to move on, to focus on his next move. Instead his mind went somewhere new, somewhere that had hit him hard in the gut and twisted into fear, a climber's worst enemy. Instead he thought of Kendall. He had seen her face etched with worry and sadness when he left her cabin.

He never thought about worst-case scenarios on the mountain. Despite the fact that death could be one slip of the foot away, he blocked it out, both as a matter of self-preservation and because embedded in the decision to take the risk was the acceptance of this possibility.

But when his foot slipped, he saw the whole thing through Kendall's eyes. Which was exactly what he shouldn't do, exactly what put him in the most danger. Lin, the camerawoman, was filming his every move, but this time, he couldn't smile at the camera. He turned away and stared at the rock under his hands. He couldn't go back in time and stay in Kendall's cabin instead of walking away. He couldn't change the path he was on. Not yet. But when he got to the top, he could do something about it. What the hell that something was, he didn't know. But he'd figure that out once he wasn't scaring the shit out of Kendall, if she was watching. And his entire team. And himself, if he were completely honest. Because every second he stalled made falling to his death more likely.

It took all of Daxon's mental strength to turn his focus back to the mountain in front of him, and those years of training were powerful. One hand, one heel hook, one toe jam, one extension, a high foot, a weight shift, exactly the way he had done it a dozen times before, until finally he was close. Just three more moves. Two. One. And then he was at the summit. Lin climbed over the last ledge, and Calvin was there, waiting for him. Daxon knew he was supposed to say something to his viewers, but he had no idea what it was. Calvin, probably sensing this, motioned for Lin to pan to him.

"That was incredible," he said, his own face lit up with joy. "Thank you to the over one million viewers who are watching this live, across the world."

Daxon listened as Calvin went through their plans for the next six months, as they prepared for the El Cap free solo. He was supposed to be happy about this. The sponsorships, the ad revenue, the worldwide brand expansion—everything that Calvin had so carefully planned was making a leap forward today. Pure Adrenaline was taking off on a whole new level.

This should've been the ultimate adrenaline rush, his moment of triumph. But instead, it was as if he had fallen into a big empty hole of uncertainty. He didn't care if a million or even a hundred million strangers were watching him right now. There was only one person that he was thinking about, and he was worried that *she* might be watching. Because if she was, he had just scared the hell out of her. Enough so that she'd never want to speak to him again.

Calvin glanced over at him, his mouth in a flat line. Then he turned back to the camera and smiled. "Lin, let's get a look at the views."

When she had stepped away, his friend furrowed his brow, his eyes serious. "You okay, Dax?"

"That slip really threw me off," he muttered.

"I bought you a couple minutes to get your shit together." Calvin tilted his head a little, staring at him. "You've done worse. Are you sure you're feeling okay?"

Slowly, Daxon shook his head. "I'm not sure what the hell I'm feeling."

It seemed an awful lot like regret. He had just successfully pulled off his best climb, but it felt like he had made the biggest mistake of his life.

Before Calvin could pry anymore, Lin turned, heading right back toward them.

Calvin swung his arm around Daxon's shoulder and whispered, "Two more minutes of being the man who just fucking free soloed Moonlight Buttress. Two minutes of being the Daxon Miles who smiles at the camera, the guy everyone tuned in for. Then you can go back to looking like your dog just died."

So Daxon took a deep breath and did it. He stood up and pasted on his camera-ready smile. As Lin came over, he flexed his muscles, just the way he was supposed to. Then he tried to slip away, but Calvin held him in place, and Lin stopped in front of him. There was no escape.

"Daxon, you've just completed the first live free solo climb of Moonlight Buttress in history. What do you want to say to everyone who joined us this afternoon to watch?"

Daxon stared into the camera, but he still couldn't think of a single thing he wanted to say to a million strangers. Even the easy platitudes weren't coming. He needed to talk to Kendall. The silence hung heavily in the air, and Lin was frowning at him. Daxon felt the smile on his face fade. There was only one thing to say, and it definitely wasn't what Calvin and Lin had in mind. As he opened his mouth, he was fully aware that this could be the stupidest thing he had ever done. Still, he did it.

"What I have to say is for one person, and she knows who she is. I'm so, so sorry. I messed up. You deserve someone who listens when you say you've reached your limit." Lin's jaw had dropped, but Daxon didn't stop. "For the rest of you out there, thank you for showing up today and every time before this. This has been Calvin's and Lin's and my dream for a while, and it wouldn't have happened without you." He swallowed and glanced over at Calvin, who wasn't bothering to hide his wary expression. But Daxon looked back into the camera and cleared his throat. "But as of today, I am officially backing out of the free solo El Capitan climb. Back in the middle of the mountain, my foothold gave out, and I'm taking that as a sign that this is no longer what I should be doing."

Lin's mouth was still hanging open, and Daxon wasn't ready to hazard a glance toward Calvin. When his friend finally spoke, his voice was filled with false cheer.

"We'll update you soon on the future of Pure Adrenaline. And thanks to everyone out there who is watching."

CHAPTER FOURTEEN

DAXON KNOCKED ON Kendall's door for the third time. Her windows were open, and he could have sworn he heard a noise from inside when he walked up the path. Kendall hadn't answered any of his attempts to get in touch. After a flurry of desperate emails, Alana had given in and told him that today was Kendall's day off. Which meant she should be here… which had led to the conclusion that she was inside but wasn't answering the door.

Had she seen the video that would forever live in Pure Adrenaline infamy? It would probably be used in future marketing classes around the world as an example of how to lose your sponsorships in less than a minute, flat. But Daxon didn't care. He'd figure that out later, after talking to Kendall. He had tried to pry the answer out of Alana, but she was tight-lipped about almost everything he had asked. She was clearly a good friend to Kendall, so she got props for that, but in this situation, he would have preferred a slightly looser moral code.

Daxon knocked again. "Kendall?"

He was trying not to make a scene, but he had flown in from Utah the day before in preparation, and he knew she didn't have another day off for almost a week. If he had to, he'd wait, but right now, he was feeling impatient as hell.

"Kendall? Please can we talk?" He glanced around. Most of the neighbors' windows were open, too, so none of what he said would be a secret. Not that he cared, but this was where she worked. He wanted to respect that...though he wasn't above a little leveraging. Not at this point.

"I know I messed up badly, sweets. But please give me a chance to talk this through. Just talk. I promise I won't..." He glanced around, wondering how far to take this in public. "I won't use other methods of convincing."

No sounds came from inside, no footsteps, nothing to hang his hopes on. Shit. Daxon swiped a hand over his forehead. Climbing through the open window was tempting...and probably a little crazy. Yeah, that definitely crossed the line, especially since she hadn't answered his calls this morning. But he could wait her out.

Daxon turned around and sat on the doorstep, running his hand through his hair. He hung his head, trying to summon his patience for the long day ahead of him. She had to leave the place at some point, didn't she? Did this count as stalking? Shit, if he had to ask himself that question, he was really not in a good place.

Not so long ago, he had sat on this very step after the best day of his entire life, his body filled with giddy hope, grasping at future possibilities. He had managed to quash all of that the moment he left the Kalani to do the thing Kendall wanted absolutely no part of. He knew this conversation would require a hell of a lot of groveling, but he had assumed that she would at least—

"Aaah, the famous Daxon Miles."

Daxon looked up, taking in the flurry of purple hair.

"Alana." He sighed, greeting her with a tilt of his chin.

"I would've come over earlier, but I was waiting to see how much pleading you were willing to do on Kendall's doorstep."

"Glad to provide you with some entertainment." He ran his hand through his hair.

Alana gave him an amused smile. "I just came out to tell you that she went for a run."

Daxon took a deep breath as a mixture of relief and hope coursed through him. Kendall wasn't inside, ignoring him. God, he was a desperate man if that little comment gave him hope. But at this point he didn't care. He just wanted to work out things with Kendall.

"How long ago did she leave?"

Alana shrugged. "Maybe five minutes before you

showed up. She might have heard you if you started calling for her a little earlier. You're pretty loud." She smiled at him like she was enjoying this. His ever-optimistic brain took Alana's smile as yet another reason to hope.

But damn, he had just missed seeing Kendall. He was definitely not going to take *that* as a sign. Hell, no. He was going to find her. The Kalani's peninsula wasn't big, and he was in great shape. He could cover a lot of territory on foot over the next hour and then turn back for her cabin if he didn't find her. But this talk would probably go best if they were somewhere private. And that sure as hell wasn't her doorstep.

Daxon stood up, envisioning the layout of the resort's grounds. "Did you see which way she went?"

"That direction." Alana pointed toward the tip of the peninsula.

It was good news. In that direction, there were only a few trails: one up to the restaurant area, one private trail to Byron Keahi's house, which he could rule out, and one more to the surfing beach where she took him on his first tour of the resort...on the path to the waterfall. Kendall's favorite spot. She told him how to get there on the tour of the Kalani, and he was pretty sure he remembered... *Yes.* That's where he'd try first.

He flashed Alana a smile. "Thanks."

"Don't hurt her," she said, all the mischief fading from her expression. "If you're going after her, you better do it right this time."

"I want to do it right, too," he said softly. Badly. Fuck, he *had* to get this right.

Daxon took a few steps and then glanced down at what he was wearing. The button-down shirt and leather shoes weren't the best choices for running, so he stopped by the red convertible he had rented and tugged off everything but his shorts, throwing them into the trunk. He pulled out a T-shirt and his new pair of running shoes, since his last ones were, in fact, ruined. The challenge was on.

Daxon headed for the resort's main road. As long as she hadn't cut out onto the beach, he'd pass her if she was heading back. The road wound past the pool and the tennis courts, beyond the guest cabins and into the undeveloped tip of the island, where it forked. Damn, he hoped he was choosing the right path. His heart was thumping in his chest, but he wasn't tired. Kendall was close, and he'd finally, finally see her again. Daxon widened his stride as hope burst through him again.

He turned off to the left, up the hill and through the lush forest to the path along the hillside that overlooked the beach. He ran past the spot where he had stood with Kendall, so eager to kiss her that day, and continued to where the path left the beach, veering into the forest. He climbed farther, and then he came to a stop. Another fork. Shit. He laced his hands behind his head, his breaths coming fast, impatience driving his pulse higher. What the hell was he supposed to do now?

"Kendall," he called, his voice tense.

Then he quieted his breath and listened. No answer…but was that a splash of water in the distance? The waterfall. He started for the trail where the sound seemed to be coming from. Thank God. He was getting closer.

Daxon ran toward the waterfall, speeding up. Like everything else he did, he had planned this day meticulously, but this wasn't going according to plan. He had been aching to talk to her for days. He had things he needed to say to her in person. But what if he had miscalculated? What if she returned to her cabin while he was running through the forest? What if she took one look at the red convertible parked outside her cabin and left again? Uncertainty was building inside, churning in his gut. He was heading down a path without a map, and still, he pushed forward.

Finally, the forest trail opened, and there, on a rock beside the river, Daxon saw her. Kendall was facing away from him, leaning back on her arms, dressed in a tank top and running shorts, showing off miles of tanned skin. She had taken her shoes off, and her feet dangled into the stream. Above her, the waterfall cascaded, splashing over the rocks.

Daxon slowed to a stop, drinking her in. He missed her. He missed laughing with her and touching her. He missed her soft, warm body, her breath teasing his skin. Kendall looked relaxed, lost in thought. Goddamn. He was about to disturb her peace, and he hoped like hell she'd think it was worth it. He knew he didn't deserve a second chance with her, but he was a selfish bastard, and he wasn't giving up. But this time was different. This time, he was willing to listen.

So he took a deep breath and started for her.

"Kendall?"

Slowly, she turned around, her eyes wide, so beautiful and full of hope. At that moment, everything he had planned to say disappeared, and he was left with a single thought: *please, please, let me be the one to keep that look on her face.*

What made a risk worth taking? Was the tipping point when the want inside became stronger than the fear? Because Kendall's rising want for Daxon since he had left was spilling over, and now that he had appeared, she was ready to do just about anything to keep him here.

It was this feeling that had kept her from calling him, despite his very public message for her. Hearing that he was backing out of the El Cap climb was an enormous relief, but it didn't solve the more fundamental issue between them: Daxon loved risk, and she didn't know if she could live with that. Right now, she was willing to, but what happened when this almost desperate need to see him dulled? What happened when that itch to push the limits came back? It would, eventually, and they needed a way to deal with this. When he made it to the top of Moonlight Buttress, she promised herself she'd figure out how to deal with this, but so far, she hadn't come up with answers.

And now Daxon had just…shown up. He had found her at her favorite spot, looking so serious and determined, setting her heart into overdrive. A rush of hope and happiness was filling her, leaking out, despite her best efforts. Where was her well-honed sense of wariness when she needed it? Trying to be rational about Daxon was a losing battle.

He walked over and sat down on a rock, so close, facing her. He lifted his hand, like he was reaching for her, but then it dropped. Instead he rested his forearms on his thighs and looked at her. He was so gorgeous, those gray-green eyes stormy, worried and hopeful. But he looked tired, too, and it had been a couple days since he had last shaved. Was he struggling to sleep at night, too?

Lord, she'd missed him.

But she couldn't forget that the last time he'd sat next to her and proposed a future together, it included two free solos. And despite his heartfelt declaration after his climb, she still didn't know what their middle ground looked like. But she had promised herself she wouldn't ask him to quit again.

Daxon ran his hands through his hair and gave her a tentative smile. "So this is your favorite spot?"

She nodded. He looked around at the waterfall and the river that passed by on its way out into the ocean. The trees shaded most of the area, but the early-morning sun filtered through to where they were sitting. There was a rock face beside the waterfall, possibly climbable, but he didn't seem to notice.

"It's beautiful." He was quiet for a long time, hanging his head, as if he was gathering words slowly and carefully. His shoulders rose and fell, his muscles showing through the thin material of his T-shirt. Those muscles were the difference between life and death back on the face of Moonlight Buttress. She wanted to kiss them, worship them, give them her deepest appreciation for the strength that had kept him alive so that they could sit here together at this moment.

"I watched your climb," she said softly.

He blinked up at her, his eyes sad. "Did you?"

The last time she had admitted watching his show, Daxon had given her his signature cocky smile. This time he looked almost pained.

"Well, some of it," she continued, pushing herself to be honest. "I spent the first half staring at the blank TV screen, wondering if you had fallen."

The stricken look on his face almost made her feel sorry for him. Almost.

"I am so sorry, Kendall," he said. His expression was grave. "I didn't really understand this through your eyes until I was up there. Until it was too late."

Kendall swallowed and nodded.

"I should have," he continued. "That day when you jumped from the cliff, you were underwater for so long, long enough for my panic to set in. You came up all smiling and happy, but I couldn't shake that feeling of you being under the water, possibly drowning. The panic didn't just go away. When I was up there on the mountain, there was a moment when I wondered if you were feeling the same thing, magnified. The idea that I made you go through that, not just for seconds but for the hours of that climb— I can't do that anymore."

She shook her head. "You can't quit for me. I saw the way you looked at me when I told you not to climb that last day. Even if you don't resent it now, you will in the future."

He ran a hand through his hair and sighed. "I've been thinking about that a lot. It's possible that I'll feel that way, even if I don't think it will happen now. But is that really enough to stop us? It's also possible that I'll have a heart attack tomorrow. Maybe you will. We can't predict all the things that could go wrong, and that's the reason you and I should push on. If something does happen to you, if you leave me—anything—the happiness of being with you, even for a little while, is worth all the heartbreak I'd feel."

Kendall swallowed the lump in her throat. She wanted this so badly. Should she take the risk and believe in them?

"I'm falling in love with you," he said, his voice rough. "I'm not sure how we'll work everything out.

All I know is that I'm willing to listen and make compromises so that I don't hurt you like that again."

Kendall's heart was so full it was bursting. "I'm willing to compromise, too."

She turned to face him and rested her hand on his cheek. The bristly scruff on his jaw felt different, but his lips were the same as she pressed her mouth against his. Then she met his gaze. "There was a moment when you slipped, and then you stopped and looked away from the camera."

Daxon pulled back, cringing. "You saw that part?"

She nodded and kissed him again. "All I could think about was that if you fell, I would have spent the rest of my life regretting that I gave up my last chance to see you. I regretted that I turned down your offer to come. Even though I was mad that you asked, that was nothing compared to the way that I felt when I thought you might fall."

"I promise I won't do that again," he said quickly. Then he blinked at her, his eyes wide. "Will you give us a chance to do this right? Try to work something out?"

"I want that," she said. "So much."

When Daxon reached for her this time, there was no hesitation. He lifted her onto his lap so she straddled him, and he wrapped his arms around her, pulling her against him. She pressed her face into his neck, and his skin tasted of salt and of him. She found his mouth, hungry, waiting for her. The kiss was slow, filled with longing and regret and something else. Was it love? Whatever it was, she felt it deep inside.

"Calvin must be angry as hell at you," she whispered.

Daxon shrugged. "He was at first, but now he has a bunch of other ideas, ways we could still keep the Pure Adrenaline brand alive. He even had this crazy idea that we should start something called Adrenaline Vacations, where I scout out low-consequence thrills, make a video and set up a vacation tour. I would do the promo video and maybe make a guest appearance, but the rest of it we'd hire out. I thought it was a pretty good idea, but I didn't want to say yes to anything until I talk to you first."

It was almost too much to take in. His words from the top of Moonlight Buttress weren't just adrenaline-fueled promises. He was making real changes.

"I don't want you to give up climbing," she said. "It's just these climbs with no ropes, or the jumping out of airplanes with no parachute—that kind of danger level."

He nodded. "I've been thinking I'll try some deep-water soloing."

She wrinkled her brow. "Sounds a lot like free soloing."

"But without the high stakes," he said, pulling her closer. "It's free soloing over deep water—like that cliff jumping area we visited. It means all of the joy of free soloing and much less worry for you. Hawaii has a lot of potential deep-water soloing sites to explore. More cliffs you can jump from, too." His soft chuckle sent a flutter of desire through her. "I'm willing to listen to your limits. I know we can work this out, Kendall."

For the first time, she truly let herself believe it.

She kissed him again. "Are we falling in love?"

A smile spread across Daxon's face as he nodded. "This is only the beginning, sweets."

He rested his big warm hands on her thighs. It wasn't a come-on, though it seemed impossible to be near him without an undercurrent of sex flowing between them. They were simply there on a rock next to the river, his skin on hers, the sounds of their breathing and the sounds of the water all coming together to make something more than the sum of these parts. She rested her hand on the back of his neck and played with the overgrown locks that curled at the ends, sun-bleached and carefree.

He smiled a lazy smile at her, like they had all the time in the world. "Do you like it here at the Kalani, making people's wishes come true?"

Kendall laughed. "I'm not usually at the front lines of the wish fulfillment business. I'm more like support staff."

"Pretty much the best working conditions I've ever seen," he said, giving her a tight squeeze. "Besides the face of a mountain, of course."

"Of course."

"You want to stay here, don't you?" His hands

had come to a stop on her thighs, the pressure of them almost possessive, and he had that intense look, like there was nothing more important in the world than her.

She nodded. "This is my dream job, and I just started it."

"I could get a place close by." He waggled his eyebrows and lowered his voice. "So I can focus on exploring the island's best attraction more intimately."

She gave a snort of laughter. "That's the line you're giving me? You're going to need to up your game, champ."

Daxon tickled her until she scooted away. "I'm working on it, sweets. And I'm going to devote as much time as I need to pleasing you."

Kendall shifted back onto his lap. It felt so good to hold him close again…and it would feel even better to be naked together. "So what have you been doing since the climb?"

He shrugged. "Packing up, putting my trailer in storage, looking at my Photoshop porn of you…"

She raised an eyebrow.

"Kidding." His eyes glittered with amusement. He was teasing her, but she could play that game, too.

"By the way, did you know there's a whole catalog of erotic fan fiction starring you?" she said, biting her lip trying not to laugh.

He blinked. Clearly the answer was no. But he recovered quickly. "Did you read it?"

"Hell, yes."

She couldn't suppress her laughter anymore, and neither could he. She buried her face in his neck, breathing him in, letting the rush of pure joy run through her.

"I could do this forever, Kendall," he whispered into her hair. "Just you and me."

* * * * *

FROM HAWAII TO FOREVER

JULIE DANVERS

To my mother, my first and best copy editor.

CHAPTER ONE

As SHE STEPPED off the plane in Honolulu, Dr. Katherine Murphy shook the last few drops of water from her snow boots. When she'd boarded the plane in Chicago, snow had caked her boots and dusted her winter coat. A few droplets of water were all that had managed to survive the flight, and now she shook them off with relish. Back home, temperatures were below freezing and the snow was several inches deep. But here in Hawaii a steady, gentle breeze rustled through the palm trees.

Goodbye, ice and cold, Kat thought, stepping into the early-morning sun.

Although she was still wearing the winter clothes she'd had on when she left, her carry-on luggage contained sixteen bathing suits, a floppy hat and sunglasses, and numerous pairs of flip-flops. At the last minute she'd remembered to throw in her white coat and a stethoscope before zipping the small suitcase shut. The rest of her belongings had already been shipped separately to her new home on the island of Oahu.

Kat couldn't believe that just three weeks ago, she had been one of the most respected physicians in Chicago. Three weeks ago she'd expected to be promoted to head of the internal medicine department at Chicago Grace Memorial, the prestigious hospital where she'd completed her residency and spent most of her career. Three weeks ago her future had seemed stable, secure and predictable.

Three weeks ago she and Christopher had been days away from getting married.

Kat glanced at the faint line on her finger where her engagement ring used to be. She still felt a hard lump rise in her throat every time she thought about the breakup.

Tears blurred her eyes, but she fought them back and tried to smile as an airport attendant greeted her warmly and placed a beautiful *lei* of purple orchids over her head. Kat shook the tears away and raised her chin. Her new job as an internist and infectious disease specialist at Oahu General Hospital was a chance for a fresh start, and there was no point in dwelling on the past.

Goodbye, old life, she thought. *And goodbye, Christopher.*

Leaving her steady, predictable life in Chicago and moving to Hawaii ranked very high on the list of things Kat had thought she would never do. But then, she'd also never thought she would lose her promotion, her job and her fiancé on the same day.

In her mind, she thought of it as the Day of Doom.

Three weeks ago she'd huddled under a thick down blanket inside her apartment, the outside world covered with an even thicker layer of February snow, trying to figure out how she could ever face the world again. Everything she'd ever worked for—her medical career, her wedding, her family's hopes and dreams for her—had disappeared in an instant.

She'd just begun thinking about how long she could reasonably hide in her apartment before she would need to forage for food when her best friend from medical school had called with an intriguing proposal. Selena was the clinical director at a small hospital in Hawaii, and she'd called to ask if Kat knew anyone who would be interested in working in Honolulu for one year, to assist with research into and treatment of a rare strain of flu.

Kat had shocked herself by volunteering for the position.

Her mother and her friends in Chicago had been equally shocked. Kat couldn't blame them. Making spontaneous, impulsive decisions wasn't exactly her strongest personality trait. From the time she was sixteen and had decided she wanted to be a doctor, every important decision she'd made had been the result of careful planning and research. Everything in her life from her career to her closest relationships had been built on a foundation of logical, practical choices.

Kat's friends told her she was "certifiably Type A," and Kat had to admit that they were right. She was never one to leap without looking first.

But that had been the old Kat. The Kat who had been blissfully unaware of how much life could change in a single day.

Kat had always thought that her cautious, well-planned approach to life would protect her from unexpected surprises. She'd believed that if she was prepared for anything then she would be able to handle whatever life threw at her. But now, as she felt the empty space on her ring finger, she realized that what people said about best-laid plans was true: you could plan and plan, but you never really knew what would happen next.

Kat had spent her life planning, but she still hadn't been prepared for the breakup. And she definitely hadn't been prepared to lose her job—a job she'd loved and had spent her entire career working toward.

Yes, m'dear, you have definitely hit a low point, Kat thought to herself as she stepped out of the airport.

And caught her breath.

She had never seen such lush natural beauty in her life. Pink and yellow plumeria flowers lined the sidewalk, their scent wafting toward her and mixing with the perfume arising from the *lei* of orchids she wore around her neck. In the distance, mountains rose to meet a cloudless blue sky. Each path was framed by tall palm trees with large fronds that waved gently in the cool breeze.

Kat stopped and took in a slow, deep breath. The air itself smelled of flowers, and she wanted to savor the scent.

As she inhaled, she suddenly wondered when she had last stopped to breathe so deeply. She couldn't remember. Her life after medical school had been all about the fast pace of the ER. Someone had always needed her time or her attention, and needed it right away. But now, for the first time in years, there was no emergency to attend to. In this moment no one was expecting anything from her. No life-or-death decisions awaited her attention.

In this moment, all she had to do was breathe.

She blinked in amazement at herself. Thirty seconds in Hawaii and she was already stopping to smell the roses— or, in this case, the hibiscus. It was a decidedly un-Kat-like thing to do, and yet she felt more like herself than she had in weeks.

After everything that had happened she'd begun to feel as though she didn't even know who she was anymore. But now, as she gazed at the fairyland-like landscape before her, she started to feel something she hadn't felt in several weeks—something she hadn't even realized she'd lost after the Day of Doom.

It was hope.

Hope and something more than that—excitement.

There was something about the mountains in the distance that suggested endless possibilities, and Kat closed her eyes and noticed that the gentle rushing sound in the background wasn't just the wind; the ocean was adding its voice to the air as well. She was well on her way to falling in love at first sight—with Hawaii.

Maybe I'm not at such a low point after all, she thought. *Maybe this is the start of something.*

As she gazed at the natural beauty around her Kat realized that she didn't want to go straight to her new apartment. Going directly to her new home and getting things settled was something the old Kat would do. The old Kat would want to carefully organize her things and research her new neighborhood for essentials like the grocery store and the post office. But the new Kat, she decided, was going to have different priorities. And the new Kat's first order of business was to relax.

But how?

It had been so long since she'd had a moment to herself that she had absolutely no idea what relaxing even meant to her. In all her years of study, after all her classes on chemistry and human anatomy and physiology, she had overlooked one important thing. She had forgotten to learn how to relax.

She resisted the urge to look up a dictionary definition of the word *"relax"* on her phone.

I guess this is what comes of all work and no play, she thought.

She hoped she hadn't completely lost her ability to live in the moment. She had dreamed of becoming a doctor at an early age, and it had been a dream that required an incredible amount of study and discipline. She'd been so focused on her medical career that she'd never had the chance to have a wild, carefree adolescence.

Well, maybe it was time. Could someone in their late

twenties still have a wild adolescence? Kat decided she would damn well try.

This year in Hawaii would be her chance to learn how to let loose and be spontaneous. She'd spent her entire life being responsible, and where had it gotten her? Jobless. Jilted—practically at the altar. If all her careful planning, her endless pro-con lists and her thoughtful decision-making had led to so much heartbreak, then maybe it was time to try a different approach to life.

She only had one year. One year away from the expectations and preconceptions of everyone who knew her. Surely there was no better place to learn how to relax and live in the moment than a gorgeous setting such as this?

She heard the faint sound of the ocean again and it deepened her resolve. This year wasn't just going to be about putting Christopher behind her, she decided. It would be about putting the old Kat behind her.

But how did one *learn* to relax?

It can't be that hard, she thought. *If I can master organic chemistry, I can master this.*

In fact, Kat decided, she might be able to approach learning how to relax and getting over Christopher in much the same way she had gotten through organic chemistry and her other difficult classes. She would make a detailed list of her goals and then follow through with each step.

A small voice in the back of her head suggested that this might be the most Type A way that she could possibly approach relaxation, but she chose to ignore it.

How to relax in an island paradise while getting over a devastating breakup. Step one: find a beach, she thought.

Kat looked down at her snow boots in dismay. Considering the cold in Chicago, and on the flight, the boots had been a sensible choice. But now that she was here they looked ridiculous. Her feet were stifled; she couldn't wait to feel sand beneath her toes.

She had her favorite blue-and-yellow-striped bikini on underneath her heavy winter clothes. She'd fantasized about going for a swim on her first day here in Hawaii, but she'd thought she'd see her new home first. Now that she was actually here, it seemed impossible to wait.

A few moments of research on her phone informed her that the nearest beach was "a pleasant twenty-minute walk from the airport." Surely there would be somewhere she could change out of her clothes?

Kat hitched her carry-on bag over her shoulder and headed toward the water, her face set with determination. She was going to learn how to relax or die trying.

Jack Harper wasn't usually an early riser, but he'd been wandering the beach since dawn. He held his father's letter crumpled in his fist. Choice lines were burned into his brain.

> *Many medical schools have a rolling admissions policy.*
> *I could make a few phone calls and you could easily start in the winter semester.*

Jack ran his hand through his dark hair in frustration. He *liked* being a paramedic, dammit. But it didn't matter how many times he'd told his father he was never going back to medical school. There was no other path that his parents could understand.

> *It's time to apply yourself.*
> *You've had your fun in Hawaii. But now it's time to come back to real life.*

To his father, real life meant Lincoln, Nebraska.

Jack couldn't imagine a place more different from Hawaii.

Lincoln was as fine a hometown as any, but he'd been glad when he was able to exchange the cornfields, cows and cold winters of his childhood for the lush mountain landscape surrounding Honolulu.

His parents, grandfather, and two brothers still lived in Lincoln, where they were all physicians. Both of his parents were highly respected, world-renowned medical researchers, his younger brother Todd had joined their grandfather's small family practice, and his older brother Matt was a surgeon.

Five doctors in the family. Five Type A personalities who were convinced that they were always right. Five people with egos larger than the Hawaiian mountains that loomed over the ocean.

In Jack's opinion, five doctors in the family was plenty. Three years of medical school had been enough to convince him that a doctor's life wasn't for him. He was much happier as a paramedic—especially here on the island of Oahu.

After dropping out of medical school to join the Navy SEALS—another life decision his parents had disapproved of—he'd completed his basic training in Hawaii and never lived anywhere that felt more like home. He'd rescue a burn victim one day and deliver a baby the next—all while surrounded by an island paradise that meant more to him than anywhere else on earth.

He loved his job—both for the adrenaline rush and for the opportunities it gave him to save lives. But his parents wouldn't take his career choices or his desire to live in Hawaii seriously, and they continued to act as though he were on some sort of extended vacation.

He and his parents were very different people.

Nowhere was this more evident than in the last paragraph of his father's letter.

You're thirty-one years old. You have to start thinking about your future.

Plenty of women in Nebraska would like to start a family, and your mother's getting older and would like more grandchildren—

At that point Jack had stopped reading. He couldn't believe either of his parents would bring up marriage after his older brother Matt's betrayal. Matt—the golden boy of the family.

Jack snorted. It had been four years since he'd spoken with Matt or Sophie, but Jack's heart still twinged every time he thought about his older brother and his former fiancée. After being betrayed by the two most important people in his life, the last thing he wanted was to get emotionally involved in a relationship again.

As far as Jack was concerned, getting emotionally attached meant getting hurt, and that wasn't something he was willing to put himself through again. Oh, he'd had his share of dates, and there were many women willing to enjoy his company for an evening, or even a few evenings. There were certainly plenty of tourists who seemed to want Jack to fulfill their fantasies of an exotic island fling while on vacation, and Jack was happy to oblige.

But he was careful never to get too involved with anyone. If protecting his heart meant that he had to keep his guard up and keep his distance, then so be it.

Jack smoothed out the letter one last time, then crumpled it into his fist again. He resisted the urge to throw it into the ocean. The sky was clear, the water was calm and perfect, and there was no point in brooding on the beach about a past he couldn't change. He and Sophie were done, and had been for a long time. Everything that had passed between him and Matt and Sophie was long in the past.

So why did all of it still bother him so much?

Sometimes Jack wondered if keeping himself emotionally distant from everyone had actually made it harder to recover from his disastrous engagement to Sophie. But when he thought about the memories it was too painful. He hadn't just lost Sophie—he'd lost his brother, too. The one person he'd thought he could count on, no matter what.

Growing up in a family full of doctors had had its own unique pressures. Sometimes it felt to Jack as though he'd begun to feel the weight of his family's expectations the moment he was born. But, as much as Jack had felt pressured to succeed at school and in his career, it was nothing compared to what Matt had gone through.

Matt, two years older than Jack, had experienced all the pressure Jack had as well as the added expectations that had gone along with being the oldest Harper sibling. Their parents had always expected Matt to be responsible for Jack, and as a child Matt had taken that responsibility seriously. Whenever Jack had been hurt, whenever he'd had trouble with friends or begun struggling in school, he'd been able to talk to Matt about it.

In return, Jack had hero-worshipped Matt throughout their childhood. If Jack was honest with himself, he'd hero-worshipped Matt for a good part of his adulthood, too.

He'd always thought that he and Matt would stand by each other, no matter what. But after Matt had confessed what had happened with Sophie, Jack hadn't been able to stand being in the same room with him. They hadn't spoken in four years.

A faint cry for help broke through his thoughts and he

scanned the water with the trained eyes of a first responder. There—a woman swimming, far out from the shore. Too far. And going farther. She was caught in a rip current that was carrying her out into the ocean, and she was going to exhaust herself trying to swim against it.

Jack snapped into action. This was one of the quieter beaches; there were no lifeguards on duty. He dialed the emergency number on his phone and let the dispatch unit know what he was about to do. Then he dropped his phone and stripped off his shirt, revealing a smooth, well-muscled chest and the powerful arms of a former Navy SEAL.

A crowd of children who had been playing in the surf began to gather on the beach, having spotted the danger the woman was in.

"Let me borrow that," he said to one of the children, grabbing the boy's body board without waiting for a response.

He ran out into the ocean, letting the rip current do the work of carrying him out to the swimmer. When he finally reached her, he could see he'd been right. She'd been trying to fight the current instead of swimming parallel to the shore. And she was clearly terrified. He knew he could get them both back to safety, but first he'd need to calm her down.

Despite the woman's terror, he couldn't help but notice her fiery red hair. He'd always liked redheads...

Focus, he thought. *She has to stay calm. Help her relax.*

"Looks like you swam out a little further than you planned," Jack teased, attempting to lighten her fear. "You do realize it's not possible to swim all the way back to the mainland, right? You'll need to book a flight for that."

The woman coughed and choked. She looked frightened, but Jack could tell she was doing the best she could to keep her fear from overwhelming her. He admired that.

Most of the time during water rescues the bulk of his work involved keeping the victim from making things worse by panicking. But this woman was doing her best to follow his instructions.

"The current…" she gasped. "It's too strong. We'll never get back to shore."

Jack forced himself to stay calm, even as the rip current continued to pull both of them further from the shore.

"Of course we'll get back," he said. "But first, I need you to relax."

He put as much warmth and confidence into his voice as he could, but for some reason, at the word *"relax"* the woman's eyes seemed to widen in terror—as though Jack had told her she'd need to survive by learning how to fly, or something equally impossible.

He decided to see if he could get his arms around her— the sooner she stopped fighting the current, the better.

"I'm going to put my arm under your shoulders, okay?" he said.

He swam behind her and slipped a firm arm under her shoulders. The support he lent her had the desired effect: once her body was directly against his she stopped struggling against the water and allowed his strength to keep her afloat.

"Can you hold on to this?"

He put the body board he'd borrowed in front of her, and she clutched at it.

"Good," he said approvingly. Her panic seemed to be receding by the minute. He had to admire how quickly she was gaining control of herself; most people would still be struggling and swallowing seawater at this point.

"What's your name?" he asked her.

"Kat," she said, with a strangled gasp.

Good, Jack thought. If she could speak, then her airways were still clear.

"Kat, I need you to listen to me," he said. "We're going to survive this, but you have to trust me. If you do everything I say I promise you that we're going to get to shore. But the first thing I need you to do is stay calm."

"I'll try," she said.

He chuckled. "I can feel you trembling." She scowled at him, and he quickly added, "It's all right to be scared, but you don't need to be—because we're going to get out of this. First time getting caught in a rip current?"

She nodded. "It's my first time swimming in the ocean. First day in Hawaii, actually."

He could see that she was trying to talk herself into a calmer state, and was doing her best to keep a cool head. She had nerves of steel. He also couldn't help but notice the lithe shape of her body as she clung to him.

First things first, he told himself sternly. Maybe they should get back on dry land before he started trying to find out anything more about her. Most likely she was one of the thousands of tourists who came each month, eager for adventure and completely unprepared for the dangers of the ocean.

"Well, *aloha* and welcome to Oahu, Kat. Can you lean forward onto this body board? If you rest on your arms, I can paddle us in. Don't worry, I won't let you go."

Somehow Kat knew that he was telling her the truth.

At first, amidst her terror and the waves going over her head, it had been hard for her to get a good look at this man who had swum out to help her. All she'd been able to sense was a well-muscled, masculine presence and a steady, reassuring voice. A voice that was warm and soothing, like a spoonful of honey.

But he'd reached her with surprising speed, and she tried to trust that he knew what he was doing.

Pressing her between himself and the flotation device he had with him, he used his body to help her gain leverage as she shifted herself onto the board. As soon as she was resting entirely on it, he let go of her waist to swim beside her, and she felt a twinge of regret as the supportive arms released her.

"Great job," he said. "Hard part's over. Now just keep holding on while I tow you in. We'll be back to shore before you know it."

He continued swimming by her side, guiding the board as he pulled them both parallel to the shore. A rough wave knocked them unexpectedly, and Kat felt a sharp pain in her leg. She must have let out a yelp because the man instantly grabbed her around the waist again.

"What is it?" he said, his face concerned.

"My leg," she said. "I must have scraped it against something. I don't think it's bad."

"Just hang in there," he said. "We're almost back to the beach."

To Kat's relief, the shore was becoming closer and closer, until finally she felt the ocean waves pushing them both toward the beach instead of pulling them away.

She collapsed in a heap on the sand and he fell beside her, one arm draped protectively over her body. They both lay there for a moment, exhausted. He was close enough that Kat could feel the heat radiating from his body next to her on the shore.

She turned to thank her rescuer.

She'd been grateful for his strength during the rescue, but now that she was back on dry land she was able to appreciate quite a bit more than just his strength.

His eyes were the exact same shade as the Hawaiian

ocean—a blue-green-turquoise. He was muscular, but his physique was track-star-slim. A shock of dark hair fell over his forehead, and Kat had to resist a sudden urge to run her fingers through it. Their eyes locked, and for a moment Kat felt an electric charge between them.

His arm still rested over her. Sheltering her. He was gazing down at her, making sure she was all right. She tried to speak, but it came out as a cough, and it was several moments before she was able to recover.

"That's it," he said. "You've had a nasty shock. Take some time to let yourself breathe."

She sat up. He pulled his arm away and leaned back from her. Was it wishful thinking, or did he seem to move his arm slowly, as though he wasn't ready to let go of her?

As Kat lay on the beach, slowly regaining her breath, she gradually became aware of her bedraggled appearance. She was covered in muddy sand and the water that she'd coughed up, and her hair hung in strings around her face. But she was alive—thanks to the man next to her, whoever he was. His eyes radiated concern, and he patted her back gently as they both waited for her airway to clear fully.

"I'm all right," she told him, as soon as she was breathing steadily. "All this attention is unnecessary, really. But I do have to thank you for saving my life, Mr.—?"

"Jack Harper," he said.

"Well, Mr. Harper, thank you," she said.

"Don't mention it," he said. "Just give your body the time it needs to recover."

Kat sat with her knees bent and her feet flat against the sand. She held her head down, trying to slow her breathing. Keeping her head down also had the added effect of distracting her from the fact that Jack Harper was still sitting quite close to her, his powerfully built body radiating heat, his eyes examining her face with concern.

"I don't know how you can be so casual," she said. "I was certain we were both going to die."

"It was dangerous, but you kept calm and that was half the battle," he said.

She shuddered, thinking of how close she'd come to being swept out into the ocean. "Maybe I looked calm, but I definitely didn't feel it. I always thought I was a strong swimmer, but I wasn't prepared for those currents. I was trying to swim parallel to the shore, but it seemed like no matter what direction I went in the current wanted to pull me somewhere else."

"You aren't the first person to be surprised by the strength of a Hawaiian rip current. It's a shame that your first swim here nearly killed you—especially on your first day. That's no way to welcome you to the islands."

"Really? And here I was hoping that almost drowning on my first day here would turn out to be some sort of tradition." She laughed. And then, before she could stop herself, she said, "Maybe a better way to celebrate arriving in Hawaii and surviving a near-death experience would be to take my rescuer out for dinner sometime."

She couldn't believe she'd said that. She wasn't anywhere near ready to date again. But she wouldn't mind hearing that rich, deep voice more often. Or feeling those arms around her again. Preferably in a situation where she wasn't about to drown.

Learning to relax. Step two, her brain piped up. *Find an island hottie to help you move on from your devastating breakup.*

Stop it, she told herself.

She'd just been jilted at the altar—well, technically there had still been three days until the wedding, but it had been close enough that she felt jilted. The last thing she needed was to get involved with anyone right now.

She needed to get her mind off Jack's voice and arms right away. What was she *thinking*, offering to buy him dinner?

Kat forced herself to shift her attention away from Jack's beach-tanned body. This was no time for distractions, she told herself firmly. She'd just come close to getting swept out to sea, and she was still shaken by the thought of what might have happened if Jack hadn't been there to help her back to shore. She needed to clear her head and get her bearings. She also needed to find a way to turn her attention from Jack Harper's taut skin and chiseled chest muscles so she could focus on what he was saying.

"I appreciate the offer, but there's no need to thank me," said Jack. "It's part of the job." He motioned to where an ambulance had arrived, further down the beach.

"Are you a doctor?" she asked.

"Paramedic," he replied. "And I'm sorry to say that any dinner plans will have to wait—because before you do anything else we need to get you to a hospital to get checked out. We're not far from Oahu General Hospital—I'll go with you."

"Oahu General? Oh, no. I can't go there."

Now that Kat no longer feared for her life, she was becoming deeply embarrassed about the commotion her rescue had caused. More than anything, she wanted to avoid being taken to a hospital—especially Oahu General.

She could think of few things more humiliating than showing up to her new hospital as a patient, wearing nothing but a bikini. And she definitely didn't think it would be a good idea to spend more time in close quarters with Jack. If she wasn't careful that voice and those eyes would start to have an effect on her. And she had no intention of diving headlong into a fling with the first man she met in Hawaii—no matter how closely his eyes matched the color of the ocean.

"Really, I'm fine," she said.

"You're bleeding," he told her.

"What?" Kat looked down at her leg, surprised. The place where she'd felt that pain in her leg while Jack was towing her to shore had a gash of about an inch that was trickling blood. "Oh, crap. That must have happened when I hurt my leg, back in the water. It doesn't look serious to me, though."

Privately, she thought that she might need a few stitches, but she wasn't about to let Jack know that.

As he leaned in closer she caught his scent: a masculine blend of sunblock, salt water and sand. He smelled like the ocean, like the hint of salt in the air that had filled her with such excitement and called her to the beach the moment she'd stepped off the plane. She definitely needed to stay as far away from him as possible if she wanted to avoid making a fool of herself.

"It doesn't even hurt that much," she said, though she was gritting her teeth through the stinging pain that was now beginning to make itself felt.

"I'm sure it doesn't, but that's the point," said Jack. "You've just had a near-death experience, and adrenaline is coursing through your system. Right now you probably feel like you can do anything—but that's just the adrenaline. It can mask a lot of problems, including pain. You might think you're fine, but humor me—it's best for you to get to the hospital so we can get you stitched up."

"There's really no need," said Kat briskly.

But she could see that Jack wasn't going to give up easily, so she decided to try appealing to him as a medical professional.

"Look, to tell you the truth I'm a doctor, and I can take care of this myself. I'm starting my first day working at Oahu General on Monday, and I really don't want their first impression of me to be...*this*." Kat motioned to her string bikini.

Was it her imagination, or had his expression seemed to change when she'd revealed she was a doctor? For a split second it had seemed as though a shadow had passed over his face. Most people seemed to be *more* at ease with her when she revealed her profession, but if anything Jack almost seemed...disappointed?

But then he sighed and said, "Doctors always make the worst patients."

Oh. He had a valid point. As a doctor, she'd always had a difficult time allowing herself to be in the patient role, and she knew many colleagues who felt the same way. It was hard to sit back and let someone else follow procedure when she could feel her own natural tendency to take charge of the situation rising within her. Also, she hated being the center of attention.

As she took in Jack's piercing blue eyes she knew she shouldn't want to be the center of *his* attention. Her knees were still shaking, and she had a feeling that it wasn't just the onset of hypothermia.

She hoped he wouldn't notice. But of course he did. He was clearly a skilled paramedic, and Kat suspected that he didn't miss much.

"Your knees are shaking," he said. "You should know better than anyone that the biggest risk after a near-drowning in water of any temperature is hypothermia. You shouldn't be going anywhere until we can make sure your core body temperature hasn't dropped too low."

Kat groaned inwardly. Her irritation was all the worse because she knew that Jack was right. She shouldn't take care of the cut on her leg by herself—especially with the risk of hypothermia. His stubbornness was a wall she wouldn't get past, and he clearly wasn't going to be intimidated by her medical credentials.

She couldn't decide whether his determination to take care of her was incredibly annoying or attractive. A little of both, she thought.

And it didn't help that the small, rebellious voice in the back of her mind was wholly in agreement with Jack, and was shouting that spending some time in the close quarters of an ambulance with him wouldn't be an entirely unwelcome experience.

Just get in! the voice screamed. *He can be your next impulsive decision!*

Enough of that, she told herself.

Jack Harper was certainly attractive; there was no question of that. Those blue-green eyes of his seemed to change shade every minute, as though their color changed with his mood.

But Kat had felt herself getting swept away by the ocean, just moments ago. That had been scary enough. The last thing she needed now was to let herself get swept away by someone she'd just met.

Although she had to admit that Jack's air of authority was rather refreshing. She could see that no matter how much she argued he was taking her to the hospital—even if she went kicking and screaming.

As a respected internal medicine physician, Kat wasn't used to having anyone disagree with her. Her decisions were almost never questioned by her team. To have someone insist on taking care of *her* for once, in spite of all her protestations, was an utterly new experience.

It was almost a little bit sexy.

But sexy was the last thing Kat was looking for.

Not now.

Not three weeks after Christopher. Not after the disaster of their almost-wedding.

"Is it really necessary?" she asked, knowing her appeal was doomed.

"You know it is," he said.

His voice was that of a determined man who would not be denied.

Definitely a little bit sexy, the rebellious voice in her head noted.

She didn't want this kind of complication right now. She didn't want to be attracted to anyone. Three weeks ago she hadn't thought she was even capable of feeling interested in anyone else, because she'd been about to marry the love of her life. She should be returning from her honeymoon now—not standing on a tropical beach arguing with a frustratingly attractive paramedic who didn't understand when to quit.

Kat saw the stubborn set of Jack's jaw and realized that she really was going to arrive at her new place of work borderline hypothermic, muddy, and wearing a string bikini—in the company of one of the most attractive men she'd ever seen.

This, she thought, was the opposite of learning how to relax.

CHAPTER TWO

KAT DECIDED THAT if there was no chance of changing Jack's mind, she would try bargaining with him instead.

"I'll go if you insist, but at least let me find something different to wear," she said.

Riding in an ambulance with Jack while wearing nothing but a bikini would be bad enough, but she would do anything to prevent her new co-workers from forming their first impression of her while she was nearly naked and dripping wet.

"Do you have anything else with you that you could put on?" Jack asked.

"Oh!" Kat remembered. "My luggage. It's right over there, down the beach."

She started to rise, but Jack pushed her down firmly. He wrapped a blanket around her and tucked in the ends as though she were a child. Kat's cheeks burned.

She started to protest, but Jack stopped her. "I'm not taking any risks just because you're a doctor who thinks she knows better than a paramedic. Sit still and I'll bring your luggage to you."

He headed down the beach while Kat fumed. As much as she didn't want to admit it, she was secretly glad that Jack had pushed her back into a sitting position. Her legs felt like jelly, and it would have been difficult to stand.

And it was nice to have the blanket. But she needed him to understand that, as a doctor, she was perfectly capable of deciding what she did or did not need for herself.

When he returned with her things she said, "Look, this is very kind of you, but all this attention just isn't necessary. I happen to be an excellent doctor. I was the youngest chief resident of internal medicine that Chicago Grace Memorial Hospital ever had."

He rolled his eyes. "I'm sure you were."

"And I graduated from Northwestern University in just three years. I was in the top five of my class at medical school."

"Sounds like you're very smart."

Now her cheeks were burning with a different kind of embarrassment. Would he think she was the kind of person who bragged about her achievements? She realized that she was doing exactly that. Why was she acting this way? It was more than just wanting to appear competent in front of a potential new colleague. For some reason she couldn't explain, she wanted Jack to think well of her.

"I'm just trying to say that you don't need to fuss over me. You don't need to treat me like a patient," she said.

"Because doctors always know best, right?" he replied.

She was flustered. "Well…yes. Frankly, I have the most medical expertise between the two of us. I think I'm qualified to decide whether or not I'm all right."

He looked directly into her eyes and she felt a jolt go through her. His gaze was really quite arresting.

"As far as I'm concerned you are *my* patient," he said. "No matter what your medical background is, I'm the one responsible for taking care of you right now, and I intend to see that responsibility through."

His voice was firm, but warm and resonant, and she felt all her resistance melt into a puddle under his gaze. She could listen to that voice all day… She made another feeble attempt to protest, but her breath caught in her throat as he continued.

"You may think you're all right but, as I said before, that's the adrenaline pushing you through. You swallowed a lot of water out there, and I'm not leaving you alone until I'm sure you're stable."

The point apparently settled, he lifted her luggage onto the back of the ambulance and began to rummage through it.

"Hey!" she cried. "That's my stuff! How about a little privacy?" What did he think he was doing, rummaging through her personal things?

"Here we go," he said, pulling her white coat out from beneath a tangle of bathing suits and flip-flops. "Looks like your sweater's all sandy—you don't want to put that back on. But you can wear this."

She pulled the white coat over her swimsuit and wrapped it around herself. "Are you always this stubborn and bossy?" she said.

"Afraid so," he replied. "Especially where my patients are concerned—no matter where they ranked in their class at medical school."

As irritating as he was, Kat had to admire his persistence. Jack Harper might have his flaws, but being lax about patient care obviously wasn't one of them. His stubbornness both annoyed and intrigued her. Who *was* this commandeering man with the arms that had fit so perfectly around her waist?

At least she had one clue: the tattoo in flowing script along his arm. "'The only easy day was yesterday,'" she read. "You were a Navy SEAL?"

He nodded, clearly surprised. "Most people don't recognize the motto," he said.

"My grandfather was a SEAL," she said. "He always said Navy guys make the best boyfriends."

She flushed even more deeply. Why had she said a thing like that? She sounded like some sort of man-hungry flirt. It was all *his* fault—he had some sort of effect on her that made her want to punch him and jump into his arms all at once.

Her resolve to get away from him before she embarrassed herself further returned. She removed the blanket and tucked her white coat around herself. "Look, it's very kind of you to offer me an ambulance ride, but I'll be fine on my own," she said.

"Be my guest," he said, clearly deciding on a different tack. "But, just so you know, it's a long walk, and I'm going to be driving alongside you the whole way."

"That's your prerogative," she said.

She stood up, prepared to march away from the beach—and immediately began to sink into the sand as her legs shook under her. Her entire body was shaking.

Just before she fell onto the sand Jack caught her and lifted her into his arms. She was surprised at the surge of relief that flooded through her as she felt his strong arms scoop her up. As much as she hated to admit that he'd been right, she could tell that shock was hitting her, and she knew that the time for trying to prove she was strong was over—realized that the adrenaline rush had indeed been carrying her through the moment.

And now Jack was carrying her through *this* moment.

"Maybe it wouldn't be such a bad idea to head to the hospital," Kat said, her voice shaking. "But no sirens, okay? I really don't want to make a big entrance. This is already embarrassing enough."

"No sirens," he agreed.

He lifted her into the back of the ambulance and nodded to the driver before hopping in himself and closing the doors behind them.

Jack berated himself for agreeing not to use the sirens as he climbed into the back of the ambulance. Kat was probably fine, but she was still a patient in his care and he didn't want any harm to come to her. She was such a typical doctor—assuming she knew best, even when she was the one who needed help.

Of course the first woman he'd been genuinely attracted to in ages would *have* to be a co-worker. And not just any co-worker, but apparently an ambitious and career-driven doctor.

Jack had one hard and fast rule when it came to dating: no doctors. After everything that had happened with Sophie and Matt, he didn't need yet another doctor involved in his personal life. But he couldn't help but notice that the white coat Kat wore over her bikini made her legs look even longer.

None of that kind of thinking, he told himself sternly.

Kat might be attractive, but it would be best for the two of them to put some distance between each another after today.

Although if they were going to be co-workers, distance might not be an option.

He wondered how long she would be at the hospital— what department she would be in. Maybe he wouldn't have to see her that much. He decided to do some casual reconnaissance, hoping she wouldn't pick up on just how curious he really was.

"So you're the new doctor at Oahu General?" he said,

as he settled himself across from Kat and pulled out his suturing kit.

But instead of responding, Kat angled her leg away from him. "Oh, no, you don't," she said, as he opened the kit. "The cut's not that bad. It just needs a stitch or two. I could probably do the suturing myself."

Jack glared at her. He had to admire her persistence, but there was such a thing as taking it too far. The fact that Kat would even *suggest* doing stitches on herself told him that she was probably still experiencing some mild shock.

Besides, it would be a crime to allow a scar to form on one of those legs.

"How about you let me be the one to take care of the patient right now?" he said, glowering at her to make sure he'd got his point across.

"It's not as though I can't do a simple stitch," Kat muttered rebelliously.

Jack gently shifted Kat's leg toward his body, so he could reach the cut. He leaned forward and locked her gaze with his. "Listen, I know you were in the top five percent of your class at Northwestern, but I promise you'll be better off if you let *me* handle this," he said. "If you'd stop being so stubborn and let me be in charge for one minute, I'd actually be able to help you."

Kat fell silent, and for a moment Jack regretted his harsh tone. She was probably mortified at the thought of meeting her new co-workers in a few moments, dressed like this. But no, he thought, it was better to be harsh. For her own safety as well as his. *She* needed to accept that she was in the patient's role—a hard thing for a doctor—and *he* needed to make sure that he didn't get carried away by the effect she was having on him. Being clear about maintaining firm professional boundaries from the start would be the best thing for both of them.

Then, in a small voice, Kat muttered, "Top five."

"What?" said Jack.

"I was in the top five of my class at Northwestern. That's much more impressive than being in the top five percent."

He was about to make a sarcastic response, but then, to his surprise, she winked at him.

"I just wanted you to know that I'm a total big shot, okay?" she said.

He couldn't help but laugh. "Noted," he said.

Great, he thought. *Smart and funny.*

Just what he didn't need. He should keep up a detached, professional demeanor—he really should. But he couldn't help teasing her back.

"With all due respect, Dr. Big Shot, do you think you can relax and let me give this cut the attention it needs?" he asked.

She groaned, startling him.

"What's wrong?" he asked, immediately concerned. "Does it hurt?"

"Oh, no," she said. "It's just…there's that word again. *Relax.* You keep telling me to do the one thing I have no idea how to do."

"What…relax?"

He started to apply lidocaine to the wound on Kat's leg. He wanted to stay detached, but he couldn't help being curious about her. Besides, if he could keep her talking it would take her mind off the stitches.

"I've never been very good at relaxing," she said. "I've gotten so used to having a busy life that I think I've forgotten how to live in the moment…or maybe I never really knew how. Just before I went down to that beach I thought to myself that I'd learn to relax or die trying. And I guess I almost did."

"*Almost* being the operative word," said Jack. "Not only did you not die, you actually handled yourself really well out there."

"Really?" she said. "Because when you came out there and told me to '*just relax*' that's when I thought we were both doomed for sure."

Jack shook his head. "No, you stayed calm in a terrifying situation. Most people make a rescue more difficult by panicking, but you kept a cool head."

He saw her let out a slow breath that she probably hadn't even realized she was holding.

"I was so scared," she said. "I didn't feel calm at all. I was lucky that you were there."

She had been lucky—that was true enough. Rip currents were incredibly dangerous. But her survival had been more than just luck. Jack had been impressed by how well Kat had stayed focused on his instructions during the rescue, despite her terror.

He started on the first stitch, trying not to notice the thin line of bare skin down her front where her white coat had fallen open.

"You're having an eventful first day in Hawaii," he said. "Do you plan on staying long?"

"Just a year," said Kat. "I used to be an internal medicine doctor at Chicago Grace Memorial, but… I was offered a job here, and…and the timing was good, so I took it."

For a moment Kat seemed sad. Jack wondered what she'd meant about good timing, but he didn't want to pry. If she was only staying for a year, then that meant her appointment at Oahu General was temporary. Maybe he wouldn't even see her that much.

He caught himself noticing how her red hair fell in delicate tendrils around her slender neck and decided that it would probably be for the best if they didn't see each other much.

He said, in what he hoped was a light tone, "You're a visiting doctor? We get a lot of those. What department will you be in?"

"Apparently the infectious diseases department is short-staffed," she said. "They need an internal medicine doctor with a specialty in infectious diseases to head up research and treatment on a new strain of flu."

So she was a doctor of internal medicine? That meant they'd have plenty of opportunities to work together—and he'd have plenty of opportunities to notice the way her hair offset her translucent skin.

He finished the stitches he'd given the cut on Kat's leg. "Infectious Diseases is always short-staffed," he said. "We get new strains of flu every year, and we're always hit by large outbreaks in the spring. It'll be good to have more hands on deck at the hospital." He gave Kat's leg a pat, trying not to think about how her skin felt underneath his fingers. "There," he said brusquely. "Good as new."

With the stitches complete, Jack realized he had no way to distract himself from Kat. There seemed to be nothing to do but sit across from her, trying not to notice that the outline of her body was clear underneath her white coat, which had become damp from the water on her skin.

He cleared his throat. *Stay professional,* he thought to himself. *Right now she's a patient, and even if she wasn't, she's a doctor. You never date doctors.*

Jack decided to keep her talking—both to break the silence, and to distract himself from the way Kat's coat was slipping off one shoulder.

"There aren't too many top med school grads taking jobs at little hospitals in Hawaii," he said.

"It seemed like a good opportunity," she replied.

"Really?" he said. "People usually don't come to the islands to practice medicine unless they've got a personal reason—maybe family lives here, or maybe they grew up in Hawaii and want to move back."

For a moment that expression of sadness crossed her face once again. But then it disappeared just as quickly, to be replaced with cool professionalism. "It was a good opportunity," she repeated. "And I won't just be seeing patients—I've also been offered the chance to lead the internal medicine unit in an administrative role. I'll be able to make some major changes to Oahu General's hospital policy in a way that I've never been able to do at any other hospital before. I wouldn't be able to do that at a larger or more prestigious hospital, so this could be an excellent stepping stone for me."

A stepping stone. This was exactly what irritated Jack about the doctors who came to Hawaii for temporary positions. They were never invested in the islands or the community. They were interested in their careers, and they loved trying out their grand new ideas at a tiny, insignificant hospital where the stakes were low. A tiny, insignificant hospital that happened to be his professional home, with colleagues and patients he cared about.

"Oahu General may not have much prestige, but it's a great hospital, with great doctors," he said.

"Oh, I know," she said quickly. "I didn't mean to imply otherwise. But there's a lot I've learned from working at Chicago Grace Memorial about how to increase efficiency and improve patient outcomes. I'm so excited to start putting some of my ideas in place—I'm sure there's so much that can be improved."

So much that can be improved? thought Jack. She hadn't even seen the hospital yet. How could she know what needed improvement?

It was obvious to him that Kat was a typical big-city doctor, assuming she would be able to change everything. As though the hospital didn't already have good systems in place, built by people who lived in and cared about Hawaii.

His ex-fiancée Sophie had been the same way. Career-driven, independent, and unabashedly pursuing what she wanted from life. They had all been qualities Jack had wholeheartedly admired...until he'd realized that when it came to choosing between her career and the important people in her life Sophie would do whatever it took to advance her career. Even if it meant that people would get hurt.

He'd only known Kat for a few moments, but that was long enough to see that she was smart, funny, beautiful... and completely certain that she knew what was best for everyone.

At least she's only here for a year, he thought. *There's no need for things to get complicated.*

He tried very hard not to notice that Kat's medical coat had fallen open just a little further, revealing another inch of bare, creamy skin. Instead, he focused on packing up the items from his suturing kit, in a manner that he thought was very detached and professional indeed.

Despite Kat's frustration at being treated like a patient, she couldn't help but notice that Jack had handled her stitches swiftly and competently. He clearly knew what he was doing. And as she'd watched Jack complete the stitches she'd felt the soothing effect that observing a simple medical procedure had always had on her.

No matter the emergency, she took comfort in knowing that there was an established process to handle things. Simple injuries like this were almost comforting to face, because it was such a relief to have a plan, to know exactly what to do.

Watching Jack work gave her another chance to appreciate just how muscular his arms were. He'd put his shirt back on when they'd gotten into the ambulance and she wondered if she'd ever be able to get another look at what lay underneath it. But then she sternly guided her thoughts back to the present.

You're still getting over a relationship, she told herself. *You're heartbroken, remember? The last thing you need is to get involved with another guy. Besides, you've already made a fool of yourself in front of this one.*

Her cheeks burned when she recalled how she'd bragged about her accomplishments. She'd only meant to reassure him that she knew what she was doing, but she'd come off sounding so stuck-up. He probably thought she was completely full of herself.

Her body, however, was pushing her in a very different direction than her cool, logical mind.

Do you see how wavy his hair is? her body screamed. *Just run your fingers through it! Do it!*

In the three weeks that had passed since the Day of Doom, Kat had felt an anesthetizing layer of numbness settle over her heartbreak. But the moment she'd taken a good look at Jack something had pierced that and gotten through to the aching heart underneath.

She wasn't ready for it. Feeling attraction to someone wasn't part of this year's plan.

This year's plan was to recover from losing Christopher and losing her job, while learning to embrace life against the serene backdrop of a tropical island setting. Eventually—*much* later—she might start dating again, if the right person came along. But for now it would be completely illogical and inconvenient to feel attracted to anyone. Especially a bossy, overconfident paramedic.

Kat liked her plan. It was a good plan. The thought of deviating from the plan made her nervous. And her attraction to Jack was definitely a deviation, so it would have to stop.

It almost came as a relief when Jack seemed to become increasingly irritated as she discussed her plans for changes at Oahu General Hospital. Dealing with his irritation was much easier than dealing with her feelings of attraction.

Although she couldn't understand what he could possibly be irritated about in the first place.

"Am I missing something?" she said. "Is there some issue with me wanting to make changes at the hospital?"

"Why would there be an issue?" he said.

She didn't buy his innocent act. "I'm not saying there is. But I can't help noticing that you've gotten awfully quiet since I started talking about my job."

"It's just…" He seemed to be choosing his words carefully. "I think you might want to actually get to know the people and the hospital you'll be working at before you start thinking about making any sweeping changes. People can get very set in their way of doing things, and you don't want to push too fast for too much change."

Kat pressed her lips together, trying not to let her emotions show on her face. Jack's words reminded her of what the administrative director at Chicago Grace Memorial Hospital had said, about thirty minutes before she'd been fired.

Kat had spent nearly a year doing research before she'd made her presentation to the hospital board. In it, she had proposed that the hospital open a nonprofit clinic to help provide free and very low-cost care to patients who struggled to afford treatment. She had the financial information to prove the hospital could support it.

All her data indicated that the poorest patients struggled to get well because of their limited resources. They came in to the hospital far too late, after their illnesses had progressed significantly—sometimes too late for help. A nonprofit clinic would be life-changing for some of the hospital's patients.

All the board of directors had to do was approve her proposal.

But, to her shock, the administrative director had told her that the hospital was there to make a profit, and that if she wanted to make such sweeping changes she should have gone into politics instead of medicine. She was pushing for too much change, too fast, he'd said. And she'd been stunned to see the other board members nodding in agreement.

And the director had been so condescending and sanctimonious. At one point he had even referred to her as "little lady." His attitude had infuriated her and, unable to stop herself, she'd shared a few choice words with him. The director had fired back, tempers had flared, and before Kat had known it, she'd been out of a job.

When her friend Selena had offered her the job at Oahu General, Kat had been honest about her firing—and the events leading up to it. But no one else knew except for Christopher. And after Christopher's reaction… Well, *that* conversation hadn't gone well at all.

If she could help it no one else would ever know how she'd lost her job. She couldn't reveal to Jack just how much his words had activated her worst fear: that her new plans for the hospital wouldn't work and that her time at Oahu General would lead to a repeat of the Day of Doom.

But that was unlikely to happen again, she reminded

herself. This time things were different. She had the full support of the hospital director. And her plans for changes in policy and procedure were good ones… She just needed a chance to prove it. Her year at Oahu General would give her that chance. And if Jack or anyone else had a problem—well, they'd just have to get used to it.

At least she didn't have to worry about losing her job *and* her fiancé on the same day again. After all, she no longer had a fiancé to lose…

She realized her thoughts were hitting too close to emotions she wasn't ready to face. Especially not while she was sitting partially dressed across from a certain dark-haired, half-shaven, irritatingly self-assured paramedic.

"You did that pretty well," she said, indicating her stitches. "You've clearly got some skills." She'd barely felt a thing, and she could already tell she was unlikely to have a trace of a scar.

He looked up at her, seeming surprised by the unexpected compliment.

"You must have gotten lots of practice in the SEALs," she said.

"Actually, I had three years at medical school. So it wasn't exactly a challenge. But it's nice to have my abilities appreciated." He cleared his throat. "You've…um… you've got good skin. So this should heal up very nicely."

His hand was very warm where it rested against her leg. He'd applied the stitches so deftly she tried not to think about anything else his hands might be able to do.

"Three years of medical school would have put you past the worst of it," she said, trying to keep her head clear. "Why didn't you keep going?"

"I happen to love being a paramedic," he said. "I knew medical school wasn't for me, so I left."

Kat was surprised by the defensive tone in Jack's voice.

She'd only known him for a few moments, but he struck her as a supremely confident sort of person. Surely he couldn't be sensitive about being a paramedic?

During her career she had met a very small number of physicians with extremely arrogant personalities—her old hospital's administrative director came to mind—who seemed to believe that doctors were somehow superior to other medical professionals. It wasn't a view she agreed with at all. Paramedics and nurses simply provided a different kind of care than doctors. Different and vitally important.

Perhaps Jack had run into a few doctors who held such antiquated views. She hoped he didn't think that she was one of them. But in her pre-hypothermic state, and in her desperation to avoid arriving at Oahu General in an ambulance, she'd probably given him every reason to think that she was as arrogant, stubborn and overconfident as... as *he* was.

"Well, in my opinion you left medical school not a moment too soon," she said lightly.

He looked up at her in surprise.

"If you'd become a doctor you wouldn't have been there on the beach today," she explained. "You wouldn't have been able to save my life. So I'm extremely grateful you decided to become a paramedic instead, no matter what the reason was."

He gave a low, dark laugh. "You're probably the first person who's ever been happy that I left medical school. Well, maybe the second, after me."

There was something more he might have said, Kat could tell. But he didn't speak any further.

Her thoughts turned again to his tattoo. "Are others in your family in the military?" she asked.

"Not exactly," he replied. "My grandfather's a doctor... as are my parents and both of my brothers."

Ah... Suddenly Jack's defensiveness was a bit more clear. With five doctors in the family, there had probably been many expectations about Jack's career options.

"I knew a few people in medical school whose parents were physicians," she said. "But lots of people don't want to do the same thing as their parents. And I can imagine that being a paramedic in Hawaii would be the best of both worlds to someone who's a former SEAL and a former medical student. You're still able to help people, but you get the rush of adrenaline and excitement that comes with the job."

"Exactly," he said, but again, he didn't elaborate.

I get it, you don't like to talk about the past, she thought. *Duly noted.*

That was fine with her.

She felt the ambulance pull into the hospital docking bay and saw the driver step out. As Jack started to open the back door Kat put her hand on his arm to stop him.

"Wait," she said. "I haven't thanked you properly. If you hadn't been there today I probably would have drowned."

She could tell that he was as surprised as she was by the softness in her voice. What was she *doing*? She had only meant to say thank you, but the emotion behind her voice had been more than just gratitude. And now that she was looking directly at him...now that he was holding her gaze with those ocean-blue eyes...that same electric charge that she'd felt on the beach was there again, keeping her eyes locked with his.

"You mostly saved yourself, by staying calm and trusting my instructions," he said, his voice soft and low. "I was just there to help."

They were by themselves in the back of the ambulance

and there was silence. His gaze met hers and Kat couldn't look away. His eyes were pools of cerulean blue. His nose was inches away from hers.

For one insane moment she thought he was going to kiss her—which was a ridiculous idea. Why would Jack want to kiss her? She was a bedraggled mess. And he probably thought she was completely full of herself after she'd bragged about her medical background.

But she'd only bragged because he'd been so bossy at first. So, really, that part was his fault.

And Kat couldn't think why *she* would want a man as irritating as Jack Harper to kiss her.

She only knew that she did.

They were so close. She could smell his sea-salt scent. She felt an undeniable pull toward him, as strong as the current that had pulled her out to sea earlier. But this time, instead of panic, she only felt safety. Calm. A sense of certainty about what would happen next.

But just as his face began moving toward hers, close enough for her to feel the warmth of his breath on her face, two EMTs pulled open the back door of the ambulance.

Kat gave a jump and a start, and she and Jack quickly pulled away from one another. She instantly regretted her sudden move away from Jack, realizing that her reaction would probably make the situation appear even more suspicious to any gossip-prone EMTs. She needed to make it clear to everyone that she and Jack were just co-workers, and she needed to do it quickly.

She pulled the white coat tightly over herself and stepped out of the ambulance. Despite her protests, the EMTs insisted she sit in the wheelchair they'd brought out to meet her.

As they left, she turned back to Jack and said, in her coolest, most professional voice, "It was nice to meet you,

Jack. It's good to find out firsthand that I can trust my co-workers to do such a competent job. I think it's great that we'll be working together professionally. Just great."

As Kat was wheeled away Jack let out the long, slow breath that he'd been holding since the driver had stepped out and left the two of them alone together in the ambulance. He had no idea what he'd been thinking in the moment before that almost-kiss with Kat. In fact, he hadn't been thinking at all.

If he had been, he would have been able to tell himself that he and Kat made no sense. That the reasons not to get involved with her far outweighed any attraction he might feel. He ticked them off in his mind. Kat had deliberately emphasized their status as colleagues as she'd left the ambulance. They'd be working together, and workplace relationships were always a mistake. And then there was his most steadfast rule of dating: no doctors.

Not since Sophie. They'd been in medical school together, and then she'd gone on to one prestigious medical research fellowship after another. He'd been fully supportive of her, but when he'd left medical school, she'd let him know in no uncertain terms that she was interested in being the wife of a *doctor*—not a military man or a lowly paramedic.

As hard as it had been to accept, he'd thought he understood. After all, he was the one who had changed, deciding that a doctor's life wasn't for him. He couldn't fault her for wanting something different than what *he* wanted.

But wanting something different was one thing. Finding out that she'd been with his brother for six months before breaking up with Jack was quite another.

Sophie had always been extremely ambitious. And

Jack's parents were well-known in the medical field, and the Harper doctors were a valuable connection.

It was one reason he disliked talking about his family with others—especially those in the medical field: he never knew if people were just trying to get close to him in order to claim a connection to his family. Had Kat made the connection? Harper was a common enough last name, but there weren't many people who had five doctors in the family. If she did suspect that his family was essentially medical royalty, she hadn't said anything.

He'd always wondered if the reason Sophie had cheated on him with Matt, of all people, was so that she could still marry into the Harper family—simply swapping one Harper brother for another.

Matt, for his part, either hadn't seen it that way or hadn't cared. Matt had always liked Sophie, Jack knew...but he'd never realized just how far that attraction went until it was too late. He'd trusted Sophie. He'd trusted both of them.

Jack didn't want to go through that kind of heartbreak again. Ever. And as far as he was concerned he wouldn't have to. There was no shortage of short-term dating prospects on the islands. Hawaii was full of tourists with romantic ideas about a whirlwind affair before they returned to the mainland. They expected nothing more, and neither did he.

As far as he was concerned love was an illusion, and the best way to protect yourself from heartbreak was to keep from getting close to anyone in the first place.

The more he thought about it, the more he realized that his attraction to Kat wasn't going to be a problem. Kat would only be here for one year. Lots of doctors came to Hawaii for brief appointments—Hawaii's shortage of doctors was well known in the medical community, and visiting doctors weren't rare—but the vast majority of phy-

sicians returned to the mainland eventually. Kat seemed
like someone who would put her career first, probably
over just about anything. She'd leave once she'd gotten
over whatever island fantasies she harbored and realized
that practicing in Hawaii meant focusing on patient care
rather than professional advancement.

He would simply wait out his attraction until she left,
and hope that she would forget all about that awkward moment in the ambulance. Which hadn't even been a moment,
really. At the time it had felt like an almost-kiss, but now
that the moment had passed he realized that she'd probably
just meant to express her gratitude. In fact, he might have
just completely embarrassed himself by assuming even
for an instant that she'd been leaning forward for a kiss.

Yes, she'd been leaning in and turning her face toward
him, so close he'd almost been able to count her individual eyelashes…so close he had noticed the tiny freckles
dotting her nose, felt her breath on his cheek. But it didn't
mean anything. Hell, she might have just been reaching
for something.

But he had no intention of asking her about it. That
moment in the ambulance was best left forgotten. He'd
simply be careful to avoid Kat while they were at work,
and then he should have no problem putting her out of his
mind. He wouldn't spend any time thinking about that red
hair of hers, hanging in dripping ringlets around her neck.

Or the tiny freckles that dotted her nose.

Or her soft, kissable lips.

No, he wouldn't be thinking about any of those things
at all.

CHAPTER THREE

"YOU CERTAINLY KNOW how to make an entrance," said Selena.

It was several days after Kat's dramatic first arrival at Oahu General Hospital, and Kat and Selena were sharing coffee in her friend's office. Although they hadn't seen each other in several years, Dr. Selena Kahale had been one of Kat's closest friends when they'd attended medical school together. After Selena had returned to her home in Honolulu, her hard work and natural warmth had helped her to climb the ranks quickly to become clinical director of Oahu General Hospital.

But apparently her esteemed professional position didn't get in the way of teasing an old friend.

Kat blushed, remembering the amount of good-natured ribbing she'd endured as soon as the EMTs had learned who she was. Despite her protestations that she was fine, they had insisted on wheeling her into an exam room, still wet, with her medical coat wrapped around her concealing her bikini.

"I wasn't planning on showing up on my first day dressed like that," said Kat, completely embarrassed.

Selena might be an old friend, but she was now Kat's boss, and Kat wasn't sure how she'd view the whole incident.

She let out a breath of relief when Selena said, "Relax. It's Hawaii. No one stands on ceremony here. You'll find things are much more informal than what you're probably used to back in Chicago. Tommy Bahama shirts are basically considered formalwear. My only worry is whether you'll be able to get used to how casual things are around here."

"It's certainly a big change," said Kat.

That was an understatement. The environment at Oahu General Hospital was sometimes so casual that she was taken aback. After her first day she'd scrapped any thoughts of showing up in a power suit—she would have felt ridiculous wearing a formal blazer here.

Back at Chicago Grace there had been a clear hierarchy among the staff, and everyone had known where they stood. Kat had often wondered if the culture of strict adherence to authority there had interfered with patient care, since some of the doctors were too afraid to question a senior physician's diagnosis, or to make changes to treatment plans that their supervisors might disagree with.

But at Oahu General Hospital the atmosphere felt completely different. Everyone seemed to genuinely respect one another, regardless of hierarchy. Doctors routinely took advice from nurses and paramedics, everyone's input seemed to be valued, and there was an easy banter among the staff.

This relaxed atmosphere presented her with a new challenge. In Chicago, whenever she'd acted as the attending physician, her team had listened to her and carried out her instructions because she was in charge. Simply being in a position of authority had been enough for her team to respect her. But here in Hawaii she saw she would have to earn the respect of her colleagues, as well as their trust.

Selena seemed to sense her thoughts. "Every hospital's

culture is a little different," she said. "Even I was a little taken aback by the informality here at first, and I grew up on the islands. But I've come to realize that Oahu General is a special place. We're like family here. You'll grow to love it, I'm sure. And I know that everyone will love you too. Just give them time to get to know you."

Selena paused to sip her coffee, and then continued.

"You might be surprised at how well you fit in here if you can just give yourself time to adjust. The Kat Murphy I remember from medical school was so idealistic, so committed to making a difference in her patients' lives. Maybe getting sacked from Chicago Grace was a blessing in disguise."

Kat blinked. "What kind of blessing involves spending a year doing research for a proposal that ultimately fails?"

"Think about it," said Selena. "Chicago Grace Memorial may be one of the most prestigious hospitals in the country, but ultimately it's a for-profit hospital. The Kat I know could never be completely happy working at a hospital where patients are seen based on their ability to pay. That's not you. It's not where you come from."

Kat mulled this over. She and Selena had been close friends at medical school, and Selena knew how important it was to Kat to use medicine to make a difference. But when Kat had first begun working at Chicago Grace she'd been so excited about the hospital's reputation and the research opportunities it provided that she hadn't thought much about how the hospital's values might differ from her own.

As she'd continued working there it had become impossible not to see the truth in front of her: there were too many patients who couldn't afford the care they needed.

She knew how that felt.

When she was growing up her parents had always

waited until the last possible minute to seek medical care. Even as a child Kat had understood that money was tight in her family. Although her parents had always taken her to see a doctor promptly when she was ill, she knew that they'd often put off their own medical care in order to save money.

Then, when she was ten, her father had come down with an illness. "Just a cold," he had said, reassuring Kat and her mother.

When the cold had persisted he'd said it must just be the flu, and that he would see a doctor when he had time to take a break from his job. He'd kept telling them that he would see a doctor in just a few days. A few weeks later, the flu had turned into pneumonia, and by then her father's condition had been severe. He'd passed away just one day after being admitted to a hospital.

So it wasn't enough for Kat simply to be a good doctor. It hadn't been enough simply to work at Chicago Grace, with all its glamour and prestige. She wanted to make a real difference in the medical community. And more than anything she wanted to make sure that no child, no family, had to go through what she'd gone through as a little girl.

Which was why she had wanted the director of Chicago Grace Memorial to accept her proposal to open a nonprofit clinic at the hospital. It would have been her chance to finally make a true difference—a contribution to medicine that came directly from her personal experience and her professional values.

She had thought that ultimately the board of directors—many of them physicians themselves—would agree that any impact on the hospital's profits would be a small price to pay for a vast increase in quality of patient care.

How naïve she'd been.

Instead of simply rejecting Kat's proposal, the board

members had expressed deep indignation at her research findings, which had shown that wealthier patients recovered faster than poorer patients. They'd complained that her findings were terrible for the public's view of the hospital, and they'd told her to bury all her data.

Kat had refused, and it had been that refusal, as well as the choice words she had exchanged with the hospital director, that had resulted in her being fired.

She'd finally had her chance to make a difference and she'd failed. She hadn't been able to convince the hospital board to open a nonprofit clinic. She hadn't been able to control her temper when the hospital director had been condescending and rude. And she hadn't been able to make Christopher understand why all of it was so important to her.

She'd expected his support, but instead he'd seemed just as shocked as the hospital board members. Instead of sharing her anger he'd been angry with Kat, for exchanging insults with the hospital director.

"How could you?" he'd said. *"You might as well have thrown away your career."*

She'd been furious with him. Devastated and furious.

Tears pricked as she remembered their conversation and how cold he'd been. She stared into her coffee mug, hoping Selena wouldn't see those tears that still sprang to her eyes whenever Christopher came to mind.

"You know, as glad as I am to have you here, I was a little surprised when you took the job," Selena said. "Hawaii's so far from Chicago. I would have thought you'd try to look for something a little closer to your family."

"I needed a change," Kat said. "A big change."

The last thing she wanted to admit to her old friend was that she'd moved to Hawaii because of the breakup.

It was such a cliché. And Selena would expect her to be professional.

She took a deep breath and tried to think of how she could explain in a way that Selena would understand. But before she could start Selena said, "It was the breakup with Christopher, wasn't it?"

Kat choked on her coffee in surprise. "How did you know?"

"Come on, Kat! *Three days* before the wedding you post online that it's over? And then there's complete radio silence from you—none of your friends can get in touch with you. That's not just a breakup—that's a broken heart."

"I don't want you to think I moved here just because of what happened with…with him," Kat said. It was still too hard to say Christopher's name. "I'm serious about this job—I'm not here just to get over a guy."

"You think I don't understand that? I'm a single mom—I know exactly how it feels to have your life change completely and unexpectedly. You don't have to go through this alone."

Didn't she? Kat was glad to have Selena's support, but now that she was nearing the end of her first week in Hawaii she was beginning to realize that she felt more alone than she ever had in her life.

Now that the excitement of moving to the island was wearing off, Kat felt as though she wasn't sure who she was. She wasn't a top internal medicine doctor at one of the most prestigious hospitals in the country. She wasn't Christopher's fiancée—she definitely wasn't his wife. And she wasn't living in Chicago, the city where her family and friends lived, where she'd planned to spend the rest of her life.

For as long as she could remember she'd tried to be the best doctor on the staff, the best fiancée to Christopher.

But if she wasn't trying to prove herself to anyone then how did she know who she was supposed to be?

Kat blinked back tears, willing her eyes to dry. "The point is, it's in the past," she said. "I came here to try to let go of him…of everything that was holding me back. But I just don't know what I'm supposed to do next."

"Oh, Kat." Selena set her coffee aside and patted Kat's shoulder tenderly. "I think you really have come to the right place." Then she gave Kat a wicked smile. "And it looks like you're already making friends. Didn't one of Oahu's most eligible bachelors fish you out of the Pacific recently?"

"Eligible bachelors? Are you talking about Jack Harper?"

"Who else? If you wanted to meet him you didn't have to nearly drown yourself—I could have set you up on a date."

"Selena! I am *so* not ready to date yet. One of the reasons I came here was to try to learn how to slow down and relax."

Selena raised an eyebrow. "Forgive me for being skeptical, but I don't think 'slow down and relax' is a phrase I've *ever* heard you use."

"Maybe I don't have the strongest reputation in that respect, but I'm trying to change that," said Kat. "I'm trying to let go of the past and do something new. Which means I'm definitely not looking to get romantically involved with anyone right now. And even if I was, Jack and I aren't right for one another."

"Okay, first of all, you *are* ready to date—you just don't know it. You've already completed the first essential step to getting over a breakup."

"Which is?"

"Getting out of the continental U.S. as quickly as possible. Now you need to move on to step two: the rebound. And for that purpose Jack is *perfect* for you."

Kat swallowed. How much did Selena know of the kiss that had almost happened between her and Jack? Had the EMTs decided that their brief glimpse of Jack and a half-clothed Kat in close quarters was gossip-worthy after all?

She responded carefully. "I'm not so sure I'd say he's *perfect* for me. He seems pretty bossy. And even if I were interested—which I'm not—he probably doesn't want anything to do with me."

"Why on earth would you say that?" said Selena. "From what I heard, you two were getting pretty cozy just around the time the ambulance pulled up to the hospital."

Damn, thought Kat. So there *had* been gossip. She needed to set the record straight with Selena as soon as possible. What had happened with Jack—or what had almost happened—had just been a misunderstanding, nothing more.

"I don't know what people have been saying, but Jack was simply taking care of the cut on my leg. Both of us were completely professional. We did get to know each other a little…"

"And?" said Selena, rapt with anticipation.

"And I don't think I'm his type. We kind of got off on the wrong foot. I hate to admit it, but I don't think I made the best first impression—I may have sounded a little full of myself. I blame the hypothermia. And I think—no, I'm *sure*—Jack would agree that since we're to be co-workers it's best not to let emotions get in the way of our working together."

Selena waved her hand dismissively. "Honey, that's all *relationship* stuff. What you need is a *fling*."

"I'm not really sure I'm a fling kind of girl."

Selena narrowed her eyes. "Kat. Sweetheart. Did you

not hear me say that I'm a single mother? When I'm not working, my days involve making lunches and spending way too much time discussing purple crayons with a toddler whom I love to pieces but who has barely mastered words of two syllables. I need some excitement. I need to live vicariously through someone else's love-life. And I need you to be that person because I don't have time for that kind of drama myself!"

Kat laughed. "Sorry, but my love-life's never been all that exciting. If you're looking for vicarious thrills you'll have to look somewhere else."

"Oh, come *on*!" said Selena. "I thought you came here to let go of the past and try new things?"

"Well, yes, but… I'm not sure I want Jack Harper to be one of those 'new things.'"

"Why not? Jack is great. And he's ideal for you right now because he's not a relationship kind of guy. Don't get me wrong—he's a good person. And I love working with him. He's great at his job, really funny, and a good friend. But he's tailor-made fling material; he never dates *anyone* for long."

"I'll just bet he doesn't," said Kat through gritted teeth. Selena was simply confirming her first impression of him.

Selena continued to gush about Jack's virtues.

"He's a lot like you, actually," she said. "He could have worked anywhere on the mainland, but he chose to come here instead. And he's not just *any* paramedic. His parents are *the* Harpers—from the University of Nebraska in Lincoln—"

"Wait a minute," said Kat.

Jack *Harper?* It was quite a common last name and she hadn't given it a second thought till now.

"You mean his parents are Michael and Janet Harper?

The famous research scientists? I still have some of their books from medical school on my shelf."

She remembered Jack had touched on the subject of his family in the ambulance, and now knew her feeling that he'd been holding something back had been spot-on. She couldn't understand how he could have talked about his family without ever mentioning that his parents were famous in the medical world.

"What the hell is the son of two of the most well-known medical researchers in the country doing working as a paramedic at a small hospital in Hawaii?" she asked.

"Shouldn't you be asking yourself a similar question?" Selena's eyes twinkled. "What's one of the most respected internists in the U.S. doing at my little hospital? I'm sure he has his reasons, just as you do. You see? You two *are* a lot alike."

"Sure, if oil and water are alike..." Kat muttered.

"I don't know why he wants to work here, but I'm glad he does," Selena continued. "He's a gifted paramedic. Most of the patients he brings in are already stable by the time they get to the hospital, no matter what the emergency."

"Yes, I could tell he was very competent. But I made it clear to him that I was a doctor and he still flat-out ignored me and did everything his own way."

"You're too used to medical hierarchy," Selena told her. "Here we're more egalitarian. We make our decisions with everyone's input rather than automatically deciding that whoever's in charge knows best. It's a team approach. It takes some getting used to, but it's one of the things I love most about practicing here. And I think you'll learn to love it, too."

Selena's eyes grew mischievous.

"And maybe you'll fall in love with something else as well. Some*one* else...with blue eyes and dark hair and—"

"Oh, my God, Selena, let it go!" Kat held up one of the sofa pillows, threatening to throw it at her friend. "Jack and I are *not* going to happen. Maybe if he were the last man on this island I'd consider it. But only then."

Selena's eyes twinkled. "We'll see," she said. "It's a pretty small island."

Kat cleared her throat. "Is there perhaps something we can discuss *besides* my love-life? Something involving medicine?"

"Right!" said Selena. "The whole reason you're here. The virus outbreaks."

Selena sat behind her desk and pulled out several files for Kat to examine.

"Because of its location, Hawaii is vulnerable to all the strains of virus that sweep through Asia, so we try to keep an eye on what's happening there in order to be prepared for what could happen here."

She drew Kat's attention to one of the files.

"We're calling this one H5N7. There have been a few isolated cases on Oahu. Catching the signs early and keeping people quarantined to prevent the spread of infection has been key. But our hospital is too small to handle a major infectious disease event. My biggest worry is that a larger outbreak would strain our resources to such an extent that we wouldn't be able to provide effective care to patients who would otherwise be cured."

Kat nodded. "On the mainland you can rely on the resources of other hospitals, but here you can't simply call in for reinforcements or send your overflow of patients to another hospital nearby."

"Exactly. Sending patients to hospitals on the other islands can be a huge hassle. And even if we could, the only Level One trauma center for all the islands is located right here in *our* hospital—there's two thousand miles of ocean between us and the next nearest one. So we're observing very strict contamination procedures with any patient who comes in."

Kat passed the files back to Selena. "As far as I can tell you're doing the best you can to stay ahead of this thing," she said. "What's the status of any potential vaccine?"

"We're working with a team at the University of Hawaii at Manoa to see what can be done. So far their results are promising. In the meantime we're following the strictest quarantine procedures for any patients brought into the hospital with signs of flu, or any health workers who have been exposed. That means full haz-mat gear when we're working with affected patients. I've put a policy in place stating that any hospital staff members who come into contact with potentially infected patients will be housed here at the hospital, in a secure holding area, until we can confirm whether or not they've been exposed to the illness. If blood tests do confirm exposure, then it's a mandatory 10-day quarantine so that we have time to observe whether symptoms manifest, and so we can start treatment immediately if necessary. Bottom line, make sure you're taking the standard universal precautions with every patient, but be on the lookout for the rash and other symptoms so that you can be extra-careful with affected patients. So far, none of our staff have been exposed yet, and I intend to keep it that way."

Kat nodded. "Like I say, sounds like you're doing everything you can."

"We are," said Selena, "but I feel better now that you're here." Selena squirmed uncomfortably. "Actually…you may have to communicate quite a bit with Jack on this."

"Why? He's a paramedic."

"Exactly. If the outbreaks do increase, paramedics and EMTs will be at the greatest risk. They're the ones who will be exposed to the victims first. So it's essential that they keep us abreast of any risk of the flu spreading because they'll be the first to know."

Kat sighed. It seemed that avoiding Jack Harper would be harder than she'd thought.

After several weeks Kat began to settle into a rhythm at the hospital. She worked with the researchers from the University of Hawaii on the flu virus and shared ER shifts with the other doctors. They were a relaxed, easygoing bunch. And as Kat got used to the hospital's informality she began to appreciate the casual atmosphere.

She made friends with Kimo, the shift coordinator, who would bring in extra *kalua* pork sandwiches his mother had made. She got to know Marceline, a cardiologist, who would regale Kat with lurid stories of her former life as a webcam girl. "Modeling" skimpy outfits in front of her computer had helped Marceline pay for most of medical school. And one of the surgeons, Omar, was rumored to be royalty in his home country, but he was very clandestine about it. Kat had the feeling that he allowed the rumor to continue because it added to his air of mystery and seemed to improve his dating prospects quite a bit.

It was a colorful cast of characters, and nothing at all like the strait-laced, buttoned-up doctors she'd worked with back home.

The patients were different, too. Kat was used to seeing patients who were seeking second or third opinions on the prognosis of serious or rare illnesses. People came to Chicago Grace Memorial Hospital when other physicians had reached the end of their knowledge and were unable to provide more guidance, and Kat had typically used her expertise there to make hard-to-call diagnoses of illnesses that were extremely rare or difficult to treat.

Oahu General Hospital ran itself more like a small general practice. She saw children who had stuck innumerable crayons up their noses, and tourists with sprains or fractures because they'd taken risks while hiking.

She also saw entirely too much of Jack.

Somehow she always seemed to be on shift when he was bringing in patients. As if that wasn't bad enough he seemed to be constantly flirting—with everyone except Kat. Every time Kat saw him he was flashing his hundred-watt smile at the receptionists, or sharing private jokes with the nurses, or twinkling his eyes at patients.

She wasn't sure why Jack's behavior should bother her so much. She didn't care who he flirted with. After all, she wasn't interested in him, and he wasn't interested in her. She simply felt that one should maintain a professional attitude at work. A casual atmosphere was all well and good, but people could take these things too far. There was no need for Jack to go winking his ocean-blue eyes at everyone in sight, or giving his bright white smile to every woman who crossed his path.

Good God, she thought one day, when Jack smiled at a nurse who'd helped him lift a heavy patient off a gurney. *Even his teeth are perfect.*

It was all very distracting. And that was the problem, thought Kat. Jack's flirting with other people didn't bother her the least little bit. It was simply annoying to be constantly distracted by his tanned skin or his muscular arms. Why did he have to wear such tight shirts?

She'd tried to avoid him, but working at such a small hospital made it difficult to avoid anyone. He brought her just as many cases as he brought the other doctors—if not more. But he seemed to delight in bringing her the most ridiculous cases he could find. And then he wouldn't simply leave, the way most paramedics did. Every time he brought in a case, he would linger, as though he wanted to see how she would handle things.

When she'd challenged him on it he'd claimed that he was merely staying nearby in case she needed additional assistance. She didn't believe him for a minute. She was certain that he was sticking around so he could watch her reaction—which, in her opinion, proved that he was bringing her preposterous cases on purpose.

She dealt with it the only way she knew how—by maintaining a distant, cool, professional demeanor. And for his part Jack seemed to have no trouble keeping his face completely deadpan. Even today, as he pulled back one of the ER privacy curtains to reveal a young couple on a gurney. The woman sat upright, and her boyfriend was lying on his side.

Kat listened to their story.

"So where are you saying the zucchini is now?" she asked patiently.

After the couple had left, with a treatment plan and some stern words of warning about the inadvisability of placing vegetables in bodily orifices, Kat grabbed Jack and pulled him behind the curtain.

"I know what you're doing and it needs to stop," she hissed.

He blinked at her innocently. "I'm just doing my job. It's not my fault if I'm bringing patients to the ER while you happen to be on shift."

"There are other doctors on shift! Find one of them! The other day you had an acute appendicitis case and you brought it to Omar. But what kinds of cases do you bring *me*? College students who stick vegetables God knows where! A toddler who's pushed thirteen marbles up his nose! An elderly woman with dementia who ate all the little cakes her granddaughter made from Play-Doh because she thought they were real!"

"Hey, I thought she was sweet."

"She *was* sweet! That's not the point. You're doing this on purpose!"

"Doing what on purpose?" he asked innocently.

"Giving all the weird cases to me."

He shook his head. "Why on earth would I do that?" he said.

"I have no idea. Don't ask me what the motives of a sociopath are. But I've got news for you, pal. I've seen just about every crazy ER case in the book. Marbles are nothing—you wouldn't believe some of the things I've seen kids stick up their noses. You're not going to shock me with anything."

He held his hands up. "I believe you—I'm sure that you're unshockable. But I swear I'm not doing this on purpose. You've had a run of strange cases lately, I'll admit, but I promise I'm just bringing the patients as they come in."

As he spoke Kat realized just how close she and Jack were in physical proximity to one another. What had she been thinking when she pulled him behind a curtain? They could have had this conversation in public. Once again she'd ended up getting herself caught in close quarters with Jack. How did that keep happening?

She yanked open the curtain, deciding that it would be best to get out of the enclosure as quickly as possible— but she was stopped short by the small crowd of hospital staff that had gathered just outside.

There were several orderlies, as well as Marceline, Kimo and Omar. They tried to act casual, but they'd clearly been listening to her argument with Jack. *Great*, thought

Kat. If their moment in the ambulance hadn't been enough, then rumors would definitely be flying about the two of them after this.

Jack really wasn't trying to hand off the most bizarre patients to Kat—it was simply a matter of bad timing. He knew they'd gotten off on the wrong foot. But he wasn't used to having his decisions questioned or challenged while he was trying to save lives. And yet, as argumentative and challenging as Kat had been, there was a strong air of feistiness about her that he admired. She didn't seem like someone who gave up easily, whatever the circumstances.

He might have come off as bossy, but hadn't Kat acted the same way? He had been trying to provide her with medical care, while she'd been trying to convince him that she knew best by waving her credentials in front of his face—as though she couldn't possibly trust his expertise over her own.

Did she think he should be impressed by her credentials rather than her competence? It was the same kind of thinking he'd often noticed among his family members, who seemed to value the achievements and connections of medical professionals more than the skill they demonstrated.

Now that he'd spent a few weeks working with Kat he could tell that she was one of the most competent doctors he'd ever worked with. But he'd had no way of knowing that before.

And, just as he'd thought, Kat had started trying to implement changes at the hospital right away. Some changes had gone down better than others. First she'd required the EMTs and paramedics to switch from a three-point to a five-point triage system, and even he had to admit that it had been a *good* change. But her most controversial decision had been to ask all hospital staff to spend eight hours a month working at the hospital's nonprofit walk-in clinic.

Granted, she'd adjusted everyone's schedules so that this didn't impact too much on anyone's working hours.

But, while he might be able to acknowledge that Kat's changes so far were an improvement on an intellectual level, he still felt frustrated. Kat's ideas might be good, but that wasn't the point. The point was that she was a big-city doctor who thought she could just walk into a little hospital—*his* little hospital—and turn his job and his emotions upside down.

At first he'd tried to keep his distance, to give his feelings a chance to subside. But, if anything, avoiding Kat had seemed to intensify his attraction toward her, and he'd constantly found himself wondering how she was adjusting to her new job, whether she was talking to the other staff members, or if she was wearing that green blouse that offset her eyes so well.

To make matters worse, as he continued to work with Kat he became increasingly certain that he wasn't just attracted to her—he *liked* her as well. She had a wry sense of humor, and she seemed to possess wells of infinite patience and compassion with even the most difficult patients. She had a warm and ready smile, and she smiled often—just not at him.

So he'd decided to change tactics. Instead of avoiding Kat, he'd started to make a point of being sure to acknowledge her each time their paths crossed. He'd been trying to keep their encounters polite and casual. But that strategy had become more complicated when the hospital had suddenly been hit with a run of cases that bordered on the absurd.

Jack wasn't surprised that Kat thought he was bringing her weird cases on purpose, but he wished there was a way to convince her that it was just a coincidence that her caseload of late had been a bit unusual.

At least she'd never brought up their almost-kiss in the ambulance. His hunch was that she was just as eager to put that incident behind them as he was. He wondered if it would be possible for them to have a fresh start. The sooner he could convince her that he wasn't bringing her strange cases on purpose—that he did not, in fact, have any special interest in her, in any way—the sooner he could start trying to convince himself of the same thing.

He wasn't quite sure how, but he'd find a way.

A few days later, the doors of the elevator in the hospital's parking garage were just closing in front of Kat when a hand reached out to stop them. They automatically shifted open again, and Kat was surprised to see Jack standing in front of her.

"May I?" he said, motioning inside the elevator.

Kat shrugged. "Plenty of room," she said.

He got onto the elevator with her, and they began their ascent from the basement to the trauma unit. But Jack surprised Kat again by pushing the emergency stop button.

Before she could speak, he said, "Look, I know we got off on the wrong foot, and I just wanted to clear the air. Back in the ambulance, I…um…"

Oh, no, thought Kat. Was Jack was about to bring up their almost-kiss? She needed to take control of this conversation, and fast.

"I was a jerk," she said quickly. "You were just trying to help, and I argued and fought you every step of the way. I blame the hypothermia. You were just doing your job."

"That's true," he said. "But I have to admit that I'm not used to treating patients who have medical experience…just like you probably weren't used to being in the patient's role."

He was trying to offer her an olive branch. Maybe she should take it. They did have to work together, after all. She'd tried desperately to deal with her attraction by avoiding him, but that strategy didn't seem to be working. If anything, she thought about him more than ever.

Maybe the problem was that she wasn't seeing Jack as a real person. The distance between them was causing her to focus too much on his physical attractiveness. Maybe if she spent more time with him, got to know him as a normal person whom she had to see every day, whom she had to work with, then he'd lose some of his luster. This man with his dark, wavy hair and perfect teeth was sure to have some flaws—she simply hadn't been around him enough to notice any of them. Maybe once she discovered a few of them her heart and stomach would stop doing flip-flops every time she saw him.

And it would be nice to stop being so distracted by his scent, as well. How did he always manage to smell like the beach? It filled the elevator now—the scent of sunblock, saltwater, and pure masculinity. Maybe she'd get desensitized if she were around him enough…

"I really haven't been bringing you the weird cases on purpose," he was saying. "I don't know why all of the odd ones have been coming in during your ER shifts, but I promise I haven't been giving them to you intentionally."

"Hmm…" she said. "Not even that toddler who swallowed the voice box from his teddy bear, and we could all hear Teddy's disembodied voice coming out of the kid's lower abdomen every time he pressed on his stomach?"

"*Especially* not that one." Jack shuddered. "That was creepy."

Suddenly Kat found herself laughing. The case really

had been ridiculous. And anyway, even if he *had* been bringing her odd cases on purpose, dealing with the unexpected was part of the job.

His relief at her laughter seemed sincere, so Kat thought that his apology probably was as well. "All right, Jack," she said. "How about a truce?"

And finally—*finally*—after all this time, she found herself the recipient of his smile. The full force of it was just as dazzling as she had known it would be. Her knees felt a little weak, but she managed to casually grip the bar on one side of the elevator, as though she were just shifting her stance.

"A truce sounds good," he said. "I have a feeling that if we're not bickering we might actually find out we like working together."

Kat wasn't sure what to say.

Certainly not, *I'd like that, but I'm very attracted to you, and that's really interfering with my ability to recover from a fiancé who practically left me at the altar just a few weeks ago.*

No, that response was probably off the table.

She settled for giving him a small smile instead.

He released the emergency stop button and the elevator began moving upward again. This would be good, thought Kat. They would get to know each other a little better, and soon enough she'd get used to him. He'd never need to know how badly she wanted to run her fingers through his dark hair.

When the elevator doors opened on the trauma unit all was in chaos. Even Selena was sweeping around the ER floor, conducting triage.

She nodded at Jack and Kat as they stepped out of the elevator. "Major car crash on the expressway," she said, by way of explanation. "We've got multiple trauma cases coming in at once. Grab one and get to work."

Jack and Kat nodded at one another. At the end of the hallway a team of EMTs were wheeling a gurney with an incoming patient on it toward the ER; Kat rushed toward them, with Jack close behind her.

"What've we got?" Kat asked Marco, the head EMT on duty.

"Man who looks to be in his late fifties with multiple fractures. His breathing was shallow when we first picked him up, but now he's not breathing at all. He got smashed up pretty bad in the expressway crash. We had to use the jaws of life to get him out from under his car."

"How long has he been unresponsive?"

"Less than a few seconds."

"His pulse is thready," said Jack. "Could be something obstructing the airway."

Kat placed her stethoscope on the man's chest. She could hear a heartbeat, but there were no sounds of respiration. "We'll need to intubate," she said. "Let's get him to an operating room."

She was about to ask Jack if he'd be able to come with her, but he'd already moved to the other side of the gurney and was helping her push it down the hallway.

"Thanks," she said breathlessly as she tried to keep pace with him. "I know they need you out there."

"You need me in here," he responded as they pushed the patient's gurney into the OR.

He immediately began attending to the pulse oximeter, and Kat was relieved to see there was no need to talk him through the procedure; he'd clearly done this before.

Before she could ask, he handed her a laryngoscope. Kat tilted the patient's head back and inserted the scope into his mouth, taking care to avoid the man's teeth. As she pushed the endotracheal tube into the patient's airway Jack began to inflate the balloon that would deliver air into his lungs. He continued inflations as Kat positioned her stethoscope first above one lung and then the other, to listen for sounds of respiration.

There.

Kat relaxed her shoulders as she identified the ragged but unmistakable sound of breathing in both lungs. They'd need an X-ray to ensure correct placement of the tube, but hearing respiration from both lungs meant that the patient should stabilize quickly.

She straightened up from where she was bent over the patient and looked at Jack in astonishment. "I don't think I've ever gotten a line into a patient so fast," she said.

He flashed a smile at her and Kat felt another pang. Just a few minutes ago she'd been hoping that spending more time with Jack would help desensitize her to his charm. But now, finding that they were able to work together so seamlessly… Kat thought she might actually *want* to work with Jack more often if it meant that her medical procedures would go this smoothly.

If she could just get her heart to stop going into overdrive every time he smiled they'd be a great team.

"One of the easiest intubations I've ever done," he agreed, looking at the patient's pulse-ox levels on the monitor. "I'd say we should take him down to X-Ray to ensure correct placement of the line, but…"

"What is it?" said Kat.

"Come look."

Kat came around to Jack's side of the gurney and was suddenly filled with dread.

The distinctive rash of the super-flu was spread over the man's legs and abdomen: small red bumps. And she and Jack had been working on him without haz-mat suits, and with only standard levels of protection between the two of them.

Kat realized that her plan to take the edge off her attraction to Jack by getting to know him better was about to blow up in her face.

She was going to get to know Jack better, all right. Kat remembered what Selena had told her about the hospital's policy regarding virus exposure.

Kat looked at Jack's face, and knew what he was thinking, too.

They might be about to spend a long time together.

CHAPTER FOUR

KAT AND JACK had only been in the secure holding room for a few hours before Kat was certain of one thing: no matter how much time they spent together, she was never going to become desensitized to Jack Harper.

She'd wondered if being quarantined with Jack would let the two of them get to know each other better. But she quickly realized he was as guarded as ever when she mentioned that the research team working on the virus had been using studies conducted by his parents for reference. She'd only meant to reassure him that she thought the team was close to developing a vaccine, but his reaction surprised her.

"Look," he said, "I deal with this every time we get a new doctor at the hospital, so I'm just going to tell you this now: I haven't spoken with any of my family members for more than four years. So if you're trying to wangle an introduction to any of the great Dr. Harpers, you're barking up the wrong tree."

"What?" said Kat, surprised. "Jack, you've totally got the wrong idea. I just meant that your parents' research has been extremely useful."

When he still looked skeptical, Kat went on.

"Selena mentioned your family during my first few days here. What I don't understand is why it should be any sort of secret. If I came from a family like yours I'd be telling everyone. With those kinds of connections in the medical field—"

"Connections with the Harpers are only useful if you're doing what they want you to do," he said. "If you're trying to forge your own path, then being a member of the Harper family is more of a liability than an advantage."

Kat nodded slowly. "I'm guessing they didn't love it that you dropped out of medical school."

"That about sums it up," he said.

She wanted to ask him more, but she could see that the subject was closed.

Why did he have to smell so good? Her plan—the plan that had sounded so good in her mind earlier that morning—was not going to work.

She'd had high hopes that if she could simply spend more time with Jack she might start to think of him as a normal person, instead of someone she felt unaccountably attracted to. But the more time she spent with Jack, the more tantalizing he became. The question of whether his eyes were blue, or more of a deep sea-green, was becoming a matter of some urgency to her, as she found her mind wandering back to his eyes anytime she tried to concentrate.

She and Jack had been housed together in a small room at the far end of the hospital's rarely used west wing. Selena had apologized for the small size of the designated isolation area and had made a halfhearted offer to try to find a way to provide separate rooms for them, but Kat could tell her friend was concerned about the hospital's limited capacity due to the influx of patients from the highway crash. Kat and Jack had both reassured Selena that they would be fine sharing a single room with privacy curtains, although secretly Kat wasn't thrilled at the idea, and from the expression on his face, she could tell that Jack felt the same way. But if sharing a room with Jack would help to make room for more patients, then Kat would cope with the situation the best she could.

Selena had arranged for the infectious disease team to run blood tests on the affected patient. It would take anywhere from a few hours to a few days to be sure. If the team confirmed that the patient did have the super-flu, then Kat and Jack would be spending at least the next ten days together, to ensure that neither of them showed any sign of having contracted the virus.

Kat hoped with all her heart that the patient didn't have the virus—both for the patient's sake and because she wasn't sure how she was going to be able to sleep knowing Jack was a mere two feet away from her.

The room was sparse: it contained two gurneys with privacy curtains, a shared bathroom, and an old television set that could access about three network channels. With their limited entertainment options Kat could tell that it was going to be a long ten days, if it came to that.

It didn't help that their close quarters only served to highlight how different they were from one another. She could tell by the way that Jack had haphazardly thrown his belongings about the room that he was the kind of person who didn't seem to mind clutter. She, on the other hand, preferred things to be neat and orderly—even if they would only be staying there for a few days.

"We should decide which parts of the room are yours and which are mine," she said. Maybe keeping their things to separate areas would help her to ignore the mess.

He blinked, looking around the tiny, five-hundred-square-foot room. "Isn't that kind of irrelevant in a room this small?" he said. "I don't think there's much we can do to avoid each other's space."

Kat gritted her teeth. She had a feeling that she wanted to tolerate his clutter about as much as he wanted to talk about his family.

"Some people might say that in a tiny space it's even *more* important to be clear about what goes where," she said.

"Fine," he replied. "How about I stay on my gurney and you stay on yours, and the rest can work itself out?"

She took a deep breath.

You're learning how to relax, she reminded herself. *You're learning how to let go and live in the moment. Maybe this is your chance to practice that.*

The Old Kat would have insisted on trying to win the argument. The New Kat was going to disengage.

She unpacked a small mountain of meditation workbooks and arranged them at the foot of her gurney in a neat stack, making sure they were organized by subject and author's last name. If she had to be in quarantine she might as well use her time productively.

When Selena had heard about Kat's mission to spend the year learning how to relax she'd provided Kat with an extensive collection of self-help workbooks, meditation recordings, and podcasts on mindfulness. Selena had termed the project "Operation Rebound," while Kat preferred to think of it as "Operation Inner Peace." She'd gotten through about a third of the workbooks, but inner peace was still proving elusive.

Learning to relax was a much more daunting task than she'd originally thought.

The key to achieving a relaxed state, according to all of her meditation recordings and workbooks, was to practice putting aside distracting thoughts in order to turn her mind to the present moment. So she sat on her gurney with her legs crossed and her eyes closed as a soothing voice through her headphones instructed her. And she tried to follow the instructions—she really did.

First she turned aside all thoughts about Jack's eyes.

Then she turned aside all thoughts about his hair, and what it might feel like to run her fingers through it.

Then she turned aside her thoughts about whether that tantalizing scent of his might have a bit of sandalwood in it. Was the smell just *him*, she wondered, or did he put on some sort of cologne?

It was strange, she thought, that she didn't have to try very hard to keep her mind off Christopher. It was Christopher who'd broken her heart, after all. Just three days before their wedding. Her heart still ached to think about it. But, even though she was sad about the wedding, and the end of all the things she'd envisioned for their lives together, she didn't find Christopher crossing her mind very often.

Sometimes she found herself feeling sad about the breakup, or angry about the way he had gone about it, but oddly she didn't find herself thinking about Christopher *himself*. She certainly didn't find herself constantly distracted by thoughts of him. Not the way she was by thoughts of Jack.

Jack's main goal, in most relationships, was always to avoid getting too close. As someone who had been overshadowed by his family and their prestigious medical careers for much of his life, it was important to Jack to be his own person. But avoiding closeness was difficult in the tiny quarantined room. It had only been a few hours, and he already wasn't sure he would be able to make it for that much longer.

At first their sharing a room had seemed practical. But now that Jack was faced with the fact that he would be sleeping just a few feet from Kat that very night... He tried to make certain his behavior was as gentlemanlike as possible at all times. If he couldn't hide his attraction from himself, then he at least wanted to hide it from her.

Kat sat meditating on her gurney. She seemed so serene. She was ambitious, just as Sophie had been, but then, he could never picture Sophie practicing at a hospital like Oahu General, focusing on patient care rather than prestigious research projects.

Kat certainly wasn't like Sophie. Usually when people in the medical world learned who Jack's family was they couldn't wait to talk to him about how his father's books had changed their lives, or how his mother had inspired them to go into medicine. But in six weeks Kat hadn't said a thing to him, despite knowing.

Except for just a moment ago, when she'd simply mentioned his parents' books and he'd assumed the worst. He wondered now if he'd acted prematurely.

Kat was obviously at the top of her field. She should be at a prestigious hospital on the mainland. Somewhere far away from him. Then he wouldn't have to think about the red curls cascading down her back. What was she doing here, on his island, at *his* hospital?

With all those books she looked as if she should be going on some sort of meditation retreat.

When he stepped over to the carefully organized set of workbooks that were piled in a neat stack at the edge of Kat's gurney she yanked her headphones out.

"Sorry if I interrupted," he said.

"I wasn't having much success anyway," she said. "It's kind of hard to focus on the present moment when you're stuck in a small room with bad lighting, waiting to find out if you've contracted a life-threatening illness."

He nodded in agreement and picked up one of the books.

"'*Zen and the Art of You*,'" he read aloud. "'*Finding the Inner Child Within Your Inner Self.*' What *is* all this stuff?"

"It's part of my project to learn how to relax," said Kat. "I thought I'd use this time to get into my Zen."

"Into your... Zen?"

She tried to explain. "It's like...trying to live in the moment. To take life one step at a time. Not to plan, but to accept what comes in each moment."

"To go with the flow?"

"Exactly," said Kat. "Only, it's harder than it sounds. Especially since I've never been a very go-with-the-flow type of person."

He raised his eyebrows in mock surprise. "You're kidding?"

She glared at him, and he briefly considered whether he might need to duck and run for cover.

But then she groaned and said, "Look, this stuff doesn't come naturally to me. I've never been very good at letting go of all the things I have to worry about. When I lived in Chicago, sometimes I tried going to the beach on Lake Michigan to de-stress—but you know what happened every time? I couldn't shut my brain off. I'd think about the patients who needed me, or the things I'd left unfinished, or other doctors and nurses I needed to communicate with. Or the hundred other things I had to do the next day. It was so hard to figure out how to let it all go that eventually I stopped trying."

"But you're trying again now? What changed?"

Her face grew sad. "The Day of Doom," she said.

That sounded pretty intense. Was that the reason Kat had wanted to move to Hawaii? He'd simply assumed that she wanted a break from her regular life, or had romantic illusions about working in a tropical setting. It had never occurred to him that she might be running away from something.

"I suppose it does sound dramatic," she continued.

For a moment he thought she might be blinking back tears, but it must simply be the way the light hit her eyes.

"It was just a bad breakup, really. That and some other things all happened at once. Just bad timing."

Ah. So she wasn't running from something so much as some*one*. "Breakups are hard," he said. "If it makes you feel any better you're not the only one who's ever run off to Hawaii after a bad breakup."

She lifted her eyebrows. "You?"

"Me. After my own exceptionally hard breakup."

She gave a soft chuckle. "So we're both unlucky in love? And I thought you and I had nothing in common."

He snorted. "I'd have to believe in love first, in order for us to have that in common."

"Oh, no, you don't," she said.

"Don't what?"

"Don't try to beat me at cynicism. My breakup was way worse than yours—I guarantee it. No one believes in love less than I do. Trust me, pal, I have given up on love."

He raised his eyebrows. "Have you?"

"What—you don't believe me?"

"You just don't seem to be the type to give up on love."

"Oh, but I have. I've given up on love way harder than you ever could."

"Wait a minute," he said. "Has this become a contest, Kat? Are we having a contest to see which of us believes in love the least?"

She laughed. "Yes. We're having a contest to see who is the saddest and unluckiest in love, because that might be the only way to cheer ourselves up. So tell me if you can top this: my fiancé left me just three days before our wedding."

"Hmm…" he mused. "That *is* going to be hard to beat. But I think I can."

"I don't know… I think when it comes to sad love stories, getting jilted three days before your wedding is going to win every time."

"How about this? My fiancée left me for my brother."

Jack didn't know why he was telling her this. He never talked about Sophie with anyone. But talking to Kat felt so easy.

She stopped laughing and grew quiet.

"It's all right," he said. "It was a long time ago."

"What happened to her?"

"She lives in Nebraska now. She's a doctor too."

He wasn't sure he was ready for this after all. He flipped the pages of one of Kat's workbooks, which seemed to contain very specific instructions on how to achieve a relaxed state.

"You know, I'm not sure you're doing this right," he said.

"Excuse me?" she said. "Is there a *wrong* way to relax?"

"I'm just not sure relaxing is something you can learn from a book," he said. "I mean, doesn't it seem like what you're doing is the exact opposite of what you're trying to learn?"

She bristled. "What are you talking about?"

He picked up the color-coded document that Kat had printed out, which outlined each major school of thought on meditation and Kat's views on their various pros and cons.

"You're meant to be trying to learn how to live in the moment, but you're doing it exactly the way you've always done things: by planning, organizing, and obsessively studying everything there is to know about relaxing. You're practically getting yourself another doctorate in relaxation."

She snatched the document from him. "That may be the case, but this is the only way I've ever been able to learn anything. I got though medical school by throwing myself at my books and studying longer and harder than anyone else."

"Yeah, but you're not in medical school anymore. You're trying to enjoy life—not study it."

"Then what do *you* think I should do, if you're so certain all my workbooks aren't going to help?"

He considered for a moment. "So much of your life is about taking care of other people," he said. "You need some excitement that's focused on *you*, not someone else. You need something that gives you a thrill."

"A thrill?" She looked doubtful. "That goes against everything I'm reading here. All the exercises in these books are about slowing down and focusing on the present moment."

"Nothing gets you focused on the present like an adrenaline rush."

He warmed to his theme. Every time he jumped out of a helicopter to reach a patient in a remote or inaccessible area, every time he resuscitated a patient from cardiac arrest, or delivered a baby on the way to the hospital, he was completely caught up in the present moment.

"Think about it," he said. "When do you feel the most calm, the most confident?"

"Hmm…" she said slowly. "Probably those moments in the ER when we're slammed with trauma cases."

"Exactly," said Jack. "It's the same for me. You get totally lost in the moment. You forget about any of your own worries and problems and just focus on what's in front of you."

"Okay," she said thoughtfully. "You might be on to something. But I can't just spend my entire life in the ER. That kind of defeats the purpose of learning how to relax when I'm not at work."

He shook his head. "You don't have to spend your life in the ER."

"Then what?"

"It could be anything," he said. "Something that feeds your sense of adventure. Something new…something exciting. Something crazy and out of the box. Hiking, surfing, cliff jumping…"

"Cliff jumping?"

"Hurtling yourself off a cliff into the ocean is a great way to gain mental clarity. You're never as certain of what you want in your life as you are when you're falling through the air."

"Um…because you're facing death?"

"Facing death? Absolutely not." Then, before he could stop himself, "I'll take you. We'll only jump in places where I know exactly how deep the water is and what the rocks are like underneath. Safety first. Safety is what makes it exciting instead of terrifying."

Wait a minute. You're supposed to be trying to spend less time with her—not more. The second this quarantine is lifted you're out of here, remember? Whether that's ten hours or ten days from now.

But she was already smiling back at him. "Spoken like a true paramedic," she said.

At the sight of her smile he could feel his resolve to keep his distance slipping away. He needed to regroup.

"Well," he said, "when we get out of here maybe a group of us can go. The two of us and Marceline, Kimo…"

He saw something change in her eyes. Was it disappointment? Or relief?

"Sure," she said. "What better way to bond than over dangerous, death-defying stunts?"

"Not dangerous—*exciting*," he said. "I wouldn't let anything happen to you."

She gave him another small smile, making her face glow. "I'm starting to believe that's true. But, since the two of us are stuck in here for now, would you happen to have any ideas about what kind of exciting thrills we could enjoy in a five-hundred-square-foot, poorly lit, windowless room?"

Jack didn't dare voice the first suggestion that came to mind. Or the second. Or the third.

Instead, he simply said, "I play a mean Gin Rummy, if that's the kind of thrill you have in mind?"

A few hour later Kat lay on her gurney, trying unsuccessfully to sleep.

She kept replaying that conversation with Jack in her head. For one moment she'd almost thought he was suggesting they go on a date. But that was stupid. What had he ever done that would even remotely have given her that impression?

He'd simply meant to help her as a friend. He'd been watching her try to relax and he'd actually come up with a pretty good idea. How had she never thought of it before? Jack had been absolutely right to notice that she felt the most like herself when she was caught up in life-or-death situations. It was one reason she loved her ER shifts so much. The intensity of getting a patient's heart going again, or rushing to alleviate a trauma survivor's pain, was thrilling for her.

Cliff jumping.

As crazy as it sounded, Kat couldn't stop thinking about it. Hadn't her entire decision to come to Hawaii been one giant, impulsive leap into the unknown? After making such a huge change to her life, jumping off a cliff might almost feel easy in comparison.

It had been kind of Jack to offer to take her. Although he'd been eager to clarify that he was only suggesting they go as friends. And he'd been so adamant in asserting that she wouldn't come to any harm. He'd seemed almost fierce in his protectiveness of her.

But that was probably because he was a responsible person. He'd be protective of any friend he was with.

So why couldn't she sleep? Why was she just lying here, feeling disappointment settle into her stomach over and over again?

She thought about when he'd told her he didn't believe in love. She'd said the same to him. But did he really mean that? And what if he did? Why should it matter to her?

Suddenly Kat couldn't stand it for a moment longer. She was done with being in quarantine.

She sat straight up on her gurney and threw off her blankets.

This ends now, she thought. *I'm not staying here another minute longer than I absolutely have to.*

She had a plan, and she had no doubt that Jack would agree with it. After all, it was what a good friend would do.

Several feet away, Jack was failing to get any sleep as well. He glared at the privacy curtain that surrounded his gurney. Why the hell did it have to be so thin?

To his surprise, he saw it was rustling. And then Kat appeared in front of him.

"Hey…" Her voice was low, husky. "Can we talk for a sec?"

"What is it?" he asked as she stood in front of him in a pair of pink silk pajamas.

He didn't want to admit just how much he'd allowed this very scene to creep into his wildest fantasies—fantasies he'd been trying to push out of his mind since the moment they'd been put into quarantine together. The ridiculous idea that she'd slip into his enclosure, gaze into his eyes, and say something like...

"We need to take our clothes off."

Jack looked at her in disbelief, uncertain of how to take in what he'd just heard. "We need to *what?*" he said.

"Strip," she replied matter-of-factly. "I don't know about you, but I can't take it in here for another minute—and I'm sure as hell not spending the next ten days here. All my research with the experts from the university has indicated that patients with the super-flu virus become symptomatic within the first twelve hours of exposure. Neither of us has shown even the slightest sign of having contracted the virus. So here's what we're going to do. You'll examine me, I'll examine you, and once we've confirmed that there's absolutely no sign of the illness in either of us we'll call Selena. After all, I'm the one who's been studying this illness more than anyone on staff. I think I should be qualified to tell whether the two of us have been infected or not."

Jack noticed that Kat was shaking. Was she really so desperate to get out of here? He wondered if she was starting to get claustrophobic in the cramped space. Or maybe she just wanted to get away from him.

"If this is about needing to get some space, I'm sure we can tell Selena that we've changed our minds and want separate rooms," Jack said.

"That won't work. The hospital's at capacity. But that

actually works in our favor. If we can convince her that we're showing no signs of the virus right now, it means one more free room in the hospital."

Jack considered this. Compared to the prospects of limited entertainment, uncomfortable sleeping arrangements, and hospital food, the thought of getting out of here was tempting.

The problem was, the idea of a naked Kat in front of him was pretty tempting, too.

The pajamas that Kat wore were pretty thin. He could see the curve of her hip underneath her pajama top. The silk shorts revealed long, slender legs.

He decided to try reasoning with her on a professional level.

"If this is about you being afraid of having contracted the flu, I wouldn't worry too much," he said. "The chances are extremely low. They've just got us quarantined in here out of an abundance of precaution. I know it's a hassle, but it's the appropriate procedure to follow."

"It's not that," said Kat. "I doubt either one of us actually has the flu. I just have to get out of here."

Jack was trying to muster his better self. In all the ways he had pictured the two of them together—and despite himself, despite every rational thought, he *had* been picturing it—he had never imagined it like this: him and Kat quarantined together in an isolated hospital room, surrounded by medical supplies.

To make matters worse, her request meant that she clearly thought of him as nothing more than a friend. She'd never ask such a thing of him if she had the slightest inkling of his feelings for her—or if she had any feelings for him.

He made a last weak attempt to do the right thing.

"Wouldn't you rather wait until morning?" he said. "The blood test results might not take much longer—maybe the infectious disease team will have some good news for us by then."

"I can't wait until morning," said Kat. "I can't wait another minute."

She hastily began to unbutton her pajama top.

It was too much for Jack.

"Hold on," he said, putting his hands over hers. He could feel her trembling, just as she had been in the water when they'd first met. "Are you sure this is what you want?"

She gritted her teeth and grabbed his T-shirt. "Jack. We are getting out of here. *Tonight.*"

There was no arguing with the determination in her voice. Or her eyes. Jack had a feeling that no one crossed Kat when she was in this kind of mood.

The authority in her voice was intimidating.

Her eyes burned into him.

He took a deep breath. His only hope was to remain as professional as possible. He didn't know how he was going to handle seeing Kat naked. He had been trying so hard to avoid thinking about her body…and now it was going to appear right in front of him. Only not in the way he'd fantasized about. The only way he was going to get through this was by putting as much professional distance between himself and Kat as possible.

"All right," he said. "If we're going to do this, we're going to be professional about it."

"Agreed," she replied. "Let's get the lights on."

Jack flipped a switch and harsh fluorescent lighting flooded the room.

Perfect. The least romantic lighting possible in one of the most sterile rooms imaginable. This is about as unsexy as it gets, and that's exactly how it needs to be right now.

He pulled a coin from the nightstand next to his gurney. "Flip to see who gets examined first?" he said.

"Don't bother. I'll go first," she said.

I hope you know what you're doing, Kat thought to herself.

She was certain that if she could prove that neither she nor Jack were showing any sign of the virus then she'd be able to convince Selena to let them leave this room. Then she wouldn't have to deal with this tantalizing closeness any more.

It had seemed like a great idea just a few minutes ago.

Now, in the harsh reality of the fluorescent overhead lighting, she was having second thoughts.

But she and Jack were both medical professionals. Surely they could be professional about this? They'd do a thorough examination of one another and then they'd be able to go home. As a doctor, Kat had long ago set aside any sense of squeamishness about undergoing or conducting examinations. This was simply what needed to be done—for the sake of her well-being and Jack's.

She couldn't stand waiting for the blood test results for another minute. She was at her absolute limit. She needed to get away from Jack as soon as possible. Seeing him naked might be a bit overwhelming, but only for a few moments. She could withstand a few moments of being close to him if it meant that she would be on her way home after it was over.

Her fingers shook so much that she kept fumbling the buttons of her pajama top.

"Here," he said. "Let me help."

He briskly undid the remaining silk buttons of her top, one by one. The top fell open, revealing the inner curves of her breasts. She kept her eyes locked with Jack's as he slipped the top from her shoulders and it fell to the floor with the quiet rustle of crumpling silk.

He cleared his throat and then, in a clipped, professional voice, said, "Let's start from the top."

Jack cupped her face, palpating her jawline.

"I'll need you to come a little closer so I can see your scalp," he said.

She stepped forward, only inches away from him. She couldn't stop herself from breathing in deeply. This close, his scent was intoxicating. She could barely stand. But Jack was pulling her inward, looking through her hair for any sign of the flu rash on the skin of her scalp and the back of her neck.

She tried to remain perfectly still. She didn't want to make the situation any more uncomfortable than it had to be. She was the one who'd asked for this, she reminded herself. And she was probably the last person that Jack was interested in seeing naked. He was doing her a favor. The least she could do was be professional about it.

After a few moments Jack stepped away from her. "Everything up top looks good," he said. "Let's take a look at the rest of you."

Was it just her imagination or had his voice seemed to break just a little at the end? Was he nervous? Kat couldn't think why he would be. He'd made it clear that at the very most he was only interested in her friendship. Examining her naked body was probably, for him, just the same as it would be when he examined any other patient.

He placed both his hands on her shoulders and ran them down her arms, feeling for any inconsistencies in her skin. Then he turned her around and ran his hands lightly over her back. His hands felt rough—rough enough to have a texture, but not too much. She could tell he used them often, both for hard work and as sensitive instruments.

They were hands that could rescue a drowning swimmer or pound a heart back to life.

Her own heart was pounding pretty hard. She couldn't help but give a small shiver.

"Sorry," he said, instantly attentive. "Are you cold?"

"N-no. I'm fine," she managed to stammer.

His hands moved faster now. Over her back and arms, rubbing her skin as though he were trying to warm her up. He turned Kat's body so that she was facing him again, and brought one of his hands up to touch her breast.

But before going on he stopped, his hand in midair. Their eyes locked.

Suddenly Kat knew that what she wanted had nothing to do with a professional examination. And it had nothing to do with any remote worry that she might have contracted the virus.

She stood in front of Jack, vulnerable, exposed, and she didn't know what to do next. She reached for him, ready to tell him that this whole idea was a mistake and that he didn't have to continue with the examination. She stepped an inch closer to him, reaching for the hand that still hovered over her breast.

Before she knew what had happened she found herself enveloped in Jack's arms. His mouth was covering hers, and she was kissing him back just as passionately. The scent of sun and salt water overtook her senses. His strong arms held her close to him, and then she was fumbling to reach under the soft gray T-shirt he slept in, which chafed enticingly against her bare breasts.

They broke for a moment as she lifted the shirt over his head, and then he kissed her again, and she lost herself in the feeling of her skin against his, his arms circling her.

He hoisted her onto the gurney and then climbed in himself. She lifted her hips so he could slide her pajama bottoms down and then off. A voice in her head cried out that *this* was what she had wanted—had, in fact, been looking for since he'd rescued her. There was no logic to it. There was only feeling: a solid, steady feeling that *this* was what she needed, *this* was the feeling she had been craving. *This* was living in the moment.

There had been no planning, no agonizing over the right decision, no making a pro versus con list and calculating her next step. She was completely caught up in the sensation of *Jack*—the roughness of his palms against her shoulders, her breasts; the strength of his chest and arms, the sweet-salt taste of his mouth crushed against her own.

Suddenly, they both froze. Someone was knocking on the door of the quarantine room.

"Kat?" Selena's voice rang out. "Jack? Is it okay if I come in?"

They leapt away from one another.

"Just give us a second!" Kat called out.

Kat stuffed her legs into her pajama bottoms at a furious pace. She tried to fasten the buttons on her top, but kept matching the buttons with the wrong hole. Finally she gave up and settled for wrapping the top around herself and folding her arms tightly in front of her, hoping Selena wouldn't see anything amiss.

Jack threw his shirt over his head and nodded at Kat. "C'mon in," he called to Selena, once he and Kat had perched themselves casually on a gurney, looking for all the world as though they'd been enjoying a casual midnight game of cards.

Selena entered the room and took in the scene: rumpled sheets, and a breathless Kat and Jack sitting next to each other on the same gurney.

"Sorry to visit you two so late at night, but I thought you'd want to hear right away," she said. "We've had a false alarm. The patient did not have the virus. It was just an ordinary case of shingles, which both of you will have been vaccinated against. So there's no need for either of you to be in here any longer."

"That's great!" said Kat and Jack, both at once.

"I had a feeling you'd be glad to hear it," Selena said. "I'm sure you're both eager to get out of here."

"Can't wait," said Kat.

"Neither can I," said Jack. "I'm not sure either of us could have handled one more minute stuck in here."

"Glad to be the bearer of good news," said Selena, turning to leave. "Oh, by the way, Jack, your shirt is on inside out."

CHAPTER FIVE

KAT FLOPPED HERSELF onto the sofa in Selena's office and let out a groan of frustration. A week had passed since the night she and Jack had been quarantined together. They hadn't seen much of each other since then, but when their paths had crossed they'd been friendly, polite, and professional with one another. There had been absolutely no discussion of their heated moment in the quarantine room.

As far as Kat could tell Jack seemed to want to pretend it had never happened. And if that was what he wanted, then she was happy to oblige.

Or so she told herself.

She might be able to stop herself from talking about that moment, but she couldn't stop herself from thinking about it. The way his hands had felt on her back, her shoulders, her thighs. The way his scent had completely enveloped her…the way his arms had enfolded her so completely.

The way he'd slipped off her pajama bottoms seconds before Selena had knocked on the door.

She was mortified by her behavior. Jack had been completely cool and clinical while he examined her—until she'd thrown herself at him like some sort of sex-crazed maniac. Her cheeks burned at the memory. He'd been trying to maintain a professional atmosphere. *She* had been the one to completely misinterpret the situation.

It was true that as their kiss had continued he'd seemed just as caught up in the moment as she had been. He hadn't objected when she'd removed his shirt, hadn't hesitated to assist her in the removal of the rest of her own clothing. But that only meant that he'd been swept away by the moment—a moment *she'd* instigated. His actions didn't mean that he'd shared the same feelings she'd had.

Kat agonized over what might have happened if Selena hadn't made her appearance.

In that moment her whole body had been crying out for Jack.

How far would they have gone?

Would having sex with Jack have cleared away all that tension, or added to it?

Kat realized that all those questions simply left her head spinning. Once again she was overanalyzing everything—trying to solve her situation with Jack like a puzzle, rather than focusing on what was right in front of her.

And what *was* in front of her?

A pile of evidence indicating that, at best, she and Jack were friends and nothing more. Two people shut up with one another for any period of time with nothing to do were bound to get confused into thinking they were developing feelings for one another.

But Jack didn't have any feelings for her that Kat could discern. She'd been practically naked in his hands and he'd been calm and collected, focusing on his examination of her skin. *She* was the one who had thrown herself at him. She hadn't been able to help herself. The sensation of his hands on her skin, of her bare breasts against his chest, still left her feeling a little dizzy.

Fortunately she was already slumped on Selena's couch, so dizziness wouldn't be a problem.

She'd wanted to keep the details of her time in quarantine with Jack a secret, but it ached to come bursting out of her. She was desperate for someone to understand, and Selena was one of her oldest friends.

Still, unburdening herself would probably be a lot easier if Selena's eyes weren't glowing with so much excitement over the rim of her coffee cup.

"I knew I should have found you separate rooms."

Despite her words, Kat caught Selena's wry smile as she sipped her coffee.

"This is serious, Selena," said Kat. "I don't know what to do."

"Why do you have to *do* anything?" asked Selena sensibly. "It sounds to me as though you like him. And, from what you describe, it sounds like he's into you as well. Didn't you say he asked you out on a date?"

"Not a *date* date. Not at all. Just a group thing…with friends."

Selena made a face of disgust. "'Group thing?' What a cop-out. If he likes you, why doesn't he just ask you out?"

"I'm not so sure he *does* like me," said Kat. "That kiss could have meant anything. For all I know it was completely one-sided. He was a perfect gentleman when I asked him to examine me. He was completely professional about it. I was the one who made it awkward by practically throwing myself into his arms."

Selena rolled her eyes. "Even if you *were* the one who started things, it sounds as though he was pretty willing to go along with it. Maybe…and I know this is a crazy idea, but hear me out…just maybe, the two of you might try *talking to each other* about how you feel."

"Oh, God," said Kat. "That's what I was afraid you were going to say. Selena, I can't bring this up with him. I just can't. What if he doesn't feel the same way?"

"Now, there's a good place to start. You say you're worried he may not feel the same way…but, Kat, do you even know how you feel about Jack?"

Kat paused and thought for a moment. How *did* she feel about Jack?

"I guess…after Christopher… I thought I was ready to swear off relationships… Not forever, but for a long time. I don't even know if I believe there's such a thing as love anymore."

Selena's eyes bored into Kat's skull. "Kat, I don't believe that you don't believe in love. I've known you for years, and that's just not you. But I *do* believe that you've been hurt, and that you're afraid of what could happen if you let yourself get involved with someone again."

Kat sighed. "I wish there was some way to test the waters without the chance that either of us could get hurt."

"Well, I guess you could just renounce love, cover your heart in armor, and never feel anything for anyone again. But that's just not you."

No, it wasn't. Selena knew her well. She was lucky to have such a wise friend who could offer her sage, sensible advice in times of need.

"Then again," Selena continued, with a gleam in her eye, "maybe there *is* a way you can find what you're looking for without either of you getting hurt."

Kat looked at Selena warily. "What are you suggesting?"

"I'm suggesting that if your feelings for Jack are purely on a physical level—if you truly don't think either of you are ready for a relationship of any kind—then why don't you just deal with those feelings?"

"Oh, come on, Selena!" said Kat. "Are you suggesting I just walk up to him and suggest that we…we just…?"

Selena raised her eyebrows. "Start doing the dirty deed? The hibbety-dibbety?"

Kat choked on her coffee. "Those are quite the colorful terms," she sputtered. "And even if I were going to act on it, I wouldn't know where to start. I don't even know if he's interested in me. Not in *that* way. If he was, wouldn't he be seeking me out? We barely talk to one another."

"You haven't been seeking *him* out, either," said Selena.

What if it was that simple?

What if Jack was just as eager as she was to finish what they'd started in quarantine, but didn't know how to approach her?

He couldn't possibly have any *romantic* feelings for her, but what if he was at least physically attracted to her?

They'd both said that neither of them believed in love... but what if there was a way to take emotion out of the equation?

She thought again of Jack's suggestion that she needed a thrill. Well, there was more than one way to seek excitement...

An idea began to form in her mind. It was risky, of course. But the only potential negative consequence was that she might feel embarrassed. And since she'd already embarrassed herself as much as she possibly could in front of Jack, one more moment of humiliation wasn't going to make much of a difference.

All she had to do was find him and pop the question.

Jack was having a hard time staying focused.

He was in one of the hospital supply closets, gathering up various medical supplies to restock the ambulance's med kit, but he was finding it impossible to keep his mind on his work.

He kept taking the wrong items, or looking down and finding that he'd put too much of something in his box.

Jack scowled at himself. He'd completely lost count of what he'd taken. Inventory was going to be pissed.

It had been like this for the past few days. He was able to focus just fine during emergency jobs. Just like always, when he was in the middle of an emergency he was at his peak performance. There was something about getting caught up completely in the moment and focusing on a medical emergency that allowed him to re-center himself, no matter what kind of emotional turmoil he might be going through.

But during the quieter times…when his mind had time to wander…it wandered straight back to Kat.

And specifically to that kiss.

He was completely mortified by his lack of professionalism. He'd been struggling to maintain a detached, clinical demeanor, and he'd utterly failed. Kat had been vulnerable and afraid and he'd taken advantage of her vulnerability. He couldn't have felt worse.

But he also couldn't keep his mind from returning to the way his hand had fit perfectly around her hip. To the softness of her skin. The way her hair had tickled his face when he'd buried his nose in it and inhaled the faintly tropical scent that wafted from her.

To make matters even worse, not only had he failed to hold himself to his professional standards…he'd *liked* kissing Kat. He'd felt…*desire*.

The plain fact was, he wanted more of Kat. And, try as he might to deny it, he knew deep down that he wasn't going to stop thinking about her. His body burned to finish what they'd started.

But would Kat even want to talk to him after he'd let himself get so carried away? They'd known each other for a little over a month, and this was already the second time he'd been unprofessional with her in a medical setting.

And yet during their kiss he'd felt her hands clutching at him, sensed her body pressing against his. In the heat of that moment she had wanted him, too.

But did she still want him? Or had her reaction to him simply been a response to a tense, pressured moment? In either case, he didn't know what to do.

More than anything, he wished he could call Matt. Even if his brother couldn't solve the problem, he would at least listen and understand.

But for the past four years that he and Matt hadn't been speaking Jack had had to work through his emotional problems on his own. He had lost his wingman and his confidant—the person he'd relied on most when it had come to figuring out his feelings.

His solution had been simply to avoid deep relationships, even non-romantic ones, and all the troublesome emotions that went along with them. But now that Kat was in the picture he wasn't sure how well that strategy would work.

He had tried to give Kat plenty of space since their time in quarantine had ended. He didn't want her to feel that he expected any more of her than she wanted to give. If she was interested in him, then she could make the next move. But he wouldn't blame Kat if she never wanted to see him again.

Which was why he was completely surprised when he turned around with his supply box and saw her standing in front of him.

"Sorry," she said. "Didn't mean to startle you."

She walked up to Jack and took the box from him, setting it on the floor.

"Well, this takes me back," she said. "It's been a couple weeks since we were in such close quarters together."

Was she angry at him?

Her face bore the same resolute look, the same determined set of her lips, that he'd noticed while they'd been in quarantine. Whatever she wanted to talk to him about, he realized there was no avoiding it. Not when she looked like that.

"I've been thinking," she said. "We're both adults. And we've gotten to know each other quickly, in a pretty short amount of time, due to circumstances beyond our control. But, no matter how unusual those circumstances may have been, they don't change the fact that we're in this situation now."

"And…what exactly *is* our situation?"

She took a deep breath. "I've been thinking a lot about that moment in quarantine."

He waited without breathing. He thought his heart might have stopped.

She went on. "You know the moment I mean. When we…kissed."

Her eyes flickered straight to his and he knew his heart hadn't stopped after all. It was pounding jackhammer-hard.

"I don't know about you," she said, "but I've had a hard time *not* thinking about it. The kiss, I mean. And I know you said that you don't believe in relationships. Neither do I. But in a way that makes us kind of ideal for one another right now."

He wondered where this was going. "How so?" he said.

"Well," she continued, looking nervous, but clearly determined to carry her point through, "anything involving emotions would probably be a terrible idea—for both of us. But then I started thinking that not every relationship has to involve emotions. Some relationships have a more… physical basis."

He was suddenly very aware that without the supply box in his arms there was nothing between the two of them.

He would barely have to reach out to slip an arm around her waist. Her nose was inches from his. It was very hard to think clearly with her standing so close.

"Emotions are complicated," he agreed, his voice growing husky. "Are you suggesting that we try letting things get more...physical between us?"

She nodded, gazing up into his eyes. He noticed that the top of her head would fit perfectly underneath his chin if she were just a few inches closer.

"I was thinking that, since we seem to have some physical feelings for each other, we could deal with those feelings on a physical level. But no deeper emotions. No romance."

It was exactly what he wanted—so why did he feel a surge of disappointment? Hadn't he been trying to avoid his physical attraction to Kat precisely because he didn't want to toy with her emotions or awaken any of his own?

He needed to be clear with her about who he was, to make sure she didn't get hurt. "I don't do hearts and flowers," he said.

"Who the hell said anything about hearts and flowers?" she replied.

"I just want to be clear about who I am. And what you're looking for."

"I know exactly what I'm looking for. Look, I was engaged to someone I thought I loved. He did the whole hearts and flowers thing. I've had enough of them. I've had enough of thinking about the future, the long term, the happily-ever-after. I want something different. You said when we were in quarantine that you don't believe in love. Well, neither do I. Love's not what I'm looking for right now. If I were, I'd be looking somewhere else."

"Are you sure this is what you want?" he said.

Despite the dim light in the supply closet he thought he could see a wicked gleam in Kat's eye.

"You were the one who said I needed a thrill," she said. "I'm trying to learn to live in the moment. And you did say you would help…"

"As long as we're clear about our expectations from the beginning."

"Crystal-clear," she said.

Kat pressed close against him. Any fleeting resistance, any reasons not to get involved that he might have briefly entertained were fading away.

And then his lips were brushing hers before he even knew what had happened. She was kissing him back, more deeply, and his tongue explored her mouth, desiring every inch of her that she could give. Her lips crushed against his, and he felt himself become swept away with the taste of her.

He wasn't sure how much time passed before she broke their kiss, pulling her head away from his. She still leaned against him, and his arms remained around her waist. As she looked up into his eyes he thought he saw flecks of gold within the green.

"So," she said, "I take it that we're in agreement? A purely physical relationship, to address an attraction that's on a purely physical level?"

"If you're in, I'm in," he said. "Purely physical. No emotions, no strings attached."

She let out a breath, as though she'd been holding it. "We should probably set up some ground rules," she said, suddenly seeming nervous. "Maybe we should make a list of what we expect from one another, to make sure things don't get too emotional…"

He pulled her closer to him again. "Here's the only

ground rule I want to work out right now," he said, his voice husky. "My place or yours?"

The next night found Kat laying out three different outfits on her bed, repeatedly accepting and rejecting each one.

It didn't matter what she wore, she tried to tell herself. She and Jack weren't supposed to be trying to impress each other. She didn't need to care if he liked what she wore. And yet somehow tonight it was unusually difficult to make an outfit choice.

The more she thought about her arrangement with Jack, the more confident she became that it was a brilliant idea. She'd only had a few boyfriends in her life, and all the way up until Christopher she'd been a serial monogamist, going through one long-term relationship at a time. Part of her was still a bit shocked at her proposal to Jack—but mostly she was excited about her first foray into spontaneous thrill-seeking. She was nervous, but excited, and she intended to enjoy every minute of it.

Even though it would be her first time having sex since before the breakup...

It's just a meaningless fling, she reminded herself. *Don't put too much pressure on it.*

Over the two years she'd dated Christopher she'd tried to meet his expectations in every way possible. He was a career-driven perfectionist, and she'd thought she'd admired those qualities in him. She'd even thought that she and Christopher were a little bit similar in that way.

But Christopher's perfectionism had always seemed to involve making her feel *less,* somehow. Every time he'd told her that she'd look great if she worked out a little more, or that her hair would look nice if she'd only wear it in a certain way, she'd believed him, and tried to do what would make him happy. But it had never seemed to be enough. And in the end it hadn't been.

Her arrangement with Jack meant that neither of them had to worry about expectations. The thought of that was wonderfully freeing. Tonight would be her first serious attempt to let loose and let go.

Kat's heart pounded in her chest as she pulled into the driveway of Jack's house on the beach. She wrapped her black leather trench coat more tightly around herself as she stepped out of the car. Her outfit was a risk; she was wearing the trench coat, heels, and not much else. She'd been a little worried about what might happen if she got pulled over, but she'd been very careful to drive at exactly the speed limit for the entire drive to Jack's house.

The nice thing about keeping their relationship on a physical level, she thought, was that now she could freely admit her attraction to Jack without worrying about where it might lead. It would lead to sex with Jack and no further. Nice and simple. No other complications to worry about. No reason to be nervous.

Two hours is an awfully long time to spend deciding what to wear when you're supposedly just interested in a purely physical relationship, a small, disloyal corner of her mind piped up as she stepped out of the car.

She considered leaving her purse inside the car, underneath the passenger seat, but then she remembered the pack of condoms she'd brought with her, color-coded by type. Would Jack have thought about protection? Probably, but you never knew... Better to be on the safe side.

She grabbed her bag and walked up the sand-covered sidewalk.

He opened the door and stood in front of her, in dark jeans and a very tight white T-shirt. The T-shirt left very little to the imagination. Even in the dim porchlight she could see the firmness of his torso underneath the shirt.

And as she looked at the well-defined muscles all traces of the worry she'd had about the wisdom of her decision melted away. Whatever happened after tonight, it was going to be worth it if it gave her a chance to feel those arms pressing her against that chest one more time. This was going to be *good*.

He stood in the doorway, leaning on one arm, and she could see him taking her in. He was looking at how tightly she had her black trench coat wrapped around herself. He raised an eyebrow rakishly, taking in her bare legs, and she had a feeling that he was drawing the obvious conclusion about what else she might be wearing under the coat.

She saw him swallow, and suddenly she felt much more confident. Whatever false bravado he might display, she could tell that Jack wanted this every bit as much as she did.

She might have thrown herself at him at the hospital, but that had been then. Right now he was looking at her as though she were a package he couldn't wait to unwrap. Or a meal he'd like to devour.

She gave a shiver that had nothing to do with the cool breeze coming from the beach.

He smiled and reached down to grab one end of the belt of her trench coat, using it to pull her forward until she was pressed against him. He slipped an arm around her and pressed her closer, nuzzling his nose into her hair.

"You really came dressed for the occasion," he said, reaching down and putting his palm against her bare thigh. He murmured the words into her hair, his lips brushing against her neck as he spoke.

Her cheek was pressed against his chest, and her nose came just to the small hollow in his neck. Kat inhaled deeply. Ah, there it was… Eau de Jack Harper. She could finally allow herself to revel in it.

It was nice to be enveloped by Jack's scent without having to try to force her mind off it. But they were still outside. There was only so much that could be accomplished.

Kat marshaled her thoughts enough to say, "You have no idea. But if you want to see the rest of this outfit you're going to have to invite me in."

As she lifted her face from his chest he bent to kiss her. He still held her in his arms, though, and as he turned back into the house, he took her with him, so that they were just inside the entrance when he shut the door. He continued to kiss her, pressing her against the wall. His kisses were soft at first, then deeper and more deliberate.

Kat was grateful for the support of the wall behind her—it kept her from melting into Jack's arms right away. Her senses were full of nothing but him. But then she heard a faint ringing sound from further within the house.

Jack stopped kissing her and said, "Oh, right…the bouillabaisse. I set the timer."

"Bouley-*what*?"

"Bouillabaisse. It's French; it's a kind of stew with seafood and herbs. It's very good."

He headed further back into the house, presumably toward the kitchen, and Kat followed. Her mind was swirling. *Jack had cooked for her?* Why? She'd thought they were just going to have sex. Having a meal together…a meal he'd *cooked* for her…didn't quite fit with her idea of an emotionless night of physical passion. But then, maybe it wasn't a big deal. Plenty of people liked to cook. It didn't mean anything special.

Jack was shutting off the timer as she entered the kitchen and he grabbed a spoon. "Here, have a taste," he said, turning the heat on the stove to a low simmer and holding the spoon to Kat's lips.

Her eyes widened as she tasted the broth. "Wow, that's really good!" she said. "I don't know what I'm more excited about: eating that delicious stew, or…or…" She blushed. "Or some of our other plans for this evening."

He set down the spoon and put his hands against her hips. "Speaking of which," he said, "we were in the middle of something before that timer so rudely interrupted us…"

He leaned in and brushed her lips against his.

"Should we have dinner first?" she whispered. "I didn't know you were going to go to all this trouble."

"Actually, I'm more of a dessert-first kind of guy," he said, flicking off the stove and giving her his full attention.

Kat felt her thoughts slowly melting away as his body pressed against hers and their lips came together. And as they kissed her need for him began to intensify. The pent-up frustration of their interrupted moments had been building for days, and finally—finally—there was nothing between the two of them.

Well, not much, anyway…

Jack's hands moved to the belt of her trench coat. It was tied tight, but with a good wrench in the right direction the coat fell open, revealing her black lace underwear and nothing else.

"Wow," Jack said. "That is *not* what I expected to see under there."

"Hmm… Well, I have a few button-up blouses in my closet at home. Maybe I should wear one of those next time?" she said.

"Don't you dare," he replied, pulling her roughly to him.

He slipped the coat from her shoulders, then began kissing her neck and breasts. He lifted one breast from the cup of her bra and she gasped as his tongue circled her nipple. An arc of pleasure shot through her as he attended to one breast with his mouth while he teased and stroked the other. Then he slipped his hands under her buttocks, and she instinctively wrapped her legs around his waist as he lifted her and took them both to his bed.

She could feel the tantalizing hardness forming under his jeans...could feel that her own body was eager for him.

He tossed her onto the bed and Kat sighed with pleasure as he slid her underwear from her. She waited for him to get onto the bed with her, but instead he simply looked at her, drinking her in with his eyes. Then he knelt down by the side of the bed and pulled her forward by her hips, dragging her to the edge. He kissed the inside of one thigh, and then the other, and suddenly she realized what he was about to do.

"You—you don't have to do that," she stammered. "I mean, I've never asked anyone to...and no one's ever wanted to..."

"Then don't you think it's about time someone did?" he said.

And after that Kat couldn't speak any more, because he was placing his mouth on the hot, warm space between her legs where she felt the most ready for him to be. His tongue attended to the small nub he found there until Kat thought she would burst with the heat and the wanting. She began to cry out, but he was relentless—he was going to make her explode. And explode she did, unable to control herself against the onslaught of his mouth against her.

Kat let herself sink into the mattress, shaking. She'd wanted him, and she'd known he was ready for her, but she hadn't expected this welcome detour.

She worried that after the intensity of the pleasure she'd just felt she wouldn't have the energy to move from where she lay, rendered immobile by the sensations that washed over her, lasting and lasting. But then she saw Jack taking off his shirt, and the sight of his washboard torso gave her renewed energy.

The faint line of hair that trailed from his chest to his stomach and disappeared into his navel suggested tantalizing possibilities. She reached out for his waistband and pulled herself to a sitting position. Fumbling with the button at his waist, she pulled his jeans and boxers off in one smooth motion, revealing his firm, erect manhood.

Something clamored for attention in a small, forgotten corner of her mind. *Oh, right—protection.* But her purse was all the way out in the living room. For the briefest of seconds she despaired at the thought of having to interrupt this moment by running out to rummage through her purse. But before she could mention it Jack reached down for his jeans, where they lay on the floor, and took a condom from one of the pockets.

Kat felt gratified that she hadn't been the only one planning for their safety—and she was especially glad that having a condom close at hand meant they wouldn't have to leave the bed right now.

He eased onto the bed with her, his body firm and warm between her legs. The length of him was hard, but velvety to her touch. He locked his gaze with hers and she nodded to let him know that she was ready. He entered her in one long thrust. She lifted her hips, pressing them against his so she could let him into her as completely as possible. Their bodies joined in a timeless dance, responding to the heat and desire each felt in the other.

It felt as if it had been ages since she had made love. And lovemaking had never felt like *this*. His rhythm matched hers perfectly, his long, slow strokes mirroring the rise and fall of her body as if they were meant to fit together.

She lost all awareness of herself as sensation overtook

her. She was lost in the smell of him, in the feeling of his hands on her hips and the backs of her thighs as he pushed himself into her. She ran her hands through his dark hair, as she'd wanted to since the moment she'd first laid eyes on him, arching her back. His chest was hard and warm against her breasts.

There was no sound but that of their ragged breaths melding together. Nothing existed outside of the sublime feelings that promised bliss was only moments away. She rocked her hips against his more quickly, unable to withstand the craving any longer, and his strokes came faster, pushing her toward euphoria.

She cried out in ecstasy as she felt herself shatter. And as she did, she felt him tremble within her, heard him say her name. As she raised her lips to meet his once more, she felt a tightness somewhere deep within her loosen.

They lay entangled in one another's arms, her head resting against his chest. She felt wonderfully free. There were no pressures, no tasks to accomplish. *This* moment was the moment she wanted to live in, and nothing could take her out of it.

CHAPTER SIX

JACK WOKE FIRST, to an unfamiliar whirring noise. Kat's cell phone was buzzing on the nightstand next to her side of the bed.

He gazed at Kat, who still slept peacefully, her back curved against his chest. It had been a long time since any woman had spent the night with him, but she had dropped off soon after their second round of lovemaking and he soon after.

He caressed the soft red waves of her hair, which spilled over the white pillow. The early-morning sunlight dappled her face, filtered by the tall palm trees just outside the window. She looked so peaceful.

When Kat was awake he could always read the worry in her face. She was so preoccupied with caring. No one could speak to Kat for five minutes without realizing that she was constantly thinking about everyone else: her patients, her co-workers, her friends…

Jack wondered if now he might have made it onto the list of people in Kat's life that she worried about. Cared about. And he wondered how Kat felt about the night before.

She'd seemed satisfied, but they hadn't really had the opportunity to discuss it. He was grateful that they'd put their arrangement to keep things purely physical in place.

Kat might deserve more, but he knew he wasn't the one who could offer it to her.

But, if nothing else, he could offer her a good breakfast.

He'd been thrilled to find that she liked his cooking. After they'd made love the first time they'd eaten the bouillabaisse with crusty French bread. He'd loved watching her eyes widen as she'd tasted her first sip of broth, and her exclamation later, when she'd tried his homemade rosemary and strawberry ice cream.

Then, after the ice cream, they'd gotten back to the reason they'd agreed to meet in the first place. He'd loved watching her other reactions as well: her eyes drinking in his body, resting on his manhood, her breath catching as he eased his length into her.

Yes, that had been nice. More than nice.

Now, he resisted the urge to kiss the nape of her neck. He leaned over to silence Kat's cell phone and then slipped out of bed, pushing back the thick white down comforter. The heavy blanket was probably overkill in the Hawaiian heat, but he liked to be warm in bed—and it seemed she did, too.

He wondered if it was a Midwestern thing. Both he and Kat were originally from places with cold, severe winters. There'd been some winters in Nebraska when he'd feel the cold in his bones. Maybe after coming from a place like that you could never get warm enough.

He went into the kitchen and surveyed the items in his refrigerator. He wanted to make something that would let him show off a little bit, but that would also look as though he hadn't gone to too much trouble. He pulled the ingredients for crepes from the refrigerator and the pantry, setting out blackberries, strawberries, and blueberries for toppings.

He'd loved to cook ever since he was young. His par-

ents had thought it a waste of time—why learn to cook
when you could hire someone to do it for you?—but Matt
had always been supportive of his hobby.

For just a moment he thought again that it would be nice
to be able to call Matt, to tell him about Kat. He shrugged
off the wave of sadness that always came over him whenever his brother came to mind, and tried to focus on the
pleasant view of the palm trees just outside his kitchen.
It was a beautiful day, as so many Hawaiian days were.
They could have breakfast out on the lanai.

He wondered if Kat would want to talk about last night
when she woke up. Try as he might to turn his mind to the
crepes he was preparing, he couldn't get his mind off what
she might be thinking…how she might be thinking of him.

As a paramedic, Jack required a certain amount of daring. He was used to running toward dangerous situations—
not away from them He had to take risks every day. But
for some reason those risks seemed a hell of a lot easier
than talking to Kat about her feelings.

Kat woke up in Jack's bed, blinking against the morning
sun. At first she was dismayed to find herself alone, but
then she noticed the noises and smells from the kitchen.

Surely Jack wasn't making breakfast?

She snuggled deeper under the covers, savoring the delicious memory of the night before. Then she frowned. The
plan had been for her to arrive at Jack's place, have some
brisk, efficient sex, and then return home.

But nothing had gone according to plan.

Instead, everything about last night had been a sensory
feast: the taste of the food he'd made for her, the feeling of
their bodies intertwined, the tenderness of his gaze matching the softness of his bed.

She'd never imagined that he would cook her dinner.

She'd been expecting a purely physical interaction, as they'd agreed: just sex and nothing more. But Jack had made it feel like a date. And the food had been so delicious it had almost felt as though he was trying to impress her. But why would he care about doing that?

She shivered underneath the warm comforter, remembering the feeling of Jack's skin next to hers and his hands exploring the curves of her body. Remembering his attention to her, the sensations he'd created, teasing her until her body sang with pleasure. A girl could get used to that kind of thing.

She'd meant to leave immediately afterward, but she hadn't been prepared to feel so utterly replete. She and Jack had lain in bed for some time after that first time, each of them basking in the pleasant glow that had radiated from the other's body.

She could have stayed like that forever, but then Jack had heard her stomach rumble. He'd wanted her to stay for dinner, and she hadn't felt she could leave without eating when he'd gone to so much trouble. And then they'd had ice cream afterward…and he'd kissed some of the ice cream off of her nose…and she'd returned his kiss more ardently than either of them had expected…

And then they'd returned to his big bed. And if the first time had been an expression of fierce need, the second time had been a slow and tender discovery of each other. Afterward, she'd fallen asleep without a second thought. But she'd never expected that she would wake up in his bed the next morning, listening to the clamor of pots and pans clashing together in the kitchen while he made breakfast for the two of them.

At least, she assumed it was for the two of them. Jack probably wasn't going to make something for himself and wave her out of his home.

Mission accomplished, Kat thought.

Her goal had been to let loose, and she had accomplished exactly that. All according to plan. Their "no emotions" agreement was working out just fine. Barely two months in Hawaii, and she was starting to get the hang of spontaneous thrills.

She shivered again, remembering the feeling of Jack's strong arms enveloping her, his hot skin next to hers. She could hear him humming in the kitchen. Whatever he was cooking in there, it smelled amazing. That clinched it. She was getting up.

She slipped out of bed, grabbed her phone and stumbled into the kitchen.

"Crepes okay?" Jack asked when he noticed her standing in the doorway.

She felt a surge of excitement upon learning that breakfast was indeed for both of them, although she tried to quash it down.

No emotions, remember? He's just being polite.

"I'm getting seriously spoiled with all this French food," she said.

For a moment he looked worried. "Do you like French food?" he asked. "I can always make something different if this isn't what you're in the mood for."

Kat lifted an eyebrow. She hoped it made her look like Marlene Dietrich, but she worried it made her look like a librarian giving a scolding.

She hurriedly let the eyebrow down, and said, "I'd hoped last night was enough of an indication of exactly what I like."

He seemed pleased.

Her phone whirred and she resisted the urge to check it, pushing it far away from her on the kitchen counter so that she wouldn't be tempted to look at it again.

"Do you need to get that?" said Jack.

"It's work. But we've both got the day off," she replied. "Whatever it is can wait until later, because I've decided that this morning is all about living in the moment. And *this* moment is all about crepes."

She popped a berry into her mouth, enjoying the sensation of sweetness as it burst over her tongue.

"Well, look at you, all relaxed and devil-may-care," said Jack, flipping the crepes in the pan. "Who *is* this woman who's so carefree all of a sudden?"

She shrugged and smiled. "I guess I finally found my Zen."

He spun more batter into the pan. "How does your Zen feel about crepes?"

"My Zen is very much in favor of delicious breakfast foods. And I'm so glad I get a chance to try more of your cooking. I wanted to last night, but I…we…kind of got caught up in some other things."

He smirked. "'Other things,' huh?"

She smiled and said, "You know…like the hibbety-dibbety."

"The hibbety-*what*? I don't think it's been called that since the Roaring Twenties. I think my great-grandparents might have used that one."

She blushed. "It's a private joke. A colorful euphemism Selena came up with a few days ago."

"You two seem pretty close?"

"Oh, yes, she's one of my best friends," said Kat. "We talk about everything with each other."

"Everything, huh?"

"Oh—well, now that you mention it… Maybe we should talk about how you and I are going to talk about the…"

"The hibbety-dibbety?"

She laughed. "Yes, that. What if people at work find out about us?"

"Well, we should probably take care to make sure that they don't."

For a moment she felt hurt, but then she reminded herself that Jack was just being practical. Their relationship wasn't really a relationship.

"Yes, broadcasting this around work would probably complicate things," she said.

"Exactly what I was thinking," he said. "Besides, since we've agreed to keep feelings out of it…well, it's not as though there's really anything to tell."

She lifted the coffee cup he'd given her. "Here's to not believing in love."

"Cheers," he said, clinking his own coffee cup against hers.

They were sticking to the plan. *Good*. Absolutely nothing had changed from the moment she had smelled the crepes from his bedroom to the moment they'd sat down to have breakfast together.

The Hawaiian sun beamed onto Jack's lanai just as brightly as ever, but if nothing had changed, why did she suddenly feel so…

Her thoughts were interrupted by her phone, which was whirring again.

"I've got a ton of messages from work," she said. "They want me to come in right away."

Jack looked at his own phone. "Looks like they want me as well. The hospital's facing a huge surge in patients, and they want the paramedics helping out in the ER with triage and first-line care."

"So much for our day off," Kat said. "It must be a major emergency if they want us both to come in. Are you ready to see how well we can keep our secret?"

* * *

Jack left first and arrived at the hospital several minutes before Kat. The ER was inundated with patients, all of whom were presenting with symptoms of the super-flu.

He joined a group of doctors and nurses at the reception desk, where Selena was briefing the staff on the situation.

"This is my worst fear," she said. "There's been an outbreak of the super-flu on the westward side of the island, and now people are coming here with flu symptoms." She paused and nodded at Kat, who had just arrived. "The good news is that thanks to Kat's great work with the infectious disease team, we were able to develop a vaccine ahead of the outbreak. All hospital staff have been vaccinated by now, which should increase the safety for everyone tremendously."

"We'll need to triage," said Kat. "Patients with no symptoms go to one wing of the hospital, where we can administer vaccines. Everyone showing symptoms goes to another wing, and from there we can determine level of care."

Selena nodded. "I want some of our more experienced paramedics staying in the ER today. Let's leave the ambulance callouts to the Emergency Medical Technicians. The patients who are going to need the highest levels of care are most likely already here at the hospital."

"It's all hands on deck," Selena finished. "Grab a patient, grab a chart, and get going."

Jack spent the rest of the morning caught up in the flow of ER triage. He administered vaccines to patients without flu symptoms, and sent those with more severe medical needs to the appropriate department.

He'd been working so hard that he wasn't even sure how long he'd been at the hospital when a woman pulled at his arm and begged him to take a look at her teenage son.

It was the first case Jack had seen that morning that

caused him serious concern. The boy's mother said his name was Michael, and reported that he'd had a high fever and vomiting since the day before. Jack leaned in to examine Michael's cheeks, which were ashen. His face was contorted in pain, and he was holding his hand to his lower abdomen on the right side.

With a sinking feeling, Jack realized the boy probably had appendicitis. He'd need a doctor to confirm it, but based on the boy's pallor and the pain that seemed to be coming from the vicinity of his belly button, his guess was that if the appendix hadn't burst already, it would soon. Even as Jack examined the boy, he could see that his breathing was labored, and he seemed to be moving in and out of consciousness.

Michael would need surgery, fast… And Jack knew for a fact that it would be at least an hour before any of the hospital's surgeons would be free.

Jack waved at Christine, one of the nurses who was also helping with triage. "We need a gurney over here," he said. To the boy's mother, he added, "Don't be afraid. I'm going to come back with one of our doctors, and we'll do the best we can for him."

Jack straightened up. He looked out over the sea of patients that filled the ER and spotted Kat at the far end of the hall.

"Kat!" he yelled, waving to flag her down. "We've got a problem."

"What is it?" she said.

"There's a kid in the ER with what's probably appendicitis. Looks like he could be close to peritonitis."

"So call for a surgical consult."

"I will—but I already know that Ernest is out sick, and Jacquelyn's already working on a patient with a coronary artery bypass. Omar's on call, but he's at a continuing education conference across the island. Bottom line: it'll be at least an hour before a surgeon can get to this kid, and I'm not sure he can wait that long."

They'd already begun walking back toward the boy. Two nurses had already wheeled a gurney toward Michael and were easing him onto it while his mother stood by, looking worried.

"He's fading fast," said Christine quietly. "We should bag him now, because we'll need to intubate the second we get him into the OR."

Jack could see that Christine was right—Michael's breathing was so shallow as to be almost nonexistent. She had already positioned a bag-valve mask over the boy's nose and mouth. The self-inflating bag attached to the mask could be compressed to deliver oxygen to Michael's lungs until he was put on a ventilator and prepped for surgery, which needed to happen soon. Jack nodded and used both hands to apply slow, steady compressions to the bag.

"I already put in the surgical call, but it's going to be a while," Christine said. "We're going to need to make some quick decisions."

Kat's lips were a thin line. "I did a year on surgical service before I switched to internal medicine," she said.

"So you've done appendectomies before?" said Jack.

"I have, but it's been years," Kat replied.

"You might be the kid's best shot," added Jack. "Think you can do this?"

Kat paused.

She looked at Jack and Christine.

It was her call.

A year ago she might have refused. Not because she couldn't do the procedure, but because regardless of her training it wasn't her place, as an internal medicine doctor, to do surgery. But now she looked at her team and realized she had their full support.

Christine was awaiting her decision; Jack seemed confident in her.

If they could be confident, then so could she. She'd worked long enough at Oahu General by now to know that its team could handle anything.

"Okay," she said. "Let's get him into the OR. Worst-case scenario: we keep him alive until a surgeon gets here." She yelled across the ER floor to the reception desk: "Kimo! Call Tom from Anesthesiology and tell him we're prepping a patient in OR Two. And stick your head into OR One and make sure Jacquelyn knows what we're doing, in case she closes early."

They wheeled the gurney down the hall to the OR, with Jack continuing to apply compressions to the bag-valve mask, keeping pace with the team. Michael's mother ran after. "Can I come in during the surgery?" she asked.

"Not during the surgery, but you can wait right outside," Jack said. "And I'll be out right away to let you know how things are going."

"Please," she said, "stay with him. I'll feel better if I know someone's in there looking out for him."

"Don't worry," Jack said. "Your son's in good hands."

Kat knew how Michael's mother felt, though. Jack had a way with patients that made his presence inherently reassuring. She'd felt it herself. In a crisis situation, he emanated a steady calm. She'd seen patients draw from it, no matter how much distress they were in, and she'd felt herself draw from it, too. As Kat and her team scrubbed in, while the patient was prepped for surgery, Tom, the anesthesiologist, poked his head into the scrub room.

"Just wanted to let you know that his fever spiked even

higher just before we put him under," he said. "My guess is the appendix ruptured."

"Then it's a good thing we're almost ready to go in," she said.

With the patient intubated, there was no longer any reason for Jack to stay, but Kat stopped him before he left to return to the ER.

"Wait," she said. "His mother asked you to stay with him."

"Don't worry," he said, nodding toward the surgical nurses. "You're in good hands, too." But Kat thought he must have seen the fear in her eyes above her surgical mask, because after a moment's hesitation, he said, "But I'll stay to observe, if you think it's a good idea."

Kat hadn't had much chance to see the surgical nurses at Oahu General in action, but it was clear that they were experienced and knew each other well. They bantered with an ease Kat didn't feel as she began her first incision.

Her hand didn't shake, but she felt nervous. It had been several years since she'd done this procedure. Still, there was no question that the boy would die without immediate intervention. As Kat continued with the procedure her confidence grew. It took less than a minute for her to locate the appendix. As soon as she had it isolated from the other organs, she asked the nurse to place the Babcock clamps at its base.

Kat eased her scalpel along the appendix, removing it from tip to base. A cheer went up among Jack and the nurses as the appendix was removed, and Kat smiled. This atmosphere was so informal compared to what she was used to—and yet a cheer and a moment to enjoy a successful surgery seemed so appropriate to her now.

She began to close, making careful stitches on the patient's abdomen.

"Nice work," said a voice behind her. She looked over in surprise, to see Omar watching her with an appraising eye.

"Omar?" she said. "When did you get here?"

He must have driven at breakneck speed to get to the hospital from his conference.

"You were about halfway through the procedure when I got in. But you were doing so well I thought I'd just let you continue. No reason to interrupt a great job. Maybe we should get you on the surgical rotation?"

"No, thanks," she said. "Consider me a one-time pinch-hitter."

"Well, you did a great job," Omar said. "That patient is lucky you were here today. We all are."

Kat looked across the patient at Jack. She didn't know if she would have been able to do the appendectomy without him, but she was certain the procedure had been made much easier thanks to his quiet confidence pulling her through it.

Jack leaned over to look at the stitches she was finishing. "Nicely done," he said.

"See?" she replied. "I told you I was good at stitches."

It had been an exhausting day. After hours of conducting triage, administering medication and vaccines, and performing a surgery she hadn't undertaken for several years, Kat was spending the last moments of the day on the hospital's roof. She'd learned it was an excellent place to take in the Hawaiian sunrise.

She was usually alone up there, but today Jack had followed her. "You did great today," he said.

"Great?" She snorted. "You must have seen how clumsily I made that McBurney incision. You must have seen how nervous I was. It's been years since I did any surgery."

"You saved a boy's life," he replied. "Try to focus on the big picture."

She gave a dark laugh. "I've never been very good at that," she said. "Why focus on the big picture when there are a thousand small details I can obsess over?"

"I know it's not always easy for you to stay in the moment, but this is a good one," he said. "I'm not saying the little things don't matter—I'm just saying enjoy the good you did."

"I'm trying to," she said, watching the sky change from gold to rose as the sun went down. "But it's never come easily to me. My family aren't all doctors, like yours. It was my father's dream for me to become a doctor, and after he died my mom had to work two jobs to help me get through medical school. It's important for me to be the best doctor I can be. Not just for myself, but for them, too."

He nodded. "But maybe sometimes you forget that you don't have to try to be the best anymore. You got there. You fulfilled your dreams and theirs. Now you can just be who you are."

"Be who you are?" she repeated. "It sounds so simple. But it's not." She turned toward him. "Do you know why I really came to Hawaii? I got fired, Jack. From my job at Chicago Grace."

"Why?"

"I had this whole plan I wanted to implement. This huge, sweeping plan. And I still believe in it. But I didn't bother to see if it was a good fit for that hospital. I just tried to push it through. The result was a complete disaster. And the worst part was that I felt as though I'd completely let my father down by losing my job. I didn't just want to be a good doctor there, I wanted to make a real difference in medicine... Only, once I got fired I wasn't on the superstar track anymore. And he'd always seen me as a superstar. So it wasn't just the firing that hurt...it was the feeling that I wasn't good enough."

"Maybe they weren't good enough for you?"

"The best research hospital in the country?"

"Yes. Maybe they weren't good enough for you." He put his hands on her shoulders, turned her to face him. "Kat, I know something about walking away from a path that everyone else *thinks* you should want so you can pursue what you *actually* want. It never makes sense to other people. But if it makes sense to you, then that's all that matters."

"It must have been hard for you to grow up in such a famous family with such high expectations," Kat said.

"You have no idea," Jack replied. "The only person I was ever really close to was my brother Matt. As far as our parents were concerned, our hobbies were going to school and doing our homework. Anything non-academic was out of the question. And then, when I did try medical school, I could never trust any of the students or professors to be real with me. No one wanted to get to know *me*. They just wanted to know what it was like to be one of *the* Harpers."

"For me it was different," she said. "My family is poor, and I'm the only one who's ever gone to medical school. I felt like I had to prove to everyone that I was good enough. And then I met Christopher, who I thought was perfect. But the more I think about what happened between us, the more I think that he may have thought he was perfect too. So I had to prove to Christopher that I could keep up, that I was good enough."

"Like I said before—maybe he wasn't good enough for you."

Kat gave this some thought. It felt different to think about other people living up to *her* expectations for a change.

"Whatever happened back in Chicago, I'm sure your

father would have understood," Jack said. "I know you well enough by now to know that if you believed in something enough to get fired over it, then it must have been important. Being fired doesn't matter. Being the version of yourself that you want to be is what matters."

The version of herself that she wanted to be.

The question came at her again. Who *was* she? Not anyone's fiancée, not a superstar... But today, as she sat on the hospital rooftop watching the sun go down, she felt as if she was exactly what she had always wanted to be: a doctor.

She slipped her arm through Jack's and wondered if, amidst all the chaos and crises of the day, she might have found a little bit of inner peace.

As Kat's first few weeks began to turn into her first few months at Oahu General Hospital, she thought that she and Jack were maintaining the guise of being in a purely professional relationship fairly well. No one seemed to suspect anything.

Selena had given Kat a few knowing looks, but had stopped after Kat had assured her with a deadpan expression that there was nothing worth discussing between herself and Jack.

It wasn't even a lie, Kat thought. She'd said there was nothing worth discussing—not that there was nothing happening. And, since she didn't want to discuss her trysts with Jack at all, her statement was technically true. Besides, Selena herself had suggested that Kat needed a "fling." If this—whatever it was she was having with Jack—was just a fling, then there was no need to discuss it with anyone.

She didn't think that she and Jack were acting any differently at work. He handed off cases to her as they came in, giving her brief, professional summaries of the patients. They nodded to each other whenever they passed in the hall, and included each other in collegial conversations.

They also slipped into the supply closet in the hospital's rarely used west wing at every opportunity.

As far as Kat could tell, no one seemed to notice how frequently Jack needed to stock up on painkillers just moments after she happened to slip in to the closet to check on the availability of gauze.

The supply closet was the perfect place for their meetings, because it was the furthest from the ER and therefore the most rarely used. This meant that not only were they unlikely to be interrupted, but that there was plenty of empty shelf space for Kat to lean against as Jack kissed her. He was a few inches taller than her, and it helped to have a clear space where she could let her shoulders lean as she lifted her head to reach his, and where he could wrap his arms around her without fear of knocking anything over.

His nose nuzzled into her collar now, as he peppered her neck with tiny kisses. "Don't...you have...a meeting... to get to?" he queried, between each kiss.

"Not until later," she said, arching her back to press herself into him, pressing her mouth to his so she could explore every nook.

He twined his arms around her waist, holding her close to him, breathing in deeply as though he could inhale her very essence.

Usually, they were able to make the most of the little time they had together. But Jack's mention of the meeting brought Kat back to earth with a crash. She'd been trying not to think about it, but now that he'd mentioned it she couldn't get it out of her mind.

She'd hoped he wouldn't notice her distraction, but as usual he noticed everything. "What's wrong?" he said.

"It's nothing. It's just…" They'd said no emotions, but she needed someone she could talk to. "I could really use some advice," she said. "Selena's great, but she's such a close friend that I worry she wouldn't be honest with me, because she'd be so afraid of hurting my feelings. I need some advice from someone whose opinion I respect but who doesn't…*care* about me."

She couldn't be certain in the darkness, but she almost thought she saw him frown.

"I know we said no emotions or personal stuff," she said, quickly.

"No, it's okay," he said. "How can I help?"

"Do you think I fit in here?" she asked.

He pulled away from her, looking surprised. "Of course," he said. "Look at how well you're doing. You've helped develop a vaccine for a serious illness threatening the island. You did an appendectomy when you hadn't done one in years. How could you think you aren't fitting in?"

She sighed. "I had a meeting with the other doctors yesterday morning. We were talking about some of the policy changes I've put in place since coming here. Specifically, the one that's had the most impact on their work: the requirement that everyone spends eight hours a month working at the hospital's walk-in clinic."

There had been lots of grumbling about that—not without justification. The doctors felt it was an unfair increase to their workload, even though Kat had tried to adjust the schedules to prevent their hours from increasing.

"That's really important to you, isn't it?" Jack said. "But you're worried about a repeat of what happened at your last hospital?"

She nodded. "At Chicago Grace I tried to get them to open up a free, nonprofit clinic. We could have subsidized the extra cost with research and grant proposals. There would have been a *very* slight impact on the hospital's profits over the first three years, but that would have evened out over time."

He winced. "I bet they didn't like hearing that."

"No, they really didn't. In fact..." her face looked more worried than ever "...that's what they fired me over."

"What? *How?*"

"They wanted me to bury all my data showing that only wealthy patients improved after leaving the hospital. Those who couldn't afford follow-up care just stayed the same or got sicker. I refused."

"I can't believe they fired you for something like that."

"Maybe I should mention that when I refused I was shouting at the top of my lungs. And I may also have told the entire board of directors that they should lose their medical licenses because of their lack of compassion for poorer patients."

"Wow! Good for you."

"And I also told the hospital's administrative director that he was a money-hungry prick."

He let out a low whistle.

Kat nodded. "I know," she said. "It doesn't really sound like me, does it?"

"Actually, it sounds *exactly* like you," he said. "I've never seen anyone more passionate about providing good patient care. I know it sucks, getting fired, but I'm glad you don't have to work with those people anymore, and I'd have thought you would be too."

"That's the thing," she said. "I thought the problem was that I was working in the wrong environment, with the wrong people. Everyone here's been wonderful—except they seem to hate my changes, too. I *know* my idea for a nonprofit clinic can work...but only if all the doctors agree to work full shifts there. And no one seems to want to do it."

"It sounds like a great idea," he said. "But did you *ask* the doctors here what they thought about it? Or did you just rush to put your ideas into place? Did you even think about asking Marceline what she wants? Or working with Omar to figure out what he thinks would help boost patient outcomes?"

"I guess I just rushed in with my own ideas," she said. "It's not that I don't care about what they want—I *do*...so much—but it's not how I'm used to doing things. Back in Chicago, the doctors and the hospital administrators held all the authority. I can't remember the last time a hospital administrator asked me what I might need instead of telling me about some new system they wanted to implement. That kind of thinking is exactly what I wanted to get away from, and instead I've just ended up recreating it here." She looked up at him. "Do you think there's any way I can fix this?"

"I *know* you can fix this," he said. "I have a feeling you can do anything. But I'll give you a tip: here in Hawaii, informality will get you further than formality. Spend some time talking to the staff about what they need. Take things slower. They'll come around once they have a chance to see how passionate you are about this and that you want what's best for them as well."

She was smiling again. "You're really good at this, Jack."

"At what?"

"Helping me figure things out. I really appreciate it. And now I *do* need to get going, so I can get ready for my meeting."

"Hold on—let's get you presentable," he said, gently smoothing her hair and tucking a few loose strands behind her ears. Then he stopped, as though a sudden thought had occurred to him. "You know, supply closets are nice…" he said.

"Yes," she agreed. "I'm developing a certain affinity for them."

"But they can be a little claustrophobic. I was wondering if you might be interested in meeting up in a non-closet, non-quarantine, non-enclosed-space-of-any-kind type of setting."

She fixed him with a steady gaze. "Jack Harper, are you asking me out on a date?"

"Yes," he said firmly. "I do believe I am."

When Kat got off work that day she was still thinking about it.

A date. A date with Jack Harper.

It wasn't consistent with their agreement for a purely physical arrangement, but maybe it wouldn't hurt to see what happened when they took their relationship outside of the bedroom. She was surprised, though, that of all the possible moments when Jack could have asked her to go on a date he'd done so after she'd explained how she'd been fired.

Christopher's reaction to the news had been quite different.

Christopher was one of the best surgeons at Chicago Grace Memorial, and Kat had always believed their relationship was storybook-perfect. While they'd been dating she'd been proud to be with someone so disciplined. Christopher had always been the one to get up for a five a.m. run. He lived off kale smoothies…ate nothing but protein and vegetables…

Kat had always felt that she fell short of living up to his

regimented lifestyle. But Christopher was handsome, he was disciplined, and she had thought he loved her.

She had never thought he wouldn't support her when she was fired from Chicago Grace.

"I thought we were people who were serious about our careers," he'd said. "I thought I was about to marry the head of internal medicine at one of the best hospitals in the country. Not an idealistic fool who would throw her career away because she can't hold back from insulting the hospital's board of directors. Well, I won't be foolish with you. You can do what you like with your own reputation, but I won't let you damage mine."

He'd had more to say, but by then she'd slammed her engagement ring on the table and left.

At the time, she'd thought she was heartbroken. But now she wondered if her heartbreak was really about Christopher at all. Her sadness had more to do with having had to let go of the expectations and the life she'd thought she'd wanted. Christopher hadn't been the love of her life after all—he'd simply been a symptom of a larger problem. He'd simply fitted in perfectly with her own high expectations and perfectionism, her misguided idea that she somehow had to earn the right to be accepted.

But since setting foot in Hawaii she'd begun to feel accepted just as she was. And the more time she spent with the people she cared about—Selena, her co-workers and, yes, Jack—the more she felt she didn't need to change herself. She only needed to *be* herself.

CHAPTER SEVEN

KAT WAS SKEPTICAL about Jack's plans for their date, but he assured her that shave ice was a beloved Hawaiian delicacy.

"You can't truly say you've been to Hawaii without trying shave ice," he said. "Personally, I think it's an absolute travesty that you've been here this long without having any."

Kat was reluctant to crush Jack's enthusiasm, but based on his description she wasn't sure she could see the appeal.

"It sounds like it's basically a snow cone," she said.

"Blasphemy," he said. "Shave ice is *nothing* like a snow cone."

"But it's essentially shaved ice covered with syrup?"

"Okay, first of all, it's *shave* ice—not *shaved*. Please try not to embarrass me when you order."

"So they shave the ice…?"

"Into a very fine, snowy powder—yes. And then you pick the flavor of syrup you want to go over it."

"So, like I said, it's basically a snow cone."

"Not one bit," he said. "Don't let anyone hear you say that. You'll get voted off the island immediately."

She rolled her eyes and elbowed him in the ribs.

But the shave ice did turn out to be different from a snow cone. In fact, it was different from anything she'd ever eaten before. Snowy, powder-soft ice shavings were packed on top of coconut ice cream, then covered with tropical fruit syrup and a topping of condensed milk. The result was an incredibly soft, fluffy confection that made Kat think of ice-cold pudding.

"What do you think?" asked Jack.

She took another bite and closed her eyes. "It's like eating a cloud," she said, "or a fluffy milkshake."

He snorted, but she could see that he was pleased that she was enjoying the icy treat.

"A fluffy milkshake, huh?" he said. "That's one I haven't heard before."

They sat down at a colorful picnic table to eat. The shave ice stand was crowded, and Kat could see that Jack was right: shave ice was extremely popular. The lawn in front of the stand was densely packed with people.

But they had barely taken their first few bites before they heard a commotion at the far end of the lawn. Kat stared, wondering what was going on, and then she heard faint cries of, "Oh, my God! Somebody call 911!" and "Is there a doctor anywhere?"

Jack leapt into action, with Kat close behind him.

A man was slumped over his bowl of shave ice and now he slid from the picnic table. He didn't seem to have fainted, but Kat could see he was in danger of losing consciousness. He was slightly overweight, aged about forty. A woman who seemed to be his wife stood next to him and two children, a boy and a girl, stood nearby. The boy appeared to be trying not to cry; he had his arm around the girl, who looked to be about five and was crying profusely.

"He was fine just a minute ago…" The woman was distraught.

"It's okay—I'm a doctor and he's a paramedic," Kat said, and motioned toward Jack, who was checking the man's vitals as best he could without any equipment. "I need to know what happened."

"He...he said he was tired. We'd been hiking, and we missed lunch because of the hike," the woman said.

"Okay, deep breaths," said Kat. "Does he have any medical conditions that we should know about?"

Given the suddenness of the man's fall, and the fact that he'd missed a meal, her money was on some form of hypoglycemic shock—possibly due to diabetes.

Just as she was forming that thought, Jack said, "Kat, he's on an insulin pump." He pulled at the lower half of the man's shirt to reveal the device.

The pump was common for people with Type One diabetes. Small and portable, it could be worn discreetly under most clothing. It was meant to deliver small, continuous doses of insulin to the body throughout the day, rather like a portable pancreas. But insulin pumps weren't always reliable, and the danger could be significant if a pump malfunctioned.

"Check to see it's functioning properly," Kat said.

"Doesn't look like it," Jack responded. "I can't even read the screen."

"Did he complain of any dizziness earlier today?" Kat asked the man's wife. "Any shakiness, sweating, rapid heart rate?"

"It's hard to say," the woman responded. "We've just been up Diamond Head. He was a little shaky, and sweating quite a bit, but so were the children and I. We assumed it was just the result of a long hike in the heat."

"Could just be heatstroke," said Jack. "Although the broken pump makes insulin shock more likely. Does he have a glucagon rescue kit?"

The man's wife buried her face in her hands. "He was

prescribed one six months ago but we never thought we'd need it. We left it in the hotel…an hour from here."

"Call it in," said Kat, but Jack was already on his phone, talking to ambulance dispatch. "What are his vitals?" she asked him.

"Pulse is fast. He's conscious, but just barely."

"Can he swallow?"

Jack looked up to see an employee of the shave ice stand among the gathered crowd. "Can you bring us a bottle of syrup?" he said. "Any flavor. We need to get his blood sugar up *now*."

A moment later someone handed Jack a bottle of strawberry syrup and a paper cup. He poured a small amount of syrup into the cup while Kat knelt by the man's head and tried to keep him conscious.

If the man could stay conscious long enough to swallow the syrup, they'd be able to raise his blood sugar enough to revive him, so that he would simply need to be stabilized at the hospital. But if he fell unconscious there would be no way to raise his blood sugar until the ambulance arrived.

Kat knew the nearest ambulance was at least twenty minutes away, and every minute counted. Every second their patient continued to suffer from insulin shock was crucial, and she desperately wanted to prevent the man from slipping into a coma and suffering all the complications that would arise from that.

"Raise his head a little," said Jack, and Kat supported the man by his shoulders.

His wife knelt down to help her support the man's weight.

"Here, let him lean back on you while he drinks," Kat said to her.

Jack held the cup to the man's lips and tipped it back slightly. The man managed one swallow, then two.

"Easy does it," said Jack. "We just want to give the insulin something to work with, so that your blood sugar can stabilize. Right now it's way too low. The good news is that you're still awake, so you can keep swallowing this syrup."

Kat was impressed with Jack's calm tone. She'd heard him use the same one while bringing patients into the ER, and she knew firsthand how reassuring his confident tone could be. She knew that he wanted to try to normalize things for the family, to reassure the children that help was here for them and for their father. Sometimes talking helped everyone to stay calm.

Jack kept on tipping the syrup into the man's mouth, one swallow at a time, until the man was able to hold the cup himself. Kat was relieved. He was probably out of danger.

After a few more minutes the ambulance pulled up. Kat recognized two EMTs from Oahu General, who nodded at her and Jack as they took over.

"You're in good hands now," Jack said, patting the man's shoulder and giving a reassuring glance to his wife.

As Jack and Kat moved back from the patient to give the EMTs a chance to safely assist him into the ambulance, the manager of the shave ice stand appeared behind them. He was holding large-sized bowls of the same ices they'd ordered.

"On the house," he said. "I noticed you didn't get to eat yours before they melted because you were busy saving that man's life."

As they were eating, Kat said, "Jack, you really are an amazing paramedic. With skills like yours...with a family like yours...why didn't you become a doctor?"

He put down his spoon and gave her a grim look. "That question answers itself."

"I'm not sure I understand..."

He sighed. "You have no idea what it's like to be constantly noticed as one of *those* Harpers. With a family like mine you always have to wonder if people really care about *you*, or if it's just about your connections and the career advancement those connections can provide. When I was in medical school I was always wondering… Does this person want to be my friend, or do they want my dad to offer them a summer internship? Does that professor really think I did a good job on that procedure, or does he want me to mention his name to my mother?"

She thought about that. Jack was right; she didn't have any idea what that would be like. She'd been the first in her family to graduate from college, let alone go to medical school. She'd known plenty of other students who'd come to medical school already having family and other connections in the field, and she'd often been envious of those connections, but for Jack it sounded like having a family that was so well-known in the medical community was more of a liability than anything else.

"I bet there were times when it really sucked," she said. "Not only would you be constantly wondering whether people liked you for *you*, but you'd also be dealing with some pretty high expectations."

"You have no idea," he said again. "Most kids get to dream about what they want to be when they grow up. For my brothers and me it was a foregone conclusion: we were going to be doctors, whether we wanted to or not. And everyone assumed we wanted to. My brother Matt was the only person I could really talk to about it."

"Do you get to see him much?"

"Not really. Have you always known you wanted to be a doctor?" he asked quickly.

She had a feeling he wanted to change the subject, and she was happy to oblige. She was curious about him, but she didn't want to push for more than he was ready to give.

"It's been a dream of mine ever since I was very young," Kat said. "My dad passed away when I was ten. Pneumonia. Maybe things would have been different if he'd been able to see a doctor sooner, but he was always working, and sometimes he'd put off going to the doctor to save money."

Jack nodded. "That's why the idea of opening a nonprofit clinic at Chicago Grace was so important to you? That's why you got so mad when they told you no?"

Kat gave a terse nod. "If there's any way I can make it so that fewer families have to go through what mine did, I'll do it."

"I can't imagine losing a parent at such a young age," Jack said. "It must have changed everything?"

"Pretty much everything," she agreed. "I think that was the beginning of my Type A tendencies. I turned into a little adult. If I wasn't the one worrying about the bills our electricity would go out. I can't fault my mom, though. She might not have been the most organized person in the world, but she worked hard to put me through school."

"It doesn't sound like you had the chance to have much of a childhood."

"Yes and no. My family was poor, but I never felt poor because I felt loved. And even though I had to work pretty hard—I started working part-time jobs when I was sixteen to save up to pay for school—I still feel it was all worth it in the end." She brightened. "And it's not as though I can't make up for lost time. Maybe I didn't get the chance to do anything wild or reckless when I was younger, but opportunities continue to present themselves." She gave him a wicked smile.

"Oh? And what kind of opportunities might those be?"

"Well, I believe I recall one of us suggesting cliff jumping as a fun recreational pastime."

He laughed. "You can't be serious."

Her eyes widened innocently. "Why not?"

Truth be told, she'd been wildly curious about the idea of cliff jumping ever since he'd suggested it. And she didn't want to wait around to see if any of their friends wanted to go. She wanted to go now—with him—before she lost her nerve.

"I think you were right when you said that I needed some excitement, some kind of thrill. This is my chance. Besides, you said it was great for mental clarity."

"That's true," he said, his face growing thoughtful. "You're never more certain of what you really want than when you're hurtling through the air at top speed. Into appropriately deep water, of course." He glared down at her. "Safety first," he said sternly.

"Of course," she said. "So—are we doing this?"

"Let's go."

Jack had been driving for about an hour. They were almost to the spot of coastline that was his destination—the perfect spot for cliff jumping. Something was still bothering him, but he wasn't sure how to bring it up.

Just say it, he thought. *You're about to literally jump off a cliff with this woman. If you're not afraid of that you shouldn't be afraid of an emotional conversation.*

He summoned his courage. "Earlier…when you were telling me about how hard you had to work to get through medical school… I couldn't help but feel guilty," he said.

"Guilty? Why on earth should you feel guilty?" she asked.

"Because I walked away from something you worked so hard for," he said. "I left medical school at the end of my third year but I could have sailed through—because of who my parents are, and because my family have money.

You had to scrimp and save and plan your whole life to get something that I gave up."

"It wasn't what you wanted," she said. "Becoming a doctor has always been my dream. But it doesn't sound as though it was ever yours. Why feel guilty just because you decided to walk away from the path that I chose?"

He was relieved to hear that she wasn't appalled by his decision. But Kat wasn't finished.

"There is something I wonder about, though," she said. "You said earlier that you were closest to your brother Matt, but that you don't see him much now. Why not?"

"My older brother and I haven't spoken in four years," he said.

He wasn't sure why he was opening up to her. Maybe because she'd been so sympathetic. His struggle was nothing, compared to hers, but she seemed to understand exactly what he was saying.

"Oh," said Kat. "This wouldn't happen to be the same brother you told me about while we were in quarantine? The one who cheated with your fiancée?"

"That's the one," said Jack.

He'd always refused to talk about Matt and Sophie. He'd simply decided to leave that part of his life behind. He wasn't sure why he felt he could talk about it now, except that there was something about Kat's ability to understand him that seemed to make his words come tumbling out.

"Matt was the only person in my family who I could really be myself with," said Jack. "I looked up to him."

"Sounds like you were pretty close," said Kat.

"We were. Matt was a great older brother while we were growing up. He always stood up for me, listened to me, and he helped me out whenever I needed it."

"So what happened?"

"It's complicated," he said. "When I left medical school to join the SEALs Sophie felt that I'd let her down. She was in medical school too, and she'd always planned for a certain kind of life. She wanted to be married to someone who was a doctor, like she was, and she wanted a big house in the same suburb my parents lived in. And then I didn't want those things anymore."

Kat placed a hand on his arm. "It's hard when people grow apart," she said. "But if you wanted such different things maybe it's for the best that you didn't end up together."

"I can see that now," Jack said. "But at the time I was heartbroken. It wasn't just that she didn't want to be with me. I could have understood that. She'd thought all along that I wanted one kind of life, and then I started trying to explain that I wanted something different... Even though I'd hoped she would understand, I would never have faulted her for still wanting a different life than the one I'd started looking for. If it had just been that I would have gotten over it in time."

He took a deep breath. "But then I found out that she'd been cheating on me with Matt. She left me for him the next day. I confronted Matt and told him that I couldn't believe he would do that to me."

"How could he?" said Kat. "How could your family accept that from either of them?"

He sighed, and then he said, "Sophie was pregnant."

Kat paused for a moment, and Jack's heart went cold at the shocked expression on her face.

"You have a child?" she said. But then understanding broke through. Her hand went to her mouth. "Oh, no. It wasn't yours, was it?"

He winced. "See? I told you I was naïve. *You* put it together right away." He gave a dry laugh. "Matt knew the baby was his. He and Sophie had been cheating on me for six months. I've always wondered if she viewed Matt and I as somehow interchangeable. As long as she married into the Harper family she'd have the connections she needed to work at any hospital she liked for the rest of her life."

"But that's not all, is it?" asked Kat.

"What do you mean?"

"Jack, it sounds to me like you and your brother were incredibly close. To lose that relationship, especially when you didn't have many other people you felt you could count on…it must have been devastating."

He shrugged, reluctant to let her know how right she was.

"Have you ever thought about calling him?" she asked.

"No way," he said. "I don't need the complication."

"Jack, family isn't a complication. It's *family*. You have a niece or nephew to get to know."

"No," he said. "I *thought* I had a family. Instead I have a group of people back in Nebraska who are interested in prestige and not much else, and who all happen to share the same last name."

He was taken aback by the bitterness in his own voice, and surprised when Kat said softly, "I can understand why you'd feel that way. It sounds like Sophie confirmed your worst fear: that people were only interested in you for your family's prestige and connections."

"Exactly. And then when you came, with your incredible reputation and your plans to change all the policies at the hospital…"

"You thought I was some bigwig who'd put my career over the people in my life."

He had the grace to blush. "I can see how wrong I was

about that now. People come here all the time, thinking they're going to escape their problems, or they're going to jumpstart their careers by being a big fish in a small pond. But it's *my* small pond, and I'm very protective of it."

She thought for a moment, and then she said, "It might surprise you to hear this, but I know how it feels to be used for your connections."

"Oh?"

"When I got fired from Chicago Grace, Christopher called off the wedding right away. We'd both thought I was going to be promoted to director of the internal medicine department, and when I didn't get the promotion, and then got fired, he broke up with me."

Jack shook his head. This Christopher guy was a complete idiot.

"Anyway, this whole year I've been trying to figure out why I'm not grieving Christopher more. I was going to marry him. I thought he was the love of my life. But I feel like I've been more upset over losing my job than losing my fiancé. *Ex*-fiancé."

"Well, your job was something you worked hard for most of your life. Your career was about you and about your connection with your dad. Who never even met Christopher. So it makes sense that losing your job would have affected you much more deeply."

"Yes, but it's more than that. I don't think Christopher and I were really meant to be. I thought he loved me... But now I think he just loved the idea of being married to a department head at a top Chicago hospital. He liked the prestige. But when it came to really making a difference in the way I wanted to he didn't care."

Jack pulled off the highway and parked underneath a tree just beside the road. They'd reached their destination.

As they both got out of the car, he said, "It sounds like we've both broken away from our old lives. And now we can figure out what to do with our new lives—what the next steps are."

They approached the edge of the cliff at the golden hour—the hour before the sun set and cast everything with a luminous glow. It was one of Jack's favorite spots in all Hawaii: a stretch of coastline on the island's north shore. This part of the shoreline was made of high cliffs, with deep water below. It was an ideal spot for cliff jumping, if Kat decided she wanted to go through with it.

Being so close to the shoreline awed Jack, as it always did. And as he looked at Kat he could tell that she was just as taken by the island's beauty as he was.

"It's incredible," she said. "I've never seen water this shade of blue before. It's like looking at liquid lapis lazuli."

Jack realized he'd never really taken in the islands through someone else's eyes. Kat's response to the wild beauty of Oahu made him feel as though he were seeing it all again for the first time.

"You love this place," he said.

"I think I do," she replied. "Even though I haven't spent much time here. From the moment I got off the plane I felt like I was home. Chicago is a great city, but it's very... flat. I've never seen a place that radiates so much natural beauty as Hawaii."

Speaking of radiating beauty, Jack thought, *she should see how her face softens and her eyes shine when she looks out over the cliffs.*

Somewhere along their hike to the cliffs she'd plucked a plumeria flower and placed it in her hair. The effect was breathtaking now, as Kat looked out over the coast, framed by the sea and sky, her tangled red hair waving in the wind. She turned toward him and somehow, before he knew what had taken hold of him, he'd reached out and she was in his arms, her face tilted up toward his.

He felt as though she'd always belonged there—as though he'd reached out for some lost piece of himself that he hadn't known was missing. But to have her so close was confusing. He couldn't think clearly with her pulled into his arms, pressed against his chest, her hair smelling of flowers.

He found himself saying, "There's no reason to be scared," and he couldn't be sure if he was saying it to her, or to himself.

"Scared?" she said. She looked up at him, confused. "Why would I be scared?"

A fair enough question. She rested securely in his arms and he would damn well *never* let any harm come to her if he could help it. She was in the safest place she could possibly be, even if she didn't know it. So why should either of them be scared?

He searched his mind for an explanation of what he'd said—something that would make sense. "I was talking about the cliff-jumping, if you decide you want to try it," he said. "It's always scary the first time, but there's nothing to be afraid of here. The water's deep, but we're close enough to shore that we can swim back safely, and the current isn't overpowering."

She looked up at him, still folded in his arms, her eyes filled with emotion. "Jumping off a cliff doesn't scare me," she said. "I know that might sound strange. But you were right, Jack! I was never going to learn to relax from a book. I need to try new things, and I need a thrill. I'm the kind of person who relaxes by finding excitement—not by sitting in a quiet room meditating. But before coming to Hawaii I never realized that about myself because my whole life has been about studying. I never even had a chance to experience an adrenaline rush until I started working in the ER. I don't think I ever realized that *that's* what I love about medicine: the excitement, the unpredictability, having to think quickly. At least, I didn't realize it until I met you."

Jack wondered if Kat could feel his heart beating underneath his shirt. He'd pulled her to him and she hadn't pulled away. She was still resting in his arms, her head against his chest, as though she belonged there. As though she *wanted* to be there. As though whatever was between the two of them wasn't about being friends, or having a physical relationship with no emotions.

She held him as though she wanted him.

She held him the same way he was holding her.

"I'm not scared of jumping off a cliff, Jack," she continued. "Why would I be? I trust you. But I'll tell you what I really *am* scared of." She locked her eyes with his. "I'm scared of the two of us hiding from how we really feel about each other."

And then she was kissing him, her lips seeking his with ardent desire, and he found himself kissing her back just as passionately, his tongue desperate to explore every last corner of her mouth and his arms pressing her against his body, right where she belonged.

Some time later their kisses became shorter and softer, until they simply held each other close, their foreheads pressed together.

"What do you think?" he said. "Should we take the leap?"

She looked over the cliff. "The relationship leap or the actual leap?"

"Both," he said.

"I want to, but I'm not sure I know how," she said.

He held her close. "I think there's only one way to do it," he said. "Take a running start, hold hands, and jump together."

Kat's head broke the surface of the water. She felt exhilarated. She looked around and for a moment was worried not to see Jack, but then there he was, swimming toward her.

The leaping off—pushing her legs up and out, away from the cliff—had been the most frightening part, but it had helped to have that running start. And it had also helped to know that Jack was holding her hand. They'd run for the edge together, holding hands for as long as they could before they leapt into the air and broke apart.

For an endless moment that had seemed to exist outside of time she'd hung in the air. It had been the closest thing to flying she'd ever experienced. With her feet springing away from land, the sea rushing toward her and the salt air surrounding her, her senses had been completely enveloped. There had been no room for her to fret about the past or worry about the future. The only moment she'd been able to completely exist in had been the present.

Then the water had rushed up to greet her and surrounded her body. She'd let herself sink, and then relaxed her body until it had naturally begun to rise toward the surface. She'd kicked her way up to the air, breaking the water's surface with a gasp.

And now Jack was swimming toward her with sure and steady strokes.

He'd been right. About so many things. About her need for excitement. About the two of them taking a chance on one another.

He swam toward her, wrapped his arm around her waist, and kissed her.

Jumping off the cliff had felt like a microcosm of her life, she thought. You could plan and plan, she thought, but nothing could prevent you from hitting the water in the end. The question was, did you want to fall off or jump off freely, feeling the sensation of flying?

She looked over at Jack. The future would come, and life would have its twists and turns, its bumps and bruises, no matter what she did. She'd never be able to completely avoid life's setbacks or challenges.

But she could choose who she'd be holding hands with when they came.

CHAPTER EIGHT

IN CHICAGO, IT had often been hard for Kat to face the cold gray mornings. If the sun made an appearance at all, it usually didn't show up until nine a.m., and then it was often obscured by clouds, unless the weather was exceptionally nice that day.

But mornings in Hawaii felt as though they were taking place in another world. The sun was up early, and as a result so was Kat. Her apartment wasn't far from the beach, and she enjoyed taking early-morning walks by the ocean as she sipped from a mug of coffee.

She couldn't believe how much she'd already changed during the time she'd spent in Hawaii. No one back home would ever have thought of her as a morning person. But the early hours before her shifts at the hospital were now her favorite part of the day. It was so relaxing to hear the rush of the ocean mixed with the wind and birdsong in her ears.

She smiled to herself. Just a few short months ago she hadn't known how to relax, let alone how to relax at the beach. She'd been worried she might have permanently lost her ability to live in the moment. She'd spent so long trying to build her career that she'd forgotten to focus on herself as a person.

But whatever it was she might have lost after the

breakup, and everything that had happened on the Day of Doom, she'd managed to get it back. Apparently she had no trouble being spontaneous anymore. Hadn't she signed up for surfing lessons just that morning?

She couldn't wait to tell Jack. He'd mentioned that surfing was something he'd never gotten around to learning. She wondered if they might be able to learn together. Or maybe she could take the lessons on her own and then teach him. Her mind hummed with possibilities as she made her way back to her apartment.

She'd left her phone on the kitchen counter so that it wouldn't distract her from her walk—something the Old Kat never would have done. In the past she'd had to obsessively check her emails and other messages before she even got out of bed, but now she liked to savor those early moments before she started her day.

She picked up the phone. It was early, but she saw that someone had already tried to call her several times that morning. The number had a Chicago area code, though she didn't recognize it as belonging to her mother or to any of her friends.

The voicemail was fuzzy and crackly, but the important parts came through. Chicago Grace Memorial had had a major overturn in staff. There was a new hospital director, and the voicemail was from the director herself.

She said she understood that Kat's recent firing had been the result of some differences in vision between Kat and the former hospital director. But now he had been let go, along with several members of the hospital's board, so would Kat be interested in having her old job back? With an increase in pay and a promotion to Head of Internal Medicine? Chicago Grace wanted her to return very much. Could she call back as soon as possible, to let them know if she was interested?

Kat gasped. Of *course* she was interested. This was everything she'd ever wanted.

And yet somehow, she felt...flat.

She thought of all the things she'd need to do, but it was as if she were going over a laundry list. She needed to pack, to talk to Selena, to transition all her patients at Oahu General to other doctors...

Her mind went through the list mechanically. Four months ago she would have been thrilled to get a job offer like this. But now she wasn't sure how she felt.

Without thinking, she pulled a suitcase from underneath her bed and began throwing items of clothing into it.

Wait, she thought. *You haven't even called this woman back yet. You need a timeline...you need to prepare...you need to make a checklist of all the things you have to do to get ready to go back...*

She froze. She had to go, didn't she? People didn't just turn down opportunities like this. Who knew when another chance would come along?

But if this was such a clear choice why did she feel so flat? She'd only intended to stay for a year in the first place. Selena probably wouldn't mind if she needed to negotiate a few months off her contract. Or maybe the hospital in Chicago could be convinced to let her stay the whole year in Hawaii and resume her work there after her contract was up.

There was so much to do. Should she call the hospital director back first or talk to Selena first? When should she tell Selena she was leaving?

Then her heart flipped over.

When would she tell Jack she was leaving?

And *was* she leaving?

She realized she was treating it as a foregone conclusion. But was it really what she wanted?

She paused for a moment and searched her feelings. She wanted to stay here in Hawaii. But she also missed Chicago.

She'd done the thing she'd been trying so hard *not* to do the moment she'd first laid eyes on Jack. She'd fallen for him. Leaving him was going to break her heart all over again. But it was her chance to get her career back on track.

Or was it?

Somehow, the idea of returning to Chicago Grace Memorial didn't thrill her the way she'd thought it would. She was just reacting automatically, without asking herself what she really wanted.

But what *did* she want?

She stood in her apartment, listening to the silence. Just a moment ago she had felt so happy. Now she had no idea what she wanted at all.

"So that's the situation," Kat told Selena later that morning. "They've had a change in the hospital administration and they've decided they want me back."

"I knew it was too good to be true," Selena muttered. "I get one of the top infectious disease researchers in the country to work at my hospital and of *course* she's going to leave after only four months."

"That's just it," said Kat. "I'm not so sure I want to leave."

Selena's eyebrows shot up. "How could you *not* want to leave? I mean, I love this hospital, but even *I* have to admit that it's no Chicago Grace. We're a good hospital, but Chicago has the researchers and the prestige and the funding—"

Kat cut her off. "I know it has all of those things. And I feel like I'm *supposed* to want those things… But I'm not sure that I still actually *do* want them."

"Well, if that's how you feel then it sounds like you have a lot of thinking to do— Wait a minute," Selena said abruptly. "Is there something you haven't told me?"

"Like what?" said Kat innocently.

"Like maybe the situation has deepened between you and a certain dark-haired, blue-eyed paramedic?"

For a moment Kat felt a sense of shock that Selena had clearly guessed that something was going on between herself and Jack.

Oh, what the hell? More than anything right now, you need to talk this over with a friend.

She felt a little guilty, because it was Jack's secret as well as hers. But she needed her friend's advice.

"Jack and I have been seeing each other—" she began.

Selena squealed and said, "I *knew* it!"

"It started out as a purely physical thing. We promised not to get our emotions involved. But then, somehow... I think our emotions *did* get involved."

"And do you regret that?" asked Selena.

"The only thing I'm certain of right now is that I don't know how I feel," Kat said.

"Have you told Jack that you've been offered this new job back at your old hospital?"

"No," said Kat. "And I'm not going to. Not yet, anyway. It's a big decision, and I feel like I have to make it myself."

"Why don't you take the next few days off while you think it over?" said Selena.

"A few days off? I don't need that. And the last thing I want to do right now is take time off when I might be about to leave anyway. You asked me to come down here to help you out. I don't want to leave you in the lurch."

"Kat, we're fine. This is actually a really good time for you to take some time off. We're not facing any upcoming outbreaks right now. Thanks to the vaccine, and your initiative with the outpatient clinic, there's been a noticeable reduction in cases coming through the ER. With better access to follow-up care patients are less likely to need emergency response, because we're catching things early instead of at the last possible minute, when things are in crisis. So, largely thanks to you, we do have a moment for a breather right now."

"Time off, huh…?" said Kat. "It was bad enough when I spent just a few hours stuck in quarantine. I don't know what I'm going to do with myself if I'm not at the hospital."

Selena put her hand on Kat's shoulder. "You don't need to connect with your doctor self right now," she said. "You need to figure out what you want for *you*."

Jack stood outside, stunned by what he was hearing. Selena's office door was open just a crack. He hadn't meant to eavesdrop; he'd been coming to Selena's office to follow up on a request for some of the EMTs' time off to be approved. But he'd stopped when he'd noticed that she and Kat seemed to be having a private conversation.

Just as he'd turned away, he'd heard Selena.

"Have you told Jack that you've been offered this new job back at your old hospital?"

He'd frozen. When had that happened? How long had Kat known? And why had she decided not to tell him?

Now, as the initial shock wore off, he realized he was still hovering outside the door. He quietly eased himself away from the entrance to Selena's office and headed into a stairwell down the hall so he could think.

It shouldn't bother him that Kat might be leaving. She'd only ever planned to stay for one year.

But she'd been on the island for…he mentally calculated the days since they'd met…a little over four months. He hadn't expected that she would leave so soon.

And if she did leave what did it matter to him? She had a life back in Chicago, and they'd both always known that she'd planned to return to it. So what if that happened much sooner than either of them had expected? They'd both agreed to have a fling. A no-strings-attached, no-expectations, no-commitment island fling.

For the rest of the afternoon he tried to avoid her as he went about his duties at the hospital. He knew he'd want to confront her if they spoke, but he didn't know why. For some reason the thought of Kat leaving seemed to have awakened something ugly in his chest—something angry and hurt and furious at the unfairness of it all. And whatever that ugly beast was he needed to hide it from Kat— because, rationally, he knew it made no sense.

He had no right to be angry. No right to confront her, to demand an explanation of what he'd overheard between her and Selena. Getting attached to one another had never been part of the plan. They'd agreed to that from the start.

But he wanted to confront her, to ask her exactly what that conversation with Selena had meant, and what she planned to do. Even though he wasn't sure if he could maintain control over his emotions.

Oahu General was a small hospital, and despite his best efforts to avoid Kat he filed a patient's chart behind the reception desk and turned to find her right in front of him.

"Supply closet. Five minutes," she whispered into his ear, and before he could respond she'd scooted away.

For a minute he considered not meeting her there. But he knew he had to. He couldn't stand not knowing if she was leaving for a moment longer.

His face stoic, he headed down to the supply closet.

Kat stood waiting for him in the darkness. She knew she should tell Jack about the job offer—she really should.

But not yet. She wasn't ready. She wanted to enjoy her time with him for just a little longer before anything else got in the way.

But when he arrived, instead of slipping quietly inside the closet as he usually did, he switched the lights on. Her stomach dropped when she saw his face. His expression was cold, even angry, she thought. And his next words confirmed her worst fear: he already knew.

"So when were you planning to tell me that you're going back to Chicago?" he said.

His voice was dull and wooden. And his eyes weren't angry, she realized. They were pained.

"How did you find out?" she asked.

"Does it matter?"

She flinched at the coldness in his voice. "For your information, I haven't decided yet whether I'll go back early or not. I did receive the offer of a job at my old hospital, with a promotion. But I made a one-year commitment to stay here, and it's important to me to honor that."

"And what happens to your job offer while you're honoring your commitment here? Are they going to wait around for you for another eight months in Chicago? I doubt it. You're going to take their offer, and you're going to take it now—because this is the kind of opportunity that a doctor like you can't stand to pass up."

"A doctor like me? What is *that* supposed to mean?"

"You know exactly what I mean. You talk a good game about healing people, but it's really all about the prestige and the glory."

She was absolutely disgusted. "I'm not your ex, Jack, and I'm not your family. Don't start confusing me with people from your past. Yes, I'm successful and ambitious, but you have no right to tell me what my priorities are."

"Is that so? You're not exactly difficult to figure out.

You come to this island a big-city doc, thinking that you know better than everyone else, and then the minute something better comes along you leave. It's all about the next step—it's never about caring about where you actually *are*!"

She glared at him. "Maybe if you'd quit living in the past you wouldn't have such a hard time planning for your future!"

"*I'm* living in the past?" he said. "You've been living in the past since the moment you arrived. You just wanted a break from your normal life—you never wanted to think about how the people who live here are actual *people*. You say you want to learn to slow down and live in the moment, but the truth is you just wanted a place to recover from the *one time* someone didn't recognize your brilliance. And now that the world is ready to shower you with applause again you're going to kick the dust of Hawaii off your heels and head back to the city as soon as possible. You talk about wanting to change your life, but you haven't changed at all. You're just going right back to the life you left behind."

Kat was ready to throttle him. He was partly right—just a little bit—and that little bit was enough to set her blood boiling. But she certainly wasn't going to give him the satisfaction of letting him know that some of his words had hit home.

"At least I was able to leave it behind—even if it was only for a little while!" she said. "*You* haven't left the past behind at all. You're living in it every day."

"I am not!"

"Are you kidding me? You let your past control every single thing you do. Because you won't face any of it. You say you don't date doctors, but that's complete nonsense. You *like* doctors. You work with them every single day.

You don't have a problem with doctors. You have a problem with the one you're related to. Matt. *Your brother*."

"What happened between me and my brother is none of your business."

"Then I'll tell you something that *is* my business. Your whole no-strings-attached thing with relationships is ridiculous. It's not the real you—it's just you trying to avoid pain."

He inhaled sharply, as though she had cut him to the quick. And maybe she had gone too far. But she felt the truth of what she'd said deep within her. Jack's whole defense system—his guardedness, his pretense of being unemotional and uninterested in relationships—none of it was the *real* him, the Jack she'd gotten to know after four and a half months on the island. Even if he couldn't see it, she could—and she had to tell him, even if it hurt.

He had grown quiet, his face dark. Then he said, "If no-strings-attached is ridiculous, then where does that leave us?"

She didn't know what to say. She wished more than anything that she could have had this conversation with Jack when she was more prepared for it. After she had made her decision and had planned everything she wanted to tell him.

The silence grew. Finally, she said, "Look, Jack, this is just terrible timing. We've been having... *I've* been having a wonderful time. I thought we'd have more of it..."

His lips were a thin line. "I don't think it's terrible timing," he said. "In fact, I think it's *great* timing. Not a moment too soon."

"Please believe me when I say that I haven't made a decision yet. I'm not sure what I'm going to do. Chicago Grace is one of the best research hospitals in the country, and I can't turn that down lightly. But when I think about my time here… I don't know what to do."

"Stay, go—it doesn't matter to me," he said. "We agreed no emotions, remember? This was never supposed to be anything more than physical. So it makes no difference to me what you decide."

"It doesn't?"

"No. In fact, I think you should go."

She felt something in her chest shift and crack. She tried to look into his eyes, those blue eyes that had so captivated her the day they met, but his face was turned away from her and his eyes appeared to be fixated on a random spot on the supply closet wall.

He cleared his throat and said, "You can't turn it down. It wouldn't make any sense. You belong at a big research hospital where you can shine—not in a remote little hospital in the middle of the ocean."

"I just…" Her voice quavered and she blinked back tears.

"Congratulations on your new job," he said.

Hours later Jack was brooding on the beach—much as he had been the day he'd met Kat. He couldn't stop thinking about their argument.

"You let your past control every single thing you do," she'd said. *"Because you won't face any of it."*

What did she know about it, anyway? What business of hers was it whether he let his past control him or not? They'd agreed to keep things on a purely physical level, so why should she care about his past or how it affected him? *She* was the one who'd proposed their fling in the first place. They'd both always known that she was only here for a short time, and she knew that he didn't like getting his emotions involved in relationships.

"Your whole no-strings-attached thing with relationships is ridiculous. It's not the real you—it's just you trying to avoid pain."

It was true. In the heat of their argument he hadn't been able to bring himself to be honest with Kat, but he could be honest with himself now. She was right. He kept himself distant and guarded from women because of the pain he'd felt over Sophie. More specifically, over Sophie and Matt.

If it had been an ordinary breakup he would have gotten over it long ago, but the fact that Sophie had betrayed him with Matt meant that he'd lost the one person in the world he'd thought would always be there for him.

Strange, he thought, how he'd tried so hard to avoid repeating the pain of heartbreak and yet here it was, as fresh as ever. Even though he'd tried to convince himself that his relationship with Kat was purely physical and emotionless, it wasn't true. It really had been just his attempt to keep himself from getting hurt.

Despite his best efforts to stay distant they'd gotten close, and before he knew it he had allowed himself to hope. When they'd tried to keep their relationship purely physical their lovemaking hadn't quenched his thirst. It had only brought about a desire for more. He thought perhaps she might feel the same way, although he couldn't be sure. And now he could never ask her. As much as he was hurting right now, the last thing he wanted to do was make it harder for Kat to leave him.

You always knew she was here for just the one year, he told himself. *What were you expecting? Don't blame her just because you got your hopes up for something you knew perfectly well was never going to be long-term in the first place.*

But even though he knew it was the right thing to do, the mature thing to do, it was hard to accept the end of their relationship so soon after it had begun. He couldn't say what their time together had meant to Kat. But for him it had felt like the beginning of something. Something he wanted to explore to its fullest extent to see where it would lead.

He knew that it wasn't realistic or fair of him to hope that Kat would change her career plans for him. After all, they'd only known each other for a few months. And when he stepped back from the hurt of it all and really thought about it he knew that he would never dream of asking her. As much as he, personally, didn't believe in putting a career over personal happiness, that was *his* choice. Kat's career was the thing in her life that made her happy.

He'd never get in the way of her happiness—not for one second.

Even if that meant that they couldn't be together.

The thought of it tore at his heart.

For almost Jack's entire life there'd only been one person he'd felt cared enough about him to help him figure out situations like this. More than anything he wanted to talk to that person now. He wanted his advice, he wanted his reassurance that things would be okay, or that even if things weren't okay they'd stick together and figure it out.

He just wasn't sure he had the guts to make the call.

"You don't have a problem with doctors," Kat had said. *"You have a problem with the one you're related to. Matt. Your brother."*

His anger flared again. Was this what she'd meant when she'd said he let the past control him? As though he was too much of a coward to face his feelings?

But now his anger was more with himself than with Kat. Because right now he needed help from someone he could trust. Even if that person had made a mistake. His inability to forgive was holding him back from getting what he really needed.

Jack picked up his phone. He dialed a number that he'd deleted from his contacts but that had burned itself into his memory long ago.

He wasn't sure if he was ready for this conversation. But, ready or not, it was time for him and his brother to talk.

The phone rang once, and then Jack heard a familiar voice answer.

"Hi, Matt," he said.

CHAPTER NINE

EVER SINCE SELENA had advised her to take a few days off, Kat had been moving nonstop. She'd been packing, calling Selena, calling her mother, and logging in to Oahu General's system to update her files. She'd been researching flights to Chicago and looking up the number of the real estate agent who'd found her apartment to see about getting out of her lease early.

She had a million things to do, and she knew, all of a sudden, why it felt as though she had to complete every single one of those tasks *right now*: it was because preparing to leave helped her to keep her mind off Jack.

As long as she kept herself busy she wouldn't have to think about the pain in his eyes. And she wouldn't have to dwell on that sensation of something cracking, deep within her chest. It was a feeling that had started as soon as she'd looked into Jack's eyes and told him about the job offer. She was trying, and failing, to ignore it.

She believed in love. She knew that with great certainty now. When she'd told Selena months ago that she didn't think she could believe in love or in relationships she'd been lying to herself. She'd been trying to figure out who she was and what she believed at the same time she'd been trying to mask the pain that she'd felt about Christopher.

The result had been a ridiculous cynical statement that she knew now wasn't true.

There was no denying her feelings for Jack. It was true that she hadn't known him for long. She'd only been in Hawaii for a little over four months, and even less time had passed since she'd given herself permission to acknowledge her true feelings for Jack. It was too soon to know where things would go if they stayed together. And yet she felt deeply enough to know the relationship deserved a chance.

She might not know how to describe her feelings for Jack, but she knew that the only thing that held her back from using the word *love* was time. If she left now she'd spend her life wondering what might have happened if she'd stayed. Wondering if he might feel the same way.

But she had to leave, didn't she? Jack had practically insisted she go. Chicago Grace Memorial was one of the most prestigious hospitals in the country. How could she possibly turn it down?

The answer was that she couldn't. Of course she had to go. People didn't simply turn down positions like this. Did they?

But if she wanted the job so badly why was her heart sinking? What was wrong with her? Normal people didn't react with disappointment when they were offered everything they'd ever wanted.

Taking the job would make her one of the leading infectious disease researchers in the country. She'd be able to do good, important work, and she'd be recognized as a valuable contributor to the field of medicine.

When she thought about that, she recognized herself. It felt like who she was. But she wasn't so sure she was as excited at the prospect of what daily life in Chicago had to offer. She knew that life well. Long, cold winters. Late nights spent at work. She knew she could handle that life, because she'd already done it for years. But handling day-to-day life and relishing it were two different things.

In Chicago, she knew she would earn respect from her colleagues, but would she be able to count on their friendship? Before working at Oahu General she'd never dreamed there could be a hospital with such warm collegiality among its staff. She'd come to depend on her regular chats in Selena's office, on the casual banter among the paramedics, nurses, and physicians. These past four months had been among the happiest of her professional life.

When she thought about returning to her old life in Chicago, she had the strangest sense of dread. But surely no one in their right mind would pass up a prestigious job opportunity just because…just because they were *happier* where they were?

Before moving to Hawaii she would have known the answer to that question. Happiness could wait. She was busy building her career. She would worry about enjoying her life after she'd retired from twenty or thirty years as a respected physician. Maybe then there would be room in her life for her to make decisions based on what she wanted for herself rather than the next logical step in her career.

But since she'd moved to Hawaii she'd been able to get a taste of what it would be like to have balance in her life right *now*. She still worked hard—that was certain. But when she came to work she wasn't just passionate about her career: she had fun, too. She would genuinely miss the staff and the environment they'd created.

Leaving the hospital would be hard.

Leaving Hawaii would break her heart.

She paused in her packing to savor the cool breeze coming through the window. There truly was nowhere else on earth that was like this place. Where else would she be able to walk to the beach from her apartment and see dolphins frolicking off the coast? And she'd gotten used to the riot of color among the flowers that lined Honolulu's sidewalks. The thought of exchanging those tropical flowers for gray ice-covered walkways was disheartening.

It wasn't just that Hawaii was pretty. If it were only that her decision would be so much easier. There were plenty of pretty places in the world and she couldn't live in all of them—it wasn't physically possible. If her reluctance to leave was simply a matter of craving natural beauty, that was a problem easily solved. She could take a vacation somewhere beautiful any time she started to feel burnt out.

No, the islands were beautiful, but it wasn't their beauty that called to her. It was something deeper than that—more primal. Something she'd known in her bones the second she'd arrived. The moment she'd stepped off the plane she'd felt a sense of coming home. She couldn't remember having had such a feeling of belonging somewhere since before her father's death.

Her father had had such heady hopes and dreams for her, and by great good fortune she had shared those same hopes and dreams for herself. It had meant so much to her to live up to his expectations—especially after he'd gone. And then, as she'd grown up, it had become important to her to live up to the expectations of her teachers, her professors at medical school, her supervisors as a student and her superiors at work.

And because many of those expectations that others had had of her were also those she'd had for herself, she hadn't noticed that her own happiness was no longer a priority. Her desire for her happiness had slipped away as she'd focused on the needs and expectations of others.

So it had felt natural to live up to Christopher's expectations of her, as well. No wonder none of her friends had liked him. She hadn't been able to understand it at the time, because it had felt so natural for her to agree with Christopher and to try to please him. But she wondered now why it had never seemed as important to please herself.

But the minute she'd stepped off the plane in Hawaii she'd felt something new. That same breeze that had brought her the scent of the plumeria flowers had also brought her a sense of glorious possibility. The possibility of being herself. The mountains and the ocean had promised her adventure; the birds, the flowers and the meandering paths had hinted at peace. And the people had offered an acceptance that she'd never thought was possible.

She'd been so nervous about earning her place at Oahu General Hospital that she'd never realized she didn't *have* to earn it because her place was already there. She didn't have to work hard to belong. Instead she simply belonged.

Jack had once told her that he did his best thinking at the beach. He'd said he'd been out on the beach to think on the day they'd met, when he'd rescued her from the rip current. Kat had decided that the beach might not be a bad idea. And, thanks to Jack, she was now an expert at using the beach as a place to think, too.

Those days when she'd felt as though she couldn't turn her brain off, couldn't stop worrying about all the people who mattered to her and all the work stresses were over. The worries were still there, occasionally, but now she could set them aside and focus on the sand and the waves.

Jack had been right about her need for excitement, too. But as she strolled barefoot on the beach, feeling the sand underneath her toes, she knew that she needed the serenity that these islands could offer her as well. She wondered if she would have been able to appreciate the stillness and the calm of the ocean if Jack hadn't shown her how much she needed excitement first.

However she'd gotten to this point, she was glad that she was finally able to relax enough to enjoy something as simple as a walk on the beach. She wanted to soak up as much of Hawaii as possible. She gazed out over the ocean, marveling at its endlessness. She took in the sun, shimmering on the water's surface, and far in the distance she could see the other Hawaiian islands, where a cloudy haze formed around the green mountains of each one.

The sand was cool under her toes and for a moment Kat felt completely at peace. She was completely absorbed in the way each part of the beach touched her senses: she could feel the grains of sand that had collected on her feet, the warmth of the sun on her skin, and she could hear the sound of ocean waves in her ears, punctuated by a few birds flying overhead and calling.

She'd never felt this way about any place she'd ever been to or any choice she'd made. The closest comparison she could think of was the day she'd learned that she had gotten into medical school. In that moment she'd felt the strongest feeling of peace and security wash over her— the knowledge that she was going to do exactly what she was meant to be doing with her life.

She had that same feeling about Hawaii—that this was where she was meant to be and that she should spend the rest of her life here and continue feeling it was meant to be.

You could almost call it a kind of love, she thought. And it had been Jack who'd shown her how to fall in love with the islands, how to take advantage of all they had to offer.

I could visit, she told herself. *I could take trips to Hawaii every so often—maybe every other year or so. I could come here for holidays and long weekends.*

You don't visit the love of your life "every other year

or so," her heart responded. *Not if you have any choice in the matter.*

But did she have a choice? At first, it had seemed as though she hadn't. She'd just reacted without thinking. She hadn't thought about how Jack would feel at all.

She felt a stab of pain in her chest as she remembered the hurt in his eyes. She hoped she hadn't sounded callous.

Jack had a hard time trusting anyone with his feelings. He'd grown up in a family that had put career above everything—even personal happiness.

When she'd gone through her breakup with Christopher her family and friends had rallied around her. True, she'd holed up in her apartment for several days, hiding from everyone, but once she'd been ready to face the world again she'd been inundated with supportive texts and voicemails from all the people who cared about her.

But when Jack had suffered the worst betrayal of his life he hadn't been able to go to the people he needed the most for support. That was the kind of family Jack had grown up in.

She'd gotten the impression that there hadn't been much importance placed on emotion when he was a child, and that that emotionless existence was one of the very things he'd come to Hawaii to get away from. Lonely, emotionally deprived Jack had known exactly what he needed, and he'd come here because he'd known that the islands could provide it.

And he'd known what she needed, too. He was the first person to have spoken to that wild part of her—the part that needed adventure and excitement. The part of herself that she'd gotten a glimpse of on rollercoasters and waterslides as a child…the part that she'd had to bury so deep underneath her cool, professional exterior.

A light breeze had picked up over the beach. It felt

like a caress over her sun-warmed skin. She picked up a handful of sand and watched it run through her fingers. She wondered if she was doing the same thing to herself: holding happiness in her hand and letting it run through her fingers.

Jack had been able to decide that his life was about living up to his own expectations of himself. And his expectations of himself were good because he was a good person. She knew that to her core. She could see that Jack felt the same way she did about caring for the people around him—not just his patients, but everyone in his life. She and Jack might have taken different paths, but they'd gotten to the same place in the end.

Maybe her life could be about not living up to anyone's expectations but her own? Not Christopher's, not those of her family, her friends or her employers. Her father had wanted her to be a doctor, but Kat was sure that he'd wanted her to be happy, too.

But what did she want for herself?

It had been so long since she'd thought about what she wanted, rather than what everyone around her needed, that her brain felt rusty as it mulled over the question.

Jack had told her that cliff jumping was great for mental clarity. She smiled, recalling that moment. He had certainly been right in saying that you were never more certain about what you wanted than when you were hurtling through the air. But right now she felt she needed something different.

She stood up from the warm sand. She could have stayed there all day, but it was time to move on. The sun was heating the sand to the point that it was almost too uncomfortable to sit on. Soon it would be too hot to touch.

She smiled to herself. It was as though Hawaii was telling her to get a move on. Hadn't the island always known what she needed? Even from the start, when she'd thought the island was trying to drown her, it had just been bringing her and Jack together.

It was just as Jack had said: she was never going to solve the problem of what she wanted by thinking about it. She could analyze and analyze, obsess and worry and make dozens of pro-con lists without ever figuring out the answer.

In order to work out what she wanted, she need to understand how she *felt*. And in order to know how she felt, she needed to be at peace.

Fortunately, while taking these past few days off, she'd learned a new skill that was great at offering her peace.

She'd started her surfing lessons just a few days ago. At first it had been difficult, but she'd gotten the hang of it quickly. She'd anticipated having to learn with a bunch of tourists, but to her very great surprise, in addition to teens and adults, her introductory surfing class had included very young children—children who seemed young enough that they'd barely mastered walking, let alone surfing.

Her instructor had told her not to worry, that she'd pick it up in time, with enough practice. And then, to Kat's great surprise, the instructor's *dog* had hopped onto a surfboard of its own and paddled out with them.

No one else in the class had seemed the least bit surprised, and as Kat's lessons had progressed she started to understand why: they saw at least five other surfing dogs every morning. Apparently the dog lovers of Hawaii hated to leave their furry friends on the beach.

Determined not to be outshone by surfing dogs and babies, Kat had thrown herself into learning to surf. After all, if she was indeed leaving the islands, she'd only have so much time to learn.

She was getting better, too.

Now, she paddled her board out to the waves and sat up on it, letting the waves rock her gently. It was a pleasant way to sit and think. She listened to the sound of the waves lapping and inhaled the salt scent of the seawater.

It was astounding, she thought, how the island seemed to have a way of knowing just what she needed. It had pushed her into Jack's arms that first day, even though she'd been so certain she didn't want a relationship. And it had pushed her toward excitement, toward new ways of challenging herself. Did the island know her better than she knew herself?

She was still thinking about that when a rogue wave knocked her from her surfboard and pushed her under the water's surface.

CHAPTER TEN

THE PHONE CONVERSATION hadn't been as difficult as Jack had expected. In some ways it had felt like old times. And by talking to his brother Jack felt as though an entire piece of his identity had come back.

But after several years without speaking things were also different. Jack wasn't just Matt's little brother anymore, forever living in his shadow. And Jack felt that Matt respected him in a way that he never had when the two of them had been growing up together. He got the distinct impression that Matt admired him for making the phone call that he had been too afraid to make.

"I'm not sorry that Sophie and I ended up together, but I am sorry for how it happened," Matt had said. "It was unforgivable. We should have told you as soon as it started. For my part I kept the secret because I wanted to protect you... I didn't want to hurt you. But I was a coward. I should have realized that the lie would hurt you more than honesty ever would."

Jack had felt tears prick his eyes. "All that was a long time ago," he'd said.

He'd told Matt all about Kat, explaining that she was really the person who had given him the courage to make the call. If he'd never met Kat he'd probably never have tried to reconnect with Matt in the first place. And then he explained that Kat was leaving, and that he was about to lose the first person he'd been able to open his heart to in years.

At which point his brother had said something that had surprised him.

"It sounds like when she got the job offer you told her to go, to follow her career," he said. "It even sounds as though you tried to push her away."

"I didn't want her to feel as though I was trying to hold her back," Jack said. "I would never ask her to make such a major life decision based on her feelings about me. I want her to do what's best for her."

"Yeah, but who are you to decide what's best for her? Doesn't that get to be *her* decision? And wouldn't she make the best decision if she had all the information?"

"What do you mean, all the information?"

"You told her to go. But is that what you really want? I thought you said the *aloha* culture was all about being real with people? But you haven't been real with her. Why don't you tell her how you really feel about her leaving? You say you don't want to get in her way, but from everything you've said she sounds like a pretty independent woman. Don't you trust her to make the right decision for herself?"

Jack had been silent as he'd thought about this and Matt had continued.

"She can't make an informed decision if she doesn't have all the data. Maybe you think you're trying to protect her by hiding your feelings and keeping them to yourself. But if there's one thing I've learned, it's that secrets only hurt."

Jack could see the truth in that, but he was still unsure…afraid.

"What if I tell her how I feel and it doesn't matter?" he'd said. "What if she still goes back to the mainland?"

"I don't know what will happen," Matt had told him. "There's no way to know for sure. But if you tell her how you feel, with no expectations of her and no strings attached, then at least you'll know that you were honest with her and with yourself."

Honesty, Jack thought now, as he worked through his shift at the hospital. Now, there was a deceptively simple concept. Hadn't he and Kat been struggling with honesty since the moment they'd met? It had been a Herculean struggle for the two of them to be honest about their feelings with one another. And then, when they'd almost gotten there, it had all been snatched away.

Matt was right, though, Jack thought. Kat was a strong woman. She could handle the truth. And he wanted to be honest about how he felt for her. Not because he wanted to convince her to stay, but because he wanted to be real about his feelings. Kat, more than anyone else he'd ever met, had taught him that it was important to be real about what he was feeling. If she was leaving now, then he wanted her to leave knowing exactly how he felt.

Then she could use that information however she wished, without any expectations from him.

The problem was he'd been looking for her all day and hadn't been able to find her. He hadn't seen her anywhere in the ER.

It was a slow day, and there hadn't been many calls coming in that morning, but when an EMT brought in a tourist with an ankle fracture Jack offered to take the patient up to Radiology for X-rays, hoping he might see Kat there. No luck.

She wasn't in the hematology lab, nor any of the operating suites. He began popping his head into individual exam rooms, but she was nowhere to be found.

He gave up searching and went back to the reception desk, where he found Selena and Marceline.

"Is Kat coming in today?" he asked.

"She'd better," Selena said. "We're planning a surprise goodbye party for her." Then she glanced at her watch with a worried frown. "She's thirty minutes late for her shift, though. That's not like her."

Jack had stopped absorbing information after the words "surprise goodbye party."

"Wait a minute," he said. "Isn't a goodbye party a little preemptive? We don't even know if she's definitely decided to leave yet."

Selena gave him a sympathetic look. "I'd like to cling to the hope that she'll stay here too," she said. "But Kat is a talented physician. I don't think she'll turn down a job offer like this just to keep working at our little hospital." She narrowed her eyes at Jack. "Unless, of course, she has some *other reason* to stay."

Jack decided he wasn't going to rise to the bait—especially as the other half of Selena's statement had started to sink in.

"What do you mean, she's thirty minutes late for her shift?" he said.

His concern started to rise. Thirty minutes was an eternity where Kat was concerned; she usually preferred to arrive for her shift at least twenty minutes early, so she could enjoy a cup of coffee while she prepared herself for incoming patients. Of course more recently that time had been used for their supply closet trysts…but no one needed to know that.

"You know how Kat feels about being on time for things," he said. "She wouldn't be late without a reason. Has anyone heard from her? Is anyone looking for her?"

"Now you're the one being preemptive," Selena said. "I

agree that it's strange for Kat to be late for anything, but it's a little early to start worrying. For now, let's keep an eye out and assume that whatever's holding Kat up isn't too much of an emergency."

Jack didn't like it, but he knew that Selena was right. Catastrophizing wasn't going to help. But he was still worried. Kat was punctual to a fault, and he knew she wouldn't be late unless something serious had come up.

He walked by the reception desk and passed Kimo, who was preparing trays of pineapple and dried coconut for the break room.

"Hey, Jack, weren't you looking for Kat earlier?" Kimo said. "They just brought her in—in an ambulance. I think you can still catch her down there, if you hurry."

An ambulance? Oh, God. The minute he'd heard she was late he'd known something bad had to have happened.

He ran at full speed to the ambulance docking bay, where he saw a few EMTs milling about by an ambulance with open doors.

Inside he saw Kat, unconscious on a gurney.

He shoved his way through and leapt into the back of the ambulance. He started checking Kat's vitals. She appeared to be breathing—good. What had happened? Why were the EMTs acting as though nothing was wrong? Why wasn't anybody taking care of her?

"Kat?" he said. "Kat, can you hear me?"

He couldn't lose her now. His jaw set. He'd do whatever it took to fix his mistakes…assuming they could be fixed at all.

She lay in front of him, her eyes closed, her breathing shallow. Her red hair curled about her neck in ringlets and he realized that it was dripping wet—the same as it had been the day they'd first met. In fact, her whole body was soaked.

Had she met with another mishap in the ocean? If she had, he hadn't been there to leap to her rescue.

"Kat," he said again. "Please wake up."

His eyes stung and he swallowed back tears, thinking about their last conversation. Now something was wrong, and he hadn't been there, and it was his fault for not being willing to take a chance, to open his heart and give himself to someone who deserved love wholeheartedly.

A wave of shame washed over him as he remembered how effortlessly Kat had leapt off the north shore cliff with him, how trustingly she'd clung to his hand. Kat had taken a leap of faith, but he'd been so scared to take a leap into a relationship that he'd pushed her away from him. And as a result he hadn't been there when she needed him most.

He felt for a pulse. It was there, strong, and that was a relief to him. But why wouldn't she wake up?

"I should have been there," he said aloud. "Whatever happened, I should have been there."

And he would have been there if it hadn't been for his stupid pride, his stupid unwillingness to trust someone who trusted him. If he'd lost her forever, it was his fault.

But then, to his utter surprise, she began to move. He felt relief wash over him—she'd been lying so still he'd even worried about a spinal cord injury, but if she could move on her own it was nothing severe. This was confirmed as she arched her back and stretched, lifting her arms over her head languorously. Then she opened her eyes with slow, sleepy blinks, saw him at her side, and smiled.

"Hey, Jack," she said.

"What's wrong?" he said, trying to hide the terror in his voice. "Where are you hurt? Why are you all wet?"

He looked out through the back of the ambulance, his eyes stormy with anger. Why had the paramedics left Kat alone? Why weren't they helping?

"Relax… I'm fine," she said. "I'm learning to surf."

"You're learning to *surf*?" He couldn't hide his confusion. What did surfing have to do with anything?

"I still need a lot of practice. Maybe we can do that together, though? It'll be fun. Did you know that dogs and babies can surf?"

Dogs and…? What?

She wasn't making any sense. He checked her pupils to see if they were dilated. Could she have gotten a head injury?

Your fault, your fault, your fault, the voice in the back of his head intoned.

She put her arms around his neck. "Jack, I'm fine. You know, you were right about my needing a thrill, but that was only half of it. I needed some serenity, too. And you know what? I found it! For the first time in my life I went to the beach and I was actually able to relax."

"That's great," he said distractedly. "But where have you been hurt?"

"I haven't been hurt," she said, less sleepily than before. "Well, I got knocked over by a rogue wave, and that was pretty frightening, but I just relaxed and let myself float back to the surface. I'm getting *a lot* better at relaxing, thanks to you. Well, thanks to you and thanks to all the practice I've been putting in, of course. And thanks to the surfing lessons. Do you want to learn? I could teach you. I feel like I should teach you something after all you've taught me."

He gazed at her, baffled. She could sit up, and she was mobile enough that she could put her arms around his neck. As Jack's fear subsided he began to take in that maybe Kat *hadn't* suffered any serious injury.

"You're really fine?" he said.

"All body parts intact." She smiled. "Not even a scrape or a bruise."

"Then why…?"

"Why am I being hauled into work in an ambulance? There actually was a medical emergency on the beach near my apartment this morning—it just didn't involve me. Well, not as the patient, anyway. There was a child on the beach having an asthma attack, and the family had left his inhaler at the hotel. I swear, we need to give every tourist on this island a firm lecture about leaving important medical devices at their hotels. What good is an inhaler if you don't bring it with you when you go exploring?"

He smoothed her hair. "Sounds like your typical medical emergency. But you still haven't answered the question I'm most interested in: why have you been brought to the hospital in an ambulance?"

"After helping the EMTs out with the child on the beach I hitched a ride with them to work. And I got up so early this morning that I thought I'd take a little nap in the back while they drove." She frowned at the concern in his face. "I must have been sleeping pretty soundly… Jack, you weren't…*worried* about me, were you?"

He was so exasperated with her. "*Worried?* That doesn't cover half of it. Do you have *any* idea how *scared* I was when I saw you lying there?"

She gazed at him soberly. "I'm sorry, Jack. I didn't mean to alarm you. It was careless of me not to think about how it might look to you, me lying here asleep on a gurney. In fact, I've been careless about a lot of things. And I need to tell you something."

"I have something to tell you, too," he said.

"Actually—" she started.

"No, let me go first," he said. "I know you've only been here a short time, but I don't need more time to understand everything I already know I feel about you. I don't ever want to stand in the way of your career. I know that's what makes you happy. So I would never, in a million years, ask anything of you that would be too much for you to give. But someone I trust has told me something I firmly believe: secrets only hurt. So, in the interests of being honest with you, and with myself, I hope you'll let me explain how I feel about you."

She looked as if she was about to say something, but he laid a finger on her lips.

"Kat Murphy," he continued, "from the moment I lay eyes on you I thought you were one of the most obnoxious, bossy, self-assured women I've ever met."

"Wow," said Kat. "Tell me how you *really* feel."

"Hold on," he said. "I'm getting to the important part. Matt was right—I need to tell you. Getting to know you, letting myself get close to you, was one of the best decisions I've ever made. I don't regret any of our time together—not one single minute—and even though it was a short time, it's impacted my life more than any relationship I've ever had. I love you. And I'm saying that without any expectations, not because I want anything from you, but because you deserve to know how I feel and—"

"Jack, I'm staying," she said, as though she couldn't hold it in any longer, and a smile appeared on her face.

"What—? But no!" he said, dismayed. "Why on earth would you do that?"

"Oh, Jack," she said. "Isn't it obvious?"

"No, it isn't!"

She laughed. "No? Okay, I'll explain it, then. I'm in love."

"Kat, you *can't* give up an opportunity like this just for me," he sputtered.

No matter what Matt had said, Jack would *not* be the

reason that Kat slowed down in her career. They could do long distance. They could Skype. He could visit Chicago. Hell, he'd *move* to Chicago if he had to.

"My, aren't we arrogant?" she said, but she was smiling gently. "I didn't mean with you. I meant with Hawaii! Although," she said, and the look on her face was tender, "it's not as though you aren't a *very* nice perk as well."

"A nice *perk*?" he said, taking her into his arms. "I suppose I'll have to settle for being a small footnote in your tempestuous love affair with the island."

She laughed, but then grew serious. "Jack. Let me be clear. I do love it here, but there's an even more important reason that I'm staying."

"And what might that be?"

"Isn't it obvious?" she asked again.

And as she leaned against his chest and put her hands around his neck his heart melted.

"I love you," she said. "I'm happy here, but I'm happiest of all when I'm with you. I don't need to be working at some prestigious hospital to be happy. I can do exactly the kind of work I love right here. In fact, I think I've done some of my *best* work here. Because I'm working right beside someone I love."

He kissed her then—deeply, passionately, trying to put all the things he hadn't been able to say until now into the kiss. When they finally came up for air she rested her head against his chest, and he twined a curl of her hair around his fingers.

"So you're really staying?" he asked, still trying to believe it.

It was so much to take in: that she was here and that she really loved him. Somehow, against all the odds, it seemed as though his dreams really were going to come true.

He'd have to call Matt later, tell him about it…

"I really am," she said. "When I thought about going back to Chicago Grace I didn't feel excited about it. I have to admit that the idea of showing Christopher that he was wrong was appealing. But none of it felt as though it'd be worth what I'd be giving up."

"And what would that be, exactly?"

She grew thoughtful. "A chance to get what I want, rather than what other people expect of me. A chance to be happy." She snuggled closer to him and looked into his eyes. "And a chance at love."

"So, after everything that's happened, you believe in love, do you?"

"Oh, Jack, I do. I really do."

He held her close to him, breathed in the smell of her hair and smiled. "I do too," he said.

He pulled her toward him and was about to kiss her again when she placed a hand on his chest to stop him.

"Wait a minute," she said. "What did you mean earlier, when you said, 'Matt was right'?"

"I guess I haven't had a chance to tell you yet," he said. "I called my brother and we had a long talk about…about everything. I wouldn't say that things are back to normal between the two of us. I don't think they ever can be. But… we're talking again."

"Wow…" Kat said, and he saw that once again her eyes were wet with tears. "That must have been some conversation."

He let out a long, slow breath. "It was. But it's really thanks to you that I was able to have it in the first place."

"Thanks to me? How so?"

"You were the first person besides Matt who I felt I could actually be real with. It reminded me of what it felt like to have someone to rely on. It reminded me that that was something I'd missed."

She smiled shyly. "I think you might have reminded me of that too."

She leaned toward him, her mouth inches from his, and Jack had a sense of *déjà-vu*. He remembered another moment, months ago, when he and Kat had almost kissed in this very ambulance. What had stopped them? What on earth had they been waiting for? Looking at Kat now, he couldn't imagine ever hesitating to kiss her—not even for a second.

They leaned in to kiss, and then, occupied as they were, there was a lengthy silence.

Finally Jack murmured, "Just so you know...there's a surprise farewell party going on for you in the hospital."

"A farewell party? Don't tell me I've been fired again."

"Are you kidding? No, the staff will seize any chance they can get to throw a luau. I'm sure it'll immediately turn into a welcome back party the moment you go in there and share the good news. Should we go and tell everyone now?"

"Maybe not right now," said Kat. "I was actually thinking that this might be a good time for another impulsive decision..."

Kat let her fingers work their way down Jack's chest, opening the buttons on his paramedic's uniform.

"Are you sure about this?" he murmured, even as he began to unbutton her blouse. "You don't want to make a pro-con list first?"

"Hmm, let me think about that..." she said.

She pressed her mouth against his, tasting the salty sweetness of his lips. And as she let the kiss linger, she felt the deep feeling in her gut that was going to guide her from now on—the feeling deep in her body that told her she was home.

That settled it.

She pulled off Jack's shirt.

"Nah," she said. "No lists necessary. Let's be spontaneous."

* * * * *

OFF LIMITS

CLARE CONNELLY

This book is for romance readers everywhere, who fall in love again and again with the characters of our creation. You give our stories life just by reading them. Thank you.

PROLOGUE

'You've got the Prime Minister calling in ten minutes.'

Jack nods, showing not a flicker of response at the prospect of this. Then again, nothing about Jack Grant is what you'd expect. For a self-made billionaire-investor-cum-philanthropist-cum-sex-god, he is wild, disrespectful of authority and the establishment, and rough around the edges. Deliciously so.

Take this situation: Jack, in his bed, naked as the day he was born, uncaring that he should have been at his desk an hour ago. That I can see most of his beautiful back and backside. That my insides are clenching with hot, steamy lust.

'About…?'

It's a lazy drawl as he flips over and pierces me with those intelligent green eyes. His accent is pure Irish brogue. Like Colin Farrell after a night of cigarettes and booze: deep, hoarse and throaty.

'The latest episode of *The Great British Bake Off*.'

I roll my eyes. We've been negotiating to buy a huge swathe of Crown land for the last six months; it's at the highest level of negotiation and, given the media interest, the Prime Minister has become involved.

'What do you *think*?'

His laugh is a rumble that barrels out of his chest. 'Well, every man needs a good scone recipe.'

'And you've got one?'

'Sure.'

He grins. It's a grin that is at once devilish and charming, and I know how easy it must be for him to get women into bed. And that's before you factor in the body, the money, the power.

'Nine minutes,' I snap.

His grin unfurls like a ribbon on his face. My heart *kerthunks*. I ignore it. Stupid heart.

'Did you book Sydney?'

'Yes.'

He arches a brow at my impatient tone and, as if to contradict it, stretches in the bed, his arms high over his head, his body gloriously on display for me.

'And, Amber?'

I don't mean to sigh but when the Prime Minister's office is calling I feel there should be some air of responsiveness. Jack, apparently, doesn't agree.

'All arranged.'

Lucy's sister is taking a year's sabbatical from her job as an executive at a bank to manage the foundation's start-up year. She's insanely qualified and personally motivated.

'Salary agreed; she'll be based out of Edinburgh, as we discussed.'

He nods, but makes no effort to move.

'Seriously, Jack. Eight minutes. Get the hell up, already.'

'Ouch. Did you get out of the wrong side of bed this morning?'

He runs his fingers down his chest, drawing my attention to the ridges of his abdomen, the flesh so perfectly smooth and sculpted. My mouth is bone-dry.

'No.'

'You're even crosser than usual,' he teases, and my lips tighten impatiently.

As it happens, he's right. I got The Invitation this morning. The one that arrives every year, beckoning me to come and pay homage to my parents' marriage.

Ugh.

It's my least favourite social event—and the one time I'm forced to remember who I really am. The one time a year my parents recall me to the mother ship, reminding me that no matter what I do, professionally or personally, I'll always be Gemma Picton. *Lady* Gemma Picton.

Ugh.

'Sit down. Tell me all about it.'

He pats the bed beside him and I roll my eyes again, hoping he won't know how sorely I'm tempted. Just once I imagine giving in to *this*—the electrical current that is arcing between us. I never would...never could. He is as off-limits as hell is hot—the stuff of fantasies and nightmares.

'No, thanks.'

'What is it?'

'Nothing. Personal stuff,' I say, and he shrugs.

But there's curiosity in his eyes. A curiosity I have to ignore. Along with desire. Lust. Want. Need.

We have our boundaries and we definitely know better than to cross them.

Jack pushes the sheet off, exposing the tattoo that curls across his lower back and snakes around his hips to the tops of his legs. It must have hurt like hell to get it done—especially on the skin of his thighs, right near his cock.

I asked him once why he'd got it. His answer? *'Seemed like a good idea at the time.'*

He doesn't care that I see him naked. It's not the first time and undoubtedly won't be the last. Sometimes I wonder if he's goading me, waiting for me to react. After all, it's classic workplace sexual harassment.

Except it isn't. Because I'm not harassed.

I'm amused. And more than a little turned on.

In the two years since I started working for Jack I've probably seen him naked on average once per week. That's over a hundred stare-fests and he is *totally* worth staring at. I don't think he used to be like this. Before *this* there was *her.*

Lucy.

His wife.

But she got sick and died, and two months later I came to work for him and he was like this. Dark and brooding and desirable and sexy and messed up and mourning and fascinating.

This sleeping with anything in a skirt is post-Lucy. Same as the copious Scotch-drinking afterwards. It's sensual self-flagellation but he won't see it that way.

So, no matter how much I want to stare at his naked arse, I know he's for looking at—not touching. Like when Grandma used to take me shopping at her favourite Portmeirion boutique and I was allowed to stare at the intricate floral and botanical artwork for hours on end, but never, ever to touch.

Because touching might lead to breaking—and, yes, touching Jack would, I fear, break me.

'See something you like?'

Another drawl—he's so good at that. He lets words slide out of his mouth like liquid chocolate.

'Nope.' My smile is saccharine. 'Seven minutes.'

I spin on my heel and leave, a smile playing around my lips as desire pools between my legs.

Gemma is staring at me, and the mood I'm in I feel about two steps away from going all 'Me Tarzan, You Jane' on her. I want to grab her round the waist and pull her down on my length. No foreplay. No teasing. Just her…taking me deep.

In my fantasy she's not wearing panties and she's left her brain at the door—because real-life Gemma would quote me a thousand reasons not to have sex even as she was moaning in my arms.

Last night was fun. At least, it started off as fun. But the woman I brought here…Rebecca? Rowena?… talked too much.

She'd wanted to be romanced.

I wanted to screw.

So I gave her cab fare and showed her the door.

And now I have a raging hard-on and an assistant— she hates it when I call her that, so I do it often, even though she's technically my in-house counsel—who seems to have moved into my sexual fantasies permanently. When did *that* happen?

I rack my brain, trying to pinpoint the moment I went from observing her to obsessing over her. From looking dispassionately at her in those suits she wears one day, and the next imagining how long it would take me to strip her out of one.

I don't think it was one *day*, though, because that implies some switch was flicked. No, I think it was a look as she got into my helicopter in Spain. A laugh over dinner. Hearing her hum as she stared out of a window, her mind obviously running at a million miles an hour.

Then there was that blackout we were once caught in at the City office. The fire alarm shut the place down, closing us inside an elevator for close on an hour, with just the dim flicker of emergency lights that made her legs look so long and smooth. By the time they cranked the doors I was about ready to pin her to the carpeted floor and screw her senseless.

Yeah, that was probably the moment I realised how much trouble I was in.

I'm not interested in a relationship. But I do want to fuck her. And I think she wants it, too. I've seen the way her caramel eyes drop to my arse when she thinks I'm not looking.

But I'm always looking lately.

CHAPTER ONE

SHE MIGHT AS well be naked. The dress is skin-tight, bright red and low-cut. Tiny straps slip over her shoulders. The dress is short, too. Not indecently short but, *Jesus*, her legs are long and smooth, and while she's wearing that dress I find it impossible to look away.

She's hotter than any woman here—and that's saying something, given that this launch event has brought together most of London's elite. There are models, actresses, singers, athletes, and lots of those women who've married for money and now make it their life's work to live up to their husbands' expectations.

And then there's Gemma.

Her blond hair is pulled into a ballerina bun, her face is serious and her body is like pale silk that I want to wrap around me.

She's said something funny, going by the way the guy with her leans forward and laughs. Is he her date? A frown pulls at my brow. I stare harder. Did she bring a date? Isn't she technically here as my plus-one?

Seeing her with another guy does something dangerous to my equilibrium. A possessive impulse threads through me, knotting at my chest.

I pull a couple of champagne flutes from a passing

waiter and cut through the room. I'm aware of people trying to get my attention but I have no time for them. Gemma is in my sights.

'Jack…'

Her lips purse as I approach; her eyes flick to me in that way she has. How is it possible for one person to imbue a simple gesture with a measure of cold disdain even when there's the hint of a smile somewhere in that symmetrical face of hers?

I hand her a glass of champagne and she takes it, her fingers briefly wrapping over mine. Immediately my mind puts them elsewhere on my body.

'You remember Wolf DuChamp?' she says. 'He manages our accounts in New York.'

I remember his stupid name, but not the man himself. Nothing memorable about blond, pretty-boy looks and that air of Ivy League he seems to wear like a coat.

'Sure.' I extend my hand, knowing I have to meet the convention even when my body is singularly focussed on Gemma.

'Good to see you again, sir.'

Gemma's lips quiver. I hate being called 'sir' and she knows it. Out of nowhere I have an image of her saying it to me, bent at the knees, her eyes moving up my body to meet mine as her lips clamp down on my length. Okay, maybe in some circumstances I could make an exception…

What the hell am I thinking? These fantasies are one thing, but screwing Gemma cannot happen.

Cannot happen. Might as well get that tattoo added to my collection.

'I was just explaining the software overhaul we're looking at to Gem.'

Is he trying to piss me off? First of all by removing the very nice image I was enjoying by talking about software. And then by referring to Gemma as 'Gem'—as though they're best buddies who paint their nails together.

'I'll summarise it for you later,' she says, sensing my impatience though I suspect not the reason for it.

'It'll make a huge difference to our operations,' Wolf pushes.

'Gem' angles her body a bit, turning away from me, giving me a chance to escape.

'I'll look into the feasibility. The problem is going to be short-term. We'll need to make sure the systems are protected during the transfer of data. You handle some of our most sensitive work—a data breach would be unacceptable.'

'I've thought of that, too,' Wolf carries on—and I am dismissed, it would appear.

Across the room a platinum blonde with a sensational rack and legs that go on forever is trying to catch my eye.

I want Gemma, but I can't have her. And I'm not one to wallow in self-pity. There's plenty of fish in the sea.

I have two rules when it comes to the women I fuck.

No commitment.

No redheads.

Commitment was for Lucy.

And Lucy was a redhead.

I freeze. A vision of Lucy is in front of me, a scowl of disapproval on her face. I messed around a fair bit before we met, but nothing like this. I've taken it to a whole new level and I don't care. Except for that scowl. Even in death I don't want to upset Lucy.

What did you expect, Luce? You left me a pretty big void to fill.

Don't blame me, I hear her snap back. *Your life. Your choice.*

Yeah, right.

My eyes wander of their own accord back to Gemma. She's got her head bent now, and Wolf's fingers are typing something into his cell phone. She nods and smiles, then presses a hand to his forearm. My stomach rolls on a surge of emotion I don't much care for.

I stalk towards the blonde as though she is the only woman in the room.

'I'm Jack Grant.'

Her lips are painted a bright red. She purrs. 'I know who you are.'

'Then you have the advantage.'

Her lips part. 'From what I hear, telling you my name wouldn't serve much purpose. You won't remember it tomorrow, right?'

I laugh, appreciating her honesty. 'No…' I lean forward so that my lips are only a whisper from her ear. My breath flutters her hair and I see a fine trail of goose bumps run across her skin. 'But you'll remember *me* for the rest of your life.'

Her laugh is husky. She's everything I would usually find sexy, but in that moment she's just passably acceptable. If I'm honest, I'm bored. It's a phone-it-in flirt. A *What the heck?* situation.

'We'll see…'

'Can I get you a drink?'

'I can share yours,' she murmurs, her eyes dropping to my champagne flute.

I didn't even realise I was still holding it. I extend

it to her on autopilot, watching as her lips shape over the glass and she tilts it back. The liquid is honey-gold. She passes the glass to me and I take a sip.

'Let's get out of here,' she says, with a throaty laugh in the rushed words.

I nod, reaching down and putting a hand in the small of her back. Gemma and Lucy are both in my head now—a fascinating occurrence. A *new* occurrence. Are they ganging up on me? Would they even *like* each other?

Lucy was so soft and sweet. She looked at me like I was her saviour and I suppose I was. I ripped her out of her old life, away from a boyfriend who used her as a punching bag, and I made all her dreams come true.

But fate is a bastard of a thing, and it only had bad news in store for Lucy. For a while she managed to jump tracks and sit on a different train, and then— *bam*. It took her. You can't outrun destiny, can you?

Gemma is nothing like her. Her personality isn't so much hard edges as a single hard face. She is smart— smarter than me by a mile—and focussed in a way that is completely familiar to me. She is also sexy. I don't know how I know that, but I do. She acts so damned cold around me—as though she's never so much as *heard* of an orgasm, much less experienced one. It makes me want her more. Want to show her for the liar she is. To make her orgasm again and again until 'cold' is a very distant memory.

'Jack.'

She catches me as I'm about to leave the room. Her eyes briefly meet the blonde's. There is nothing beyond a polite acknowledgement of her existence. That iciness is there. I want to push Gemma backwards against the wall and kiss the hell out of her. Right here.

'You're scheduled to speak in twenty minutes.'

Whoops. Even for me that's a bit of a slip. I don't usually let anything get in the way of business—even my sex life.

'We'll be back by then.'

Blondie surprises us both. Her meaning is unmistakable.

Shit. I can't remember the last time I had a quickie in the car. Is she seriously suggesting it?

Gemma shifts her attention to her phone. She runs that iPhone as though she designed the thing. Her fingers fly over the screen like it's a part of her. Her complacency pisses me off.

'Okay. The talk can be brief. Just an outline of what the foundation is hoping to achieve, thanking the commercial partners, yada-yada-yada.'

'Yada-yada-yada?' I grin slowly, my eyes linking with hers, daring her to forget the coldness and complacency.

She looks at Blondie and her smile is perfunctory. 'Have fun.'

Of course Jack nails the speech. Not so much as a hair on his head looks out of place. The tuxedo is immaculate. The white shirt crisp. The bow tie in place as though glued. He speaks eloquently about the foundation and he also speaks with humour, so the crowd laughs.

I don't.

I am wondering about the blonde.

No. I'm thinking about Jack—but they're thoughts that I need to run a mile from. This *can't* control me.

I've worked my arse off in this job, twisting myself in mental knots to stay on top of my workload without breaking a sweat, and I am *not* going to let the fact that my boss is impossibly hot get in the way.

Instead I let my attention drift to Wolf.

He's talking to someone else now—no doubt about that bloody software. His face is serious, and that makes me smile. Because Wolf is pretty much always serious.

Warning! Warning! Warning! It flashes inside my mind. Because I don't *do* serious, and if I let the flirtation with Wolf keep going I think he's going to see roses and candy and wedding bells.

God help me, I can't think of anything worse.

I am suffocating at the very *idea* of being a bride in white, having Wolf waiting for me at the end of an aisle. He would definitely want children, too. Three of them. And he'd expect me to be the obliging baby-maker and carer. He'd look at me with those puppy-dog eyes, sadness and disappointment on his features, if I so much as dared suggest we get a nanny.

Maybe I could be like Marissa Mayer and have a nursery built into my office? The nanny could be based there, so I could still be one of those hands-on Pinterest-type mummies. Wolf would never even need to know I'd hired someone to help.

But Jack would. He'd *hate* that. A baby crying when I'm trying to talk to him about tariffs on our Chinese imports? No, he'd probably seduce the nanny and then I'd have to either fire her or kill her.

Okay, *now* who's getting ahead of themselves?

But Wolf has caught me watching him and his heart is so on his sleeve he might as well be a cartoon character, with one of those thought bubbles popping out

of his head. I *have* to let this opportunity pass me by.
He's not right, and when he realises that I'm not going
to leave Jack and move to Manhattan, working with
him will become a nightmare.

I look away.

Right at Jack.

He's standing in front of me.

The band has started to play and I've been so lost in
imagining the hell of my future with Wolf DuChamp
that I haven't realised.

'Did you like the speech?'

'Looking for compliments?' I sip my champagne,
pleased at how quickly I'm able to recover. 'What's the
matter? Wasn't she suitably impressed?'

His eyes clash with mine. He's angry. *Ooooh.* Why?
Have I hit the nail on the head somehow?

'Are you wondering if I can please a woman in fifteen minutes?'

He shifts his body infinitesimally, but enough to
spark something low in my abdomen. Anger. Resentment. Heat. Warmth. Need.

Fuck.

'Believe it or not, I haven't given any thought to your
bedroom prowess,' I lie, shifting my attention back to
the room of people. London's elite swirl around us, and
I am wanting to swirl away with them.

'Liar,' he says, so softly I think I've misheard.

Because we can't go there! He knows that—I know
that. Every bone in my body wants him, but my brain
is still in charge. I don't want to screw up my career,
but it's more than that. I *love* Jack. Not in *that* way. I
mean I love working with him. Even when he's at his

assholiest, he's become one of the biggest constants in my life. How stupid would it be to rock the boat?

I imagine, briefly, that we indulge in an affair and it ends—because Jack doesn't do permanent—and then I imagine not seeing him again.

It makes me ill.

I don't want to think about it.

I don't want to risk it.

'The speech was good.' I bring the conversation back onto far safer ground, trying to fold my desperate realisations away neatly into a box I won't open again.

'Tell me something, Gemma,' he says, and the tone of his voice is still dangerous to me.

He hasn't got my silent memo, obviously, because his words prick the blood in my veins until it gushes and gurgles through me—he's flirting with me.

I use my most businesslike tone. 'Oh, I don't know if you really want me to do that. You might not like what I say…'

His eyes lance mine. It's like being sliced through.

'What's the deal with you and that guy from New York?'

Who's he talking about? Oh. Right. 'You mean Wolf?'

His lips curl derisively—that's one of my favourite of his expressions. I don't know if he realises how devilishly sexy he looks.

'Who calls their kid after an *animal*? Especially when he's the least wolf-like person you can imagine.'

'I don't suppose they knew that when he was born,' I say, but a smile is pushing at my lips. He's right. Wolf is handsome, but in a very neat and tidy kind of way.

'Is he a wolf in the bedroom?'

The question catches me completely off guard. It's

wholly new territory for us. Invasive in a way I don't know if I like but am worried that I might.

Still, challenging Jack is what I do. That's who we are.

I tilt my head to one side, assessing him for a moment, before volleying back, 'How was the blonde?'

'She was dull,' he says with a shrug and no hesitation, apparently having no qualms discussing his sex-life with me.

'Where is she?'

'At her house. Waiting.'

'For you?'

He shrugs. 'I said I might stop by. It seemed like the only way to get rid of her.'

Wait. He *hasn't* slept with her? No, not slept with. Fucked. The thought is oddly elating, though I can't help but feel sympathy for the woman he flirted with and then sent packing.

'You really are a bastard,' I mutter. 'Are you going to go to her?'

His eyes are probing mine now, and I feel like every single one of my fantasies, my dirtiest, hottest dreams, are playing out between us like a kinky Pensieve for his pleasure.

Yes, I'm a Harry Potter diehard. Hermione was one of my first role models.

'Maybe.'

My stomach turns. I am used to this feeling with Jack. In the first six months we worked together I wasn't so adept at dealing with his vivid love-life. I blushed whenever I found evidence of his nocturnal activities, and I couldn't always meet his eye. But now? Well, now I've had two years to practise acceptance.

I smile blandly. 'Well…' I shrug as though my

heart's not racing and my nipples aren't throbbing. 'Have a good night.'

'Wait.' His words are commanding, and so too is the hand he clamps around my wrist.

I jerk my face towards his, the breath exploding out of me. We *don't* touch. No more than an accidental brush of fingers from time to time. That's impossible to avoid when you're together as often as we are.

Definitely not like this.

His thumb pads across my inner wrist, and when I don't say anything he pulls me, hard and fast, so that my body rams into his. We are surrounded and yet we are alone. There is a void that engulfs us. Like a sensual electric fence.

This is all new and all wrong. And so right.

His body is tight. Hard. Hot. Just as it is in all my fantasies. It takes every single ounce of my willpower to close my mouth and let my breath return to normal. To look at him as though he's lost his mind, not made me lose mine.

'Yes, sir?'

His eyes flare. I meant it to put him back on his guard, to remind him of the boundaries of our relationship, but I might as well have struck a match over gasoline. He doesn't let me go.

'Dance with me.'

The air around us is charged with expectation and I just know he's asking for more than a dance. Does he expect me to say no? I don't like living up to expectations, and I'm not going to give him a reason to think I'm afraid of what's going on between us.

'Fine.' My smile is tight. It stretches over my face like sunburn.

He expels a breath, long and slow, and places a hand in the small of my back. No…just at the very top of my arse. His fingers are splayed wide and they press into me firmly, so that I'm propelled towards him. His other hand links with my fingers, wrapping through them.

I focus on the band, my eyes taking in the details of their appearance while I concentrate on looking completely calm. I'm not, though. I'm weak when I want to be strong, and I need something that I shouldn't.

'This dress is sensational,' he says, immediately shattering my attempts to find calm.

'Is that your informed fashion opinion?'

Too tart. I soften the snap with a smile. It's a mistake. His eyes are mocking, his own smile sardonic.

I look away again immediately.

'It's my informed opinion as a red-blooded male.'

'What do you like about it?'

Warning lights are flashing in my mind, clamouring for attention. They are bright and angry. What am I *doing*?

'Let me see,' he murmurs. 'The colour. The way it's literally glued to your skin.'

He drops his head closer and heat spirals inside me; my blood is a vapour of steam in my veins.

This isn't right. It's not us. He sleeps with other women and, sure, he flirts the heck out of me, but that's harmless.

This doesn't feel harmless.

The music slows and I slow with it, putting some space between us with what I tell myself is relief.

'Get me up to speed on the New York situation,' he says.

'I intend to.'

I'm snappy because I'm uncertain. I'm completely wrong-footed by his nearness, his touch, and my own desire for him is swamping me. I need a minute to re-group, but his fingers are giving me no time. They're throbbing across my spine, my arse, and I am heating up by the second.

'Tonight. Now.'

I angle my head towards Wolf unconsciously. He's still locked in conversation. I have no intention of going home with him, and yet I resent Jack's implication that I don't have a life of my own.

'It's not urgent.' My words are stiff. 'It'll keep till tomorrow.' And I force myself to pull completely free of Jack's grip.

It's the equivalent of grabbing a lifeline from the side of a sinking boat. It's slippery, and I'm pretty sure I'm not strong enough to hold on to it for long enough to save myself. Drowning is inevitable.

'I want to hear about it tonight.'

It's a challenge. A gauntlet. He gives me a lot of latitude in my job because he knows how much I do. And I do it well. But at the end of the day he's my boss, and I don't know if anything is to be served by refus-ing him this request.

'Fine,' I say with a shrug of my shoulders. But I'm not going to let him think he's won. 'I just need... twenty minutes.'

I disconnect myself from him and try not to register how my body screams in frustration.

I saunter off towards Wolf before I can see if Jack's reacting in the same way.

Wolf is deep in conversation when I approach. 'May

I have a moment?' I look with a hint of apology towards the men he's with.

'Sure.' He grins at me. A nice grin. He really is good to look at. Not groundbreaking, earth-shattering, but *nice*.

He puts a hand on my elbow but I am leading *him*, walking quickly out of the ballroom, seeking privacy for no reason other than to give Jack a taste of his own damned medicine. That and to send a loud and clear message. He doesn't control every part of me.

'All good for later?' Wolf asks.

I smile. 'No, it's not. I have to work tonight, actually. I'm going to brief Jack on the software situation.'

'Tonight?' He arches a brow, his voice rich with disbelief.

'He micromanages *everything*,' I explain. It's true. 'And he's impatient as hell. I just want to make sure I have all the information.'

He nods, not quite hiding his disappointment. 'Let's recap.'

And that's how I spend the nineteen minutes I have. Well, eighteen… I allow myself one minute to pull a bit of my hair loose from its bun and to pinch my cheeks, making them appear flushed with pleasure.

Jack is waiting for me in the limousine twenty-five minutes after I left him. I imitate breathlessness as I step inside, and enjoy the way his eyes sweep over me with undisguised speculation.

'Ready?'

It's not what I expected. I nod, but as I do so I feel like maybe I'm agreeing to something I don't understand. Like there's a hidden meaning I don't yet know.

'Yeah. Let's go.'

CHAPTER TWO

I'LL SAY THIS for Jack. He knows how to do *this*. Late-night entertaining is clearly his forte.

His office is dimly lit and he's switched on some kind of acoustic guitar album that's humming low in my abdomen. The vocalist has a husky rasp and it's doing very strange things to my equilibrium. He mixes two martinis with a maraschino cherry in each.

I arch a brow as he hands me mine. 'I hate cherries.'

'Interesting,' he murmurs, his eyes hooked to mine. 'Why?'

I stare at it and swirl the glass, sipping the alcohol and wincing as the slightly medicinal flavour assaults my back palette. 'They're weird. Plasticky.'

'Not the real ones.'

'No.'

I swallow, wondering at the way my gut is churning and my pulse is racing. I need to bring it back to business. It's the reason I'm here with him.

'The server in Canada can pick up the slack, but it's going to slow things down.'

'By how much?'

'Just a few seconds' lag. It's unavoidable, given the distance.'

'A few seconds?' He shakes his head. 'There's no-where closer?'

'Not that can handle this amount of data.'

He throws his drink back in one motion. 'And *Wolf* thinks that's acceptable?'

He says his name with obvious derision.

'You think he'd go to the effort of flying out here to propose it if he did?'

'Well, he's banging you, right?'

I can't hide the angry intake of breath. Sure, he's always rude. And demanding. And I've learned not to give a shit. I don't expect the same courtesy from Jack Grant that most people pepper into life. But this is too far even for him…even when we've been flirting all night.

'His suggestion is professional,' I return softly. A warning lurks in my words. Does he hear it?

Apparently not. Jack is like a cat with a mouse.

'But you are fucking him?'

'God, Jack,' I snap, standing up.

His eyes follow the fluidity of my movement. They're narrowed. Assessing. He's reading me like a book. But I'm too angry to care. Too worked up, as well. He's halfway to being drunk, and he's obnoxious, and since he pulled me hard against his body I'm a bit mushy.

I hide my mushiness, though. I hide it behind a veil of anger. 'That's none of your damned business.'

His eyes flick to mine. There's a lazy arrogance in his features but anger palpitates off him.

'He works for me. You work for me. If you're fucking him I want to know.'

'What I do in my own time, and with whom, is up

to me. Until the day it starts affecting my job performance you should just butt out.' I jut my chin, my eyes
sparking with his. 'Got it?'

He looks calm, controlled, but I know there's an
undercurrent of emotion just beneath the handsome
surface. Because I know Jack. Probably better than
anyone else on earth.

'You don't strike me as coy,' he says.

'Because I'm not.'

I step backwards. The wall is behind me. I brush
against it, feeling cornered and unbelievably confused
and turned on by this strange turn of events.

'So answer the question.'

'Am I fucking Wolf?' My question emerges as a
husk in the night.

'Yeah.' He moves forward. An infinitesimal step.
'You know everything there is to know about me, don't
you? So why keep your secrets?'

I open my mouth to say something snappy, but shut
it again. He's right. I know a lot about him. Not the 'everything' he claims, but a lot.

'You could always lock your door if you want to be
more private about your love-life.'

'*Sex*-life,' he interjects swiftly, on autopilot, and I
know it's because of Lucy that he's so emphatic on
this point.

I don't know anything about his wife. I presume
she was a nice enough person—although agreeing to
marry Jack does make me question both her sanity and
her judgement. But maybe he was different before she
died. Maybe his bastard impulses weren't so apparent?

'So you're going to live out the rest of your life like
this? Moving from one woman to another, never get-

ting to know a thing about them beyond their cup size and their sexual proclivities.'

His eyes drop to my breasts and I can tell he is assessing *my* cup size. *Crap.* My nipples strain hard against the flimsy fabric of my dress—it's too tight for a bra, and sadly I don't really need one.

His smile is self-satisfied and I want to slap it off his face. I fight the urge to cross my arms and cover my involuntary reaction.

'I'm trying to get to know more about you right now,' he says.

My pulse is hammering hard in my veins. His revolving-door bedroom flashes before me in an instant. The number of mornings I've arrived to find him asleep after a busy night of... Best I don't imagine that right now.

'Are you afraid I'll judge you?'

I open my eyes to find him right in front of me, his head bent, his body just a hair's breadth from me. A soft moan escapes me before I can catch it.

'You? You think you'd have any right to judge me after parading half of England through here?'

'Not half of *England*,' he murmurs, a smile shifting over his face. 'Half of London, maybe.'

'How do you justify it?' I ask, feeling a dangerous pull towards a line of questioning my brain is shouting at me to back away from. 'You think Lucy would be happy that you're fucking your way through a smorgasbord of women just because you won't have an actual relationship? Is there a sliding scale of monogamy that the dead expect?'

A muscle jerks in his cheek. I recognise that I'm stirring him up and still I don't stop. I'm angry, too!

He doesn't have a monopoly on thwarted desire and pent-up frustration.

It feels good to goad him! *So* good!

'You think what you do is fair to these women?'

His smile spreads slowly, but it is cold, angry. 'I don't hear any complaints.'

Boom! It's the proverbial match to the fuel of my anger. I explode.

'You boot them out before you even know their names half the time! Where, exactly, would they lodge their complaint? My God, Jack. Of all the chauvinistic, selfish, careless—'

He lifts a finger to my lips, silencing me with the touch. His eyes on mine are intent. Heat builds inside my blood, at fever pitch now.

'You know...' His fingers dip into my drink, fishing out the bright red orb at its base. 'You have a tendency to be judgemental.'

My sharp intake of breath is dangerous, given his finger's closeness to my mouth. He runs it across my lower lip and I don't pull away. He holds up the cherry with his other hand. My eyes slip to it of their own accord.

'Haven't you ever discovered that you like something you thought you hated? Haven't you ever been wrong?'

I shake my head, not really sure of the question he's asking. He surprises me by lifting the cherry to his own lips and sucking it into his mouth. I watch for a moment, and as his finger drops from my mouth I try to say something. I'm not sure what, and I'll never have a chance to find out. He brings his lips to mine, press-

AH THE KNIGHT

ing the cherry into my mouth, rolling it around before sucking it back into his and crushing it.

The flavour is all around me and I no longer care. Because it is dwarfed by something else: the taste of *him*. Cherry flavour is on his tongue, evaporating in the flame of our kiss.

His lips crush mine, silencing any words, sucking them out of me, and a new heat spreads in my body. His kiss is punishment and it is possession. I cannot explain it better than that. It is a moment of clarity in which my anger seems to evaporate temporarily before it is back and I am kissing him—just as hard, with just as much fury.

My tongue lashes his and my hands are in his hair, rough, pulling at him, and I am kissing him as though I am still shouting at him with my touch.

He groans angrily and his body weight holds me to the wall, his strong legs straddling me, pinning me where I am. I think my brain is trying to tell me something, but I can hear nothing above the pounding of my heart and the rushing of my blood.

Desire is a whip, and it is lashing at my spine.

He drags his lips lower, nipping the skin of my shoulder with his teeth and teasing the racing pulse-point in my neck with his tongue. I groan, tilting my head back, knowing I need to stop this madness but accepting we are past that.

A line has been crossed. Not just crossed! Obliter-ated! There is newness to this. But I want to shape it, not be shaped *by* it. I need to be in charge—at least to some extent.

'Why do you care?' he asks, bringing his mouth back to mine and kissing me with enough force to hold my head hard against the wall. His hand drops to my dress, lifting the hem, and his fingers slide between my weak, shaking legs.

'Care…?' I mumble. What is he talking about?

He breaks the kiss but I have no space to think—not when his fingers are sliding inside me, his hand easily pushing aside the barrier of my flimsy underpants.

Oh, my God. I'm about to come. I swear, I'm this close. He swirls his finger around my wet muscles, teasing me, feeling me, and I am his. Completely.

'Why do you care who I fuck?'

The question is a gruff, deep demand.

I blink my eyes, trying to think straight. But he moves his thumb over my clit and I shiver, trembling in every bone of my body as I feel the wave building around me.

'I don't,' I snap through gritted teeth, sweat sheening my brow.

My eyes are shut, so I don't see him dip his head forward. It is a surprise when his mouth clamps over my breast, his teeth biting down on my nipple through the silky fabric of my dress.

My stomach lurches as he drags his teeth along my nipple, pulling, making me throb with pleasure. And his finger pushes deeper, then draws out. My own wetness glides across my clit as he thumbs my nerves, and I am lost. Exploded. Gone.

Heat shoots through me, bursting me apart, and I am panting loud and hard as he moves his head to the other breast.

Shit. It's too much. My muscles are clenching and my legs are hardly able to hold me up. I have had amazing sex, but something about this has blown all my experiences out of the water. Is it the illicitness of being with my boss?

My boss.

Jack Grant.

I groan in awareness of a moment I will undoubtedly regret, and then I groan at my weakness because I can't stop. There is a compulsion—no. An awakening. It is an acceptance of a truth I have fought too hard and for too long.

Two years of looks, laughs, infuriating arguments and differences of opinion have been leading to this. Two years of finding him in bed and fantasising about climbing in with him. I have resisted because he is my boss and I love my job—and because he's Jack-bloody-Grant. I have resisted acting on my deepest desires, but now I find it is impossible not to welcome his.

His hand drops to my side. His fingers dig into my flesh just enough to make me arch my back forward, but his hips rock me against the wall, crushing me with strength and passion. Hell, he's good at this. So, *so* good. So much better than I imagined.

And I've imagined a lot.

I whimper—a sound I don't think I've ever made in my life—as he brings his mouth back to mine, but the ghost of his kiss lingers on my breasts, making them painfully sensitised.

'Now do you think women complain after they leave me?' he asks, and he is stepping away, backwards, his eyes glinting in his handsome face as he stares at me with a confusing lack of passion.

There is colour in his cheeks and his chest is shifting hard, as is mine, with the pain of laboured breath. But his voice is steady and his eyes are cold.

His question doesn't make sense. I lift a finger to my breasts. They're tingling and swollen. I stare at him, unusually slow on the uptake.

'I give them what they want. What *you* want.'

And he turns sharply, stalking across the room and grabbing another drink. His back is to me as he throws back the glass and swallows, but I hardly register the movement. Shock is seeping into me. Shock at what we've just done.

Holy hell!

Was he proving a point? I am trembling, moistness slicks my underwear, my dress bears the marks of his kiss, my mind is tumbled—and he is *nothing*?

Feminine pique stirs in my gut. I fantasise about slipping the dress from my body and storming across the room. About pushing him to the floor and strad-dling him, making him admit he wants me.

I know he does. I felt the proof of his desire hard against my stomach. But sanity is returning, and with it the realisation that we have done something very, very stupid. There is no turning back. No unwinding time. I need to salvage my pride and get the hell out of his office before I do something really stupid. Like ask him to finish the job he started.

'I'll email you a full report on the server's feasibil-ity tomorrow.' My words are pleasingly stiff.

He grunts. 'There she is. My cold-as-ice assistant.'

I straighten my back. I have *never* been his assis-tant and he knows it. He's goading me. Spoiling for another fight?

I narrow my eyes. 'Oh, I'm not cold,' I hear myself say. 'I'm very, *very* turned on.'

Perhaps my honesty surprises him. He turns his

face, angling it towards me without actually looking in my direction.

'If you'll excuse me, I'm going to go and…blow off some steam.'

I walk out of there calmly, even though I am awash with doubt. Let him make of that what he will. If he imagines me going to Wolf… So what? If he imagines me going home to masturbate, looking at a picture of him, then let him.

I don't know if I give a shit.

It is cold when I emerge from The Mansion, and drizzling with rain.

One of the decisions I made within six months of coming to work for Jack was to move to Hampstead, where he lives. The hours I work, I don't want to lose any more to a lengthy commute.

The Mansion is at the end of a long lane that comes out near the Heath, and just around the corner from a happy little school is my townhouse. A Dickensian brick with a shining red door and window boxes that have been sorely neglected over the summer. I should have planted them with pansies and strawberries, as they were when I first moved in, but I've never got around to it.

I shoulder the door inwards and slam it closed behind me with true relief.

But then I make the mistake of shutting my eyes and there he is. Jack Grant…head bent forward…mouth moving over my breast. I curse darkly—a string of angry words that would have knocked my mother sideways if she thought I even knew such language—and stride to the mirror in my entrance way.

My breasts are covered by two dark, wet marks. I

lift my fingers to them and trace their outline, shuddering at remembered sensations, desperate for more. More of him. More of this.

I groan loudly and stomp through to the kitchen.

What the hell just happened? He's my boss. My *boss*! And I know what he's like. I know how messed up he is. For two years I have kept all this swirling desire at bay. Why couldn't I control it tonight?

I pour myself a glass of wine in the hope that it will somehow reach back through time and wipe the experience not only from my memory but also from existence. It doesn't. Each sip reminds me of him, and the faint overtone of alcohol hits the back of my throat, making me crave him.

This is *not* good.

I walk more slowly through the house, up the narrow stairs—two flights. The house is tall and skinny, with one or two rooms on each of its five storeys. My office is on the first floor; my bedroom and bathroom are on the next. There are three bedrooms on the next few levels, and a roof terrace right at the top. I love it, but I am not here nearly enough.

I kick my shoes off, then flick the light on with the base of my wineglass, narrowly avoiding spilling Pinot Noir on the beige carpet. I pad over the carpet and strip off the dress as I go. I'll give it to charity as soon as I can.

In just my still-damp underpants, I climb into bed and pull the duvet up to my chin. Wineglass in hand, I stare at the wall.

It's not *that* bad, is it?

People must do this kind of thing all the time. We

work together. Hell, we practically live together. Something like this was kind of inevitable.

I cringe.

It's so *not* okay. Wasn't I just congratulating myself a few days ago on the Very Important Lessons I've learned from watching female bosses get derided and demoted over the years? Surely the cardinal sin for any woman in the workplace is to get involved with a colleague? And definitely not a senior, super-rich, super-yummy, fuck-around kind of colleague.

Ugh!

There are only a handful of us that work at The Mansion. Jack's two assistants, his driver, a bodyguard and me. We are all bound by a strict notion of confidentiality, and I think most of his staff are too afraid of me to get on my bad side anyway. So it's not gossip I fear.

It's Jack. And it's me. It's the respect I suspect I have sacrificed by letting this happen.

Letting it happen? My brain is outraged. My brain, after all, *did* try to stop it.

Sorry, I wasn't listening. I won't make that mistake again.

I pour the wine into my mouth, wincing at the astringent taste I really don't enjoy. I'm tired. It's been a long day and a weird night.

The last thing on my mind as I fall into a tortured, sensual sleep is a question about what tomorrow will bring.

He's at his desk when I arrive the next morning, coffee steaming in front of him, dark head bent. I move past, telling myself I would never do anything as cowardly as tiptoeing even as I hold my breath until I'm past his doorframe.

'Gemma? Get in here.'

Shit.

I squeeze my eyes shut, suck in a deep breath. I can do this. We just kissed.

You didn't 'just kiss'. He stuck his finger deep inside you and made you come.

Shut up, brain.

He sucked on your breasts and you fell apart at the seams.

Seriously, I'm going to lobotomise myself.

'Gemma?'

With a silent oath, I spin on my you-can-handle-anything Jimmy Choo heel and stride into his office with my very best appearance of calm.

'Oh, hi, Jack.'

Crap. He's wearing the pale blue shirt that makes his eyes look like bloody gemstones. It's unbuttoned at the neck and I can see a hint of dark hair curling above the top button.

'I didn't realise you were here.'

His smirk shows my lie for what it is.

'Sit.'

I arch my brow, staying exactly where I am, ignoring the wall to my left. The wall he pressed me against while he explored me intimately. My eyes stray to the bar instead. To the cocktail he was drinking last night.

'Sit,' he says again, and there is something in his voice that makes my nerves twitch.

There is promise in that command. Promise and heat.

'How are you?' The question, softly asked, makes everything inside me tremble.

'I'm fine,' I snap, to counteract that response. 'And busy. What do you need?'

His smile spreads slowly across his face. It is fire and it is flame and my brain is beginning to get very, very anxious.

'How did you sleep?'

Does he know I dreamed of him? That in my dreams he did very, very bad things to me?

I swallow, crossing my arms over my chest as the memories nip at my heels. They are in the room with us, swirling around him, me and the things we did. I can't give them more air.

'Did you want something?'

He stands up, and I am frozen to the spot as he moves confidently across the room, shutting the door and clicking the lock in place.

'I slept badly,' he says, ignoring my question, his voice sunshine on my cool flesh.

'Mmm…?' I murmur, making sure no warmth conveys itself to him. 'Maybe you should have tried a sedative?'

He strides to the chair across from his and holds it out. Shooting him a look laced with my fiercest resentment, I sit down, careful not to so much as brush against his fingertips. Fingers that have now been inside me—that have not just touched me, but have breached my barriers and found my throbbing heart.

Fingers that have undone me.

I am holding my breath again. Is that how I'm going to get over this little hurdle? Suffocate myself? Is that even possible? I'm pretty sure we have some breathing trigger in our brains, but my brain is a bit pissy with me so maybe it would conveniently forget about the button.

I push air out consciously, quietly, and he takes his seat.

'Anyway…' I prompt impatiently.

His smile is a flicker. Is he *laughing* at me? Arrogant arsehole! That'd be just like him. See? That's the problem! I *know* him. I'm not one of his other women. I know that he is as bastardy as he is sexy.

'How did you sleep?'

I blink at him, my eyes wide. 'You've already asked me that.'

'You didn't answer.'

I expel a sigh that speaks of anger. 'Like I always do. Seriously, Jack. My desk is covered in paper. I have to get to work.'

'*I'm* your work,' he says with a shrug.

Insolent bastard.

He leans forward, and while his face is casual there is an urgency in the flecks of gold that fill his eyes. 'Did you see him last night?'

I want to remind him of the salient fact I pointed out the night before. It's not his damned business. But I'm not sure I can say that with such conviction now that I've tasted his mouth; now that I've been stunned by his desire.

Can I skirt around his question?

'*You're* my work? Okay, the thing is I have the New York guys waiting on contracts, you have a meeting in a week that I have to prepare for and Athens wants your input—which means *my* input—on a lease agreement. And I need to—'

'Quiet.'

God! Don't hate me, but when he's bossy I *love* it. And he's almost always bossy.

I glare at him across his desk; it's best if he doesn't know that this is just about my favourite version of him.

'You're fucking telling *me* to be quiet?' I lean forward, and we're close now: almost touching. 'Seriously?'

'You're pissed off.'

'Damn right, I am.'

His laugh is soft. Throaty. Hot. 'Because we didn't finish?'

I flick my eyes shut. My cheeks are hot. 'What do you need?'

'Are you in a relationship with him?'

'Who?'

'Wolf DuChamp?'

I hide a smile. 'So you *do* know his name?'

'*Now* I do.'

His expression is unreadable. But deep inside me something stirs. *Hope.* Because isn't there an implication there that he knows about Wolf because of *me*? Because he wants to know about *my* life?

'So? What's the deal?' he asks.

'Are you jealous?' The words are a challenge; they escape unbidden.

His response is razor-sharp. 'Why would I be jealous?'

Crap. A stupid challenge, apparently.

'Forget it.' I scrape the chair back and stand, my eyes not inviting argument. 'Is that all?'

'You haven't answered me. How can it be *all*?'

I expel a breath angrily. 'I like him.' I shrug.

It's true. Not romantically, necessarily. But he's a nice guy. Good-looking. It doesn't matter that I've already ruled out a relationship.

'Are you fucking him?'

My expression is ice—even I can feel the chill that spreads through the office.

'Isn't this the question that got us into trouble last night?'

He stands up, slamming his palms against the desk, his eyes lashing me. 'Are you *fucking* him?'

It's loud. Not quite a roar, but close to it. I'm startled. This is outside the bounds of anything that's happened between us and we both know it. Then again, I guess we've obliterated boundaries now. They—like me— are in a state of flux. Changeability that is unpredictable and not good.

'Go to hell.'

I turn around and walk out of his office, but my knees are shaking and I feel really weird, as if I could cry—which, for your information, I haven't done in years. I *literally* don't cry. Not at sad movies. Not when my cat died.

But I'm shaking, and if he follows me I'll be really lost.

He doesn't.

I storm over to my desk. I wasn't lying or exaggerating. Piles of paper clutter every available inch of the thing. I turn my back on them and stare over the Heath, my eyes brooding.

This is a damned nightmare, isn't it?

My brain nods along smugly. *Told you so.*

CHAPTER THREE

IT HAS BEEN a week and I'm still here. What's more, my brain and I are almost friends again. I have been behaving. Working hard, speaking politely, keeping my sexy, kinky 'if only' thoughts hidden behind a mask of disinterest.

Of course it helps that I've hardly seen Jack.

He's been in Tokyo for four days, on a trip I would usually do with him.

Here's how it would go: Private jet. Limousine. Luxurious hotel accommodation—his apartment there is being remodelled. Meetings. Late-night debriefing.

You get the picture, and you no doubt see the risk.

'I have too much on,' I said when he'd decided he needed to go personally. 'Seriously, there's no way I can leave the office now.'

He ground his teeth together, looked at me as though I were pulling some soppy, emotional crap and then he nodded. 'Fine.'

He's due back today and my desk is no clearer—it's just a different heap of papers that covers it now. My phone bleats and I grab it up, my nerves not welcoming the intrusion.

Perhaps my impatience conveys itself in my brusque greeting.

'You sound like shit.'

The cackling voice brings an instant smile to my face. 'Hi, Grandma.'

'Where've you *been*, lovey?'

'Oh, you know…' I eye the paperwork dubiously. 'Living it up.'

'If only. Let me guess. You're at work?'

'You called my work number, so I suspect you know the answer to that.'

Another cackle. 'Are you coming to see me any time soon? I have something for you.'

'Another lecture on my priorities?'

'You're a smart girl. You know your priorities are out of order.' She sighs. 'Take it from a woman at the end of her journey. There's a big, beautiful world out there, and even if you devote your life entirely to travelling you'll still never get to see everywhere and everything.'

'God, that makes me feel both nauseated and claustrophobic. It's saccharine and overly sentimental even for *you*, Grandma.'

She laughs. I love her laugh. My grandma shines a light with her smile alone.

'Everyone's allowed a bit of sentimentalism at some point, aren't they? Especially at *my* age.'

'I travel *everywhere*,' I point out, flicking my calendar onto my screen and scanning it. 'In fact I'm off to Australia next week.'

Crap. With Jack.

'Oh, yes? That wouldn't be a work trip, would it?'

I grin. 'No. And by no, I mean yes—but I imagine I'll still get time to pet a koala.'

'You know they're not just crawling around the streets? You actually need to go bush to find one.'

I burst out laughing. '*"Go bush"?* Grandma, you're a Duchess. I think it's in the manual that you're not allowed to "go bush"—or go anywhere, really.'

I'm not joking. Grandma really *is* a Duchess. She married my grandpa, who was a decade her senior and had come back from the Second World War with what we'd now know as post-traumatic stress disorder. She was a nurse, and his family hired her to care for him—to "fix" him. She quit on the first day. There wasn't anything wrong with him, she declared. He was just different.

They got engaged that afternoon.

It's the only fairytale I believe in—and only because it has a macabre degree of reality to it. Grandma *did* fix him. He made her a princess—of the social variety—and she made him whole in a different way, just like she said.

We lost him years ago, and now *she's* the one who's a little bit broken. But still amazing. The most beautiful person in my life. My other constant.

Jack and Grandma. *Great.* An emotionally closed-off sexy widower that I should definitely know better than to want, and a champagne-swilling octogenarian, relic of the aristocracy. These two are the anchors in my life…

I shake my head, my smile rueful.

'Pish! I'll have you know I went bush and did a great many other things in my time.' She sighs heavily. 'And now it's *your* time—and you're spending it in some ghoulish house on the edge of the moors.'

'It's a mansion, actually, with state-of-the-art offices. And it's Hampstead Heath—not a moor.'

'Still…' A huff of impatience. 'You'll come this weekend?'

'I promise.'

I click in my calendar and make a note. Without entering my plans straight into my calendar I'm running blind. My eyes are dragged of their own accord to the entry for my parents' anniversary. *Ugh.*

'I suppose you got your invitation?'

'Mmm…' It's a noise of agreement that could mean a thousand things. 'Very elegant paper.'

I stifle a laugh. 'Stiff and unyielding.'

My implication hangs in the air, unspoken.

'Ah, well. At least there'll be booze.'

'And lots of it.'

I run a finger over my desk. Grandma and I got rather unceremoniously sloshed at the previous year's anniversary affair. If we hadn't been related by blood to the bride *du jour* we definitely wouldn't have been invited back.

'We'll do a rehearsal at the weekend,' she says, and I hear the wink in her words.

'Perfect. See you then.'

'Good, darling. Ta-ta.'

My phone rings again almost as soon as I hang up, and the smile is still playing on my lips as I lift the receiver and hook it beneath my ear. 'Yeah?'

'Gemma.'

His voice gushes through me like a tidal wave crashes over the shore. We've been in constant contact while he's been travelling—but only via email or text, and only in the most businesslike sense.

At no point has he reminded me of the way his mouth pushed me back, tasting me, robbing me of comprehension and hammering every last one of my senses. At no point have we discussed how he made me come against the wall of his office.

Hearing his voice now is as intimate and personal as if he strode into the room and straddled me, reached down and kissed me...

'I'm meeting some clients in the City. I need that presentation on the Tokyo project, as well as an up-to-date cost analysis and the report I had done. Meet me in an hour.'

It almost sounds like a question, but we both know it isn't. My body hums with vibrations. *I'm going to see him again.* It's the most alive I've felt in a week. My abdomen clenches in anticipation. Of what?

My body is getting carried away, but thankfully my brain is still lucid-ish. 'Fine,' I hear my brain say, cool and unconcerned. *Liar.*

There's a pause and I wonder what's coming next. 'Good.'

The little tick of approval sends a thrill along my spine. I hate that. I repress my pleasure.

'And, Gemma? Rose has something for you.'

I gather the documents he needs and quickly run through the project presentation, then step out of my office, laden with files and my MacBook Air.

Sophia and Rose are in the office they share, heads bent, and I smile crisply at them. 'I'm meeting Jack in the City. He says you have something for me?'

I address the question to Rose, who reaches into her

desk and pulls out an envelope. It has his dark, confident writing across the front. My name, scrawled in his handwriting. I resist the urge to run my fingertip over the letters.

'Thanks.' I nod crisply and Sophia reaches for her phone before I've said another word.

'Hughes—Miss Picton is travelling to the City.'

'Thanks.' I nod, pleased that things are working efficiently.

I hired Sophia to replace the last of Jack's assistants to quit. He's run through about six since losing Lucy; my own job has been filled a dozen times at least. I think it kind of bonds Sophia and me—a similar determination not to fail runs through us both.

'Will you be long? Shall I move your two o'clock?' asks Rose.

I can't reach my phone and can't remember off the top of my head what I have at two. I guess my blank stare conveys that, because Rose smiles at me kindly. How she's managed to work for Jack for three years is beyond me. She's a butter-wouldn't-melt kind of woman, and yet there's a quality to her that makes her oblivious to Jack's demanding requests and lack of charm.

'Carrie Johnson.'

'Right.' I nod distractedly, thinking only of the mysterious envelope. It's small and there's something inside.

Carrie is my friend who's looking for a new job—I have her in mind for something with the foundation, though I don't know exactly what yet. She was made redundant in the last round of restructuring at her company, and she's brilliant and incisive—far too clever to let go.

'Yeah, shift it to tomorrow. Thanks. Please apologise for me.'

'Here.' Sophia scrapes her chair back and walks towards me with outstretched arms. 'I'll help you to the car.'

I hand over some of the papers gratefully. The offices are in a separate wing of The Mansion, and we step out onto the short path that winds through a manicured garden before opening out into a gravelled courtyard. It's really well designed to keep business away from personal life—not that Jack has much of a personal life outside his fuck-fests.

At least, not that I know of.

I slide into the back of the limo, distracted; I don't think I even acknowledge Hughes, which is unusual because I like him and we usually have a nice banter going.

You know everything there is to know about me.

I'm startled. The words come from nowhere and I look over my shoulder, half expecting to see Jack's cynical smile. Is that even true? Do I *really* know him that well?

We've spent a heap of time together, that's true. But I don't know if I would say I consider us well acquainted. Out of nowhere the memory of his lips on mine sears me, pressing me back into the leather seat with a groan.

I reach for the envelope, and now I give in to temptation, running my finger over his scrawled writing before tearing the top off.

My emotions are mixed as the object inside falls into my palm.

The distinctive dark red foil denoting a Cherry Ripe confectionery bar is instantly recognisable. I check the envelope for a note; there isn't one. But his meaning is clear.

I can't help it. I tear the paper off the bar and inhale.

Cherries will remind me of Jack forever. I don't think I can say I hate them anymore.

My gut clenches as I recall the intimate way his finger circled me, teasing every nerve ending, finding where to press to make me moan.

Fuck.

A shiver dances along my spine and it is still pulsing even as the car pulls into the underground car park of the City high-rise that houses Jack's offices. I gather he used to be based here a lot more. It was only after Lucy died that he set up shop, so to speak, at his home.

I make a point of smiling brightly at Hughes as I step out of the limo, laden with documents.

'Need a hand, ma'am?'

'I'm fine,' I demur.

I can't help but wonder if my cheeks are burning after the delicious thoughts that have travelled along with me.

Why did he stop? What happened to push him away from me?

I wanted everything. I wanted *him*. That technically makes me a complete idiot, right? Because I know he's a total man-whore, and I know it would make my job pretty untenable to be fucking Jack, but in that moment none of it had mattered.

Which only goes to show that I need to be even more on my guard with him.

I am *not* going to let this get out of hand. There are plenty of hot guys out there. Plenty of men who can kiss you like you're their dying breath.

Except I don't think that's necessarily true...

I've dated a fair few guys—most of them smart, handsome, powerful. I have a thing for that sort of man, I suppose. But none of them has done *this* to me. My mind is still mushy. I only have to close my eyes and remember the way it felt to have his body pressed hard to mine, almost holding me up with the weight of his strength, and I'm having palpitations and flushing to the roots of my hair.

The lift whooshes up and reminds me of the glass elevator in *Charlie and the Chocolate Factory*. It seems to be building up speed as we get nearer the top, and my tummy lurches as I imagine it bursting through the ceiling and flying into outer space.

It doesn't.

Is it wrong that I'm just a teeny bit disappointed? I always thought that looked to be so much fun—the way that elevator flew all over London's skyline.

The offices are buzzing, and it's so strange to be back in this kind of environment that I freeze for a moment, simply soaking in the noises. Anywhere else I've worked, it's been like this. I was like a headless chicken most days, surrounded by people who were every bit as harried and exhausted as I was. Exhaustion used to bleed into energy, so that I fed off a state of perpetual tiredness.

Someone rushes past, arms full of papers, and that reminds me that I need to do something with the files

I'm carrying. I begin moving quickly down the carpeted corridor, eyes straight ahead lest I be called upon to answer a query. The problem with being Jack's right-hand woman is that people see me as a substitute for him. I cannot visit this office without being waylaid with a dozen queries at least. Only I don't feel like talking to anyone at this point in time.

The conference room is at the end of the corridor. Two enormous timber doors provide entry to it. I shoulder my way in, making straight for the table, and I've just dropped the files down onto its glass top when I realise I'm not alone.

There's a movement to my right. No, a shadow more than a movement. But it captures my eye and I turn around slowly, careful to keep my expression neutral, because deep down I know who it is.

'You're here already,' I murmur, pleased with how unaffected I sound.

Especially when he's wearing his charcoal Armani suit with a crisp white shirt. And a dark grey tie. *Oh, God, help me.* I turn around, on the pretext of straightening the documents, but I feel the moment he starts to walk towards me and sweep my eyes shut.

My heart is pounding and my blood is gushing. What happened to pretending not to be affected by him? To keeping him at a distance?

'I'd say it's quicker to get here from City Airport than it is from my place.'

His voice is barely above a growl. It's primal and animalistic and a slick of heat runs through me.

'How was Tokyo?' I skirt around the table, laying information packs down as I go, checking each space has a glass of water.

He shrugs. 'Fine. And here?'

But his eyes are dropping. He's looking at my breasts as though he wants to take them into his mouth. As though he's remembering the way it felt to suck my nipple through the fabric of my shirt.

I moan, low and soft, so soft I don't think he catches it, but his lips flicker and I am in serious trouble. They are beautiful lips. Not full, but rather sculpted as if from stone. His face is peppered with stubble, as though he hasn't shaved the whole time he's been away.

I turn away, my breath uneven. I don't know what to do.

'As usual,' I say, no longer dispassionate, no longer smooth. My voice is jerky and unnatural.

I want to kiss him.

I *need* to kiss him.

I realise it in an instant and I turn around, back towards him. Our eyes meet and I feel a pulse of heat that I know I'm not imagining. It's a need so deep, so desperate, that I instantly imagine us fucking on the glass-topped conference table.

Is he thinking the same thing?

He takes a step towards me, his eyes latched to mine, his expression almost haunted. I part my lips on a breath and he stops just in front of me, catching that breath with his chest, and I can almost feel his lips on mine. It's a phantom kiss, but no less mesmerising than a real kiss because he's so close I can smell him…I can feel the warmth emanating from him.

'Did you get the chocolate bar?' he asks, and I feel my skin heat with memories.

I nod.

'Did you miss me?'

His voice is low and hoarse. I should laugh at him. That's what I would usually do. So why does his question fill me with a dawning despair? I can't ignore it. I'm suffocating under the realisation that I *have* missed him.

'Yeah, right,' I mutter, hoping it sounds more convincing to him than it does to me. 'I've been sitting in my office pining for you every day. One kiss and I've been writing your name in my notebook with little love hearts around it.'

I roll my eyes for good measure and so miss the moment he narrows his.

Jack isn't a man to be mocked. I know that, but honestly I wasn't intending to goad him. And yet I'm in no way surprised when his mouth crashes down on mine—for real this time, nothing phantom about it.

His hands pull through my hair, letting it out of the bun I looped it into earlier this morning. His fingers fist around it, holding my head under his so that his mouth has full access to me. And he *plunders* me. There's no other way to describe it. His mouth is a weight on mine and his tongue is angry.

Fierce heat pools between my legs.

He pulls on my hair as his mouth pushes mine, bending me backwards until my spine is on the conference table.

'Did you miss me?' It's a demand now, as he separates my legs and stands between them.

His cock is hard. I can feel it and unconsciously I writhe lower, trying to press myself against him, to connect myself to him.

His laugh is a dark imitation of the sound. 'Not now.'

It's a gruff warning, but insanity is cutting across me. I need him. If I don't have him I am going to scream. Sense is gone. Rational thought impossible. Even my brain seems to have momentarily forgotten itself.

I'm wearing a grey woollen dress and he rubs his hand over my breast, cupping it, holding me tight as his fingers graze my nipple. The fabric of the dress is coarse and the friction is unbearable.

His kiss is an insufficient prelude. I need so much more.

'More?' he murmurs, and I realise I must have spoken aloud.

He pushes my dress up my legs, and groans when he connects with the lace tops of my stockings. He digs a finger under one of my suspenders and then snaps it, hard, so that I make a sound of complaint. It's quickly muffled by a groan of pleasure as his fingers find my panties, pulling them roughly down my legs.

He stares at me and I wonder if I look as wanton as I feel. Hair tumbling around me like a golden halo, face pink, dress hitched up around my waist, legs spread around him.

His eyes are mocking as they meet mine. 'Haven't missed me, huh?'

I know I should say something sassy, pithy. Put him in his place. If his hard-on is anything to go by he's missed me, too. Or fantasised about me, at least.

'Like a hole in the head,' I murmur, but it's lacking spark.

He laughs, his hands firm around my calves as he spreads my legs wider, and before I can anticipate what he's going to do he brings his mouth down on me, running his tongue across my opening, lashing me with that same intensity he's just kissed me with. He pummels me, his tongue flicks my clit, and I am crumbling. I arch my back and stretch my arms over my head, my whole body trembling as wave after wave of need builds inside me. I'm so close to coming that I have to bite down on my lip to stop myself crying out.

'Have you missed me?'

He brings his mouth higher, dragging his tongue over my belly button, and his fingers push my dress up my body. His fingers find one of my nipples through the fabric of my lace bra and I jerk, because I am too sensitive already. I am only seconds from falling apart.

'Please…' I groan, moving my hips nearer to him, needing him to release me from this sensual torture.

'Please what?' he asks with a quiet anger I don't understand.

'Please,' I insist.

'Say it.'

Our eyes clash; it's a battle of the wills. I don't care enough to try to win it. At one time I would have fought tooth and nail, but not now. Now only one thing matters to me.

'Fuck me, Jack.'

'Here? In the boardroom at my office?'

I am going to hell. I don't even want to think about what my brain's going to have to say.

'Yes. Now. Please. Fuck me,' I whimper, so hot that I need him to *do* something. To fix this.

I drop my hand to my clit, but when I touch myself he grabs my wrist and pulls it away.

'No, that's cheating,' he whispers, his eyes on me as he loosens his belt and pushes his pants down just enough to release his gorgeous, glorious cock for me to see. I've seen it so many times, but now…? It's for *me*.

'Please…'

His eyes hold mine as he layers protection over his length, quickly, easily.

I push forward on the table, seeking him, and then he thrusts inside me, slamming me hard, and I feel the coiling of a pleasure that I cannot control. It is hot and fierce, and I cry out at the invasion that is so much better than my wildest fantasies.

His hands on my shoulders pull me up; he's so strong and I am lost in the moment. He pulls me against him and lifts me off the table so I can take him deeper, and I have a fleeting moment of gratitude for the heavy tint on the windows that surround the boardroom. His cock is spearing me, and I am wrapped around him, and he kisses me again—a kiss of such ownership and possession that I don't think I'll ever be able to lie to him again.

I *did* miss him.

'You want this?' he asks me, lifting my hips easily, gliding me up his length before pushing me down and making me cry out, my back arched, my nipples hard.

I nod.

'I didn't hear that.'

'I want this,' I groan, my fingers tearing through his hair, my mind completely scattered.

His laugh is throaty as he lifts me once more, but this time he eases me down to the floor, stroking up my dress as he goes.

I know outrage must show in my face, and I know he appreciates that.

'You want me.'

Mortification, anger and impatience are firing bullets across my desire.

I reach down and cup his hard-on, my eyes issuing him with a challenge. 'And you want me.'

He nods slowly, his eyes locked to mine. There is no mockery there now; instead I see something darker. Resentment.

'I want you.'

He turns away from me, pulling his pants up, buckling his belt, his shoulders set square.

He turns to face me, his expression suddenly businesslike. 'We'll talk after the meeting.'

I blink. The meeting. *Shit.* It's the reason I'm here but how quickly I've forgotten its existence.

My eyes fly to the clocks on the wall, each showing a different time zone. There are minutes to go before the others are expected, which means they could literally arrive *now.* I run my hands down my dress, then neaten my hair. No time to pin it back into a bun so I just smooth it with the palms of my hands until it sits neatly around my face.

I turn to face him, intending to ask for my underpants back. But the look he gives me is so fulminating that I lose my voice.

'You look like you've just been fucked,' he says darkly, and I sweep my eyes shut, shame spiralling through me.

What the hell has come over me?

I stalk towards him, my hand extended, waiting for the scrap of lace he must have somewhere, but he grabs my hand and jerks me against him once more.

'I like the way you taste.'

And he pushes me against the glass, and his hand pushes between my legs, and he pads a thumb over my clit. I'm already at breaking point. His body traps mine, but he doesn't kiss me. He watches me from a distance as he torments me with his thumb, moving faster until my breath is ragged and my eyes are huge.

'I want to taste you tonight. I want to spread your legs and dip my tongue inside you. Then I want to flip you over and take you from behind. You are so fucking hot when you're turned on.'

I whimper—a sound of pure confusion—because the pleasure of his words combined with the torment of his touch is almost more than I can bear.

I swear—a low, throbbing whisper—as my pleasure bursts like a waterfall. I come. I come hard. And as I do he slips a finger deep inside me, swirling it against my walls as my muscles contract. He stays there as I fall apart and then he glides his finger out and lifts it to his mouth, sucking on it while his eyes watch me.

The door is pushed inwards. It happens so quickly. I am still breathless, and I'm sure my orgasm is written all over my face. It's not like it was my first time, but this was *Jack*. He's Jack Grant—seriously sexy.

He should come with a health warning.

I hear my colleagues move into the room and I turn away on the pretext of getting myself a coffee from the back of the room.

He still has my underwear, and the tops of my legs are wet with the evidence of my own satisfaction. My breath is uneven.

God, this is going to be the longest hour of my life.

'Gem.'

Is that what everyone in the universe except me calls her? Her back has been towards me for at least three minutes and I've gone through the greetings and I'm waiting for her to turn around. I want to see her full red lips, her messy hair, her passion-soaked expression, and I want to know that I did that to her.

She angles her head sideways to greet Barry Moore, one of the transition team consultants on the Tokyo deal. 'Hey...'

Her smile is cool, her expression calm. The only sign that she was ravaged by me only minutes ago is that her nipples are straining against the fabric of her dress—something that might be explained by the ice-cold air conditioning.

'You did a great job on the summaries—thanks.'

'You got my email, then?' Her voice is calm and clipped, as always, those haughty, aristocratic syllables like plums in her mouth.

'On the flight over.' He nods, his eyes briefly dipping to her breasts so that I am flooded by an urgent need to bodily shove him aside.

'Jack? Shall we begin?'

I draw my attention away reluctantly, turning to the manager of the takeover team. 'Yes. Take a seat.'

I nod towards the table and find myself drawn to one seat in particular. I press my hands to the table-top, right where Gemma's legs were spread, and my eyes seek hers.

She meets them with fierce resentment.

She's pissed at me.

I just made her come in what I gather to have been a spectacular fashion and she's angry with me. Mind you, I guess I didn't really choose my time or place well. Leaving her breathless and wet right as some of the company's most senior staff filed into the room might explain her anger with me.

I sit down, my eyes not shying away from hers.

She chooses a seat at the other end of the table, on the opposite side. I cross an ankle over my knee and something catches my eye. Something dark and small. With a smile, I reach down and lift her underpants off the floor, palming them thoughtfully.

Her eyes are watching me and I see embarrassment creep along her cheeks, creating a hole in the armour of her professional composure. Her beautiful neck moves visibly as she swallows. And while I have her attention I lift my finger to my mouth and run it over my lower lip thoughtfully, tasting her openly.

Even from this distance I hear her sharp intake of breath and I smile.

I'm going to make her do that a *lot*.

CHAPTER FOUR

'I BELIEVE YOU have something of mine.'

Like my dignity. My self-control.

The meeting took almost two hours, and I managed to concentrate for the most part. But every now and again my insides would clench, reminding me that Jack had driven himself inside me—that he'd made me come against the glass windows of his boardroom and he hadn't experienced the same pleasure. I should have felt satisfied by that, but instead I was annoyed. Like he had proved how easily he could tear me apart and I hadn't done the same to him.

'Yeah…'

His smile makes my heart pound. Desire is slick in my blood, heavy and needy.

'So?' I put my hand out, then retract it, remembering belatedly that he has a habit of yanking me towards him when I give him the chance.

'So…' He reaches into his pocket and retrieves the underpants. 'I like the idea of you not wearing them.'

I roll my eyes. 'What a cliché. Do you expect me to dress a certain way for you from now on?'

His smile is a flicker at the corner of his lips. 'No…'

He wraps an arm around me easily, pulling me to

him. Of course he doesn't need my hand as an invitation. He has arms and hands of his own, and if he wants to touch me Jack Grant isn't going to wait for a bloody invitation.

'But if you did I'd enjoy doing what we just did over and over.'

I'm wet again. I can feel it building and I know that only fucking him—properly—is going to release this beast of need inside me. But I'm still fuming with Jack. How dare he do that to me right before an important meeting?

'No way,' I snap. 'Never again.'

He raises a brow, his smile genuinely amused. 'Really?'

And he reaches around for my hand, dragging it to his cock. I stare at him, challenging him, showing him I'm not afraid, as he curls my fingers around his length, rock hard inside his suit pants. My heart begins to bang into my ribs so hard that I absent-mindedly wonder if anyone has ever broken a bone that way.

'You *don't* want me to sprawl you out on the table and fuck you so hard you forget your own name?'

I want that so badly—but I have enough self-respect to know that he's playing with me. That the way he can knock me sideways is insulting.

And so I shrug. 'I think you've got a pretty fucking exaggerated idea of your abilities in bed.'

His laugh sends sparks of warnings through me. 'Really?'

'I'm not telling you anything you don't already know.'

I jerk away from him but my hand forms a fist; it wants to go back. To grab his cock and hold it tight.

'You want a demonstration of how wrong you are?'

'Arrogant son of a bitch…' I mutter, my eyes scanning the room until they land on my vintage Balenciaga bag.

I scoop it up, sending him a fulminating look. 'Keep them.'

I want him to chase me. To follow me and slam the door shut. To press me against it and moan into my mouth. To beg me to get on the floor and let him take me. Because at the smallest sign of conciliatory, normal behaviour I would do anything Jack asked of me.

But he doesn't.

I leave and I don't even know if he watches me go—I am too proud to turn around and check. My knees are shaking as I make my way through the corridor. It's only early afternoon, and I have a mountain of work to do, but suddenly I'm not in the mood.

I don't want to be near Jack.

Oh, really? my brain prompts sarcastically, rolling its eyes with such force that my head starts to throb. *Really?*

Really.

I jab my finger onto the lift's 'down' button and wait. As I step in I see Jack emerge from the boardroom, looking every bit the confident billionaire bachelor.

Ugh.

I press the button for the car park impatiently, and slam my palm against the 'door shut' button, holding my breath and praying I can avoid a shared lift ride with Jack to the basement. I'm not sure if I'd shout at him or jump him but neither is advisable.

I tell myself I'm glad when he doesn't arrive, jam his hand in the closing doors, out of breath from racing to catch me like men do in movies. The lift cruises downwards, taking my plummeting stomach with it.

Hughes is waiting in the limousine. I smile at him tersely as he steps out and opens the door for me, grateful to slide into the luxurious leather interior. I stare at the screen of my phone and that ridiculous sense that I might cry is back.

What the hell is happening to me?

I tap out a quick email to Sophia, asking her to clear the rest of my afternoon—from memory I had a phone conference scheduled and I'm really not in the mood. Nothing won't wait until tomorrow.

I double-check the itinerary I've been sent for the Australia trip—it's jam-packed, but that makes sense. Jack's too busy—and so am I, come to think of it—to go halfway around the world on holiday.

He's setting up an office in Sydney, which will start with a staff of almost four hundred to oversee two of the companies he's recently acquired there, as well as a winery in New Zealand that he's bidding on, should he be successful. It's a huge venture, and it's the first time I've been involved in anything like it.

Challenges like this are another reason I love working for Jack. Really, I was hardly qualified for this kind of job when I started working for him—my background in law and then banking give me excellent corporate insights, and yet this just works. He's always challenged me. Trusted me. Thrown down gauntlets and stood back to watch me pick them up.

He's doing it now, isn't he? Pushing me in ways I could never have imagined. But instead of meeting his challenge I'm acting like a terrified child.

A frown tugs at my lips. Why have I just run away from him? He wants to fuck me and I want that, too.

The car door opens abruptly and I tilt my head upwards, expecting to see Hughes's face. It's Jack instead, and he's visibly pissed off.

Ignoring the way my pulse immediately starts to fire in my veins, I send him a look of barbed curiosity. 'Yes? Can I help you?'

He doesn't answer. Instead he leans forward and taps on the glass that separates Hughes from us, then settles back into the seat beside me. The car glides out of its parking space, moving through the underground car park with finesse.

'Jack?' I snap, angling in my seat to face him fully.

'Not now.'

My eyebrows shoot upwards. Even for the dictatorial side of Jack, this is a tad too much. *'"Not now"?'*

'No.' He turns to face me, and there's such a searing… *something* in his expression that I blink several times, trying to understand him. This—us.

But I get *nada*.

'Okay, but I think we need to talk,' I respond after a moment.

He glares at me and my temper bubbles. 'I don't want to talk. I want to fuck.'

My jaw drops. 'You don't just get to *say* that!'

A muscle jerks in his cheek. He turns away from me, sits back in the seat, his body rigid, his face tight.

'Not another word.'

I'm not afraid of Jack. Not even a bit. Many times I've gone up against him, arguing my case until he either sees it my way or at least understands my perspective. I won't do that now. I'm too fond of Hughes, and the idea of subjecting him to the tirade I'm about to unleash doesn't appeal to me, so I bite my tongue—

literally—curling my fingernails into my palms as I
stare out at the City.

It takes me a moment to realise we're not going towards Hampstead.

'I want to go home,' I say coldly.

His look is one of silent impatience, but before he
can say anything the car pulls into yet another underground car park and comes to a stop right near the lift.

I can't describe how lost and confused I feel. I'm
a swirling tempest of rage and insecurity, uncertainty
and doubt. It's as though I'm in the middle of a swamp,
reeds tangled around my ankles, water rising.

I want to fight with him. I'm angry. But I don't know
what about! Putting into words what I feel seems impossible.

And then he speaks.

'Come with me.'

Three simple words, but they are enough because
there is a plea in their depths.

I nod slowly, and there's a plea in that, too. *Please
don't hurt me. Please don't use me.* I haven't even realised I feel it until this moment, but the idea of becoming to Jack what all those other women are is
unpalatable. I weigh that against my need for him, and
desire wins. I can only hope I won't regret it.

He pushes the button for the lift and then swipes
a keycard. Soon the elevator is soaring towards the
heavens—I'm in another lift, only this time with Jack
Grant by my side.

'Am I allowed to talk now?'

He glares at me, then stares ahead until the lift doors
open.

I guess not.

I stand with my hands on my hips, angrily admonishing him with my look. 'Nuh-uh. I'm not getting out until you tell me what's going on.'

'What's *going on*?' His tone shows incredulity.

He turns back into the elevator and lifts me easily, throwing me over his shoulder in a way I have only ever fantasised about. He carries me into an apartment—a palatial space. I gain a brief impression of glass, steel, white leather furniture and a state-of-the-art kitchen before he's storming down a tiled hallway and turning into a room.

A bedroom.

With an enormous bed in the centre and floor-to-ceiling windows that show a glinting view of London below.

'You are driving me crazy—that's what's going on. And I don't want to want you like this. I'm sick of waking up about to fucking explode because I've been dreaming about you. I'm sick of looking at you and imagining you naked every time we're in the same damned room.'

He drops me onto the bed but I'm too shocked by his angry confession to care. So he *does* feel it, too—this burning, all-consuming, unwanted, unwelcome, unasked-for need.

'So, if it's all the same to you, I want to fuck you properly—right out of my head—so we can go back to working together like damned adults instead of horny teenagers.'

My breath is burning my lungs, exploding out of me in fierce bursts. 'You think you can *fuck me out of your head*?'

'Yes.' He stares down at me, flicking his shirt open button by button.

My eyes follow his movement and though I've seen him naked before it was never like this. He's never been naked *for me*.

'Why? Why now?'

'Because I need you *now*.'

Still, my brain is shouting at me and, having ignored it in the past and had it lead me into disastrous temptation, I push up on my elbows and roll off the other side of the bed.

His eyes stay trained on me even as he continues to undress, and my throat is dry, parched. I feel like I've been dropped from a great height; I'm in free fall with nothing to grab. Gravity no longer exists.

'How *dare* you? You drag me here, to your…your…lair…' I spit angrily, only to have Jack burst out laughing.

'My *lair*?' He throws his head back.

He's so sexy. God, this isn't fair. I know what I should do. I know what I *need* to do. But he is laughing at me, and my pride is being thumped with each sound he makes.

I jump back onto the bed, storm across it quickly and step off the other side, surprising him with the force of my body against his, knocking him partway to the floor. He catches his balance, his hands steadying me even as I keep on pushing until we are at the wall.

'I'm not some nuisance you can get rid of. An itch you can scratch and lose.' I push a fingernail into his chest and glare up at him, my eyes firing at his.

'So what *are* you?' he demands roughly, his chest moving with each strained breath. 'Why are you all I can think of lately? Why do you consume my every damned waking thought? What sort of magic is this?'

I have needed to hear these words and they fill me

with something I don't understand. There is awe and confusion, and anger, too—because he is just like Mr Darcy, telling me he loves me against his will.

Only Jack's not promising love so much as sex, and Mr Darcy would *never* have made Elizabeth Bennet come pressed hard against a glass window on the forty-second floor of a high-rise in the City of London.

You know what else Lizzy wouldn't have done…?

I drop to my knees in front of him, and before he can guess what I want, or say anything to stop me, I move my mouth over his length, taking him deep—so deep that I feel him connect with the back of my throat.

'Holy hell, Gemma,' he groans, but he doesn't pull away.

His hands drop to my hair, tangling in its blond lengths. It is still wild around my face from when he almost fucked me in his office. His fingers pull at it and I glide my mouth over his shaft, rolling my tongue across its tip and tasting just enough of him to make my insides clench with fevered desire. I squeeze my fingers around his length and then take him deep inside my mouth again, my eyes travelling up his honed body to meet his. I see the swirling depths of emotion in them…I see that he is as lost as I am…and it is all that keeps me going.

If I'm going to feel like I have no clue who I am anymore then he should, too.

I move my mouth faster, rolling my tongue over his sensitive tip each time I am close to pulling away completely, and then his hands on my hair tighten, slowing me down, holding me still. His breath is rough, and I taste more of him spilling into my mouth.

I try to take him deeper but his fingers hold me still, the pressure on my scalp almost painful.

'This isn't going to end that quickly,' he says darkly, pulling me away completely and staring down at me before reaching beneath my arms and lifting me to stand. He stares into my eyes and there is so much triumph in my face that he must see it.

'Holy hell, Gemma,' he says again after a moment, and pulls me back towards the bed.

My heart twists achingly in my chest. He pushes me backwards, onto the middle of the mattress, and bends down, grabbing for something off the floor.

A second later I see what it is: his belt. He's naked—spectacularly so—and so hard and firm. He runs his hands over my arms, catching my wrists and pinning them over my head.

'Do you trust me?' he asks—deep, throaty, gravelled.

I shake my head but my lips are twitching. 'I trust you to make me come. I don't know if I trust you with anything else right now.'

His laugh is soft as he loops the belt in and out of the bedposts, and then grabs my wrists and incorporates them into it, pinning my arms behind me and above my head. It's not particularly comfortable.

'Then let me make you come again and again and again, Gemma.'

Gemma. The way he says my name like that—rich with passion and want—makes my body catch fire. Like it's not already an inferno!

He pushes at my dress, his hands on my thighs intimate. I still have no underwear on and he smiles to see my nakedness.

'You are beautiful,' he grunts, almost as though he's never noticed me before.

He brings his mouth down against me and I jerk my arms, wanting to touch him.

He laughs. 'And you're mine.'

Butterflies ravage me angrily. I *am* his. For this moment…for this night. Is this how it always is with him? When he makes love to those other women does it feel to them as though they are the only woman in the world?

The idea of being one of *them* is anathema to me.

'Remember what I told you in the boardroom?'

He pushes the dress higher, over my breasts, then leaves it bunched under my arms while he turns his attention to the scrap of lace that covers me. He doesn't bother to unclasp it—just lifts my breasts out of the delicate cups, bringing his mouth close to one of them and breathing warm air over the sensitive, erect nipple.

I arch my back instinctively and he laughs. 'Do you want this?' he murmurs, flicking it with his tongue, then circling the darker flesh slowly, teasing me, taunting me.

I nod, incoherent with need. 'I want *everything*,' I say seriously.

'Everything?'

'All of this,' I agree, pulling at my hands again, not caring that I am conceding all that I am to him. 'Please,' I add.

'Do you remember what I said?'

He is insistent. What *did* he say? 'Not to wear underpants again?'

He laughs, and then his teeth clamp down on my nipple and I cry out. The pleasure radiates through my body, slick in my abdomen.

'That, too.'

He rubs his stubble over my nipple and it's so sensitive from his mouth that I make a soft sound of surprise.

'I said I am going to fuck you until you can't remember your own name. Okay?'

I nod. I am lost, and I need him to see that. 'What's happening to us?'

His smile is haunted as he slides a condom over himself once more. 'What's happening? I think I've finally found my cure—that's what's happening.'

And he thrusts into me, so deep and hard and fast that the peculiar statement is lost. *I* am lost. I jerk my wrists so that the belt pulls against my skin, and I cry out in frustration that I can't touch him like I want to.

He is so big, and his dick reaches places inside me that I didn't know existed. He moves his mouth to my other breast and lashes his tongue against me as he pounds me hard. My hands jerk above my head. I am his prisoner, but even without the belt at my wrists I would be.

'Are you on the pill?' he demands, and I nod.

I am incoherent with pleasure, saying his name over and over again. My body is on fire. He is its master. His hands are rough on my smooth skin. He touches me everywhere as he moves inside me, thrusting deep, and still I want more.

'Please!' I cry out, not even sure what I'm begging for now.

But he knows what I need. Somehow he has mastered my body already, even though we are so new to one another. He pushes inside me and rolls his hips. I lift mine to meet him and I'm exploding, falling apart and flying at the same time, dropping through the earth's core as my body tries to cope with these sensations.

I groan loudly, wrapping my legs around his waist, holding him right where he is. But before the waves of my pleasure have begun to subside he guides my legs over his shoulders, so that I am bent over myself and he is so deep I see stars. Pleasure is tingling through me and he blows through it, rocking me in rhythm with his needs, kissing the sensitive flesh behind my knees before running his fingers lower to cup my arse.

I am shuddering with the strength of what he's doing to me. Then he pulls out, and I almost sob with the emptiness that threatens to cut me in half.

His laugh is dark. An acknowledgement that he understands.

His hands on my hips are strong; he flips me easily onto my stomach and my arms are crisscrossed, my dress tangled around my breasts and my neck.

I don't have time to tell him this, or to shift and adjust myself. He spreads my legs wide, puts an arm under my belly and lifts me higher. And then he drives into me from behind. He brushes against new nerves, makes me feel new things, and I gather from the muttered string of dark curses that fill the room that this is different for him, too.

His fingers dig into my hips as he holds me steady, thrusting into me and making me *different*, somehow. He drops forward, kissing my shoulder, dragging his mouth down my back before biting me on the arse— gently, but enough to make me groan. And then he's sucking the flesh at the small of my back, and I wonder if I'm going to have a mark there afterwards.

His finger between my arse cheeks surprises me. It is not somewhere I've been touched before, but it's only the lightest suggestion of a touch. A finger lightly pressing against my butt. A curious flash of wonder flies through me. But instinctively I shy away from it and he understands, laughing and moving his hand to my clit.

He strums me as though I am a guitar, and it's so intense that I almost cannot bear the pleasure. But I don't dare ask him to stop because perhaps he would and I couldn't bear that. It is like being prodded by a hot iron, though: I am burning up.

I explode angrily, loudly, my body shaking from head to toe, glistening with sweat.

He holds me tight, waiting for the waves to slow, to recede a little, and then runs his hands over my flat stomach to my neat breasts. He rolls my nipples between his finger and thumb, plucking them in time with his dick as he takes me again and again.

'It's not fair…' I moan, resting my head on the pillow, trying to catch my breath. 'I want *you* to feel this.'

He makes a noise. It could be agreement or amusement; I'm not sure. 'Do you think I'm not enjoying myself?'

No. I know he's having a good time. But that's not enough. I don't want to think I'm like all those other women, just being 'had' by him. I want to rock his goddamned world.

'Do I get to tie *you* up?' My words are as fevered as my sex-stormed soul.

He laughs and shakes his head, his chin gravelly against my back. 'No.'

'Why not? What's good for the goose isn't good for the gander?'

'Not in this case.'

'Isn't that a bit sexist?'

'You don't like it?'

My cheeks flame and I'm glad I'm facing away from him.

He brings the flat of his hand down on my arse, just lightly, but enough to spark the fire back into me, to make me forget what I want to do to him momentarily and enjoy what he's doing to me instead.

I push my arse higher and he massages me with his fingers, digging hard into the muscles there. I moan, low in my throat, and then he pushes inside me. I'm so wet. I drop my head lower and now he reaches up, unclipping the belt and freeing my wrists.

He pulls out of me. 'Turn around.'

A command. I obey, even though a part of me wants to tell him to stuff it purely as a point of pride.

Flat on my back, I stare up at him, my breath rushed, my lower lip sucked between my teeth.

'I want you to see what you do to me.' The admission is hoarse; as though drawn from deep in his throat.

He pushes my legs up again, lifting them over his shoulders as he drops into me, and I welcome him as though he's been absent for months, not moments. He laces his fingers through mine, pinning my arms either side of me, and he stares down at me as he takes me once more.

I sweep my eyes closed as another wave begins to build, but he drops his mouth to mine and pulls my lower lip between his teeth, pressing into it just enough to startle me into looking at him.

'I want to see you. And I want *you* to see me.'

Mesmerised, I can't look away. I watch as his face contorts with pleasure and he rocks inside me, and my own pleasure rides high with his until we are climaxing together, my body flaming to his, leaping with his, burning like his. It is him and me, and no one else in the world exists or matters.

He explodes inside me—a powerful release that makes him cry out loudly…a guttural sound that rips through the room. And I echo it deep within my soul. I am as overwhelmed as he.

He stays above me, his breath uneven, his eyes almost accusing as my own climax recedes, and I am left weak and confused by what the hell just happened to us.

I stare up at my boss, at the man who's just given me—I don't know…four orgasms? Five orgasms? I've lost count. It's still the afternoon and my body is covered in goose bumps.

Holy shit. Is this what it's like with his other women?

They are like ghosts, immediately hovering on my subconscious. I hate it that they're there, but my brain clearly needs me to remember them. To remember what Jack's like.

'So I suppose you don't get complaints after all,' I murmur, running my fingertips down his back. Like mine, it is wet with perspiration.

'Not so much.'

He pushes up, with a smile on his face that somehow doesn't fill his eyes. He presses a light kiss to my forehead and then stands.

'I'll get Hughes to take you home.'

The words seem to be spoken in a foreign language for all the sense they make to me. He'll get Hughes to take me home? Is he fucking *serious*? Am I being *dismissed*?

I smile, even as my mind is reeling from the sheer rudeness of that statement. 'I need to finish something at the office.'

I am amazed by myself. How do I sound so unbothered? So casual? It's a bald-faced lie, but it's the best I can come up with while my body is numbed by shock and fulfilled desire.

He nods. 'Fine. He can take you there.' Another tight smile. 'You're okay to let yourself out? I'm going to grab a shower.'

Jesus fucking Christ. *Is* he indeed?

'I think I can find a door without a map,' I drawl sarcastically, reaching for my phone without so much as a smile.

I flick it to life and load my emails, but the words swim before me like one big puddle of grey matter.

Which is what his brain is going to be against the crisp white wall if I don't get the hell out of there.

He walks towards a door across the room and I continue staring at my phone. Yet I know he's paused and is watching me. So I smile at an imagined joke on my phone, then pretend I'm typing a reply.

If you'd asked me an hour ago what could go wrong I would have said exactly this. Pushing past the boundaries we've always wisely obeyed, only to have Jack reinstating them just as fast as he's able—brick by brick, blocking me out.

My fingers move over my phone but I'm play-acting, doing what I can to distract him from the fissures running through my heart, my hopes and my confidence.

Eventually Jack moves into the bathroom and I hear the shower running.

Arsehole.

It might have been the best sex I've ever had, but I'm pretty sure it was also the biggest mistake of my life.

CHAPTER FIVE

'AMBER.' I SMILE, meeting the redhead's eyes with genuine interest.

Lucy's sister is ten years older than Lucy was, and she has the same pale skin and dainty features—at least going from the photographs I've seen. Her eyes are enormous and brown, her smile slow but genuine. She is naturally plump and attractive.

I like her instantly.

'The angelic Gemma,' she responds, her Scottish accent thick. 'I've been looking forward to meeting the woman who's tamed my brother-in-law.'

Tamed him? Not bloody likely.

Flashbacks of the previous afternoon flood my brain and I push them away. I cannot think about how it felt to be made love to by Jack Grant. No—*fucked* by him. Fucked hard. So hard, so hot… Oh, my God. My insides clench with remembered need. It's a visceral awareness, and actual biological need throbs through me on a cellular level. It's every bit as compelling and real as thirst, starvation and fear. It is a need strong enough to fell me at the knees.

I swallow, hoping to calm my raging, insatiable desire. 'I'm pretty sure he's untameable,' I say, with only a hint of desperation, gesturing that she should take a seat.

I've moved us to the small conference room on-site at The Mansion. Thankfully it's nothing like the office in the City, with its modern decor and imposing outlook. This is a room far more fitted to an ancient home on the edge of Hampstead. Still expensive, with luxurious leather recliners, but homely, somehow.

'Put up with him, then. You must have the patience of a saint.'

'I must,' I agree.

'Gemma is actually very impatient.'

His voice enters the room before he does, and I straighten in the chair.

'If I don't give her what she wants straightaway she begs me until I give in.'

My cheeks flame and I'm grateful that Amber is standing and moving across the room towards Jack—arsehole that he is. How *dare* he say something so bloody obvious? I know we're both thinking of how I begged him to make love to me the day before.

My eyes cling to Jack and Amber, morbidly fascinated, as they embrace. It's a hug of true affection and, yes, grief is there, too. He's wearing navy blue pants and a pale blue shirt which he's rolled up to just below the elbows. It's a linen material, and it's crinkled a little around the chest, showing he's been sitting in it for quite some time.

He keeps an arm around Amber's waist as they walk deeper into the room. She takes an armchair opposite me and he sits beside her, facing me, aligning himself with her.

They are family. I'm the outsider.

It hurts. Possibly even more than the showering-straight-after-sex thing.

Did he need to drink copious measures of Scotch to forget me last night?

My eyes drift to his face to find him watching me. Intensely watchful, I would have to say, peeling away my skin and analysing each beat of my heart.

I blink, careful not to react, and then turn back to Amber. 'How's everything going with the launch preparation?'

'Aye, good. We're getting there. I've staffed the main headquarters and we're just getting the international charitable recognition worked out to allow foreign donations.'

'Advertising?' Jack chimes in.

'We're meeting with two agencies next week to select a final campaign. It's looking like it will be print and digital-heavy, with the possibility of sponsoring a major sporting event over the summer—possibly the cricket.'

Jack pulls a face. 'Bloody hell. The *cricket*?'

'Oh, come *on*. Lucy would have wanted it.' Amber grins, pushing a finger into his shoulder in a further sign of their casual camaraderie.

It's strange that I don't often think of Jack like this—as a member of other spheres.

Here, it is him and me and the work we do together. It consumes so much of my life that I must admit I'm surprised to realise he has other people, things, memories and hobbies. Jokes and history.

Did Lucy watch cricket while Jack groaned about it? Did they laugh about his aversion to any sport other than rugby?

I blank the thoughts—or try to. But they're gnawing at my mind, unfolding like a concertinaing piano accordion that's ever so slightly out of key.

'It'll be a good show,' Amber says loudly, her smile encouraging as she winks in my direction.

Despite the fact that she's forced me to walk through a door that shows me the ghosts of Jack's Happy Past, I like her immensely, and the more she speaks about the foundation the more I know we've absolutely made the right decision. She's intimately informed on all the matters I need to consult with her about. She's thorough and quick and funny. And she's uniquely motivated to make the fundraiser a success.

She's Lucy's sister, and Lucy is dead, but I am jealous of Amber suddenly. It's ridiculous. An emotion entirely unworthy. But watching her talk, with her big red lips and her animated face, I feel wan and boring in comparison.

I would have been bland compared to Lucy, too.

I look downwards as Amber launches into a description of the view from her office. I'm wearing one of my favourite dresses—a shift in olive-green with bell sleeves and a boat neck. Oh, but it's so conservative and drab! Just the kind of dress my mother would adore. I chose it for the length of the sleeves, which fall to partway down my hands, because my wrists—which I see I've now accidentally left uncovered—have a dark band of bruising around them.

Belt-burn. *Thanks, arsehole.*

I nod at something Amber's said, my eyes moving of their own accord to Jack's face.

He's looking at my wrists, too, and the colour has drained from his face. I shift self-consciously, uncrossing and crossing my legs and drawing my sleeves lower in the process.

'Amber, we can discuss the rest over lunch. I know Gemma's got a desk full of crap to deal with.'

'*Your* crap!' Amber laughs good-naturedly, totally relaxed.

'That's her job,' he says pointedly.

Amber rolls her eyes. 'How you put up with him is beyond me.'

But she stands, straightening the crinkles out of the front of her skirt as she moves towards me. I hold out a hand to shake but she ignores it and pulls me into a hug instead.

'We've spoken so many times I feel like I already know you. But it's been lovely to finally meet you.'

'Likewise,' I murmur, stepping away from her with cringe-inducing coldness. Something else my mother would approve of! Standoffishness is a bland green dress. *Great.* I'm everything I swore I'd never be.

'Gemma? I need a moment with you, please.' He turns to Amber. 'Why don't you wait for me in the car? This won't take long.'

'I have a few calls to make,' she says, and nods, clipping out of the room.

He walks behind her, but only so far as the door, which he pushes shut emphatically and slips the lock across with equal force. And then he is prowling towards me. Yes, *prowling.* That's absolutely the word.

I have about four seconds to pull myself together. Four seconds to ignore the hammering of my heart and the throbbing of my libido. Four seconds to remind myself that he's my boss, and a total ass to boot. To remember how I felt when he rolled off me and all but asked me to leave his bed not two minutes after deserting my body.

No one has the right to make me feel like that. *No one*. And certainly not twice.

'That went well,' I say efficiently, leaving no room for the personal. 'I'm thrilled she's going to be at the helm of the foundation.'

A muscle jerks in his cheek—as though he's grinding his teeth or something. He catches my wrists and lifts them, pushing my sleeves up my arms to reveal the full extent of my bruising. He closes his eyes as he runs his finger over them, as though fortifying himself to look properly.

'You're hurt.'

I swallow, not liking this side of him any more than I do the bastard side that showered as soon as he'd pulled out of me. This is scarier, because it's doing really odd things to my heart and my tummy, seeing him show this kind of humanity and compassion.

I jerk my wrists away. 'Yeah… Can't you tell? I'm in agony.' I roll my eyes for good measure. 'It's just a couple of bruises.'

He nods, but there's a look in his face that I don't know if I ever want to see again. 'Listen, Gemma…' The way he says it rolls my stomach. 'About yesterday…'

'It's fine.' My smile is a flicker across my face and then it's gone. 'I *know* you.'

He shakes his head. 'No, you don't understand.' His frown is one of frustration. 'Let me explain.'

I swallow. *Be strong. Remember Shower Gate.* 'You don't need to explain,' I say firmly.

Please don't let him explain. Without an explanation there's ambivalence. But if I have to listen to his regrets, worse, his apology…?

'It was good. I had fun. Let's leave it at that.'

I walk towards the door, needing an escape. My legs are unsteady and my throat is parched and sore—like it's been flamed with a blowtorch. I walk away from him because my sanity depends on distance.

But this time he follows. He puts a hand on either side of me as I reach the darkly panelled door, so that I'm trapped by him. I freeze, staring straight ahead while my body goes into overdrive, his nearness impossible to ignore.

'You want to leave it at that?' he asks, his hand dropping to my hip.

I close my eyes, waiting for the hammering of my pulse to slow. As if it's going to.

'You want to forget what that felt like? Never do it again?' His fingers run lower, down my leg to the hem of my dress. 'Say the word and I'll step backwards. I'll stop touching you. For good.'

I nod, but 'the word' clogs my throat.

'Spread your legs apart.'

You do that and I am outta here. Love from your brain.

'Jack…' I say, his name thick and hoarse.

'I've been wondering all morning,' he says quietly. 'Did you listen to me?'

And his hand creeps under my dress, up my leg towards my bottom, where he finds the fabric of my knickers and flicks at it, hard enough to make me jerk.

'No, you didn't. Shame… Because if you weren't wearing underwear I could take you right now. Here against the door. Would you like that, Gemma?'

I groan, completely frozen by the imagery of his words.

'I'm going to fuck you now unless you tell me not to.'

Not only can I not find the words, I nod my head in total surrender. I hear his exhalation of breath and smile weakly. I move to turn around, but he keeps his hands on my hip—firm.

'No. Like this.' And he pulls me backwards, bending me at a ninety-degree angle.

He doesn't remove my underpants. He links both hands around them and pulls until they tear, dropping them to the ground.

I stare at them with surprise and impatience. 'They were really expensive,' I say darkly.

'They were in my way.'

I hear him unzip his trousers, then the familiar sound of foil being torn, rubber being snapped onto his length, and then he's inside me. No preamble, but—let's face it—the whole morning's been a total exercise in tantric delay. He runs his hands over my back as he thrusts into me and I splay my fingers wide against the door, my body taking his possession as though it's what I need to stay alive.

I am hot and cold all over, and about to come when he pulls out. It is so like the torment of the day before—the utter outrageous shock of desolation—that I cry out hoarsely into the room.

'You'd better not fucking stop,' I say angrily.

He straightens me and turns me around, pushing me hard against the door and kissing me until my knees are about to give way.

'Think of that as an IOU.' He pulls away, his eyes

meshing with mine. 'One I intend to collect.' He scoops down and grabs my underwear, dangling the scrap of fabric by one finger. 'And no more of this.'

I gape at him. 'Is that an order, *sir*?'

'You'd better damned well believe it.'

'Okay, I'll call HR and have it added to my contract.'

He kisses me again and my body sways towards his; I give up the sass immediately.

'Fuck me more,' I say into his mouth.

'Wild horses won't stop me.' It's a growl. 'Later.'

Five minutes later, I'm staring at my desk, a frown on my face.

What just happened?

It's like some kind of cyclone came into the room and settled down on top of us. All that's needed is for us to be close to one another and *bam!* The world loses its usual governance and we are wild, unshackled animals.

I tilt my head forward, catching it in my hands.

I've never felt like this.

I've always been able to control the men in my life, and I've always, *always* known what I want from them. Relationship decisions have, historically, been made by the same part of my brain that runs my career and all other aspects of my life.

I know some people talk about 'love at first sight', but that's always been a good clue to me that those people are batshit crazy.

Oh, I'm not saying I think I'm in love with Jack! I'm sexually tormented, not a sadist, and loving Jack would be stupid. But I don't have any brainpower or willpower around him.

He has all the power. *Sex* power. It makes me uneasy to acknowledge that and to accept that I would walk headfirst into whatever it is we're doing just to be with him some more. He's that good.

My body is a livewire, arcing through space, waiting to be grounded by him. But he doesn't ground me—he flares me into a violent electrical storm.

I drive him crazy, too. I remember, in a drowning attempt to have faith in my own abilities, that when I went down on him he was mine. Completely.

I don't think Jack welcomes this development any more than I do. I think his brain is probably giving him as hard a time as my own... What we had before *worked*. Sure, I pretty much had to pull up my big girl pants in the form of Maid Marian's chastity belt to make sure I didn't give in to the sexy man-pull of Jack Grant. But professionally we're a great team.

And losing that is far riskier for him. I'll get another job when I want one—I'm forever being headhunted, in fact.

My frown deepens as I open my second drawer and rifle through it, my fingers curling around the card of the most persistent caller. Andrew Long from Saatchi & Long. He's offered me some seriously awesome job opportunities in the last year, and every time I demur he tells me I must be on an incredible package.

Little does he know! I *am* very well-paid; Jack knows he can't afford to lose me. But, more than that, I get to stare at Jack-fucking-Grant all day.

Oh, God.

This is hopeless. I scrape my chair back, dropping Andrew's card back into the drawer and pushing it closed, scooping my bag up and pulling the strap over my shoulder.

'I'm going out,' I call as I pass Sophia and Rose. 'Back soon.'

Sophia waves in acknowledgement. I keep walking, my bare ass making me feel both turned on and self-conscious as I step out into the weather. It's cold, but I forgot my coat and I don't really care.

'Ma'am?' Hughes straightens from where he's been leaning beside the limo.

'Do you just lounge about out here all day, waiting for me to walk past?' I ask teasingly. I know how busy he is.

'Better than watching paint dry. You can actually *walk* in those things?'

He nods down at my Louboutins with a smile on his lips. They're two-inch spike heels and, yes, I'm very, very good in heels.

'I could run a marathon in them,' I say, and wink. My hair is in a ponytail today and the wind blows past, flicking it against my cheek.

'Well, save yourself the effort today.' He reaches for the door handle. 'Where to?'

I look at him blankly. It's a fair question; one to which I have no answer. 'I'm just going to go for a walk,' I explain. 'I need a coffee.'

'A coffee?' His look is one of sardonic amusement. 'You mean that spaceship's stopped working?'

I shake my head. The high-end pod machine Jack's had installed makes great coffee and we both know it. 'Okay, you caught me. I want a *pain au chocolat*.'

'Really?' He grins, arching a brow. 'A weakness for patisserie goods…interesting.'

I shrug. 'Certain days,' I say in explanation.

'Say no more.'

'See you soon,' I say in farewell. Then, as an after-thought, 'Need anything?'

'No, ma'am.'

So, I've banged her against a door in the conference room of my home office *and* against a window of my boardroom in the City. And while my sister-in-law was waiting in the car for me, too.

Jesus.

The Gemma Conundrum is getting out of hand. I woke up this morning knowing I had to apologise for yesterday, to tell her I'd regretted having sex with her the second we were done. That it had been a colossal, asshole mistake.

And then she walked away from me and I panicked.

Apparently Gemma only listens when I'm inside her.

So? What? I'm going to have sex with her any time we disagree? Any time she gets annoyed?

Amber laughs at something and I smile, but my mind is on Gemma and the promise I made her—that I'd collect on my IOU later today. The thought of not doing so makes some part of me want to shrivel up. So I accept the inevitable. We're going to fuck again.

My cock tightens instantly, straining against the fabric of my pants. Is she still naked beneath her dress, waiting for me? Wanting me?

I sip my wine, and say something in response to Amber's question—I'm amazed that any part of my brain is ticking on as normal, absorbing what's being said and answering in kind, even while most of me is absorbed by the question of my assistant.

I *love* sex. I love it because it lets me forget about Lucy and what I no longer have. But Gemma is different—because I can't just fuck her and walk away for good. I have to see her every morning—and what if she starts to want more from me than I can possibly give?

'Hey, Grandma.' I can't help but smile as she answers the phone in her sunny little room.

I hear her sip her tea and imagine her lips smiling against the bone china rim. 'What's up, lovey?'

'Nothing's up. How are you?'

'It's the middle of the day on Friday and you're calling me. What's up?'

I shake my head, but those damned tears that have been dogging me for days are threatening to fall. I blink my eyes angrily, staring at a family as they walk past me. Mum and Dad holding hands and three small children of varying degrees of growth and ruggedupness run past, looking as though they're being pulled back by a magnetic force when all they want is to sprint along.

'And is that birdsong in the background?'

I bite into the *pain au chocolat*; crumbs flake down my front. Absent-mindedly I brush them aside. 'I'm on the Heath.'

'You mean you've unshackled yourself from that desk?'

I laugh. 'Yes, Grandma. From time to time I *do* get out.'

'Have you spoken to your mother recently?'

I furrow my brow. Grandma is the only person on earth who understands my relationship with my parents. She understands that I love them, but in a dutiful way—they did give me life, after all. They also gave me self-doubt and insecurity and a sense that I'd never be good enough for anything other than the life they envisaged for me. Grandma tunnelled me right out of that existence, though.

'Not for a week or so.' Actually, it's closer to a month. 'You?'

'They called yesterday. They're in Cambodia.'

I arch a brow, imagining my perfectly manicured, elegant mother in Cambodia, of all places. 'I trust the Shangri-La's penthouse is sufficient?'

Grandma laughs. 'Well, you know—they're doing volunteer work.'

I burst out laughing at this ongoing joke between us. My parents are incredibly wealthy, incredibly entitled aristocrats and they have apparently reached a point in their life where they're bored with that and are looking to 'make the world a better place'. So far this has involved paying a lot of money to buy shoes for children in Africa, travelling to Lithuania to learn about child smuggling and now a trip of Southern Asia to 'help provide vaccinations' to the poor.

I wonder how helpful my mother—who faints at the sight of blood—and my dad—who can't stand heat, mosquitos or poverty—are actually capable of being.

'I think they're going to cut their trip short,' Grandma says, almost managing to keep the droll amusement out of her voice.

'Oh, I'm *so* surprised by that.' I fail miserably. 'I daresay the philanthropic community of Cambodia will breathe a sigh of relief when they board their flight home.'

'Yes, well… Their hearts are in the right places,' she murmurs, and I nod.

Perhaps.

'They'd do better to donate to a foundation,' I say. 'Money is what these people need. And then trained staff can do their jobs without westerners assuaging their guilt over the quality of our lives getting in the way.'

'Phew, that's been building up for a while, has it?'

'Sorry. I just can't stand volunteer tourism. If I see one more photo of a schoolfriend posing with emaciated children in Africa I'm going to punch something.'

'Darling, it all brings attention to good causes.'

'Yeah—and it makes rich people feel better about their rarefied existence in the process.'

'Mmm...'

Grandma is nodding. I just know it.

'So nothing's going on, then?' she asks.

The children on the Heath are running now, and the mother and father are watching, holding hands, laughing as the littlest one tumbles down and lands in the middle of some wet grass. One of the older siblings scoops him up, cradling him and spinning in circles until the little one's laughter peals across the grass towards me, hitting me like a slap in the face.

I'm not clucky. I don't want children. The agony of my own childhood is one I would never inflict on another. Oh, it's not like I was abused or anything. My parents loved me. Loved me enough to hire only the best nannies and tutors and horse-riding coaches. To send me to the very best schools... Clue: the best schools for meeting handsome, eligible husbands-to-be.

And they loved me enough to question my sanity when I enrolled in joint honours at Oxford and then post-grad at the LSE. But there was Grandma in the front row when I accepted my Master's degree.

'I'm just flat out,' I say quietly. 'Work's crazy at the moment.'

Grandma is quiet, taking this in. Then, 'You're coming for lunch tomorrow?'

Tomorrow? *Shit*. It's almost the weekend. But the idea of seeing Grandma makes my heart soar. 'Lunch? Yeah, sure.'

'And you'll bust me out of this hellhole again? Take me out for so much champagne I get woozy and disgraceful?'

I laugh, because the 'hellhole' nursing home Grandma is in costs more per year than most people earn in a lifetime and is the last word in luxury. She has a *personal butler*, for crying out loud. But the staff there don't entirely approve of her love of bubbles, whereas I am more than happy to serve as her occasional enabler.

'Yep. You betcha.'

I stand up, giving one last look at the family as they move over the crest of a hill and disappear out of sight, then I walk across the grass, making my way to the gate nearest the lane that leads to Jack's mansion.

I try not to think about whether Jack will be in the office when I get back.

CHAPTER SIX

It's just as well I'm busy. Between running one last glance over the Wyndham contracts, checking the files I'll need and locking down the details for Australia, responding to some urgent emails and looking at some high-level staff CVs for the foundation, the day passes quickly.

It is evening before I know it and I am still at my desk. My phone bleeps just as I'm packing up.

I'm in the City. Hughes will bring you here when you're done.

I read the text three times, my bemusement growing with each moment. True, I'd basically begged him to fuck me earlier that day, but this is hardly a masterpiece in flirtation and seduction.

Do you need me for something?

I fire the message back, lifting my bag over my shoulder and switching the lights off at the door.

You know what I need you for.

I don't reply. I don't know why. But I make my way outside and smile at Hughes—possibly the only guy in the company who works hours as long as Jack and mine. He doesn't have a family. He was in the army and returned from three tours of Iraq ready for a change. He's smart, safe and we trust him implicitly.

We.

I do that a lot, but I don't mean 'we' in a romantic sense. It's just that we've almost become partners over the years without either of us realising it.

'I'm meeting Jack at his place in the City,' I murmur.

When I was sixteen my dad caught Roger Cranston and me fooling around in the kitchen. I was so mortified with embarrassment that I spent the next week making up elaborate stories that would explain exactly why Roger had been kneeling in front of me, my skirt pushed up my legs.

He dropped a pen and...um...I was reaching for another...

I feel that now. That same sense of embarrassment— like I've been caught doing completely the wrong thing and need to explain. To *Hughes*, of all people.

My cheeks flush pink and I don't meet his eye. 'I need some documents signed.'

He pulls the door open and smiles. 'Long day?'

'Yeah, you could say that.' I sit down, careful not to flash my naked self to him, then sink back into the leather seat.

I read the news on my phone as we drive, catching up on what I've missed while I've had my head down the Jack Grant wormhole all day, and discover that a police manhunt has ended with the suspect being shot, and that a chain of supermarkets is at risk of bankruptcy.

We're at his apartment block quickly, though, and the door opens to the familiar bank of lifts. Hughes presses a button, then swipes a keycard so that I'm granted access to the floor Jack's penthouse is on.

'Thanks. Goodnight, Hughes.'

'Goodnight, ma'am.'

I laugh. 'You know I hate it when you call me that.'

The doors swish closed on his wink.

I'm still smiling when the lift opens—but it's transformed into a frown of curiosity as I step into Jack's place. A couple of lights are on, casting an ambient glow, but otherwise it's dark. There are lights coming from beyond the glass and, curious, I walk towards it.

'Hey.'

Jack's voice comes from down the hallway and I turn to see him emerging from one of the rooms, a towel knotted loosely around his waist.

'I didn't know you were on your way.'

My eyes have dropped to his bare chest. To its rhythmic rise and fall as he breathes, to the smooth tan that covers him and the hint of ink I can see above the towel.

I swallow, my throat dry, and force myself to meet his eyes. 'How was your day?' Crisp, professional. Safe, good.

'Fine.'

He unwraps the towel, uncaring of his spectacular nudity, and brings it to his hair, towelling it dry. He's semi-hard, and God knows I want to jump him then and there.

But I don't. I'm not sure why, but something holds me immobile.

'Good meeting with Amber?'

'Yeah. You were right about her. She's a good pick for the job.'

'I think she's got the perfect combination of experience and passion.'

His nod is droll. 'She sure has, Miss Picton. Cocktail first?'

Damn it. I like the way he says that. It's such a formal name, but when he says it I sound like a courtesan or something.

'First?' I can't help teasing.

He drops the towel, hooking it around his body once more, and I'm glad even though it means I can't perve at him so easily. It stops my blood from simmering itself into a fever state.

'First. As in first, before I fuck you senseless.' He grins, pulling me to him.

Something about this feels so right, and it should feel wrong. And awkward. I shake my head, my eyes dropping to the floor before I remember that I've known Jack for two years and that whatever happens we work together and I won't be cowered by him and what we are.

'Cocktails sound perfect.'

His smile is a flicker and then, his eyes holding mine, his smile just a smudge across his handsome face, he lifts my dress with the same reverence a groom might lift his bride's veil and finds my nakedness.

He groans approvingly. 'You've been waiting for me all day?' His hands curve around my butt, pulling me tight to him.

'Well, you did tear my underpants,' I point out.

'Sorry about that.' His voice shows that he is anything but.

He releases me and I have to stifle a noise of impatience, watching as he saunters into the kitchen and pulls something from the freezer. It's a bottle, but I don't recognise it—nor the label. He shakes it, then opens the top. As he pours it into two glasses I realise that it has a thickened consistency, like a Frozen Coke.

I taste it tentatively, my eyes latched to his. 'Cherry?' I raise my brows, taking another sip.

'It's my new favourite flavour.'

My cheeks glow pink to rival the drink. 'Mine, too.'

'Good to see we're both re-evaluating our opinions,' he says with a wink. Then, almost as an afterthought, 'How was your day?'

'Busy.' I don't want to talk about work. We do enough of that. 'I spoke to my grandma and sat on the Heath, though.'

He laughs. 'Am I not giving you enough to do?'

I shoot him a look of dismissal. 'It was a short break.'

'I'm kidding.' His eyes are thoughtful. 'You never talk about your family.'

'Yes, I do,' I retort, perhaps too quickly. 'Just not with *you*.'

'I see. Why not?'

I'm pretty sure I'm scowling at him. 'Well, for starters, because up until recently our relationship has never remotely veered away from the professional...'

'That's not true. You've seen me naked. You wake me up most days.'

'Yes, I know.' Thoughts of his body sprawled over his bed make my blood simmer. 'You're my boss…'

'Then take it as a command.'

The thought of Jack commanding me is instantly memorable. My lungs are filled with thick, hot air.

'A *command*? You're my boss—not royalty.'

He shrugs. 'Is there a difference? Tell me about your grandmother.'

I laugh. A soft sound of disbelief. 'My grandmother? That's *really* what you want to talk about right now?'

'Why not?'

He sips his drink, his eyes locked to mine. It's a challenge! Just like always, he's finding my boundaries and pushing at them with a persistence I find hard to ignore. And I do like to rise to his challenges.

'Grandma is one of a kind,' I say after the smallest of pauses. 'Revolutionary. She worked until well into her seventies and has always been my biggest ally. She encourages me to push myself as hard as I can in everything I do.'

'What did she do?'

'For work? She was a nurse. Still is, actually.' My lips twitch. 'Just last month she saved a man in her nursing home after he had a heart attack. She threw off her cardigan and performed CPR until the staff got there.'

'Sounds like you're just as proud of her as she is of you.'

'Mmm…' I make a smooth noise of agreement, absent-mindedly running my fingers over the bones of my wrist.

His eyes catch the gesture and he steps around the bench towards me. Before I can guess what he's planning he dribbles some cherry daiquiri from his glass onto the skin I've just rubbed, then brings his lips to it, sucking it and kissing me gently.

'I'm sorry about this.'

Jack? Sorry? That's a novelty.

My heart squeezes at his gentle admission. My voice is soft when I speak. 'I told you, it doesn't hurt.'

'The bruising would say otherwise.'

I shrug, but the way his mouth is moving over me is making thought difficult. 'I'm fine. I would have told you if I didn't like it, believe me.'

'I do.'

He brings my thumb to his mouth and sucks on it. I shudder; the pleasure rips through me.

'So? What *do* you like? Usually?'

'With other men?' I clarify, and there is a strange darkening of his features before he wipes them clear and nods.

'Yes.'

I tilt my head to the side. 'Oh, you know—kinky shit.'

'Such as…?'

It's a calm, measured response beyond what I expect.

'I'll show you soon.'

He clears his throat. 'You bet your sweet arse, you will.' He grins and sips his drink once more.

'Anyway,' I ask throatily, 'what do *you* like? With other women? Or is the only prerequisite that they submit to your *wham-bam, thank you, ma'am* form of sex?'

He shakes his head. 'Not the *only* prerequisite, but it's an important one.'

'Why?' I push, taking another sip.

He presses his finger under my chin, tilting my face towards his. 'Because that's what I want.'

'One-night stands.'

'Two-night stands, in your case,' he says, pulling me forward.

At the same time I reach for his towel and push it down his body. He lifts me easily, settling me on a bar stool, his eyes holding mine as he slides on a condom, and then he takes me totally, driving deep inside me and winding my legs around his waist. Even as the bliss of his possession moves through me I feel a strange distaste for his statement.

A two-night stand on its second night means it's the end.

But don't I want that?

Aren't boundaries a *good* thing?

I bite down on my lip, unable to process it any more. He holds me tight, gripping me against him.

'I like being able to be inside you like this. Whenever I want.'

His fingers grab my dress and lift it up my body, over my head, so that I'm wearing only my heels and a lace bra. He disposes of the latter easily and then, true to his word, grabs his daiquiri glass and trickles ice-cold liquid across my breasts.

His mouth on my nipple is warm and I arch my back, giving him greater access. He chases it down my body as he thrusts into me again, his ownership of me both thrilling and frightening at the same time. His chin is stubbled and rough against my neck. He takes an earlobe into his mouth, wobbling it between his teeth, and I groan, desperate for him to move faster, deeper.

'What do you want?' he asks softly.

'More!' I call the word out loudly, an incantation or an invocation, scoring my nails across his back, marking him as mine even when I know he isn't.

'Like this?'

He moves a little deeper, so that I nod, but it's not enough.

'More...'

He laughs, pulling out of me and guiding me off the stool at the same time.

'Turn around.'

'Has anyone ever told you you're a bossy son of a bitch in bed?'

'We're not in bed,' he reminds me frankly, and there's a sexy, sardonic smile at the corner of his lips.

'You're a bossy son of a bitch to fuck,' I correct dutifully, and he laughs.

'You're complaining?'

I shoot him a look over my shoulder and do as he says, turning around.

'Those fucking heels...' he says, bending me at my waist and spreading my legs before taking me from behind, his fingers digging into my naked arse. 'You have no idea how hot this is.'

But I do, because he's driving me to the point of distraction with every single move. Fire spirals inside me, coiling, spinning, taking me and making me fall apart in his arms.

The kitchen bench is marble and cold beneath my fevered palms. And then he brings the palm of his hand down on my arse and I jerk, crying out as both pleasure and pain radiate through me.

'Did you know you have a mark here from me?' He

presses into what I presume must be a hickey from the last time we were together.

I shake my head and he catches my ponytail in his hand, pulling it with just enough pressure to hold me still as he thrusts inside me. His other hand trails down my spine, chasing each knot, each groove, until he reaches my arse. Once again he presses a single finger against me, and there is something so illicit and forbidden about it that I come—out of nowhere.

The orgasm is intense. He's only touching my skin, there is nothing invasive about his finger, but just the idea of what I'd let him do to me makes me fall apart.

'Shit…' I swear under my breath, sweat across my brow.

His finger pushes in a little way and I buck hard. His dick thrusts into me and his hand around my hair pulls. It's too much. The pleasure is making me weak.

'I can't…' I say, my breath coming in pants, my eyes fevered, my body wet.

'You can do whatever you want,' he contradicts, and brings his mouth to my back.

But he moves his hand away, bringing it to cup my breasts and torment my nipples. I have never known sex like this. I have never been an instrument of pleasure. I always call the shots and yet now I am his to control, to command, and there is something so hedonistic about that I know I will never be the same again.

'You are so much more perfect than I imagined,' he groans, and now he thrusts deeper and harder and faster, and I rock my hips with him until we fall apart together, him exploding inside me while I tremble and squeeze him tight.

I bring my weight forward, pressing my head onto the marble kitchen bench, not wanting to lose him.

He belongs inside me.

It's an erroneous thought. No one person can belong to another—inside or out.

'I needed that.'

He steps away from me as though he's sated, when I'm satisfied and still needy all at once.

'You and me both.'

I walk around the kitchen bench on legs that are wobbly as all hell. I sip some of my drink, my eyes linked to his. But he's staring at my breasts. Bemused, I look down and see that they're red from his stubble.

His jaw is clenched and he looks away.

Something jars in my mind. A memory I can't quite grab, like finding soap in the bath.

'What is it?'

His smile is tight. 'I ordered Japanese.'

'Great. No karaoke, though,' I tease, referring to my last drunken night with Jack.

He nods. But something is wrong.

'What is it?' I insist.

'I've marked your entire body,' he says after a beat has passed. 'You're literally covered in marks from me.'

I frown, running my hands over my breasts, and then I shrug. 'So?'

His eyes, when they meet mine, are haunted. 'It doesn't bother you that I *like* fucking marking you? That I'm turned on by seeing proof of me on you?'

I tilt my head to one side, pretending bemusement, but my heart is accelerating and again I wonder at the risk of broken ribs in the face of a particularly aggressive heartbeat.

I shake my head slowly.

'Jesus…' He drags a hand through his hair unsteadily. 'All this time I thought you were Miss Moneypenny and you're actually Air Force Amy.'

'Who?'

He doesn't answer, just reaches down and picks up his towel, wrapping it around his waist, then walks into the kitchen to stand behind me. He runs his finger down my spine.

'There is a line here.' He drops his finger lower and presses it against my butt. 'And here, where I sucked you until you bruised.' Then he cups my arse. 'And here, where I slapped you hard enough to redden your skin.'

I swallow. This description of his touch is erotic and dangerous.

I suck my lip between my teeth. 'Don't you get it?' I don't look at him as I speak. 'When I'm here, I'm yours. I trust you. And I want this. This—what you do to me—is what turns me on. More than anything I've ever known.'

He drops his forehead to my shoulder, and then he grabs me and turns me around to face him. 'It doesn't bother you that I'm just using you?'

It's not what I expect him to say. I look at him with an obvious expression of confusion because he shakes his head.

'Not *you*, per se. Sex with you.'

I try to play the lighter side. 'Do I seem like I mind?'

He exhales, frustration and anger communicating themselves in the weighted breath. 'I don't want you to be another one of *them*.'

His eyes are hollow. No matter how I stare at him, I can't intuit his meaning.

'Another one of whom?'

'Them. The women I fuck to forget about her.'

I know instantly that he's referring to Lucy. Sadness wells inside me. Sadness for Jack, for Lucy and the whole sordid mess.

'But that's all this can be.'

There's a determination in his statement that fills me with ice.

I nod, but his words are exploding in my mind like tiny little bombs.

'I know,' I say. Because I do.

That's the worst thing. I have known this about him for a long time and yet here I am, fucking him and letting him drive me crazy when I should be running a mile in the opposite direction.

'So what are you doing here? How can you be okay with that?'

A great fucking question! One I wish I'd asked myself sooner.

'Hasn't that horse already bolted? We've had sex together. Does it really matter why?'

'I don't know.' His laugh is uncertain, his eyes cagey. 'I'm not usually this…*barbaric*.'

He drops his mouth to my shoulder and bites me gently.

'But with you…I don't know…it's like some animal instinct kicks in. I feel like I want to carry you over my shoulder and tie you to my bed.'

'You've already done that. Check and check.'

A flicker of his lips acknowledges the truth of my reply. 'I mean for days. I mean I want to feed you when it suits me. Let you drink the champagne that I tip into your mouth. But otherwise you'd exist for my pleasure alone.'

'Maybe you just want that because you know I'd never go for it,' I say hoarsely, hiding the fact that his words have evoked a powerful emotional need in me.

'Maybe.'

Suddenly, his need gives me an idea. No, it gives me a bartering chip. 'What if I let you go all Neanderthal?'

'You think I haven't already?' he asks, the words full of hoarse self-condemnation.

I shake my head. 'I think you've just scratched the surface.' I cup his face, rubbing my thumb over his stubble. 'So give me what I want and I'll give you what you want.'

'And what *is* it you want, Gemma Picton?'

I swallow my anxiety. What's the worst that can happen? He'll say no?

'I want you to answer my questions. I want to understand you better.'

The shower is warm against my skin. I rub my body all over, letting the soap bubble and froth before turning the heat off and stepping out into an enormous soft towel. I dry myself and then reach for one of the luxurious robes hanging behind the door.

I'm nervous, as though I'm on a first date. But that's stupid.

Because Jack doesn't date. Come to think of it, I don't really date either.

What we're doing is fucking—sure, the best sex of my life. But still just sex. Two nights? Maybe more? But definitely not any form of happily-ever-after.

It's sex. And it's discovery.

I'm getting my curiosity answered—and I have been curious about Jack for as long as I've worked with him. I've wondered about the demons that drive him. The ghosts, real and imagined, that play on the edges of his mind.

Besides, it's kind of win-win for me. I love the animal passion in him. So much so I'm terrified of myself. This way I get to find out more about the beautiful darkness of Jack Grant, and I get the beast in bed.

Perfect.

When I step out of the bathroom he's arranging containers on an enormous dining table. It could easily seat twelve people, but he's placed us at one end and, in a gesture that makes my heart thump, he's even lit a candle.

'Expecting company?' I murmur with forced sarcasm, desperate to cover the trembling emotion in my chest.

'That's not what I'd call you,' he responds in kind, but he winks at me and my heart pounds harder.

'We've covered that already with—who was it? Amy someone?'

He grins. 'I called you Miss Moneypenny first.'

'Yes, and that's equally wrong. I'm not some wallflower assistant.'

'You assist me,' he says with a shrug, but he comes to a chair and pulls it out, his eyes meeting mine, silently inviting me to sit.

Electricity sparks between us like a current neither of us can control.

I'm nervous, and that makes me angry! I don't want to be nervous around Jack, like this is a date or something. I've agreed to let him ravage me so that he'll tell me stuff. It's not a date. If it were he'd tell me all that stuff without the promise of animalistic sex.

It's only when I sit that I pay attention to the kind of food he's ordered. There's sushi, sashimi, a Katsu curry, edamame and a couple of miso soups. I try not to think he's remembered that Katsu curry is my favourite thing in the world.

He takes the seat opposite mine and lifts a glass. I tilt mine towards his and then rest it back on the table.

'It's bad luck not to drink after clinking glasses.'

'I haven't heard that.'

I lift the drink to my lips and taste it. Of course it's delicious.

He rests back in the chair, his hands linked beneath his chin. 'Well, Miss Picton. We have a deal. What is it you'd like to know?'

'You'll tell me anything?'

'And you'll let me *do* anything.'

I nod, my throat dry as I wonder just what his idea of 'anything' encompasses.

'How do you know I won't chicken out, out of interest?'

His laugh makes my gut vibrate. 'Because you're you. I can't imagine you backing away from anything in your life. You're fearless.'

'Not entirely,' I say under my breath.

'No? What are you afraid of?'

I sip my wine again, and then snap my chopsticks in half reaching for a piece of salmon *nigiri*. 'I'm afraid of lightning,' I say softly. 'Terrified of it.'

'As in thunder and lightning?'

I nod. 'Yep. That one.'

'But why? It's just atmospheric discharge.'

'Yeah. It's just a weather phenomenon. But I will still hide under my covers during a storm, waiting for it to pass, without fail.'

'Why? Since when?'

My smile is lopsided. 'Since I was a girl.'

'What happened?'

'How do you know *anything* happened?'

'I just do,' he says with a shrug of his broad shoulders, lifting his own chopsticks and taking a piece of chicken *karaage*.

He's right, of course.

'I was seven years old and locked out of our home. I'd gone to pick apples and my parents presumed I was in bed. They were out to dinner with friends and Nanny Winters thought I'd gone with them. The house was locked up and I couldn't get in.'

I shiver. It was one of the most horrifying nights I can recall.

'I climbed into my tree house and waited it out there. But a flash of lightning came down so close and so loud it smoked on the ground at my feet.'

He nods thoughtfully, but I can tell he's unravelling the story.

'When did you get back into your home?'

'Not until morning. I fell asleep eventually, and it wasn't until Nanny discovered me missing and the alarm was raised that I heard the staff looking for me. I woke up and all was well. Except that I can't stand storms now. Even the smell of rain in the air makes me afraid.'

He strokes his chin thoughtfully.

'So I'm not entirely fearless,' I finish lamely.

'Lots of people are afraid of thunderstorms.'

'Are *you*?'

'No.' His smile is perfunctory. 'There isn't much I'm afraid of.'

'But…?' I ask, sipping my wine, curious to the point of distraction.

'Yes, I have fears,' he admits grudgingly.

'Like…?'

He makes a deep, guttural noise. 'This was a crappy idea.'

I laugh softly. 'Ghosts? Spiders?'

'No.' He's quiet for so long I wonder if he's not going to answer, and then he continues, his voice hoarse. 'I'm afraid of powerlessness. Of watching someone I love die.'

His grief hits me like a web and I am caught in it.

'You've watched someone you love die and you've survived.'

'Barely.' He shakes his head. 'Try the chicken. It's great.'

I don't move. The ghosts of his admission linger between us, haunting our table.

'Were you with her when she died?'

He recoils as though he's been slapped and I briefly regret the agreement we've made. But I want to *know* this stuff. It's so important to me to understand. I feel like I've got only half of the picture and bit by bit I want to piece him together.

'Yes.'

'I'm sorry.'

'I wanted to be with her.'

'Of course.' I nod. 'How long were you married?'

'A year.' He clears his throat. 'Can we talk about something else?'

Sympathy is thick inside of me but instinctively I

know talking about this will help him so I don't back down. 'You told me I could ask what I want.'

'And this is what you want to know?'

'You told me you're fucking me because of her—so, yes, I want to know.'

His face pales. 'Fine.' His teeth are gritted. 'What else?'

I drink some wine and eat another piece of sushi, chewing on it thoughtfully. 'She died of cancer?'

He nods.

'And…?' I prompt.

'And *what*, Gemma?'

'Well, what kind?'

He expels an angry breath. 'Chronic Lymphocytic Leukaemia. Stage Four. It was a terminal diagnosis.'

I wince. 'I'm so sorry.'

'Why? It's not your fault.'

I understand his anger and aggression.

'Nothing could be done?'

His eyes meet mine and he shakes his head. I feel like he's holding something back, but I don't want to push him anymore. Not about this.

Sympathy trumps curiosity. So I let it go.

'This is delicious,' I say instead, reaching for another piece.

And he visibly relaxes, as though he's been in hell and I'm unlocking the gate.

'Yeah.'

'Do you spend much time here?' I look around the palatial apartment, seeing it almost as if for the first time.

'I used to.' His smile is tight. 'So…Nanny Winters, huh?'

'No, no—*you* don't get to change the subject.'

He laughs. 'I can do what I want.'

'That's not our deal.'

'Your parents worked full-time?'

It's so like Jack to push on with his line of questioning just because it suits him.

I stare at him. 'Not really.'

'Yet you were raised by a nanny?'

'I had three nannies,' I say, grabbing a piece of avocado sushi and eating it, then sipping my wine. 'Nanny Winters oversaw the other two.'

'*Three* nannies?' His voice is bordering on a scoff. 'So you were a handful even as a child?'

I roll my eyes. 'Did you not hear my thunderstorm story?'

'A runaway and a handful?' He nods with mock seriousness.

'Yep.'

'Your parents were rich?'

'*Are* rich,' I agree.

'Funny… I didn't have you picked as the daughter of some loaded guy.'

I arch a brow teasingly. 'Technically I'm the daughter of a loaded guy *and* a loaded lady. Duchess Arabella Picton, in fact.'

'No shit? *That* I did not see coming.'

He laughs then—a sound that relaxes me because it's so like us to laugh together that I am reminded of the years we've spent working together, getting to know one another. Not like this, admittedly, but in a different way.

'Why not?' I ask.

He laughs again and my gut clenches.

'So you slaving away for me is like a vanity job?'

I frown. 'No!'

'But you're going to inherit a fortune?'

I shrug, deciding it's better not to talk about my trust fund with Jack. I figure he won't really appreciate the amount that's sitting in my name in a Swiss bank account.

'One day.'

'Fascinating.'

'Not really.'

He nods, but I can see the wheels of his brain turning. 'You studied law, right?'

I roll my eyes. 'I'm your in-house counsel, what do you think?'

He grins and my tummy tilts off-balance. 'I don't pay too much attention to what my assistants do at university.'

I shoot him a look of disapproval but bite my tongue. He's goading me, and I won't give him the satisfaction of knowing he's been successful. 'I studied law and economics at Oxford, thank you very much.'

'Let me guess…you did well?'

My gaze doesn't falter. 'Double first.'

He tilts his head back, his laugh a soft caress. 'Not at all surprising.'

'How do you not know this about me? You hired me to work for you.'

'Yeah… Expecting you to last about three seconds.'

'Really? Why?'

'Because that's how long all my other assistants lasted.'

I grit my teeth. 'Counsels.'

'Your job is pretty much unfillable.'

'Because you're such a charm to work with,' I point out.

'Whatever the reason, no one stays around. So why have you?'

'Because I like a challenge,' I say honestly, my chin jutting out, my eyes holding to his. And he is still. Watchful. The air between us thickens.

'I'm a challenge?'

I laugh. 'You're kidding, right?'

He reaches for a piece of sushi. I watch him eat it and my stomach squeezes. How can I want him again already? I am fire and flame, bursting with need.

'Were you always like this? Or is it just since... Lucy?'

He frowns and doesn't answer right away. I can practically see the cogs turning in his brain. 'I don't know.'

'Well, before she...she died, did you have a constantly changing stream of staff?'

He shrugs. 'No.'

I nod, slowly. So this *is* a hangover of Lucy's death. My job, my being here, it all comes back to her. To Lucy.

The emotional strangulation of that is not something I think I'll easily comprehend, and so I stand up slowly.

'I've had enough for now.' My eyes meet his and now I am the one issuing a challenge. 'So show me.'

'Show you what?' he asks with a purposeful glint in his eye.

'Show me what *you* want.'

CHAPTER SEVEN

I'M IN LIMBO.

Not asleep…not awake. I lie in his bed, my body throbbing with pleasures untold, my mind exhausted.

It is late. Somewhere between midnight and dawn. And I am his.

I lift up on one elbow, my eyes hazy as I look down at him. He is beautiful and he is sexy. He is groggy. Almost asleep. But his eyes flick to mine and I see blank speculation in them.

Confusion.

Wariness.

'How are you?'

I smile—I hope it's as reassuring as I intend and not maniacal as I suspect. 'Good.'

He nods tersely, pushing up out of bed, dragging a hand through his hair as he stalks across to his wardrobe. He emerges after a moment, boxer shorts on. At least he's not showering me away immediately.

But he will soon enough. I know Jack too well to misunderstand his mood now, and it pisses me off as much as it worries me. I don't want a relationship, but I don't know how we can go from white-hot sex to awkward silence in the space of minutes.

'Do you need anything?' His voice is husky. 'Drink? Coffee? Shower?'

A flicker of annoyance draws my lips into a frown. 'No, thanks.'

I stand up, feeling as though I've run ten marathons. My body is sore and stiff, but still throbbing with pleasures previously unknown. My dress is—where? Out in the living area?

I walk towards him slowly, and pause just in front of him. What *he* wants is crystal-clear; my own needs are far more difficult to interpret but I *do* want to interpret them.

Self-preservation draws me inwards, away from Jack before he can push me away. 'I'm going to go.'

I see the emotions that flicker on his face and I recognise only one—relief.

'Are you sure?'

I laugh—a soft sound that covers whatever that heavy pain is in my chest. 'Come on, Jack. We both know how this works.'

I press a kiss against his cheek and move into the lounge. Our sushi feast is still on the table—a relic of our attempt at a date. Like normal people date. But we're *not* normal. Not on our own and definitely not together. We're misfits, both of us, operating outside the normal realms of this kind of relationship thing.

I scoop up my dress and bra and pull the dress on over my naked body, stuffing the bra into my handbag as I step into my shoes.

My hair I pull over one shoulder, brushing my fingers through its tangled length to neaten it somewhat.

'Martins will be on roster now,' he says, looking at the clock over the oven and referring to one of the junior staff drivers.

I shake my head. The last thing I want is for a company driver to see me like this, post-Jack-Grant-ravaging. 'I'll get a cab.' I walk towards him again and press a single kiss to his cheek.

'I'll see you Monday.'

'Monday...' He nods and there are more emotions in his face, these harder to comprehend. 'Right. It's the weekend.'

I swallow past a lump in my throat. 'And then Australia,' I remind him—probably unnecessarily.

'Yeah.'

His eyes probe mine. I feel like I'm escaping prison and one of those enormous floodlights has landed on me, full beam.

'You're okay?'

'I'm fine,' I reassure him.

We've just had pretty much the best sex in the world—I doubt it has ever been better for anyone than it is for us. But I know I need to go. It's important. My self-preservation instincts are blaring loudly, demanding I put some space between us.

He nods, and it's only then that I realise he's got a glass of Scotch in his hand.

It hurts. There's something about seeing him with a drink that reminds me of what he does—how often he does it and how he reacts afterwards. And I don't want that to be the case with us.

Those self-preservation instincts join forces with my brain and they pull the strings to make me smile brightly.

'Thanks for tonight. I had fun. See you soon.'

And I turn and walk slowly towards the door, my heart thudding, my mind foggy.

* * *

I watch her leave with a certainty that I'm messing up my life in a monumental way. What the *hell* am I doing? Sleeping with Gemma *once* was a disastrous cock-up. But again and again? Showing her all my dark spaces and hauntings?

No one needs to know the demons that lash me.

I am in control. That's me. It's the persona I've built and I don't like the idea of someone knowing that it's not completely true. Lucy knew, of course. And I guess Amber does; she's seen me in a pretty fucked-up state, right after Lucy died. But Gemma? Now?

Her eyes, big and intelligent, are assessing, always understanding. And the way her face scrunches when she's about to come... The way her body trembles beneath mine... Jesus. I want her now—again—more.

I turn to the door. If I chased her what would she say? God, would she think it means I want more than sex? Ironic, given that I *just* want sex. With Gemma.

An obsession is building inside me. Bit by bit it is closing me in. But Gemma Picton is hardly going to let me turn her into my own personal sex slave. Although I think she's about as caught up in all of this as I am...

All the more reason for me to fight harder, to control it.

I grip the crystal tumbler in my hands, feeling my anger and determination surge, and I pitch the glass hard against the wall. It breaks with satisfying immediacy, shattering into thousands of tiny pieces that mix with the slosh of amber liquid running fast down the wall before landing with a thud against the tiles. I drag my hand through my hair and stare at the destruction with a sense of satisfaction.

I'm good at ruining things. At breaking them.

That's what I need to stick to.

I don't think I'll ever eat again. Grandma has no such qualms. She reaches for another oyster—it must be her tenth—and swirls it inside lips she's painted bright red for the occasion.

'What's in Australia?'

I stare out at the little street, watching a small black car reverse—badly—into a narrow parking space. 'Work.'

'Always work...' She sighs.

I nod absently.

Jack will be there, too. After not going to Tokyo, I don't suppose there's the smallest hope I can get out of it.

'I promise I'll do something fun. Just for you.'

My insides quiver as I imagine what that could be. *Jack*. Doing Jack would be fun.

But even as my pulse is stirring and my heart is beginning to race my brain is demonstratively reminding me of Jack's particular brand of cold fishery. His ability to walk away from me right after we've shared mind-blowing, simultaneous orgasms is as offensive as it is unique.

Am I crazy to be letting this happen?

Yes, hisses my brain. *He's told you he's using you. He still loves his dead wife. Jesus. You're a fool.*

'Grandma...' I pause, my lips tight as I dismiss whatever the heck I'd been about to say.

She swallows the oyster—Grandma is the only person I know who actually chews the slimy little devils first...*shudder*...like phlegmatic explosions...*ugh*. Her gaze is cool and direct.

At eighty, Grandma is every bit as beautiful as she was in her youth. Lined, ephemeral and pale now, but with a glimmer in her eyes, a wave to her silver shoulder-length hair and a smile that is punctuated by straight white teeth—all her own. Her nose is straight, her eyes wide-set, her figure as svelte as ever. And she dresses in a fashion which somehow straddles the latest in trends without coming across as an attempt to be youthful.

'Something's on your mind.'

I shake my head and reach for my bread roll. Only I've already fingered it anxiously, reducing it to a pile of wheaten crumbs and ash.

'When Grandpa died, did you think about finding someone else?'

She snorts. 'There is no one else.'

The words make me smile, yet they are also sounding the death knell for the hope I hadn't realised I've been carrying.

'No one?' I tease.

'No one.' She expels a sigh. 'Your grandfather was... What we shared is impossible to explain.' She sips her champagne, her eyes growing even more intensely watchful, if that's possible. 'Have I ever told you about how we met?'

I shake my head, even though I know the story backwards.

'Liar!' She chuckles.

We're interrupted by a waiter, but Grandma dispenses with him quickly, placing an order for another bottle of champagne and then fixing me with that steady grey gaze of hers.

'He was sitting on the lawns at Huntington, his knees bent, his chin resting on them. His face was resolutely turned away from me, but as I approached his eyes shifted, locking to my face. It was as if he was telling me all his secrets and begging me to help him in that one single second. He looked at me as if he knew that I was the only person on earth who would be able to dig through his shit and find the kernel of the boy he'd once been.'

Grandma is looking over my shoulder now. The story is one she's told so many times that it comes out word for word as I remember it. Still, I lean forward, the invisible threads of magic and history curling around me.

'That enormous oak tree was just to his side—far enough away to prevent shade from darkening him, but close enough to dwarf him. He was a big man, your grandfather. Tall and strong—built for battle.' Her lips twist with undisguised disgust. 'But not strong in spirit. His spirit had been broken and the tree made that obvious to me.'

Her eyes flick back to mine and I feel it, too. Just like she did. The weight of silent communication and understanding.

'I loved him instantly.'

My heart does a weird little palpitation in my chest. 'I can't imagine that.'

'Why?'

'It's just unfathomable to me.'

'That's because you haven't met someone worth loving yet,' she says with a shrug of her elegant shoulders. 'One day you'll know just what I mean.'

I quirk my lips, hoping my smile seems dismissive. My pulse has speeded up. I try to quell it.

'I don't think it always works like that.'

'Perhaps not. Your grandfather *was* special.'

'What you shared was special,' I murmur, reaching across and squeezing her hand.

Grandma's eyes flicker, her lips tighten and she nods, as if to dismiss the conversation. The waiter appears, brandishing a bottle of champagne, and begins to unfurl the foil top. Grandma stares resolutely at the view as the waiter performs his ministrations, and doesn't smile when he pours two fresh glasses.

She is very much the Duchess in instances like this: a woman who has become so used to service and being served that it isn't even an act she needs to be grateful for.

I smile my thanks as he leaves.

Grandma waits until we are alone again. 'You will never meet anyone—no lover, no special friend, no one—if you are behind your desk all day.'

Out of nowhere I picture Jack. I picture the way he drapes himself against the doorframe, the way his body is so languid and sensual, and my stomach flops.

'Have I told you the foundation is almost ready to launch?'

Grandma tilts her head to one side. 'I admire your commitment to that…' she says, clearly trying to frame whatever she's thinking carefully. 'But you have money. If philanthropy is your aim, why not set up your own charity?'

'Perhaps I will—one day. But my job is more than

just one thing… You know that.' I expel a sigh, frustration gnawing at me. 'You've always championed my work.'

'You're very clever. And I know you're brilliant at what you do. But you're sacrificing too much now. I championed your work because I hoped you would find a way to pursue your career and still live your life. You, more than anyone I've ever known, have the ability to keep multiple balls in the air at once. So why aren't you doing it?'

I drop my head, my eyes not meeting hers. There is so much truth in what she's saying, but the criticism hurts.

'I…I am.' It's a lie. We both know that. But reality is not something I want to face.

'*All* of you is focussed on that job. On that man. I'm worried you're going to wake up one day and realise what you've sacrificed. And all for *him*.'

My heart bumps against my ribs, banging them with its frantic racing. 'He's brilliant.'

'And a bastard, by all reports.'

Yes. A beautiful, arrogant, brilliant, sex-obsessed bastard.

Was it only yesterday he was inside me? It feels like forever ago. I am at a fever pitch of want—want only he can answer. My insides clench instantly, remembering him, needing him, craving his touch, smell and taste…

'He's not that bad.' The words are hoarse, punctured by breath and memory.

'With him and that job in your life you're never going to be truly happy.'

Her pronouncement is spoken in a way that is almost prophetic. A shiver dances down my spine, spiralling coldness across my flesh like a breath from the North Pole.

'Travelling and living off the family trust would be better?' I arch a brow. 'You know me better than that. I *live* for what I do. I *love* it. Maybe *that's* the love of my life.'

Silence prickles between us. Silence that is suffocating and unwelcome.

'Very well,' she clips, dismissing this conversation, as well. 'I don't like the way they've trimmed those hedges. It's so severe.'

I breathe again, but my heart is still twisting and thumping. The truth sits heavily in my mind but I step away from it.

There is no ulterior motive to my working so hard for Jack. There's no mystery as to why I don't feel like I've sacrificed a damn thing for him. It doesn't mean anything that I am fulfilled and alive, energised every time I speak to him, see him, do his bidding. But my stomach drops. Because actually I think there probably *is* a meaning—just one I don't want to appreciate. *Fuck.*

His jet is the last word in space-age luxury. Cream leather armchairs on either side of the aisle, thick carpet a pale beige and lamps that would look at home in a five-star hotel make the perfect night-flight reading environment. USB docks are in every armrest to charge phones and iPads, and there are several bedrooms, a boardroom and a small cinema.

There is also a brooding billionaire sitting at the back of the plane, his head bent over a stack of files, apparently engrossed.

I ignore him. Or pretend to.

We've hardly spoken since I left his apartment on Friday night.

That was easy enough over the weekend. After sharing two bottles of champagne and being drilled in life's lessons, Grandma and I shopped in the high street, selecting a new clutch purse for Grandma to take to the anniversary dinner and pretending we weren't both dreading the damned thing.

I didn't hear from Jack, and it wasn't until I got back to my own place on Sunday evening that I realised I'd been expecting to. That I'd thought he'd text or call or email or something.

Those two days away from him, without seeing him, stretched interminably.

The knowledge prickled down my spine so that on Monday morning I steeled myself to be as standoffish and unaffected as possible. To fight coldness with cool unconcern, with no care.

But I didn't see him then either. He arrived late, left early and didn't speak to me.

And I didn't speak to him, despite the fact I needed his signature on some papers.

I chickened out and actually hid from him when he walked past my office, ducking beneath my desk.

Crazy, right?

Not so much.

We've moved into dangerous territory. I don't know if he realises it, but there are warnings blaring in my head. I don't want to need Jack Grant like I do. I don't mean sexually. I mean in every way.

Only I can't imagine my life without him.

We've been flying for the better part of a day now,

and hardly spoken beyond a perfunctory, polite 'Hiya' as he boarded the flight, ten minutes late and looking like sex and seduction in a ten-thousand-pound suit.

I have been telling myself I don't care with varying measures of success. Did I expect he'd storm up to me and kiss me? Take me passionately in his arms and hold me close? Tell me he never wants to go three days without seeing me again?

He's made it abundantly clear what he wants.

It should be what I want, too.

I shut my eyes for a moment, crossing my legs in the armchair, and am surprised when I'm woken a moment later.

'We're landing.' Jack's hands are at my hips and I bat them away instinctively.

He grabs the seatbelt and clips it across me—tight—his eyes flicking to mine. The hint of a smile on his face makes my heart flip-flop.

'Have I ever told you that you snore?'

Warmth invades my face. 'I know. I have mild asthma.'

He grins and takes the seat beside mine. My body is instantly aware of him and my brain is pretty pissed off at the rapid response.

I shift a little, looking down at my watch. I must have slept for over an hour. I blink, opening the world clock function on my phone. It's six o'clock in Sydney, which means I want to be tired—not refreshed after a quick nap on the flight.

Silence stretches between us. Debbie, one of his flight attendants, clips out efficiently, 'We'll be touching down on schedule. Can I get you anything before we land?'

'Water, thanks.' I smile at her, turning my attention back to the papers I'd been reading.

Well, half my attention. A quarter of it. A sliver. The tiny part that's not completely drawn to Jack and his nearness and his hypermasculine fragrance. The part of me that isn't all wrapped up in the way he's sitting, legs spread, arms relaxed, body warm and large and so close I could push out of my seat and sit on his lap. Unzip his pants and take him.

God. I want that.

'Dr Pepper.'

His response to Debbie's question shakes the desire from my mind, but he looks at me and my toes curl. Does he guess what I'm thinking?

I tap my pen against the side of the page I'm reading in an attempt to focus my thoughts in a more appropriate direction.

But Jack reaches across, his hand curling over mine. My pulse goes into overdrive.

'Did you have a good weekend?' he asks.

I laugh. I can't help it. A short, sharp sound of weary frustration. 'Yeah.'

He nods, and a frown pulls at his lips. 'I don't know how to speak to you now.'

And I feel sorry for him. Sorry for me. Because we're both in the middle of a patch of uncertainty too wide to navigate.

'I'm still me.'

'But it's different.'

'Yeah… I don't know if you ever asked me about my weekend before we had sex together.'

I lower my voice as Debbie walks back into the

cabin. She places a glass of water on my side table and a can of soda on Jack's.

As Debbie disappears once more he winks at me. 'It's cherry flavour.'

Damn him. He knows what he's doing to me.

My pulse fires and I give him a tight half-smile before returning my attention to the document I'm partway through reading.

'You've got a breakfast meeting at seven o'clock with the mayor. While you're with him I'm going to be going over the premises. Then I'll meet with your Australian CEO, Clint Sheridan, to touch base on recruitment matters. The broker for the New Zealand deal is meeting us for lunch at Aria, and Clint's asked you to his place for dinner, with a few of the other executives.'

'Asked *us*, you mean,' he corrects, his eyes hooked to mine.

I frown. 'It's just social. You don't need me—'

'I want you there,' he says firmly, and I remember that he *is* actually my boss.

Plus, if it weren't for the fact that we've had sex I wouldn't have ever thought of *not* going. It's my own way of not blurring the lines, but he sees right through it.

'You've done most of this deal. You *should* be there.'

I pull my lips to the side thoughtfully. 'Sure.'

It's not worth arguing about. We've gone to hundreds of this kind of thing in our time. I'm sure this won't be any different.

He nods, but he's distracted. 'Do we need to talk?'

His suggestion sets off a kaleidoscope of possibilities. Talk? About what? About us? What would I say? And him?

I swallow to hide my confusion and return his question with one of my own. 'Do we?'

He reaches across and wipes his thumb over my lip. Butterflies bounce around my gut.

'I guess not. It doesn't matter.'

I stare straight ahead, moving out of his reach. Because maybe this *doesn't* matter. Maybe this is just one of those things and in a few weeks I'll wonder what the heck I got so worked up about. Why I let him get under my skin like this.

I hope it's true even as I know how unlikely that is.

CHAPTER EIGHT

I LOVE AUSTRALIA. We don't get here often—though with Jack opening this office that will probably change.

The heat and humidity hit me as soon as the doors open. Even in the air-conditioned airport there's a sultry oppressiveness that makes me ache to find the nearest swimming pool and dive straight in.

A limo is waiting for us, and a couple of reporters from the broadsheet newspapers. I forget sometimes that Jack is a 'Person of Interest', especially in the business world. Working with him for over two years has made him just 'Jack' to me, but to the world he's an enigmatic tycoon and philanthropist.

I remember feeling awestruck before I knew him. The prospect of working for him was one I pinned all my hopes to.

Now it's just my life.

Jack and I have been pretty much inseparable this whole time. I'm his right hand. Despite having been hired as his in-house counsel, my job has morphed and varied and now incorporates a wide variety of duties. I'm across his workload and can step in at any point, finishing negotiations, speaking on his behalf. When we travel together we either stay in adjoining rooms or in one of his apartments. It depends on how long we're in town and what's required of us.

This unfettered access has been helpful when we needed to proof things late at night or discuss early morning meetings. It's never been an issue. But the thought of sharing his penthouse at Woolloomooloo is filling me with a sense of apprehension. Not because I'm afraid of him. I'm afraid of what I want from him—what I need. Of what living in close confines, even temporarily, will force us to confront.

My sense of foreboding doesn't improve once we arrive and I remember how stunning the place is. How glamorous and romantic.

The thought is errant and I quash it immediately. Romance be damned. We're colleagues who happen to be sleeping together. That's all.

The penthouse is in a big converted wharf building. He bought the whole top floor from some Hollywood celebrity about five years ago, converting several luxurious flats into one enormous sky home. It has panoramic views of Sydney Harbour. From where I'm standing I can see the bridge and a beautiful little island. There's a balcony that wraps all the way around and a lap pool in a glass room to one side.

I look at the water, my temptation obvious.

'Plans for tonight?'

Jack's right behind me. I don't turn around but I can feel his nearness. My body quivers; I want to jump him.

'None. Getting into the time zone.'

'I'm *in* the time zone, baby.' He grins, and strolls towards the enormous glass windows that overlook the harbour. 'I'm also hungry enough to eat a horse.' He turns to face me, his eyes dragging from my head to my toes and then back up, slowing down over my cleavage. 'Shall we go out?'

My body is sticky from the humidity and I am weary. Wary, too. Instinctively I understand that we need to keep some boundaries in place. Going out, just the two of us, is an unacceptable boundary erosion.

I smile—hopefully politely. 'I'm going to have a swim before I do another thing. Don't feel you have to wait for me to eat.'

I walk back towards the door, to where our suitcases are, and wheel mine along beside me down the corridor.

I find the room I used last time I was here and step into it, shutting the door behind me with an emphatic click. I lean against it and suck in a deep breath, then open the case and pull out my swimsuit. A simple black one-piece. I slip it on, pausing to check my reflection before wrapping a towel around my middle and walking back into the apartment.

I hear him before I see him and my stomach twists. His powerful arms are pulling him through the water, and if you told me he had trained as an Olympic swimmer I would believe you. His tan glistens like gold beneath the Australian sun.

Trying valiantly to ignore the heat between my legs, I drop my towel onto a lounger and dive in, long and low, holding my breath for as long as I can before kicking to the surface and swimming all the way to the end. I rest my arms on the sun-warmed coping and stare out at the harbour beneath us.

It looks like someone has shattered a thousand diamonds and thrown them over the water's top. The way it glistens is almost impossible to believe.

He swims up beside me. 'You're angry at me.'

He doesn't touch me, but the words feel like finger-prints on my chest.

I turn to him slowly, my hair wet, my eyes sur-rounded by clumps of black lashes. 'No.'

His expression is one of impatience. 'I'm no good at this. Tell me what I've done so I know.'

'What you've *done*?' It's so ludicrous that I almost laugh, but an equal urge to cry rises in my chest. 'You haven't "done" anything, Jack. I thought we'd agreed that this is our deal? Sex—fine. Work—fine. Nothing in between.'

But out of nowhere I remember the way my grandma talks about meeting Grandpa. I look at Jack and my heart hammers. *Damn it.*

He stares back at me. I can practically see the cogs turning. 'You're in your late twenties?'

'Twenty-six,' I clarify, and the distinction is a small but important one, for some absurd reason I can't com-prehend. Am I vain about my age? *Really?*

'And you've never been in a relationship?'

'Why do you say that?' I ask, though he's right.

'I just don't see you as someone's girlfriend.'

'Gee, thanks,' I mutter, turning my attention back to the view.

His fingertip on my shoulder is so light that I al-most wonder if I've imagined his touch. But then he runs it down my wet arm, all the way to my elbow, and cups me there, squeezing gently. I turn towards him once more and he pushes out from the wall of the pool, bringing me with him, deeper into the water.

I'm a good swimmer, and I tread water without his help. But he stays close, his handsome face mesmeris-ing me with ocean-green eyes and darkly tanned skin.

'Am I wrong?'

I shake my head. 'Not necessarily.' A smile flicks across my lips without my permission. 'I've dated. And been with men when it's suited me. But I've always had demanding jobs, and not a lot of time to do the whole dinner-and-a-movie thing.'

He laughs. 'That sounds boring as shit.'

My thoughts exactly. 'How did you meet her?'

I don't need to say his wife's name. We both know who I mean. He expels a breath and looks away, his jaw clenched.

'It's fine if you don't want to talk about it,' I say, making to swim away, but he grabs my wrist and pulls me towards him. And I'm glad. I need him to need me, and it's a sign that he does. My heart smiles.

'You keep running away from me when you don't get your own way—did you know that?'

Do I? 'I'm not running away. I'm swimming away,' I say, in a very lame attempt at humour. 'And it's not because I don't get my own way—it's because talking to you is like talking to a brick wall. It's easy to…to run away when you're being pushed.'

His eyes widen in non-verbal acknowledgement of the point I've made. 'She was working at a restaurant in Edinburgh.' His eyes flash with remembered pain. 'I'd just wrapped up a meeting and was heading to the hotel. Thought I'd stop for a late dinner.' He clears his throat, but his voice is still gravelly. 'And I saw her.'

Jealousy fires inside me at the look of total wonderment that briefly crosses his eyes.

'She was finishing up and I made her nervous as hell.'

'Nervous? Why?'

Though, I remember belatedly my first meeting with Jack and the trepidation that lived in me. I hid it beneath a layer of finely honed bravado but, yes, I was nervous, too. He has a machismo and dynamism that is at once overpowering. I have truly never met anyone like him.

'She hadn't had a lot of good experience with men,' he says tightly, a muscle jerking in his square jaw.

'I'm sorry for that,' I say quietly.

'Yeah. I was, too.' His smile was haunted. 'The guy she'd left just before meeting me seemed to have thought of her as his own personal punch bag.'

I nod slowly, imagining what that must be like. I have nothing to reference it to. It's beyond my remit even to comprehend that kind of fear and pain.

'I'm sorry,' I say again.

'Yeah.' He nods, too. 'Anyway…'

'So you guys started seeing each other?'

He winced. 'I proposed to her a week after we met. I'm not good at the whole dating thing. I don't have the patience for it.' His smile is shaded with self-deprecation. 'I steamrollered her rather than dated her.'

I can't help the soft laugh that escapes me. 'Why does that not surprise me?'

It's further proof that when Jack wants something he goes after it—immediately and unequivocally. But it's taken him two years to realise he wants my body, and there's no sign he wants more than that. He felt the same love for Lucy that my grandma describes having for Grandpa. So perhaps it is normal and common and I just don't realise that because I've never felt anything like it.

It's pretty obvious Jack doesn't feel it for me. Jealousy bubbles in my gut.

'I wanted to make her life better. I wanted to fix it all. To take away her pain and make her smile and laugh.'

'I'm sure you did,' I say, with truth.

I've only seen a few photos of Lucy around the mansion and, yes, on the internet, when I've allowed myself the morbid indulgence of looking her up. And in all of these pictures she is smiling.

'I killed her, Gemma.' His eyes meet mine for a second and then he looks away. 'If she'd never met me she'd probably still be alive.'

I freeze, ill-equipped to deal with this kind of confession. Nothing about it makes sense. And yet the way he drinks after he's slept with someone... Is it possible there's a darker truth at play? No. I know Jack. I know him through and through. He's being dramatic, not literal.

'What are you talking about?'

He swallows, then closes his eyes. 'She was pregnant. We'd just found out and then the tests showed that she had cancer. I wanted her to start treatment immediately, but it would have meant her having an abortion.'

Sadness for Jack, for Lucy and for the baby they would have had fills me all the way to the top of my soul. I don't consider myself maternal, but I know instantly what decision she made and why.

'She didn't want to do that.'

'No.' His face is grim. 'Even with treatment she had pretty much no hope.' He clears his throat. 'But still... There would have been a chance. If she hadn't fallen pregnant.' He shakes his head angrily.

'Then she wouldn't have found out about the cancer until it was too late,' I say softly.

Sympathy makes me crumble. How can I be strong in the face of his loss? I cup his face and draw him to me, kissing him gently, tenderly, hoping to reassure him and wipe away this baseless and yet unending guilt.

He is still. Not kissing me back. His guilt is still cloaked about us, but then something clicks into gear and he groans into my mouth, cupping my butt and lifting my legs to wrap them around his waist, holding me against his arousal and letting me obliterate his sadness. For one more moment. One more night.

I see now that this is how he's getting through.

A night here and there to stop feeling this weight of responsibility.

A different woman to bury himself in and forget that he got Lucy pregnant and that because of her pregnancy she refused treatment.

His words swirl through my head. *'I wanted to make her life better. I wanted to fix it all. To take away her pain and make her smile and laugh.'*

It's exactly how I feel about Jack.

And I know one sure-fire way to bring him back from the haunted brink of the misery he's inhabiting. I kiss him hard, moving my mouth over his as I press against his cock. My hands tuck into the elastic of his swim shorts, curving around his arse, holding him tight against me.

He knows. He knows which way salvation lies and he powers through the water, walking easily to the edge and lifting me so that I'm sitting on the coping. He barely breaks our kiss as he climbs out, pressing his body over mine, his weight and wetness making me writhe against the tiles as need explodes in me.

It's the need to remove this burden from his mind, sure. But it's my own need, too. My need to *feel* him. This is what makes sense right now.

'You are like an angel,' he mutters, stripping my swimsuit from my body. The fabric is wet and stubborn, but his hands are strong and determined and dispose of it easily, rolling it down my flesh, my legs, until I can kick it off my feet. He brings his mouth back to mine and I kiss him once more, my hands grabbing his cock and guiding him towards me.

He pauses, though, his eyes seeking mine as though he's asking me something, needing something else.

I smile at him—a slow-spreading smile—and I whisper, 'Please...'

He moves inside me and something is shifting around us—changing—as tangible as the pleasure that rolls through me.

We want this to be clear-cut, yet it no longer feels that way. It's not just sex this time... It's a slow exploration that curls my toes and, I'm afraid, shakes my heart to life.

CHAPTER NINE

'I LOVE THIS CITY.'

His eyes meet mine, his smile disarming, and my body responds. I swear my breasts grin at him. Happiness settles around my shoulders.

'It's beautiful.'

A pizza box sits between us, the contents half-eaten. He reaches for another piece and I watch his fingers curl over the crust.

Making love by the pool broke something inside me and I'm glad—because it's rebuilt me in a different way. *I'm* different. *He's* different. Nothing is the same now.

'It's clean. New.' He smiles. 'Nothing like where I grew up.'

I have to shake myself into the conversation. I'm genuinely interested in where this is going, but the cobwebs of lust are hard to ignore.

'Dublin?'

'Yeah. Just outside it, anyway. A grimy little town to the east.' He wrinkles his nose.

'Do you ever get back?'

'Nah.' He throws the crust back into the box and stands up, holding his hands out to me.

I stand and put my hands in his. When did I stop questioning him and just become a part of him? And why doesn't it bother me more?

'My parents moved to Kerry—a little house over-looking the ocean, as far as you can see. It's beautiful there.'

'But you like cities?' I say as he pulls me towards him and holds me close.

He begins to sway, dancing with me on the balcony of his apartment as the moon casts a silver light over the Sydney Opera House.

'I like the pace,' he agrees. 'I'm not one for small towns.'

I tilt my head to the side. 'I don't know...' I say thoughtfully. 'I think cities can be almost slower than towns. It just depends on how you spend your time. There's certainly a lot of anonymity in a city. Haven't you ever just wanted to get lost? You can walk down Oxford Street on Boxing Day and not be seen by anyone.'

He presses his cheek against mine. There it is again. That clicking inside me as I acknowledge how right this feels. I know it's a very dangerous thought—one that will certainly lead me to pain.

'I can honestly tell you I have *never* contemplated walking down Oxford Street—let alone on Boxing Day. Are you fucking mad?'

I smile against his chest. 'Yes, well, I suppose you'd send someone to get whatever the hell you need, right?'

His smile indicates agreement.

'Anyway, you live in Hampstead. That's basically as small town as it's possible to get inside London.'

'But so close to everything. And might I point out that you live there, too?'

'I moved to Hampstead because *you* live there,' I say sensibly, and then stop moving, looking up at him with obvious embarrassment. 'Because my *job* is there,' I correct, but my cheeks are pink and my eyes can't quite meet his. 'You know…with the long hours it just made sense.'

'I know what you meant,' he says, his smile sending fire through my body. 'Where did you live before that?'

I let my breath out slowly, glad he's giving me a pass. 'Elephant and Castle.'

He laughs—a gravelled sound. 'Your parents must have *loved* that!'

They hated it. His insight shakes me. 'Why do you say that?'

'You had three nannies growing up, and a tree house big enough to sleep in. My guess would be they felt it was a bit of a fall from grace for you.'

I hide my smile by dipping my head forward. He lifts my hand and twirls me in his arms, as though we are dancing to a song that only he can hear.

'It wasn't their idea of sensible, no. But it was easy to get into work from there, and I had good friends in the area. Plus, I loved spending my Saturday mornings at Borough Market and it was an easy walk.'

'A closet foodie?' he prompts.

'No. I'm too busy to cook. But I'm a sucker for fresh flowers.' I exhale. 'And cheese. I would go from stall to stall buying whichever cheese took my fancy, savouring it that afternoon with a matched glass of wine.'

'Sounds pretty damned good.' He grins.

'Yep.'

'And you gave all that up to work for *me*, huh?'

'Not all of it,' I say with a wink. 'There's a pretty amazing cheese shop on the high street, you know.'

'And flowers?'

'Always.' I tilt my head up to his and then immediately look past him, to the glittering view of Sydney by night. There is something in his face that calls to me, and I know it would be foolish to answer it.

'Let me guess. You like white Oriental lilies?'

I'm surprised that he even knows a variety of flower, let alone is hazarding a guess as to which would be my favourite.

'No.' I shake my head. 'I love peonies and ranunculus. There's something so wildly chaotic about them that it makes my heart sing.'

'So poetic!' he teases, curling me against him and holding me tight.

I can feel his hard edges and planes, so familiar to me, but my heart is racing as though it's the first time we've touched.

'I think they're naughty,' I say with a grin. 'As though someone has said to them, *"We're going to make you the most beautiful, chubby little flowers in the world, but only if you grow straight up towards the sky."* And then they looked at each other and said, *"Nah."* Have you ever really paid attention to their stems? The way they wind round and round as though they're dancing in a thunderstorm?'

His smile is mysterious. Enigmatic. He is, at times, impossible to read.

'No.'

'No? You don't agree?'

'No, I've never looked at their stems to the degree you have. Nor have I anthropomorphised them.'

'Then you've led a very deprived life, sir.'

I feel his laugh rather than hear it: a rumble from deep in his body. 'Apparently. Do you want some dessert?'

'I can think of other things I want more.'

He laughs and shakes his head, stepping away from me and disappearing.

Thwarted desire flames at the soles of my feet.

He returns a moment later, two coffee cups in his hands. Except there's no coffee in them. They're filled with a single scoop of vanilla ice cream each.

It's sweet, but truly dessert is the last thing on my mind. Before I can tell him that he pulls a hand from behind his back and holds out two perfect fresh cherries.

I grin as he places one in each cup.

'The cherry on top,' he explains unnecessarily, and my heart turns over in my chest at this gesture that is at once both sexy and sweet. Sexy, because how can I *ever* see a cherry as just a cherry again? And sweet because it is *our* thing.

We have *a thing*.

He digs a spoon into the ice cream and brings it to my lips. I taste it, but as on that first night, with our first kiss, his mouth is on mine immediately, his tongue tasting me even as I taste the ice cream.

Dessert is forgotten.

His kiss is unlike anything I've felt with him. It's soft. Tender. Gentle.

He breathes in as though he's inhaling me and I do the same, smiling against his lips.

Despite everything we've shared, it feels like the most intimate we've ever been. As if we're connected on every level.

But then our desperate hunger takes over and his hands are pushing at my robe, connecting with my naked flesh with the same intensity that marked our first coming together. It's as though he's punishing himself now—punishing himself for wanting me in any way other than animalistic and wild.

He presses me back, his kiss hard against my face, his body firm against mine, until I connect with the glass balustrade that runs along the edge of the terrace. He drops his kiss lower, to my neck, and lower still, his stubble grazing along my front until he brushes a nipple, taking it into his mouth and sucking it, spinning whirls of pleasure through me.

He drops lower, and finally falls to his knees. His mouth against my clit is a welcome invasion, his tongue what I have been needing. I grip the railing, my hands tight around its edge, as he glides his tongue down and I moan, pressing deeper against him. He knows exactly what I like now, and it takes him only moments to stir me to a fever pitch of awareness.

I make a small sound in the night air, tilting my head back and staring up at the stars above Sydney as I fall apart against his mouth, my orgasm spellbinding in its intensity and strength. I sway, and almost fall forward, but his strong hands are gripping my hips, pulling me to him as he stands.

'You are beautiful,' he murmurs, pressing a kiss to my forehead.

My breath is burning hard in my lungs, supercharging my body. Everything about this moment is just that: beautiful.

I meet his eyes and—ridiculously—feel a stinging in the back of mine. *Don't let me cry!* How embarrassing. But there's something in his look that's spinning my gut, shifting through me with a sense of unreality. As though he's thinking something and doesn't know how to say it.

I watch him, waiting for my breath to settle and my pulse to slow. He opens his mouth. My heart is still. Then, with one of those rakish smiles I've come to love, he says, 'Let's go to bed.'

'So you're his other half? Professionally speaking.'

I smile at Clint Sheridan but my eyes are glued to Jack. Across the room he holds court easily, and a group of men and two women stand hanging on his every word.

'Technically, I'm his in-house counsel,' I say, with a sideways smile.

'But word has it that you pretty much oversee his entire workload.'

'Really?' I arch a brow and sip my champagne. 'His workload is pretty immense.'

'I can imagine.'

I like Clint. Given that he's going to be running the Australian operation, I'll have to work closely with him—certainly in the start-up phase. He's a bit nervous, but I think once he settles down into the role he'll be funny and fast. He's definitely relaxed a little, even over the course of the few hours we've been at his expansive apartment on Sydney's North Shore.

The view is spectacular—different to that from Jack's penthouse—and by night the city shimmers before us. The famed Harbour Bridge has been lit red, for some reason, and there's something almost eerie about the way it seems to glide over the water, an angry sentinel or a protective beacon. In the far distance there's a flash of lightning, and that only adds to the spectacle.

'Night show!'

Clint grins, as if following my gaze. Or perhaps he's seen the involuntary shudder—a response to the suggestion of thunder. I don't give in to temptation and ask if a storm is forecast. I'm not a little girl any more. I can recognise my phobia as just that—an illogical pattern of fear.

'Have you lived here long?' I ask.

'A few years.' He rests his hand on the back of a dark timber chair and sips his beer. 'Bought it off the plan. Thought I'd use it as a renter, but then—divorce.' He grimaces, as if the single word should communicate his entire backstory.

'I'm sorry. I didn't know.'

'Why would you?'

His smile is disarming. He's handsome, I realise. Strange that I didn't notice sooner. *Oh, yeah?* My brain is rolling its eyes again. It has a point. Finding another man attractive when I'm sleeping with Jack Grant is like taking a shower in the middle of the Niagara Falls. But there's no denying it. Clint has got eyes that are almost as dark as night, a thick crop of black hair, a swarthy tanned complexion—and he's built like a tank. Thick neck, muscled arms—like he'd be as at home on a rugby field as he would the boardroom.

Mmm.

'True. It's not really our concern if you're married or not.'

'Are you?'

My eyes lift to his, my smile hinting at a laugh. 'Definitely not.'

'That's funny?'

His eyes scan my face and there's curiosity there. I suppose I am of an age where women are generally on that path somewhere. Either dating, engaged, planning the wedding, married, just married, sick of marriage… I'm none of those things. In fact, marriage really hasn't entered my head as a desirable state into which to enter.

Out of nowhere, the wedding anniversary party fizzes into my mind. I could definitely attribute my lack of faith in the whole institution of marriage to my parents. The silence of my childhood sits like a dull weight on my periphery.

'Only in that I barely have time to plan a holiday, let alone something as monumental as—' I wave my hand in the air and the gold bangles I'm wearing jangle '—that.'

'Smart move. The whole thing's overrated.'

I arch a brow, sipping my champagne. My eyes travel across the room distractedly. They're just skimming faces and people, travelling out of habit rather than on any specific quest. But they glance across at Jack and meet his eyes and everything inside me lurches almost painfully. A primal ache of possession unfurls in my gut.

With effort, I turn my attention back to Clint. 'I suppose it's easy to feel that when you've just come out of a divorce.'

'Should never have got married,' he says with a shrug of his shoulders. 'Taught me a valuable lesson, though.'

'And what's that?'

'Gemma?'

I tilt my head, my eyes locking with Jack's once more. He's right beside me, his face unreadable.

'Am I interrupting?'

'I've never understood why people ask that. You obviously *are* interrupting.' I soften the words with a smile, but Clint tenses beside me.

'Then by all means continue,' Jack invites, his eyes challenging me silently.

'Clint was just telling me why marriage is a huge mistake.'

I turn my body away from Jack, giving Clint my full attention. Only I've made a crucial error. Jack's right behind me, and my back is completely hidden from the room. His hand curls around my arse and I have to bite my tongue to stop myself drawing in a sharp breath.

His fingers stroke my flesh, and even I can feel his warmth through the dress.

My knees are shaking suddenly.

'For me it was,' Clint backpedals, his smile dismissive.

'Sorry to hear that,' Jack says, pressing his fingers in a little deeper, shooting arrows of desire through my flesh. 'I need Gemma for a conference call I'm expecting. Is there somewhere private we can go?'

My heart is racing, beating so hard I'm surprised it can stay lodged in my chest.

'Yeah, of course—my office.' Clint nods, turning on his heel and moving through the lounge area.

Jack runs his hand higher up my back and then drops it to his side as he moves to follow Clint through the luxurious apartment. Three doors down a long, well-lit corridor, Clint pauses, his smile professional.

It's clear he has no clue how Jack's been touching me, nor what Jack and I want.

'Make yourselves at home,' he invites. 'Need water? Coffee? Anything?'

Jack shakes his head and Clint leaves, pulling the door shut behind him. The office is large, and offers another view of the harbour. There's a desk in the middle, a sofa pushed hard to the wall and a bookshelf that holds a coffee machine and a bar fridge.

My inspection is cut short by Jack.

His lips find mine and his arms curl around my back, lifting me up and bringing me closer to him.

'What are you doing to me?' he groans into my mouth, the words both a plea and a hope.

'I don't know what you mean,' I manage to say. But his tongue is fighting mine and no further conversation is possible.

His hands find the hem of my dress, lifting it just enough for Jack to be able to cup my bare arse. He groans as his fingers connect with naked skin and he pushes his arousal towards me, his cock hard and firm. My body is desperate to feel more of him. But he grinds against me and I grip his shoulders, my body weakening at this contact that is so good I can barely think straight.

He lifts one hand to my hair. It's loose around my face and he tangles his fingers in its ends then pulls up from my scalp, his fingers holding me against his mouth. His other hand slips between my legs and finds my warm heat. He runs a finger along my seam and I whimper into his mouth, so wet and hot for him.

He pushes into me—just a finger, and just enough to make my body throb. I need something. Space. Breath. But his tongue lashes my mouth as his finger teases my insides, and pleasure is a spiral I cannot escape, cannot control. It spins in my gut, my chest, my heart, my blood.

I whimper again—a tiny noise locked in the back of my throat—and his fingers tighten in my hair. I am trapped by him, by this, our need for each other. His finger swirls, finding my most sensitive cluster of nerves, and I am shaking all over, from head to toe, my body his to please and command.

'Come for me,' he instructs into my mouth, as though he has heard my thoughts and knows I will do anything he asks of me.

My knees can barely hold me. Without Jack's support I would be a puddle of bones and haute couture on the elegant carpeted floor of Clint Sheridan's office.

Jack kisses me in a rhythm matched by his finger's invasion and I am falling apart in his arms, with no chance of reprieve or pause. No break in the assault of pleasure he is inflicting on me. He kisses me as I moan, my breath snatched, my blood fevered. And even as my muscles clamp around him, squeezing the pleasure from my body, his finger continues to tease me, so that the pleasure and awareness is almost unbearable.

The first orgasm is crashing around me even as a second, bigger one builds, and I grip his lapels, holding him as my world shatters in a mind-blowing moment of sexual awakening. I am fevered and limp, broken and whole.

But he's not done with me. Even as wave after wave of pleasure crashes across my brow his hands reach down, finding his zip and freeing his arousal. I know I have only seconds to regain my senses. To exercise my control in this situation that is eating me alive.

'No,' I say, and the word is thick with desire, fevered by need.

He stops, his eyes locked to mine, anguish clear in his expression. But he stops. Waits.

'Sit down,' I say, nodding towards the sofa.

Something like relief spreads over his face as he nods and moves to the sofa.

'Do you have a...'

He's reaching for his wallet before I can finish, fishing out a foil square. I groan as I slide it down his cock and then I am on top of him, straddling him, taking his length deep inside me, revelling in his possession and in his look of wonderment. Seeing that he is as lost to this pleasure as I am.

I move up and down his length, rocking on my haunches. His fingers dig into my sides, moving with me, but I am in control. When I feel him pump, so close to coming, I sit higher, so that only his tip is inside me, and he groans, tilting his head back as waves of pleasure engulf his being. I laugh softly, lowering myself back onto him and leaning forward, kissing his neck, his throat, tasting the desire that has overheated us both.

He holds my hips, keeping me low against him, and thrusts into me. My body is already on fire. It takes nothing for further flames to take hold, spreading like wildfire through my blood. My cry is muffled by his kiss, and he kisses me as together we explode.

Lightning flashes in the sky—closer now—but I barely notice. Even as rain begins to lash the windows I am aware only of *this*. Our own little storm, raging through our souls.

CHAPTER TEN

HE'S WATCHING ME, so I try to subdue my reaction. But as lightning and thunder burst almost simultaneously, and rain hammers the enormous windows and the roof of the pool room, I am quivering.

'You're actually terrified,' he murmurs with bemusement, his fingers brushing my shoulder as he removes the lightweight jacket I wore to Clint's.

'I'm not,' I lie, stepping away from him before he can detect the fine tremble in my body.

I dig my fingernails into my palms, staring out at the raging storm. It's furious and I can't stand it. If I was alone I would put earphones in and dig myself under my duvet to wait it out. But I can't, and he's still watching me.

My voice is scratchy when I speak. 'It was such a nice day. Where did this come from?'

'It's the tropics,' he points out, stepping out of his shoes and shrugging free of his jacket at the same time.

His jacket is slightly crumpled at the front, from where I curled my fingers into it as he drove me to multiple orgasms.

'Heat builds up, then it breaks in a storm.'

'Why does *that* sound familiar?'

His half-smile shows he agrees. We are our own tropical weather system. Sultry heat, storm clouds and flash floods without warning. And plenty of lightning and thunder, too.

A spike of lightning floods the lounge with an eerie glow and I jump. 'God!'

'It's only a storm,' he murmurs, closing the distance between us, his eyes locked to mine as his thumb presses beneath my chin, lifting my face to his, exposing me to his curiosity and inspection. 'It will pass.'

My stomach twists painfully now as the metaphor takes on new resonance. Is he trying to be cryptic? Is he talking about the surge of awareness that thunders between us? About us? Of course this will pass. What else do I expect?

'Sit with me.'

He squeezes my hand and draws me to him, holding me to his side as we cross the lounge to the white leather sofa that offers the most spectacular view of the harbour. The opera house is ghoulishly lit in white, and the rain lashing against it creates the impression of fog and apocalypse.

'Even the air smells different.' I inhale the acrid, electrical thickness of the atmosphere.

'Yeah…' The word is hoarse.

He sits, and I go to take the seat next to him, but he pulls me closer, landing me softly on his lap. And now his kiss is gentle. Soft. A kiss of reassurance that scares me all the more because of the way it shakes my heart to life.

I panic. This is too much. *Everything* is too much. I'm in the eye of two storms and I don't know if I'll survive either one of them.

'Tonight went well,' he says, his hand stroking my bare arm, comforting and confounding all at once.

'What do you think of the team?' I ask, finding what I hope will be common ground in our established business dynamic. Some reassurance from the familiarity of that life.

'Competent,' he says thoughtfully. 'I'm not sold on Ryan being a good fit.'

'What makes you say that?'

I feel him shrug, the movement brushing the crispness of his shirt against my skin.

'Instinct.'

'He comes highly recommended.'

'I know.'

He runs his hand over his chin and I hold my breath as I'm seared by the memory of him pressing his finger inside me, holding me as I fell apart. My gut clenches and my insides are slick with a swirling tempest of knowledge of what we've done.

'There's just something about him that seems wrong. I can't explain.'

I think back to the evening, trying to capture the same sense Jack has, and shake my head. 'We'll see, I suppose.'

'His contract has a three-month probation period?'

'Yes. I'll make a note to come over and review him at two months, though, if you're concerned.'

'Great.'

Lightning bursts again and I jump automatically.

He presses his forehead against my shoulder, the strangeness of the gesture not taking anything away from how reassuring I find it.

'Were your parents cross with you?'

'My parents? When?'

They'll be back in England now. I should probably go and see them. The thought cools the warmth in my body.

'The night you slept in the tree house.'

'Oh.' I shift a little, angling my body closer to his. 'Furious.' Then I shake my head. 'Actually, that's not true. They were disappointed.'

'Disappointed?'

'Disappointed that I'd not been cared for to their standards. Embarrassed that people might think they'd hired substandard domestic staff.' I grimace. 'Perhaps ashamed they hadn't thought to check on me when they got home—most parents would, after all.'

'You're not close to them?'

'Why do you say that?'

'Just the way you speak of them.'

'No. I'm *not* close to them. They're not that thrilled with my life choices.'

'Really? Graduating with a double first from Oxford isn't what they had in mind?'

'Hell, no. I was supposed to marry someone fancy and respectable, with a country estate to match but not better our own. And to appear in *Harper's Bazaar* articles...have tea at Kensington Palace.' I can't help rolling my eyes. 'I'm exhausted just *thinking* about what they wanted for me.'

'You don't strike me as someone who's into the society scene at all.'

'I'm not.' I shake my head. 'Their wedding anniversary is in a week, and it'll be a who's who of the British aristocracy. And, yes, *Harper's Bazaar* will be there.'

'You don't want to go?'

'I *have* to go,' I say. 'It's just—'

Thunder rolls around the apartment and I swear the windows shake in their frames. *We're going to die.*

He holds me tighter. 'It's just…?'

I don't know if he's trying to distract me from the storm or if he's really interested in my dysfunctional family, but talking *is* distracting me and distractions are good. Besides which, having opened up to him, I'm not finding it easy to curtail my thoughts.

'I'm always trotted out as proof of their happiness. Their marriage is a success. They've had a child. An heiress. I swear they actually *call* me their heiress during their toasts every year—like that's my soul function in life. To inherit.' I shake my head. 'I *hate* that. I've hated it for as long as I have understood their expectations. Or lack thereof. My existing is sufficient for their needs. My ambitions are irrelevant and slightly offensive to them. And my working for *you* is definitely tantamount to slashing the family tapestries.'

'You make them sound like selfish bastards.'

I laugh. 'Do I?'

'*Are* they?'

His fingers are glancing over my skin, stirring warmth and desire inside my chest.

'They're products of their upbringings,' I say, and then shake my head, for it's disloyal to Grandma to implicate her in my father's cold-fishery. He's really a grump of his own creation. 'Or perhaps of society's expectations. I don't know. They're very…stiff upper lip. Cold. Emotionless.'

His lips twist. 'Funny. That's just how I would have described *you* a few weeks ago.'

My eyes widen and I look at him. 'There's a huge

difference between maintaining a professional distance and being cold.'

'Yes, there is.' His finger lifts higher, running a line over my cheek. 'You were doing both.'

'I was *not*,' I deny, offended by his description.

'You made ice look warm.'

I move to stand, but his hands still me. 'Why?' he asks. 'Why did you act like that around me?'

'It wasn't an *act*.' I sniff, staring out at the storm-ravaged harbour.

But Jack's insistent. 'You're not like it with anybody else. I never really noticed that until I saw you talking with Wolf DuChamp. And now I've paid better attention I see you weren't like it with anyone but me.'

'I…I was. That's just how I am.'

'No.' He's adamant. 'The guys from the Tokyo transition team all call you "Gem", like you're some long-lost buddy of theirs. You're friendly with Rose and Sophia. Amber raves about you. It's just me.'

I open my mouth to deny it, but how can I? He's totally right. I met Jack Grant and every single one of my defences was raised because I *knew*. I knew there was trouble on our doorstep: a chemistry we would need to work our butts off to deny.

'So what *is* it about me, Gemma Picton, that had you acting as though I were the plague incarnate?'

My heart hammers hard in my chest. There is danger in this conversation. Danger of truth and honesty and far too much insight.

'Maybe I thought you'd see friendliness as encouragement,' I murmur, my tone light, going for a joke.

'But not with Wolf or Barry or Clint?'

My expression is calm, but inside I'm shivering. 'No.' It's a whisper.

God. What is he doing to me? He seems to have become 'just Jack', but my brain reminds me forcefully that the man made a billion-pound fortune virtually from scratch. He's brilliant, ruthless and incisive. And determined.

'When did you realise this was going to happen?' He runs his finger higher, teasing my nipple through the flimsiness of my dress.

I arch a brow, my breath trapped in my throat. 'Um… around the night you kissed me and…touched me…'

It's a lie. I knew it from the moment I accepted the job. Proximity would feed inevitability. On reflection, I can't believe I stalled it for two years.

'I think you've wanted me longer than that.'

'Do you?' I clear my throat, and this time when I stand, he doesn't stop me.

I feel his eyes on my back as I walk into the kitchen and pour a glass of mineral water. The bubbles are frantic—hypnotic, even.

'Yeah.'

He stands, and I look at him helplessly.

'What do you want me to say?' I lift my shoulders. 'I knew you, Jack. I *know* you. I know that you're in love with your wife. I know that you sleep with women to forget her. Do you blame me for wanting to keep this insanity at bay?'

'No.' He drags a hand through his hair and his smile is ghostly on his face. 'I blame myself for not letting you.'

His shoulders are broad, and an invisible, enormous weight is upon them.

'I blame myself for not being strong, like you were. You wanted me, but you were never going to do a damned thing about it—were you?'

'Of course not. Apart from anything else, you're my boss. And that's *before* I think about the steady stream of women filing through your bedroom. This is probably the dumbest thing I've ever done.'

'Yes.' He nods, his eyes locked to mine. 'But you don't want it to end.'

I shake my head, seeking refuge in honesty at last. 'Do *you*?'

'No.' And now his smile is broader. 'Turns out I'm scared of something else.'

'What's that?'

'How much I want you. Need you. And I'm scared of hurting you, Gemma.'

'You won't.'

He nods, but I know he's not convinced. Nor am I. In fact, I would say Jack hurting me is as inevitable as the morning that will break over the harbour in the next few hours. But I don't care. Having given in to this, I am just a tree in the middle of a storm, trying my hardest to hold on, to stand tall even as it threatens to uproot me for good.

The mood is oppressive. Suddenly I want to lighten it. To make him smile. To feel his warmth and contentment.

'I bet you were a real little shit growing up.'

The ghost of our conversation lingers, but he makes a visible effort to push it away. 'Why do you say that?'

'Hmm…remember who you're talking to? You're stubborn and selfish…'

'Selfish, huh? I always look after *you*…'

My face burns hot and I'm sure it's flame-red. 'I didn't mean in bed,' I mumble.

His laugh is my reward. Sweet and husky, it makes my nerves quiver.

'I see...'

Perhaps he takes pity on me. He strides across the kitchen and props his arse against the kitchen counter. I imagine his tattoo through the tailored cut of his trousers and absent-mindedly slide my hand out and curve it over his hip.

'I was a good kid, actually,' he says, not reacting to my touch visibly.

I like the intimacy of this, though. Perhaps more than I should. Of being able to reach out and feel him, to sense his nearness.

'So your recalcitrance came later in life?'

He laughs. 'I guess so.'

His hand lifts and wraps around my cheek. I inhale. This moment, his fragrance—everything. I fold the memory away and store it for later delight. It is a perfect slice of time.

'I went away to school.'

'A boarding school?'

His nod is a small movement—just a jerk of his head. 'I won a full scholarship.'

'And you call *me* an overachiever?' I tease.

His smile is indulgent. 'I had no choice. There was only one way out of the backwater I grew up in. I succeeded because the prospect of failure was too depressing to contemplate. You, on the other hand, m'lady, are motivated by something I don't understand. You had everything... You were born with a fortune and a family lineage that dates back to the Magna Carta...

It would have been so easy for you to stay within the boundaries of that life. And it would have been a *good* life.'

'It depends on how you define "good",' I say simply. 'I've never fitted in.'

'I find that impossible to believe.'

'Why?'

'You could fit in anywhere.'

'Trust me—I didn't want to feel at home in *that* crowd.'

His frown is just a very slight twist of his lips. 'So your parents are stuffy. What about your friends?'

'Most of my closest friends I met later. At university. Then at Goldman. Deloitte.'

'And here? With me?'

For a second my heart skids to a stop, because I think he's talking about himself and there is something so delightfully needy about the question that I ache for him.

But then he continues. 'Wolf. Barry. You seem to know everyone who works for me.'

'Oh, right…' Emptiness is a gulf in the pit of my stomach. 'That happens. *Your* parents must be proud of *you*.' I shift the conversation to him, hating the vulnerabilities he's able to expose in me so easily.

'Yes.'

He moves a little, bringing his body closer to mine, and then, before I know what he's doing, he lifts me onto the bench, spreading my legs and standing between them.

He's so close I'm sure he must be able to hear the thundering of my heart; it is surpassed only by the storm outside.

'My parents thought I would—at most—become an accountant. Like my father and his father before him. I was always good at numbers. It fair skittled them when I told them I'd bought my first company.'

'Yeah, I can see how that would bowl them over.'

His laugh is husky. He brushes his lips against the soft skin at the base of my throat, chasing the wildly beating pulse-point with his tongue. I moan, deep in my mouth, the sound strangled by my own hot, thick breath.

'You make it sound easy. Like you didn't want to be an accountant so you did this instead.'

'This?' He laughs, flicking the strap of my dress so it falls haphazardly down my arm, revealing my shoulder to him.

His kiss is sweet, like nectar. He finds the exposed skin and possesses it as only Jack Grant can, gliding his mouth over it, making me feel I have never before been kissed. It is at once intimate and simple and my back arches forward. Or backwards. Who can tell? The normal rules of gravity and physics seem not to apply.

'How do you know my family dates back to the Magna Carta?' I ask, though the words are squeezed tight from my chest, not quite coming out clearly.

But he hears. He understands. 'I looked you up,' he says unapologetically.

'You…?'

His mouth drops lower and at the same time he lifts my hand, drags the kiss to my inner wrist. I squeeze my eyes shut as he finds another pulse-point, tracing it with his tongue.

'I searched you on the internet,' he confirms, dropping my hand gently and cupping my arse, pulling me closer to him.

I wrap my legs around his waist. 'Why?'

'Because you surprised me the other night. I realised I should have known this stuff.'

'What stuff?'

'All of it. Your dynastic birthright.'

I laugh.

'What's funny?'

'Just… Only *you* would want to know more and decide to look it up rather than ask.'

'Asking would have taken time,' he says with an unapologetic lift of his broad strong shoulders.

'And we don't have time?'

'I'm impatient.' He grins.

'I had no idea.' Sarcasm is rich in my murmured tone.

His hands are on my knees and then they're tracing higher, his fingertips barely brushing my flesh as he searches for the softness of my inner thighs.

'Is that weird?'

I pause, concentration almost impossible. 'Is *what* weird?'

His lips are buzzing mine, just the smallest hint of contact making every nerve ending in my body sing. 'That I ran an internet search on you.'

'Oh.' I frown. 'It should be. But, no. For you it makes sense.'

His laugh is breathed across my skin, sending it into a break-out of goose bumps.

'Because I'm weird?'

'Because you're *you*,' I correct. 'Domineering, determined, somewhat wonderful you.'

He's still for a moment. Frozen by the compliment he didn't expect. Then he relaxes again, his lips are on my skin and my heart is flying out of my body, soaring above me. This is so *right*. So *perfect*. Out of nowhere I am in heaven.

'Are you saying you haven't done a search on me?' he teases, his hands lifting to the zip at the back of my dress and catching it lower, snagging it over my spine. My body is hypersensitive; I feel every single kink of his touch.

I have. I've looked him up *and* his wife. Something I am naturally hesitant to confess.

'I applied to work for you,' I say with a shrug. 'Of course I did.'

His laugh shows he knows me to be lying. Or at least being liberal with the truth.

'Why did you move your office from the City?' The question is blurted out of me before I even realise I've been wondering.

He pauses, the zip halfway down my back, his mouth so close to mine I want to push up and find him. But he's still, and the question hangs between us, and I realise I do want to hear the answer.

'Sorry?'

'I just… Speaking of questions…' My throat thumps as I swallow. 'Is it because of Lucy?'

His expression flashes with something. Anguish?

I shake my head quickly. 'Forget it. I shouldn't have asked.'

'No.' It's a gravelled denial. 'It's fine.'

But I might as well have lashed him with a stick dipped in lava.

'It *was* because of Lucy. She was sick at the end.

I set my home up so I could be near her all the time. The room…the bedroom near my office… That was her room.'

Oh, God. How did I not know that? His little 'den of sin' held his dying wife's sickbed.

A shudder rips through me as the macabre sadness of it all washes over me.

'After she died I just… I didn't want life to go back to normal. I resented the implication that it would.'

He expels an angry sigh and now his fingers are pushing my zip down almost dispassionately.

'There's no textbook on grief.'

'Of course there's not.'

'But I expected to cope better than I did.'

His eyes sweep shut. He's shielding himself from me, but at least he keeps talking. That's enough. It *has* to be enough.

'We had months to prepare. To brace ourselves. She was ready. Her life at the end was…' He changes direction, as though he's somehow betraying Lucy. 'She was ready to go. My therapist tells me I spent so long being strong for Lucy that I had nothing left to give myself.'

'You have a therapist?'

'I did. Until he spouted *that* piece of pretty bullshit. As if there's a finite amount of support to give. As if I should have ignored Lucy's needs in favour of my own.'

'I don't think he meant that. Lucy's sickness must have been draining on you. I can imagine that you spent so much of your energy focussing on what she needed that you had no idea what to do with yourself once she passed.'

'It shook my world,' he said simply.

I'm so sorry for him. But I don't say that because

I've said it before. My dress is loose around my waist. I'm not wearing a bra and his hands run up my sides and cup my breasts as though holding them is his only form of salvation.

'It still does,' I say softly.

'It's different now.'

He runs his thumb over my nipple, his eyes drawn downwards, his attention focussed on the physicality of my body, rather than me.

'Different how?' I need to know. I want to understand.

'I grieve for her, but I can function. The hardest days aren't the ones that fill me with sadness.'

'No?'

'No, Gemma.'

He lifts me up, off the bench, wrapping me around him as he walks through the apartment, towards his bedroom. But I don't want him to close this conversation down.

'What are the hardest days?' I push as he shoulders the door inwards.

He lays me down on the bed and I scramble into a sitting position, not caring that my dress is simply a belt at my hips and my body is exposed to him completely.

'Days like this. Days when I am happy and distracted. Days when I forget to remember her. The worst days now are the days when I realise I haven't thought of her at all. Days like today, when all I've had room for on my mind is *you*.'

My heart turns over and, God, I am the worst kind of human because I delight in his admittance even as I realise I am triumphing over a dead woman.

Telling myself Lucy would want him to be happy,

I stand up onto the tips of my toes so I can kiss him, and then pull him backwards onto the bed.

'Being happy doesn't mean you loved her any less,' I promise him softly as I flick his buttons open and run my fingertips over his chest. 'It just means you're human and that time is moving on. It's normal. It's natural.'

He doesn't answer, but his kiss is all the response I need. It is sweet and it is gentle and it is a promise from his body that I know he's not yet ready to make with his words.

The first week Gemma came to work for me I pushed her like a demon. I was so sick of the string of quitters before her that I'd developed a foolproof way to flush them out. I started them at six o'clock each morning, demanding different sets of information in advance and then what I actually required. This was to see how they thought on their feet.

She was amazing.

When she didn't have a ready answer she would procure it easily and without fuss. She was honest about what she didn't know and she stared me down when I tried to imply that her inefficiencies were a result of a flaw in her preparation.

She worked late, travelled to Paris with me on a minute's notice and never once complained.

And then one day I went into her office and found her asleep, just like she is now. Her head dropped on the desk, her hair like golden silk across her keyboard.

That was the first time I told myself she was off-limits. I wanted her even then. My body responded instantly, and in my mind I fantasised about acting on my desire. Making her mine. But it would have been a transient pleasure. And even then, when I hardly knew her, I knew she was a rare, fascinating object—someone I could never touch. Never hurt.

Yet here I am.

Here *she* is.

At some point during the night, after I'd fallen asleep, Gemma must have stirred and taken herself back to her room, respecting those unspoken boundaries we've erected even after I told her more about myself than I ever have another soul.

And that angers me. It angers me that she accepts those limitations even now.

It is not yet dawn, but the sky is glistening with the promise of morning and a hint of golden light steals through the blinds, marking her cheek and her arm. I wonder what it would be like to lift the cover and lie beside her. To wrap her to my chest and kiss her awake softly. To stir her body with mine.

But the day is breaking, and she is just as off-limits to me now as she was two years ago.

CHAPTER ELEVEN

My plane lands at seven. How soon can you be at my place?

I SMILE AT the text but my heart sinks. A week after I returned from Australia and Jack is almost home. A problem with the winery in New Zealand required his urgent personal attention, and as a result I have been in sexual purgatory for seven days and nights.

I am aching for him physically and, yes, I miss him. I miss him so much I can no longer doubt just what form my feelings take.

I love him.

I am in love with him.

And, just like Grandma described, it has hit me out of nowhere. It is a realisation and it is also an incontrovertible law of nature now, as unquestionable and rock-solid as gravity, helium, oxygen and rain.

I run a hand down my pale green sheath dress, feeling its silkiness and wishing like hell it was his hands, not mine, on my body.

Tomorrow morning…?

I wait for a moment, but he doesn't reply. Jack has Wi-Fi enabled on his jet, and he's always in contact, so I don't doubt he's got the message. I imagine his lips drawing down at the corners as he contemplates the fact that I'm not simply fitting in with what he's suggested.

By 'tomorrow morning' do you mean 7.05 p.m.?

I laugh and shake my head, reaching for my bronzer and giving my face one last flush of colour. My make-up is exquisite—I didn't do it, so I can say that. My hair has been styled into a rather vintage crimp, and a diamond clip is tethered just above one ear, adding to the *Great Gatsby* look.

I grab a stole and slip into my shoes, then scoop up my phone.

I wish. It's my parents' anniversary party, remember?

I thrust the phone into my bag and press it beneath my arm.

My driver is waiting. Not Hughes. *My* driver. The one I use when I have family stuff on and Mum and Dad like to know I'm observing the little rituals that matter to them. Like being chauffeured.

'Hey…' I smile distractedly, sliding into the back seat. I look at my phone.

Shit. I forgot. Skip it?

I laugh.

I wish.

What are you wearing?

I grin, lift the phone up and take a shot of myself. I examine it quickly—one chin, eyes open, passably attractive—and then send it to him.

His response is almost immediate.

Smoking hot, Lady Gemma.

My heart turns over in my chest and for a minisecond I contemplate blowing the party off—to hell with the consequences—and going to Jack instead. My parents would be furious, but I suspect it would be worth it…

I text him back.

What are YOU wearing?

A few seconds later I am rewarded with a photo of him. I stare at the screen and my heart thumps hard in my chest. He is gorgeous. So beautiful. So dangerously, darkly, distractingly beautiful.

I stare at his eyes and feel as though I really am looking at him.

You're flying in a SUIT? What happened to comfort?

He doesn't respond immediately and I put my phone into my bag, letting my eyes catch up with the passing scenery. The anniversary celebration is to be at The Ritz—where else?—and the car eats up the distance from Hampstead into the West End, skirting Kensington Gardens on one side.

I check my phone again as we pull to a stop—nothing.

Disappointment fills me, but I will see him soon. Tomorrow. And we'll make up for lost time.

Just looking at that photo is enough to get me off. But I need more than that. I need to be held by him. To feel his arms wrapping around me, to look up at him and know that his heart is beating for mine...

'Madam.' The driver opens the door and I smile at him, stepping out into the cool night air.

Flashes go off in my face. I'm unprepared. Foolishly, really, given the high-profile nature of the party and the venue that's designed to draw attention. I just haven't been focussing on it at all. I plaster a smile on my face as I dip my head forward and clip towards the large glass doors.

The party is in The Music Room. I've been there once before, for my grandfather's birthday, I remember as I step over the threshold. The room is the very definition of elegance, with gold and pink highlights, enormous floral arrangements and curtains that look like they weigh a tonne.

I'm late. Only ten minutes or so, but the room is full. The music is a perfectly refined string quartet, and my parents are at the end of a receiving line, like a scene from a Jane Austen book.

I pause, wondering if I can sneak away before they see me, go and find Grandma. I'd put money on her being near the bar...

But my mother's eyes meet mine and her hand lifts, waving me over.

I swear under my breath, plastering a smile on my face. 'Mum.' I kiss her cheek. 'You look lovely.'

She does. Mum is always stunning. And now, after her jaunting about—rather, her international philanthropy—she's acquired a caramel tan. Her outfit is almost bridal—a cream lace prom dress that falls to just below her knees. Dad is in a tux.

'Welcome home,' I say.

'Oh, yes. That's right. We haven't seen you since we got back.' Her lips pucker in disapproval.

'I've been in Australia,' I explain awkwardly, then wish I hadn't. Why the heck am I apologising? It's not like they've been tripping over themselves to organise a reunion. 'Was it a good trip?'

My father grumbles something I don't quite catch.

'Quite.' Mother nods. 'We're thinking of going again next year—aren't we, darling?'

His look is one of long-suffering tolerance. 'We'll see.'

'Is Grandma here?'

My mother nods, her eyes flitting across the room. 'In that direction.'

'I'll go and check on her,' I say, as though it's a service I can offer when in fact I am serving only myself.

'Is your speech ready, darling?' Mother calls to me as I leave.

I wince. *Shit*. Why didn't I remember I'd have to do a speech?

I cut through the crowd until my eyes land on Grandma. Her wiry figure is perfectly framed by a jet-black dress and a bolero that has a fine silver thread to it. She's wearing dark silk flowers at the collar and she manages to look rather funereal.

I laugh as I approach. 'Hey!'

'Oh, thank fuck. Someone I actually *like*.'

Several people hear her curse and move away disapprovingly. I grin, kissing her papery cheek.

'Tell me about it… I think this is an even duller crowd than usual.' I tap the bar, my eyes catching the bartender's. 'Champagne.'

He pours a glass of Bollinger and hands it to me. Grandma signals for a top-up and I wonder, with a disguised smile, how many glasses she's already knocked back. She can hold her liquor like a sailor, and age isn't slowing that down.

'Where's my koala?'

'Your…huh?'

'You went to Australia, didn't you?' she asks impatiently.

'Oh. Yeah, right. Guess what? Turns out you *do* have to go bush to see one.'

'And let me guess? You were working too hard for that?'

'Mmm…'

It wasn't all work. My body flushes with remembered pleasure. Jack's touch was worth travelling to the other side of the world for.

'I did see dolphins from Jack's balcony, though. They were amazing. A whole pod of them, just gliding and…frolicking.'

'They were on the balcony?'

'No, Grandma, they were in the harbour.' I laugh.

'Obviously, dear.' She takes another sip of champagne. 'Remember your grandfather's birthday?'

I nod. 'I was thinking of it when I came in.'

'He was so happy that night. To be surrounded by

his loved ones.' She sighs, her eyes a little watery as she looks around the room. 'The mayor's here.'

I follow her gaze. 'Yes. Dad and he have been doing some work together, I think.'

Grandma's brows lift skyward, as if imbuing even that with a response of disapproval. I sip my champagne.

'You had a good time, then?'

'Yeah. Australia's beautiful. I like Sydney.'

'So why did you come back?'

I laugh. 'You're turning into a one-track record.'

'Darling, life's too short for pleasantries, and I love you too much to lie.'

'I live *here*. I'd miss *you*, apart from anything.'

'I'd come and visit.'

We're interrupted by an old friend of my father's, and for the next twenty minutes Grandma and I make polite conversation, all the while subtly—and, I fear, not so subtly—nudging one another's ankles and trying not to roll our eyes.

There is someone else after that, and then my grandma's goddaughter Laurena—another story altogether...*ugh!* And then, before I know it, it's half past seven.

Jack will have landed by now. In his suit. So handsome; such a waste.

I sigh and refocus my attention on the conversation I'm half involved in, nodding as required, and then I'm actually grateful when my father asks me to dance with him. There's only a small makeshift dance floor—a concession to the fact that there are so many guests and most of them are not interested in dancing.

But Dad and I have always danced. He wraps his arms around me and it reminds me of when I was a little girl, standing on his feet, moving in time to the music. And it's a hell of a lot better than shooting the breeze with my parents' friends.

I feel a wave of sympathy for Grandma, whom I have deserted and left to the well-heeled wolves. I look over my shoulder to see her holding court and wonder, with a distracted smile, what she's talking about.

'How's work, pumpkin?'

I blink back to my father. 'Great.'

'Really? That's a shame.'

'It is?'

'Sidney was just saying he could use a consultant with your skill set.'

'Mayor Black?' I prompt, my smile wry.

'He's admired your career for a long time. Asked if I'd set up a meeting.'

'I've got a job, Daddy. A job I love.'

And then, as if I have somehow conjured him from my longing and imagination, Jack is beside us, his eyes intense as they lock solely to mine, his expression inscrutable. It is him and me—*us*. Just us.

'Jack?' I stop dancing altogether and take a small step away from my dad. I can hardly catch my breath. 'What are you doing here?'

'You invited me. Remember?'

I did no such thing, and we both know it, but I'm not going to point that out in front of my father.

'Right, of course.' I nod. Blood is roaring through my veins. 'I forgot. Dad, this is Jack Grant. My...er...boss.'

Jack extends his hand and shakes my father's with his natural confidence. 'My Lord.'

My father is in awe—like most people who first meet Jack. It pleases me. For all he hates the hours I work, and the commitment I have to my job, he obviously understands the unique thrill that comes from working with someone like Jack.

'Mind if I cut in?'

'Oh, I... Of course not.'

My father steps back, but I don't see him move away because Jack wraps his arms around me and consumes all my senses.

He overpowers me with his nearness and his uniqueness. He moves in time to the music but I feel his body, tight and hard, and my gut clenches.

'What are you really doing here?'

There is something I don't understand in his features. A haunted expression. Anger?

'You seem kind of uptight about this. I've never seen you like that about anything.'

I nod slowly. Does he think that explains anything?

'So...?'

'I was at a loose end.'

'Oh.' My heart thumps painfully. 'Right.'

What was I expecting? Flowery declarations of love?

'You were my plan,' he says gently, his fingers running over my back. 'I wanted to see you. And you were here.'

'So you came here?' I murmur, crossing over into unnecessary repetition and not caring.

Because my heart is floating away from my body, thumping high in the sky over us.

'Pretty much.'

His smile makes my stomach flip and flop and twist and turn.

'Well, I'm not so sure I want to be here now.'

His laugh undoes the last stitch of my sanity. I want to strip my clothes off and cry out, *Take me now!*

'My evil plan.' He grins. 'How's your week been?'

Is this really happening? Is Jack Grant at my parents' wedding anniversary party, dancing with me, stroking my back, asking me about my week, telling me he's missed me? Or am I somehow dreaming this up? It doesn't make sense.

'Busy. Yours?'

Wow. I sound normal. Good job, me!

'Perfect.' He winks—so sexy. 'New Zealand is stunning; the winery is incredible.'

My sigh is wistful. 'I'll bet.'

He chuckles. 'You'll see it for yourself next time you're over.'

'Yeah…'

I try not to get too swept up in fantasies that involve Jack and me skipping down the rows of grapes, holding hands, laughing into the sunset. Fantasies are nice, but they're not real life.

'Jack Grant?'

I feel his sigh but he hides it well, turning to look at the man who's come to address us. I recognise him, but can't think of his name in that moment.

'Adam.' Jack nods, not relinquishing his grip around my waist. 'How's it going?'

'Jesus, I haven't seen you in *years*. I've kept up with you, of course. Amazing career. Got a moment? I'd love to talk to you about a project I'm in the middle of.'

'Actually…' Jack says, and my heart leaps.

But we're attracting attention, and I'm not sure either of us is ready to deal with that yet.

I clear my throat and step backwards. 'It's fine.' I

wince inwardly when I hear the ice-cold tone that bleats from my lips. I soften it with effort, stretching my lips into a smile. 'I want to go check on my grandma, anyway.'

'Ah, she's here?' Jack's eyes glint with shared knowledge. My gut somersaults. 'I look forward to meeting her.'

His gaze holds mine for a moment too long and the universe vibrates differently—just for us.

I smile as I walk away, swinging my butt, knowing that not only is he here with me tonight because he cares for me, but that soon we're going to be making love and I cannot wait.

'Things are making a little more sense now,' Grandma murmurs, her eyes trained on Jack's profile.

He's locked in conversation with the man—Adam—his expression instantly businesslike. My heart thumps.

'What do you mean?' I reach down and sip her champagne, taking the seat beside her.

Grandma taps my knee. 'It isn't just a job.'

I contemplate denial, but it's Grandma. She'll see through it.

'Meaning?' I say instead, cautious. Waiting.

'You're seeing him?'

Trust Grandma. I bite down on my lip. 'Not really. Kind of.'

'You love him?'

My heart throbs. I look at her and shake my head, but my smile tells a different story.

'I see.' She tilts her head, her eyes pinned to Jack as though she's pulling him apart, piece by piece. 'Interesting…'

'Not really.' I shake my head. 'And it's very…early. New.'

'Secret?' she supplies, her eyes flitting to mine and sparkling with the hint of mystery I've evoked. I sigh. There'll be no stopping her now.

'Yes, secret,' I say after a beat.

'Fine. I can do secret.' She winks at me and taps my knee once more.

It's more than an hour before I get near Jack again, and by then I am *desperate* to touch him. To kiss him. To be alone with him. I'm almost there—just a few people to navigate—when my parents take to the stage and the music goes silent. The guests follow suit.

My mother is a natural-born performer. She speaks easily to the crowd, playing the part of happy wife perfectly. My father toasts her and then they introduce me. Their heir.

Ugh.

I paste a smile on my face, sashaying close enough to Jack on my way to the stage that his hands brush my hip and my body charges with electricity.

I'll do the damned tribute speech and then we'll go. Him and me. Alone time with him is the talisman on the periphery of my mind.

There are a heap of people looking back at me, but I see only Jack. His eyes seem to caress me, even from this distance. A pulse throbs between my legs. Desire is a tangible force, wrapping me in its determined grip.

'I've been thinking about love and marriage a lot lately. About the leap of faith required to take that step. We can enter into a relationship with the best of intentions and find that it doesn't work out. That our love alone isn't enough—that it doesn't go the distance. Or perhaps we lose the person we love most on earth, and feel robbed of our soul mate. Our love.'

My eyes hold Jack's and I blink, my heart twisting.

'Or perhaps we fall in love and marry and everything is perfect. A true happily-ever-after.'

I turn and smile at my parents, hoping that these vague descriptions of love will somehow mean something to them. It's hard to tell. Botox has rendered my mother's range of visible reactions down to single digits. There's disapproval, impatience, wry amusement and boredom. I don't know which of these she's feeling, so I turn back to the assembled guests.

'My grandma talks about meeting my grandpa almost as if the moment was divined by fate. There was an inevitability to their life and love—one she couldn't have fought even if she'd wanted to.'

I smile at Grandma and the tears in her eyes make me proud, because she understands that I *know*. I know what she felt.

'I think marriage is a remarkable thing, and I congratulate my parents on thirty years of it. To Mum and Dad.'

I lift the glass in my hand and smile at them.

My mother nods her thanks. Dad blows me a kiss. The crowd repeats my toast and I walk off stage.

I set my champagne flute down on the edge of a table and don't look at another soul. Instead I walk towards the doors, my stride meaningful, my attention unwavering.

I don't say goodbye to Grandma, and nor do I acknowledge any of the guests looking to congratulate me on my toast. I stare straight ahead until I am out. Free.

I continue to walk—down the stairs to the foyer and then, my heels clipping noisily, across it. I am conscious only of my own breath, my own footsteps, until I reach the glass doors and wait. And wait.

Not for long. Not even a full minute in reality.

He doesn't speak. His hand on the small of my back is warm and intimate and my stomach dips. My knees almost buckle.

He guides me out of The Ritz and I smile at Hughes. I am prepared to step apart from Jack, to put some distance between us. But he doesn't let me. His hand stays glued to the base of my spine, and the moment I step into the limousine he catches my shoulder and spins me.

His eyes are charged with emotion, but I cannot fathom what he's feeling. I know only that he wants me with the same burning desperation that rips through me.

'We're going?' I prompt, my eyebrows raised.

'You'd better fucking believe it.'

And then, as if he has no choice, no free will, no say in the matter, he drops his head and presses a bone-meltingly lovely kiss against the tip of my nose.

As if I didn't love him enough already.

CHAPTER TWELVE

'CARRIE?'

My voice is croaky and my eyes sting as I answer my phone. I'm tired. What bloody time is it?

I peer into the darkness of Jack's room and panic sets in.

I've slept in his bed. With him. All night.

Or have I? He's not in the space beside me and his pillow is cool to the touch.

I look beyond it to the clock on his bedside. It's not as early as I feared—just gone eight. But it *is* Sunday, and I probably only got an hour's sleep the night before.

My cheeks flush pink as I remember the way our bodies rediscovered one another. Desperate at first, we came together as soon as we walked in the door of his apartment. Then slower, more sensually. An exploration. A reacquaintance. And finally dominatingly, Jack using my needs to control me and me letting him, loving it.

Still, I realise I haven't spoken to my friend in weeks, since our rescheduled catch-up. 'Is everything okay?' I ask.

'Um, shouldn't I be asking *you* that?'

'Why?'

I frown, running a finger over the crisp white duvet. *Where's Jack?*

'What's up?'

'I take it you haven't seen the papers yet?'

I shake my head, scrambling to remember which of Jack's business deals was at a crucial stage. What could have gone wrong?

Cursing under my breath, I find my feet are halfway to the ground when Carrie reads aloud:*'"Beauty and the Billionaire..."'*

Oh, shit.

'What is it?'

'Want me to read it?'

'Give me the gist,' I murmur urgently, dipping my head forward.

'"Renowned billionaire philanthropist and widower Jack Grant may be ready to get back into the swing of things. Spotted out and about with Lady Gemma Picton at The Ritz last night, blah-blah-blah..."' Carrie says under her breath, and then resumes reading. '"The pair have worked together for some years, but it appears their relationship has moved to the next level. Is it possible Britain's favourite billionaire is about to be taken off the market?"' She pauses, letting the words sink in. 'There's some photos, too.'

'I'll bet there is.'

I stand, reaching for Jack's robe, which hangs on the back of his door. It's dark blue towelling and falls all the way to the floor on me. It smells like him; my senses respond predictably.

'Which paper?' I cinch the robe tightly around my waist, my hand on the doorknob.

'The *Daily Gazette*.'

'Oh, well,' I say with relief. 'That's okay. What the hell are you doing reading *that*?'

'My cousin emailed it to me. She knows we're friends.'

'Great. But no one else I know will read it.'

'Sorry, mate. It's in the *Telegraph*, too.'

My eyes sweep shut. 'Shit.'

'Is it true?'

There's earnest concern in Carrie's voice.

My denial is as swift as it is untrue. 'No.'

'You guys look pretty cosy in the picture…' she says softly.

'Pictures lie. Look, I'll… Let me get back to you, okay?'

I disconnect the call before she answers, wrenching the door open.

Jack is fully dressed, a cup of coffee cradled in his hands, his attention focussed on the view of London revealed by the windows of his apartment.

Several newspapers sit on the table. I move towards them, instead of him, and cringe when I see that one of them has given us a whole page spread. Photos of us separately and photos of us working together make it look as though this has been going on for a long time.

And, yes, there's the obligatory photo of Jack and Lucy, taken on their wedding day. I'm drawn to her eyes, her smile, her kindness that shines through the picture.

There we all are—the three of us, together in print media for posterity, for anyone who cares to look us up in the future.

'I'm sorry,' I say softly, though I don't know what I'm apologising for, exactly.

'Why?' He turns around, a muscle throbbing in his jaw.

He looks both incredibly handsome and utterly awful at the same time. His skin is ashen beneath his tan.

'This—' he jerks his head towards the papers '—isn't your fault.'

'I know…' I shake my head slowly from side to side. 'But still…it's not ideal.'

His nod is curt agreement. 'I've left a message for Amber,' he murmurs, dragging the palm of his hand over his stubble. 'To explain.'

I nod. It makes sense that he'd want to give Lucy's sister the courtesy of a heads-up.

'Fucking paparazzi *scum*!' he says loudly, and he makes me jump when he slams his hand against the chair nearest to him. 'I wish they'd fuck off!'

'You're kind of famous,' I point out gently, and despite the palpable stress in the room my lips twist into an awkward smile.

But he's not in a joking mood. I sober.

'I guess my parents' thing…'

'I shouldn't have bloody come.'

The intensity of his reaction surprises me. I understand that he's upset; I am, too. This is invasive and unwelcome. And the timing couldn't be worse—just as we're finally morphing into something else, something perfect, we've been put in a position of needing to define what we are. But still…

'Jack.' I command his attention with a clear voice. 'This isn't the end of the world, is it?'

He stares at me, and I don't know if he's trying to work out why I don't get it or trying to calm himself down. But he doesn't speak.

I cannot make sense of this without caffeine—that much is certain. I move to the kitchen and fish a pod out of the canister, slip it in place. The whir of the coffee machine is the only noise in the cavernous apartment. I let it run through and then sip it, strangely pleased when it scalds my tongue.

'Jack?' I say again.

He's looking at me like he doesn't recognise me. A month ago this would have cowered me, but not now. Not after what we've shared.

'Damn it, Jack. You're freaking out for no reason. This is just a stupid gossip story. We can ignore it.'

'No reason?' he repeats, the words quiet but infused with angry disbelief. 'No *reason*?'

'Yes—no reason. So what? So what if you and I are seeing one another? Who cares? What's the big deal?'

'Jesus…' He spins away, his back to me, rigid as hell.

'I mean it.'

I take another sip of coffee, but when he continues to stare out of the window I slam the cup onto the marble benchtop, cross to him and grab his arm. I yank on it, drawing him around to face me. He's holding on—being CEO, cold, professional, unfeeling. But he's feeling *everything*. I know that now.

'We've been sleeping together for over a month. We had sex in Clint-bloody-Sheridan's home office. Did it never occur to you that some time, somehow, it would come out?'

'I never thought about it,' he dismisses. 'Or I sure as hell would have been more careful.'

I change tack, folding his admission into a part of

my brain that will later want to analyse all that is being said and done.

'*Why* is this a big deal?'

My eyes stare into his even as he looks away. I see every flicker of emotion on his face, and it's a little like watching a ship sink all the way from shore. I can't reach him. He's being devoured by an ocean that I cannot cross.

'Apart from the gross invasion of my privacy?'

I dismiss that immediately. 'You're a big boy and you're used to that. What else?'

'It's too much.' He shakes his head with weariness, running a hand over his stubbled jaw. 'Gemma, look… I have a thing this morning. I'm already running late.'

His sentence sits between us like a little row of tiny bombs. I can't help the look of disgust that crosses my face. 'A *thing*?' I ask, scorn deep in my tone.

'Yes, a thing. A breakfast.'

'You're *kidding* me?'

I lift a hand to his chest. He stands there for a moment, a tight smile stretched on his face, and then he steps back, dislodging my touch, breaking our contact.

His voice is coldly authoritative. 'Don't feel you need to rush off. You can let yourself out when you're ready. Hughes will…'

'*Fuck* Hughes!' I shout, moving behind him. 'You aren't getting rid of me like that. *God*, Jack! I have put up with this for long enough. You blowing hot and cold. You want me one second—then we fuck and you're nowhere to be seen.'

That same muscle twists in his face, and it might as well be a bullseye for how badly I want to slap it.

'So we were photographed leaving a party? So people think we're an item? Well, guess what? We *are*.'

He steps back as though I've given in to temptation and cracked my palm across his cheek.

'We're sleeping together. Working together. We know each other inside out. What's the big fucking *deal*?'

'I can't do this right now.'

The louder and more screechy I become, the calmer he seems. And that just makes me even angrier! It's like a horrible hamster wheel and I don't know how to get off.

'We have to talk,' I snap, my voice quivering like an arrow striking a tree.

'Yes, we do.'

It's a softly spoken confession that fills me with more fear than it does relief.

'But not now. I really do have a thing this morning, Gemma.'

But I know his diary, his movements, and I can't for the life of me remember a single entry for today.

'What? *What* thing?'

He looks away from me, guilty, and, *God*, I am fuming. Is he lying to me? To get rid of me? Is he so desperate to avoid having an adult conversation about what our relationship's become that he's inventing reasons to get rid of me?

Fine. I'd rather go than beg him to love me—which is what I feel like doing.

But just when I'm about to flounce off like a teenager in a strop, at the very last minute, he says, 'It's Lucy's birthday.'

Boom! The bombs explode and, predictably, I reel.

'I always have breakfast with Amber on Lucy's birthday. Given this—' he gestures with outrage towards the papers '—I think it would be in poor taste to be late.'

'It's Lucy's birthday...' I say with a nod, but inside my stomach is turning and my heart is shrivelling.

Had I noticed the glass before? My eyes find it easily now. A single Scotch glass on the edge of the table.

My eyes sweep shut.

He sleeps with women to forget Lucy. And that's what last night was.

Oh, God. *Oh, God.* Panic is like bile in my mouth.

'That's why you needed to see me last night,' I say thickly. 'It wasn't about me at all, was it?'

And I was so sure we were moving to another level—that he sought me out because he needed *me*. Because he missed me.

But it hadn't been that at all, had it? It was about Lucy. Always Lucy.

His eyes are swirling with anguish and emotion. But I don't care. I grab the belt of the robe and loosen it, pushing it off as I walk back into his bedroom. My clothes are strewn all over the place, where we flung them the night before, and they've landed haphazardly—the roadkill of our passion; the pathway to his penance.

I pull my dress on without bothering with underpants; my fingers tremble. He's standing in the doorway. I hear him before I see him, but I don't pause. I slide my shoes on.

'God! I'm such an idiot! You needed to *forget*. You needed to obliterate all your grief and whatever and *that's* why it had to be last night. Right?'

He doesn't answer my question, but mutters, 'Can this wait until tomorrow?'

Obviously it's just about the worst thing he can say.

I clench my teeth together and nod—because while I'm fuming I know better than to make any rash decisions.

'You're an asshole,' I mutter, pushing past him, taking satisfaction from the way my shoulder jams against his chest as I pass.

I stalk towards the front door but then change my mind and spin around, moving back towards him. My hand pushes at his chest and tears sparkle in my eyes. I push him and then I lift up on my tiptoes and I kiss him. *Hard.*

My mouth punishes him and I sob into the kiss, hating him, hating Lucy, hating it all so much but needing him to understand.

I rip myself away, my breath dragging ferociously from my lungs, my eyes whispering warm droplets from their corners.

'That is about *you* and *me*. Nothing else. No one else. It's *us*, Jack. Got it?'

He is infuriatingly immovable. His hands on his hips, his breathing even.

'Tomorrow,' he says softly, like a plea, and I nod.

But I know what tomorrow will bring.

Tomorrow is the dawning of a new day; tomorrow will be our end.

She is everywhere I look, despite the fact no visible sign remains. She's in the rumpled sheets of my bed, the towel I dry myself with after the shower, the toothbrush next to mine in the bathroom vanity unit. She's in the half-drunk coffee on the bench and the pool of coffee beside it, from where she presumably slammed it down.

I didn't noticed at the time but she must have been angry to do that. Gemma doesn't waste coffee.

My expression ghosts with a smile but I blank it.

I find myself standing in front of the newspapers once more and I look at Lucy. It's like I've been stabbed through my heart, a pain familiar to me. She was so happy on our wedding day; we both were. How could we have known what darkness was in store?

I press a finger into the page, as though I can touch Lucy's hair in real life if I press hard enough. But she's just a collection of black dots on cheap grey paper.

Fuck.

My finger moves to Gemma's face and lingers there, just beneath her chin. It's a larger photograph—almost half the page. The way she's looking at me… My gut twists and my throat aches.

Fuck.

The way *I'm* looking at *her*! How did I let it go this far? What madness has overtaken me?

I curl my fingers around the newspaper's edges and fold it back together, then collect them all into a stack that I carry to the wastepaper bin.

I get rid of them, and wish I could do the same to this mess.

I have to end it.

Gemma deserves better than this—to be jerked around by a man who can never give her what she wants. She wants my heart and it's no longer a part of me. I gave it to Lucy… She took it away with her.

The stars are not wanted now: put out every one;
Pack up the moon and dismantle the sun;
Pour away the ocean and sweep up the wood.

He's at my desk when I arrive the next day, looking immaculate in that blue shirt that makes me throb with the desire I partly want to cave in to. But I'm too angry, too sad, too hurt.

Grandma called me earlier, to enquire about my 'friend'. I didn't have the heart to tell her that the first 'friend' I'd had in years was about to put an end to things. Or that I was. That things had run their course.

'Coffee?' He nods to the mug in front of him.

I shake my head. I'm pretty sure I'll be ill if I eat or drink a thing.

'How was breakfast yesterday?' I ask, not meaning it to sound bitchy but suspecting it does.

'Fine.'

I'm pretty sure it *wasn't* fine, but Jack doesn't want to talk about it. And if Jack doesn't want to talk about it, then that's that.

I drop my handbag onto the floor with more force than is necessary and reach down, pulling out my Mac-Book case.

'I was blindsided by the press.'

'You and me both.' I move back to the door and click the lock in place.

'I've been careless. I shouldn't have let things go this far.'

'Bullshit,' I snap, a frown pulling at my whole face. 'Neither of us could stop this. It is what it is. We've worked together for two years—I *know* you. I'm not one of those women you bring home for a quick fuck.'

'You're not that,' he agrees, his eyes holding mine with an intensity that supercharges my blood. 'But there's no future for us.'

The words are spoken clinically, almost as though he's rehearsed them.

'Why not?' I'm not going to give in to my breaking heart and let him end this. Not just because he's afraid.

'This was never meant to be serious.' It's a short declaration.

'So? That doesn't change what we are.'

'Lucy—'

But I cut him off, shaking my head abruptly from side to side. 'Lucy and you… I don't want to infringe on that. I'm not asking you to renounce your love for her. I think you can love me, too. I think you can stay true to what she means to you and still make room for me.'

He clenches his jaw. 'I married Lucy for life.'

I nod slowly, my heart whimpering somewhere near my toes now. 'Even though she passed away?'

'Yes.'

He is so certain, so intractable.

I try a different approach. 'What would Lucy have wanted?'

He clears his throat and turns away from me. 'It doesn't matter.'

'I think it does,' I say with quiet determination. 'If you're going to invoke this woman as your reason for shutting this down, then I think you should at least pretend to consider what she would have wanted.'

'Lucy had only months to come to terms with her condition,' he says. 'She didn't grapple with how I'd live after she died.'

'Bullshit,' I dismiss angrily.

He's resigned. Frustrated. Tired. 'You didn't know her, Gemma.'

I move closer towards him, my voice a whisper. 'I know that anyone who has been in love would want their partner to be happy. Not to live out their life in a hollow, empty wasteland as some kind of sick tribute.'

He squares his shoulders as I speak, as though he can make my words bounce off. 'It doesn't matter.'

It's so arrogantly defeatist that I almost laugh. But I'm weary. So weary now. Deflation has set in and is sucking my energy.

'What are we *doing*, Jack?'

He turns to face me slowly. 'I've been asking myself that same question.'

'What do I mean to you?'

I look at him as he sweeps his eyes shut, the truth apparently not something he's ready to communicate to me.

'You're my in-house,' he says, with so much gentle concern that I feel tears sting the back of my throat. The use of my actual job title makes everything worse, somehow. 'And my lover.'

I am very still while his words sink in. 'You can't compartmentalise me. I can't be your employee at work, your lover after hours and nothing in between. It doesn't work like that.'

'Why not?' he demands with husky urgency. 'This is *good*. Those things are good.'

'But I want more.'

'That's all I have,' he says honestly. 'It's all I can give you.'

A muscle jerks in his jaw and I lift my finger to touch it lightly. 'You've already given me so much more. Don't you see that?' I say gently.

'It's not possible.'

His eyes are dead ahead, his jaw locked. I know Jack Grant—I understand him. I know when he's made his mind up and when it's useless to argue. I see his determination and in it is the answer I have been waiting for.

It is the end.

And yet knowing that and truly accepting it are two different things.

'How can you think this is just sex?'

He shakes his head. 'I should have been more careful. I'll never be what you want.'

'And what's that?' I push, approaching the precipice of what we are.

He meets my eyes; there is bleak reality in them. It breaks my heart.

He reaches for my hand and squeezes it. 'I'm not your boyfriend. I don't want to be. And I don't want us to get more serious. I just want to fuck you.'

Oh, God. The pain is like ten thousand blades running over my spine. It's unbearable and yet I revel in it, because somehow I feel I deserve it. It makes it easier to accept the truth.

My head jerks upwards. My eyes are clouded by grief. 'So that's it?'

His expression shows that he too understands the inevitability before us. 'Yes.'

His voice is pleasingly roughened by emotion so I know he's not unaffected.

I don't trust myself to speak. Not for a moment. I wait, counting to twenty in English, French and Russian, and then I reach into the neoprene case for my laptop and pull out the crisp white piece of paper I printed that morning.

'This is Carrie Johnson's CV. She'll be in at lunch-time to meet with you.'

He frowns, as if the sudden change in conversation has surprised him. As though he expected me to argue for longer, to fight for what we were.

'What for?' He doesn't look at the CV.

'For my job.'

A second passes while we both absorb the reality of that.

'She's excellent. Highly qualified. You'll like her.'

His face drains of all colour. 'What the *hell* are you talking about?'

'Obviously I can't continue to work for you,' I say with quiet determination, zipping my laptop case. My fingers are shaking, making a mockery of my calm delivery.

'Stop. That's bullshit, Gemma. Utter nonsense.'

'That you think so underscores why I need to leave.'

Fuck it. Tears are rolling down my cheeks now but I don't bother to check them. What does it matter?

I stuff the laptop into my handbag with relief.

'You've worked for me for two years. You can't just…because we…you *can't* quit this job. You can't quit on *me*.'

Quit on *him*? The nerve! *He's* the one who's quitting. I bite my tongue. More tears are stinging my throat and I don't want to indulge them.

'I can't work for you, Jack. Not for another minute.'

He's truly aghast. 'Why the fuck not? We're a team, aren't we?'

'Yeah. In bed. In the boardroom. But not in real life. No, thanks.'

He waves the résumé in the air. 'I don't want this… Carrie Whoever.'

'You'll need someone, and she's got what it takes to put up with you. She's got killer legs and a great rack. You'll probably get her into bed in a week or so.'

Jealousy rings in the statement. I don't care about that either.

'*Christ*, Gemma.' He drags a hand through his hair and it spikes in a way that makes my stomach roll. 'Don't *do* that. You're making it seem like that's all we were…'

'No. That's what *you* did,' I say angrily. 'You just said it. We're lovers. We work together.'

He tilts his head back, a growl escaping his lips. 'At least stay for the week. Let's just let the dust settle on all this…'

'I can't.'

I'm emphatic; my life depends on his acceptance of this.

'Why not? It's just a week. Seven days.'

'It's so much more than that. It's all of me. It's my heart. Don't you *get* it? This might have been just convenient sex for you, but to me… It's *everything*. I've fallen in love with you, Jack. I love you completely.'

I wait. And a part of me waits in hope. In the desperate, unfounded hope that he will say it back. That he feels it, too.

But he says nothing. He stares at me, and I stare at him, and finally—well beyond the time I should have given him—I lift my bag onto my shoulder and walk out of my office. I keep my head bent and I don't even acknowledge Hughes when I pass.

I'm so fucking *done*.

CHAPTER THIRTEEN

We need to talk.

THE MESSAGE BUZZES into my phone at three the next morning. I stare at it, my heart pounding, tears leaking out of my eyes. They make me angry.

I delete the message and turn my phone off.

When I wake up I've almost forgotten about it. I make my coffee, switch my phone on and it buzzes immediately.

Four messages from Jack.

You can't just ignore me.

I was surprised yesterday. I didn't handle it well.

Meet me for lunch today.

Please.

I turn my phone off again and leave it at home when I head out. After being tied to Jack—tied to my phone, my emails, my laptop—for the last two years, I'm looking up. Finally. And seeing.

I walk from Hampstead through Regent's Park to the British Museum. I don't think I've been in since I was a teenager, and strolling amongst the exhibits now gives me the perfect dose of perspective. Seeing the ancient Egyptian tombs, the mummies so perfectly preserved, the sarcophagi all shining and morbidly beautiful, I am reminded that I am just one person.

That Jack is just another.

That life is long and its adventures many.

I am philosophical enough to smile as I leave, but my heart is broken again when I walk past a man who is wearing something a little bit like Jack's aftershave.

Dejected, I head to my favourite restaurant in Dean Street and grab a counter spot, eating a roast lunch with a bucket of wine and staring out at the street as people pass.

A matinee show after that, and a slow walk home.

I'm exhausted when I finally get to my front door, and in no mood to see a huge bunch of ranunculus waiting on my step. I know they're from Jack without even looking at them, so I step over the arrangement, careful not to touch it with even the toe of my shoe.

I'll deal with them in the morning. When I have more energy. Hell, maybe I'll get lucky and someone will steal them to save me the hassle.

I stare at my phone as if it's a lit fuse. I'm torn between switching it on and throwing it in the bin.

It's cowardly, I know, but I leave it off. I send a quick email to my mother and grandmother, telling them I've lost my mobile and that they can contact me on email if there's an emergency and then I go to bed without eating dinner.

I'm too wrecked.

The next morning, I am woken by his knocking at the door.

I know it's him because who else knocks with their whole palm? As though they have a God-given right to disturb you whenever the hell it suits them?

I ignore him, but my throat is thick with more damned tears and my heart is spinning in my chest.

His voice is muffled but it speaks directly to my soul. Deep and dark. He's calling my name.

I burrow deeper under the duvet, pulling the pillow over my head.

I can still hear him swear loudly.

Finally, though, he's gone.

I stay in bed all day. I doze, and I stare at the wall, and then I doze some more. I have never been in love before, and I've certainly never had my heart broken. I have no concept if this is normal.

I feel as though I've been torn into a dozen pieces, ripped apart piece by piece, and as if my brain is too sluggish to remember how to rebuild me. Some time after dark my tummy groans. I'm hungry. That's a good sign, surely?

I shove my feet out of bed, grabbing a pashmina as I pass my wardrobe and wrapping it around my shoulders. I catch a glimpse of my reflection in the hallway mirror and grimace.

Pale face. Bed hair. Red-rimmed eyes. Puckered lips. *Ugh*.

I haven't grocery-shopped in days, but there's a pack of soup sachets in my pantry. I check the date on them warily. Only two months past, and surely there's enough sodium in these things to outlast a zombie apocalypse?

I tip the contents of one into a mug and stare at it while waiting for the kettle to boil.

It's a proverb, I know, so it shouldn't surprise me that it feels like I am waiting for ever, staring at the kettle, waiting for it to click off and signal that the water is hot enough. After several minutes I realise I haven't turned it on at the wall.

I curse under my breath and rectify the oversight. The kettle immediately spurts to life. I drum my fingers as I wait some more and finally, when I can hear it's near enough to boiling, I slosh a little water into the cup and whisk it noisily with a fork.

Halfway through the surprisingly *not* awful soup, I remember I told my mother I'd be available on email. I doubt she's tried to contact me, but I feel honour-bound at least to take a peek. I open my laptop and wait for the emails to come in.

Jack's I delete without reading.

Curiosity is burning in me, but I know he has nothing to say that will change what has happened. However he wants to make himself feel better, I won't allow it. He *did* hurt me. He *should* be sorry. It's not my job to assuage his guilt.

I force myself to concentrate on the other emails, to put Jack from my mind. There is one from Grandma and I smile weakly, imagining her typing it on the iPad I gave her for Christmas. It probably took her an hour.

Darling.
I'm worried. I can't explain it in any way that makes sense—I've had the heaviest feeling in my heart for days.
    I'm sure it's connected with you.

Can you call me tomorrow?
Gma Xx

My heart squeezes with affection for her. And the sense that she and I are connected in some way floods through me.

Trust Grandma to just 'know' when things aren't right in my world.

Everything's fine. But I'll call you tomorrow. Love.

I switch my computer off and finish the soup. I'm exhausted, but not sleepy. I've dozed all day, so I suppose that makes sense. I turn on the TV and stare at it for a few hours before going back to my nest.

I wake up with the sun, and only the thought of Jack coming again spurs me on to get out of bed. I doubt he'll be content to bang on my door a second time, and I don't particularly want to press charges for trespass.

I dress in running gear—for a quick getaway rather than any genuine interest in exercise—and pull the door open. The breeze slaps me in the face. I take care to step over the flowers, resolving to deal with them when I get back—really this time. I lock the door and begin to jog around the corner and up the narrow laneway that leads to several cafés.

Only I don't plan to stay in Hampstead. It's too close to Jack.

I catch a cab into Soho and lose myself in the throng of people and busyness. But as I kick out of Tottenham Court Road and get pulled into the riptide of shoppers on Oxford Street I have to stop walking and grip the brick wall beside me for support.

The pain is visceral and sharp.

The realisation that it's over—whatever we were, whatever it was—is deep and sudden. It ruptures my chest like barbed wire pulled at high speed.

I no longer want to be around people.

I move towards the road, lifting my hand and flagging down a cab. It pulls over on a double yellow, blocking a bus that lets us know its displeasure by sounding its horn loudly. I wave in acknowledgement and hurl myself into the back, giving my address and collapsing against the seat.

I must doze off because the cab driver speaks loudly as we arrive home and I'm startled as if from a deep sleep.

'Thank you.'

I tap my credit card and step out. It's early afternoon and my tummy groans with hunger. The breakfast I planned on didn't happen and I have only just realised. I step over the flowers once more, promising myself I'll throw them out soon, and push the door shut behind myself.

I've been home ten minutes when a knock sounds.

My heart thuds heavily.

I know it is Jack.

My eyes fly to the mirror opposite. I am still pale, but I brushed my hair this morning, and at least I'm dressed in something other than ill-fitting pyjamas.

'Open the door, Gemma.'

My heart twists. I have never doubted my strength in all my life, but now…I don't know if I can do this. Can I look at Jack, knowing I can't touch him? That it is over? That we are over?

'Gemma? I will stay here all goddamned day if I have to.'

I don't doubt the sincerity of his statement.

Sympathy for my neighbours has me wrenching the door inwards.

And the sight of him causes me to suck in a huge breath. Because he looks so much like *himself*—so strong and powerful, so confident, so *unaffected*—that any lingering hopes I've nurtured of his being as destroyed by this as me die an immediate, suffocating death.

He's staring at me. His dark eyes are haunting my face, dragging over my cheekbones, my lips, down to my throat and then back up again. He blinks as if to clear his thoughts.

'You're home.'

I frown, keeping my hand firmly tethered to the door, holding it in place as if my life depends on it. 'Yes.'

He bends down and lifts the flowers. A pool of dark brown has formed on one side of the waxed paper, where the overnight dew has set in. I look at the once-cheery blooms and am sorry for them. Sorry I gave them such a cold reception.

None of this is their fault.

I narrow my eyes, my heart pounding and breaking at the same time, like one enormous wrenching storm inside my chest. 'What do you want, Jack?'

I see his throat bob as he swallows, and I resist the urge to make this easier for him.

'May I come in?'

Just the question alone sets fire to my veins. It's so

unlike Jack that I am surprised enough to consider relenting. But I don't.

I have seen his dark places. All of them. And he has birthed new ones in me.

'No.'

Exasperation flickers on his face. 'I reacted badly the other day. I'm sorry.'

He did. But it doesn't change the facts. Perhaps at another time he might have found a softer way to let me down, but nothing will alter the truth. I love him completely, and when I told him he made it obvious he just wanted me to go.

The memories strengthen my spine and fire my determination.

'It's fine,' I say, even managing to dredge up a smile. 'Let's just chalk it up to life's experience and move on.'

He groans and shakes his head. 'I don't *want* to move on.'

'And yet you ended it.' I swallow, afraid I'm going to cry yet again.

'I didn't fucking *end* it.' His eyes are earnest as they meet mine. 'I didn't *mean* to end it.'

My heart screws down inside me. 'You freaked out when our story went into the papers.'

'It was Lucy's birthday,' he says softly. 'I think it's fair to say I wasn't in a good headspace.'

'That night...' I look over his shoulder, my throat thick and tasting acrid. 'You used me to forget her.' My eyes sweep shut. I can't bear this anymore. 'I thought you were there to see *me*.'

He takes advantage of my temporary weakness to push the door inwards, to catch my face with his hands and hold me steady, and then he kisses me as though his whole life has come down to this moment.

As though it is the most important thing he's ever done.

He kisses me with hot, fiery need and I sob in my throat as I kiss him back—but only for a second. And then my hands are on his chest, pushing him, and my back is against the wall, holding me upright as my breath is dragged out of me. He stares at me for a moment and then pushes the door shut. The flowers are discarded once more, but inside now, nestling against my shoes.

'You said you love me.'

He says it like a challenge. A cold line of truth that I can't take back.

'Yeah. I remember. I was there.'

His eyes narrow at my sarcastic retort. 'And? Is it true?'

I screw my face up and drop my head into my hands. 'Fuck you, Jack.'

He grabs me by the wrists, pulling my hands away so he can see my face, and he's so close that I take comfort from his body even when I know I shouldn't. When I know I should be demanding he get out of my house.

'Because I've been thinking about love, and how it's not something you can just walk out on.' He pauses, perhaps waiting for his words to sink in. 'You think you love me? Prove it.'

I suck in a breath and lift my eyes to his face. He's stroking my wrists, his strong legs straddling me. Without him and the wall I think I'd slide to the floor.

'Don't walk away from me.'

'Why should I stay?' I whisper, the words coloured

by a thousand shades of sadness. 'You told me in black-and-white terms there's no future. I can't be with you. I sure as hell can't *work* for you.'

He nods, but his hand lifts and strokes my cheek. 'When I met Lucy I fell in love with her straightaway.'

I spin my head away, twisting it to the side, hurting as though he's punched me in the gut. The pain is no less intense. I want to shove him away from me, but there's such earnestness in his voice, and I am obviously such a glutton for punishment that I stay, my mind absorbing the fact that the man I am hopelessly in love with is now telling me about his wife.

'But it was partly a selfish love. I loved her because she needed me. She made me feel like I was her entire world and I was addicted to that.'

His eyes hold mine, staring deep into my soul. I am exposed and self-conscious, because I find it hard to feel anything but resentment for his poor late wife.

'I wanted to save her. She needed me and I thought that was what love *was*. I didn't know it could be so different.'

The words form a crack. In my certainty and in my heart. 'What are you saying?'

'I feel like someone has cut inside me and excavated the very middle of my chest.' He grabs my hand and holds it against him. 'I'm empty *here*. I wake up and I can't believe I have to get through another day without you.'

His eyes probe mine deeper, deeper, watching and waiting.

'It's been three days. I can't do another one without you. I don't know when you became my reason for being, Gemma, but you *are*.'

Tears are burning my throat. I look away again, swallowing, hurting, *hoping*. But my brain won't let me be such a fool. Not again.

'It's just good sex,' I say stonily.

'I've *had* good sex,' he dismisses with deep-voiced urgency. 'I know the difference between that and what *we* are.'

My cheeks flush pink and I shake my head. 'You think that now because you didn't expect me to leave you. I *believe* you miss me. I believe you miss *fucking* me. I believe you miss me at work. But none of that is love.'

I force myself to meet his eyes and am instantly burned by the lie I've just told. Because I love him enough for both of us.

'How can you *say* that?'

It is a groan that perfectly echoes my own frustrations.

'How can *I* say it? *You're* the one who said it! And I think you spoke the truth. I think that's how you feel.'

'I was wrong. An idiot. I hadn't expected to love anyone ever again, and after two years you blew up my whole world. Everything I thought I knew and wanted exploded in front of me. I fucked up. *I fucked up.* I should *never* have let you walk away from me. I should never have let you quit.'

I swallow, my mind rushing to comprehend what he is saying, my brain working overtime trying to pick faults with his rationale.

'I don't believe you. You had so many chances to make this work. I think you can't stand that I've left you, but that's not the same as wanting this—us.'

'I wanted to convince myself that I could contain

our relationship. That we could be lovers and work together without any emotional fallout.'

I nod, and then I shiver. I realise belatedly that I haven't turned the heating on and the house is frozen.

'I know that. You did a great job. You were able to flick a switch and turn yourself off when it suited you. That's not love either.'

'No,' he groans. 'I couldn't. That's the problem. From the first time we kissed you have been all I can think about. That whole trip to Tokyo I was counting down the minutes till I could see you again. God, when you walked into the boardroom and you were so fucking *cold*—as though you could barely remember my name, let alone the fact I'd made you come against the wall of my office… Gemma…you've had me since then. I have been yours completely.'

A sob is silenced by my throat.

His voice is gravelly and I hear his sincerity, but my brain doesn't buy it.

'I'm messed up. I *know* that. What happened with Lucy was a shitstorm I never braced myself for. There are going to be days when I don't cope as well as others. Days when I am reminded of the tragedy of her loss.'

'I know that,' I whisper. 'That's natural.'

'Lucy's birthday—it's hard. It's a day that should be spent celebrating her chalking up another year and instead I just… I really feel her absence on those days.'

His eyes are bleak when they meet mine.

'The hardest part about realising I love you is accepting that I'll always feel like this. Like I'm betraying her by being with you.'

'No.' I shake my head, sadness for him filling me

up. 'I don't want that. I don't need you to choose between Lucy and me. We're different, and how you love us is different. You never have to hide that sadness from me. Don't you get it? I love *all* of you, Jack, and that means loving your grief and your sadness. Loving you even when you are lost and alone. Loving Lucy, too, and honouring your relationship.'

His eyes are wide, as though he has never imagined I could say that.

'She'd have been as pissed off as all hell at the way I've jerked you around,' he mutters. 'She'd have been glad I've fallen in love with you. She would have liked you.'

He strokes my cheek, his lips close to mine. So close. I breathe in deeply and can almost taste him.

'*I* like you,' he whispers against my mouth. 'I like the way you drink almost as much coffee as I do. I like the way you can't hold a tune to save your life. I like the way you don't put up with my bullshit. I like the way you use that magnificent brain of yours and make me exhausted just trying to keep up with you. I like the way you see me and know that beneath all the fucked-upness there's something about me that you actually like. That I'm worth loving.'

He is. He *is* worth loving, and I do completely. But it is all so complicated.

I bite down on my lip, staring at him through new eyes. 'I just don't… I braced myself for this to end. But for me it was never just sex.'

'No.' He cups my cheek, his smile a secret communication from his heart to mine. 'It was definitely never that.'

He kisses the tip of my nose, like he did after my parents' party, and as then my heart soars.

'I know there are no guarantees in life or love, Gemma. I know that better than anyone. But I'm not going to waste another second when we can be together. You mean too much to me. So? What do you say?'

'About what?' I ask, my lips twitching into a smile.

'Let's *do* this.'

'Do *what*?' I prompt, shaking my head slightly, feeling a sense of bemusement wrapping around me.

'Life. Together. You—me. For as long as we have. Never wasting a day or taking it for granted.' He pulls me into a bear hug. 'I want this. I want *you*—so much.'

I expel the breath I've probably been holding, in part, since I stormed out of my office three days earlier.

'Let's do this,' I agree, my smile stretching my face.

I have known happiness and sadness, but I have never known such perfect, utter rightness before. It settles into my heart and brings me peace and pleasure.

I am Gemma, he is Jack, and we have found each other at last.

EPILOGUE

'GEMMA? ARE YOU in here?'

Strange that in all the time I worked for Jack I never came to this side of his home. The mysterious 'Private Wing' of his mansion. And now I am here almost all the time—in his bedroom, his kitchen, his living room. We have barely been apart since that afternoon three weeks ago, when he came to my home and broke down all my defences.

'Yeah?'

I set down my laptop and stand, butterflies bouncing about in my stomach as though it is a forest and they its sole occupants.

He sweeps in and I hold my breath—as always, bowled over by his physical perfection. In dark jeans and a simple white T-shirt he is hypermasculine and edibly delicious. The idea fans my stomach and I'm walking towards him before I realise it, itching to touch him, to taste him.

He sees the intent in my eyes and chuckles. 'Wait until you've heard me out!'

But he pulls me to him, his hands seeking the hem of my shirt and lifting it so that he can hold my bare hips. He makes a small sound of relief at the contact and I echo it in my heart.

I understand.

This—being naked, touching—this is how we need to be.

'Remember my hunch about Ryan?'

It takes me a few seconds to remember the guy in Australia he didn't think would work out. 'Yes?'

His eyes are sparkling with something I don't understand. 'Well, it occurs to me that you would be an *excellent* candidate for his job.'

I blink, confusion and excitement at war within me. 'He's left?'

'Yeah. Just wasn't up to it. The job is difficult. I need someone I can trust.'

Of course the idea is instantly appealing. Building the Australian office from scratch would be a challenge to relish. And yet...

'It's a long way away,' I point out, as though perhaps my sexy, brilliant lover doesn't comprehend the logistics of geography.

'From London, yes. But we'd come back whenever you wanted.'

I freeze, my eyes flying to his face. 'We?'

A smile cracks over his face and I hold my breath.

'Why not?' He pulls at my top, lifting it over my head so that his hands can roam my bare back. 'Do you *really* think I'd let you move to Sydney without me?'

I stare at him and wonder if perhaps he's lost his mind a little bit. 'Jack...your business is *here*.'

'*I* am my business,' he says with a shrug. 'I can fly here whenever I need to. Fly people out to us. But I have it on good authority, my beautiful, distracting, brilliant Gemma, that you need to spread your wings before you settle down.'

'What?' I blink my eyes, realisation settling. 'Grandma?'

'Mmm…'

He drops his mouth, dragging his lips along my collarbone. I dig my fingers into his shirt front, a feeling of bliss spreading through me.

'She called me when she heard about our "developments".'

I laugh. 'That sounds about right.'

'She's given me a list of her requirements for when she comes to visit.'

'Oh, God.' I groan and laugh at the same time.

'I've told her she's welcome to come for as long as she wants. I think she's fancying a year or two in our guest room.'

I laugh and shake my head, but Jack leans closer, whispering, 'I've got an apartment downstairs. I think we'll set her up there so we can continue to enjoy our… *privacy*.'

I nod, grateful for his understanding. 'But, Jack, it's such a big move. Are you sure…?'

'Life's too short, Gem. You want to travel? To see the world? Let's do it. If we don't like it we'll come back.'

He lifts me up around the waist, carrying me easily to his bedroom.

His *real* bedroom. *Our* bedroom, I suppose, seeing as I have been with him here nonstop since the day he came to my house.

'Of course, if you need some extra convincing…'

I don't, but his lips around my nipple make speech impossible. I nod and murmur something incoherent, and as he kisses me until my body is vibrating and my insides are heated with need I see our future.

I see our home in Sydney, our love, and I fall apart in his arms, knowing that wherever we live happiness will surround us.

For as long as we both shall live.

* * * * *

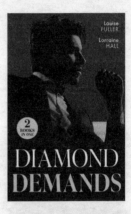
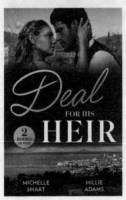
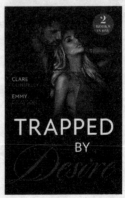

afterglow **BOOKS**

Afterglow Books is a trend-led, trope-filled list of books with diverse, authentic and relatable characters, a wide array of voices and representations, plus real world trials and tribulations. Featuring all the tropes you could possibly want (think small-town settings, fake relationships, grumpy vs sunshine, enemies to lovers) and all with a generous dose of spice in every story.

♪ @millsandboonuk
📷 @millsandboonuk
afterglowbooks.co.uk

#AfterglowBooks

For all the latest book news, exclusive content and giveaways scan the QR code below to sign up to the Afterglow newsletter:

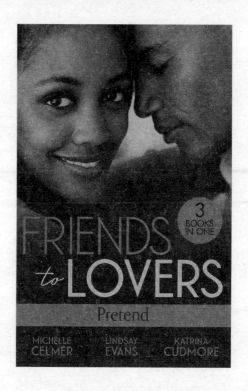